THE POSITION

the
Position

A Novel

MEG WOLITZER

Chatto & Windus

LONDON

Published by Chatto & Windus 2005

First published in the United States of America by Scribner 2005

2 4 6 8 10 9 7 5 3 1

A portion of this novel in a different form appeared in *Ploughshares* and
Best American Short Stories 1998

First published in Great Britain in 2005 by
Chatto & Windus
Random House, 20 Vauxhall Bridge Road,
London SW1V 2SA

Random House Australia (Pty) Limited
20 Alfred Street, Milsons Point, Sydney,
New South Wales 2061, Australia

Random House New Zealand Limited
18 Poland Road, Glenfield,
Auckland 10, New Zealand

Random House (Pty) Limited
Endulini, 5A Jubilee Road, Parktown 2193, South Africa

The Random House Group Limited Reg. No. 954009
www.randomhouse.co.uk

A CIP catalogue record for this book
is available from the British Library

ISBN 0 7011 7890 6

Designed by Kyoko Watanabe

Papers used by The Random House Group Limited are natural, recyclable prod-
ucts made from wood grown in sustainable forests; the manufacturing processes
conform to the environmental regulations of the country of origin

Printed and bound in Great Britain by
Mackays of Chatham plc, Chatham, Kent

for Richard

THE POSITION

Chapter One

THE BOOK was placed on a high shelf in the den, as though it were the only copy in the world and if the children didn't find it they would be forever unaware of the sexual lives of their parents, forever ignorant of the press of hot skin, the overlapping voices, the stir and scrape of the brass headboard as it lightly battered the plaster, creating twin finial-shaped depressions over the years in the wall of the bedroom in which the parents slept, or didn't sleep, depending on the night.

The book sat among a collection of unrelated and mostly ignored volumes: *Watership Down, Diet for a Small Planet, Building a Deck for Your Home, Yes I Can: The Story of Sammy Davis, Jr., The Big Anthology of Golden Retrievers,* and on and on and on. It was casually slipped in, this one copy of the book that the parents brought into the house, for if they'd stored all their copies, including the various foreign editions, in taped-up boxes in the basement marked "Kitchenware" or "Odds and Ends," that would have sent a message to the children: Sex is filth. Or at least, if not exactly filth, then something unacceptable to think about anywhere except beneath a blanket, in pitch darkness, between two consenting, loving, lusty, faithful, married adults.

This, of course, was not the view of the parents, who for a very long time had loved sex and most of its aspects—loved it so dearly that they'd found the nerve and arrogance to write a book about it. When they thought of their four children reading that book, though, they brooded about what kind of effect it would have on them over time. Would it simply bounce off their sturdy, sprouting bodies, or else be absorbed along with the fractions and canned spaghetti and skating lessons—the things that wouldn't last, wouldn't matter, or perhaps *would* matter, coalescing into some unimaginable shape and gathering meaning inside them?

But the parents' concern was mostly overshadowed by confidence, so why not put the book on a shelf in the den, a high but reachable shelf where the children could get to it if they wanted to, and the chances were good that they would want to, and that no one would be struck dead by it, and life would just go on, as it always had.

Michael Mellow, age thirteen and the second oldest of the Mellow children, was the one to find it. It was a late Friday afternoon in November 1975. He had wandered into the den of the house only moments after his father had stuck the book into the opening on the shelf and then retreated back upstairs. Michael was hunting for his Swingline mini-stapler in order to join together the many sheets of paper that constituted his essay on egg osmosis. Why his little red stapler should have found its way there, into the den, could not be answered. Things levitated and floated from room to room in this house: A stapler, which ordinarily was kept in a boy's desk, might inexplicably turn up open-jawed under the coffee table in the den; a box of Triscuits, empty or full, might make its temporary home on a bathroom counter. Objects moved and shifted and traded places, seemingly as restless as the people who owned them.

Walking through the den, Michael became aware of the presence of something new. It was as though he possessed one of those freakish photographic memories and could feel that something was here that should not have been, that had not, in fact, been here earlier in the day. He experienced a *fee fie fo fum* moment, smelling human blood—or more to the point, inhuman blood, something not quite earthly. The stapler, which was nowhere to be found, did not call out to him, but the book did, and he stood blinking and casting his eyes farther and farther upward, onto the shelves, moving among the familiar titles, the comforting ones that together over time defined his family life, just the way the UNICEF wall calendar tacked up inside the broom closet did, or the kitchen drawer filled with nothing but batteries that rolled freely when you opened it.

The Mellows' family life was also defined by a song, which had often been sung on vacations. For years, as they barreled along expressways toward Colonial Williamsburg with its candle-dippers and loom-sitters, or else toward a sleepy, shabby resort in the Poconos called the Roaring Fire Lodge, with everyone and their stuff packed tight into the Volvo station wagon, they would sing it:

"Oh we're the Mellows," they sang, "Some girls and some fellows . . ." And then they would continue in such a vein, using names of other families from the neighborhood: "We're not the Gambles/'cause we'd be covered with brambles." Or: "We're not the Dreyers/'cause we'd be liars." Or: "We're not the Rinzlers/'cause we'd be . . ." A stumped silence descended upon the car, while everyone tried to think their way out of this one.

". . . *Pinzlers!*" shrieked Claudia, the youngest, and though this made no sense, the whole family paused for a moment, the older children making derisive groans that were quickly evil-eyed by the parents, and then they all gave in and sang Claudia's rhyme.

Every family in the world had its own corny, pointless song, or a set of ignored books, or a wall calendar, or a rolling battery drawer, all of which resembled, but only in part, those of other families. These details had been introduced into the Mellow household long ago and they were there for good. Here in the den, Michael Mellow leaped onto the couch barefoot, summoned silently, and there, second shelf from the top, he found it.

The book was white-spined, hard-backed, thick, sizzling, with a colophon of a mermaid gracing the spine, hand on hip, bifurcated tail flipped up in insouciance; it was this mermaid herself who seemed to be speaking to him. What she said was this: *Pick it up, Michael. Go on. Don't be afraid. You have nothing to fear but fear itself.* This last line was one that he had learned in social studies that very week.

Pulling hard, he yanked the book from its vacuum, glanced at his spoils briefly in terror, and then tucked it under his shirt, feeling its glossy surface against his bare, matte skin, forgetting the mini-stapler forever, forgetting the step-by-step progression of egg osmosis. Then he clambered up two flights of stairs and disappeared into the murk of his bedroom for one solid hour.

What he saw in the book was something that, Michael Mellow began to realize during that hour, he could not tolerate alone. He would have to bring Holly in on it, for he often brought her in when something was simply too difficult or perplexing or exciting or opaque to process on his own. She was older, she knew things, she had a worldly, cynical perspective that he lacked. But then he thought, no, it can't be *just* Holly, for she would think it was strange, even perverse, for her brother to invite her to sit with him and look at this thing. So he would have to invite the two others to look at it too, and it could become an important moment of sibling closeness, an eternal bond. That was what he would do. For if your parents write a book like this, one that's just burst out into the world, there's no way you can read it on your own and *not* discuss it, just as there's no way you can snub it entirely, act cool and indifferent in its presence. There's no way you can exist in the same house with that book, walking by it in the den while it's up there burning on the shelf, and tell yourself: *I'm not ready for this.*

Michael sat on the bed in his room, the book open on his lap. Sweat had formed in the notch above his upper lip, and he licked it quickly away, but already this innocent gesture seemed some-how sexual, and so did the taste of human broth in which bodies were basted. His own sweat had taken on a new quality, and so had his tongue, which seemed thick and alive. What would be next, his thumb-pad? The knob of his knee? Was everything that belonged to the body up for grabs and reinterpretation?

A little while later he returned the book to its proper place and said nothing to anyone. But already he had set his plan in motion, and now he waited. The following day, early in the afternoon, Michael said to the others, "They're gone. I heard the car."

It was a wet Saturday, and they were all corralled inside the house. The whole suburb of Wontauket seemed to be in an early hibernation, with children from other families trapped and stunned in their own homes, everyone inexplicably made helpless in the face of rain or a falling thermometer. In summer this town knew how to react, knew how to break out the timed sprinklers and sparklers and domed backyard grills and show a little spirit, but on a day like today it always seemed to plunge into a regional clin-ical depression. Nothing moved. Shades stayed down. Inside vari-ous white or avocado or copper-tiled kitchens, bread was dropped listlessly into the slots of toasters, dogs were fed from cans, news-papers were spread wide in front of faces, forming individual cubi-cles that neatly divided members of a family sitting together at one oval table. Things that had long been broken would perhaps today be fixed, at least partially. There was initiative, followed by boredom and then abandonment.

Such inertia seemed, at first look, to exist here in the large red-wood house on Swarthmore Circle. Out front, leftover rain plopped rhythmically from paper birch trees, rendering the brick walkway leaf-slick, while inside, the Mellow children sat or lay on paisley throw pillows on the floor of their older sister Holly's hot-pink room. Long stretches of time passed during which no one spoke, though within the room, specifically within Michael, there was a covert stirring of energy and direction.

Dashiell, eight years old and the second-youngest of the four, sang to himself a song of his own design, something about an electric can opener that came to life and danced, while the three others played a somnolent round of the game Life, with its elaborate menu of choices: go to college, pick a career, buy a car, get married. (Why did you have to *do* things all the time? one or another of the children wondered sometimes. What did the world want from you? Why couldn't you just be left alone to *exist*?)

Michael Mellow, the cunning planner and decider of his siblings' fates, was thin and dark, good-looking though slightly adenoidal, destined to be considered bookish his entire life even if he were to become a forklift operator. He glanced across the game board at his older sister Holly, the person who occupied many of his thoughts, though this was not something that could ever be spoken. He would have to bury it like a bone. At fifteen, Holly fascinated everyone with her metallic blonde hair and aggregate of freckles that had collected on her face and arms and chest during many summers of sitting on a folding chair at Jones Beach with an unlistenable record album *(Mitch Miller's Stars and Stripes Sing-Along)* covered in Reynolds Wrap and splayed open before her. The sun connected with the sheet of aluminum and bounced back off onto the fair, vulnerable face of the girl who lay there. This was long before SPFs or melanoma death-warnings, and the sun created such a wall of light that even with her eyes closed, she seemed to be looking at something silvery white: falling snow, an enormous wave.

Now, in cold late fall, with the summer long done with, the reflector closed and put away in a third-floor closet among deflated inner tubes and thin, punishingly rough beach towels, Holly Mellow sat on the floor of her room, yawning, thinking not at all of her brother, or of anyone in the family except herself. Her feet were encased in spongy lime green socks. She was always cold, like many girls at age fifteen. It was as though female skin thinned out with the advent of puberty, leaving girls open to every stray thought and fear and desire, and in need of layers. Suddenly Holly had to have crocheted shawls wrapped around her, and ponchos with long fringe. Lately she had begun to feel she needed the draping of the warm, hairy arm of a boy, the pressure of which would create a contentment inside her that she couldn't find on her own up here in her pink room, which she'd long ago chosen for its frilly, undiluted girliness, but that lately seemed more like the color of inflamed desperation.

Adolescence had arrived recently and separately for both Holly and Michael, accompanied by the usual complement of sebum production and wild moods. Without consulting each other, they had taken on the roles of junior father and mother to their younger siblings Dashiell and Claudia, who sported giant new teeth dwarfing their baby ones, a series of untucked shirts, and vitamin breath each morning. Michael and Holly jointly ruled the third-floor duchy where the children all lived, coexisting with an assortment of animals that no one could really love: a ferret, a gecko, a tank of sea monkeys (technically brine shrimp, though the ad from the mail-order place had depicted the sea monkeys with mouths and eyes and even long, curling eyelashes), and an iridescent blue fighting fish with a decomposing tail that left fragments behind as it swiped like a blade through the rapidly clouding water.

The parents, always loving to their children but lately preoccupied by the sudden, massive success of their book, almost never came up to the third floor of the house, and as a result the place had become a kind of anarchic menagerie, dense with the dark stink and wall-fingerprints and equipment of child-life and animal-life, so different from the floor below, the *parents'* floor, which was a Danish-modern oasis. To a visitor, the parents' floor of the Mellow household seemed to suggest sex, or at least to suggest a sophisticated medium in which sex could grow unimpeded, a quivering, translucent agar where a man and woman could lie down together on any surface, blond wood or brass bed, and begin the overture of willing, playful, goal-free fucking.

The Mellow children, at the urging of Michael, who'd said to them that it was time they all saw it, time they "grew up, myself included," emerged from the bedroom and all went downstairs, *clump-clump*, down the groaning oak steps with their faded Persian runner, past the gallery of historically accurate, life-is-short family photos and school pictures, and, on the first-floor landing, past the penciled height demarcations that documented the children's rise from the size of fire hydrants to the size of, in Michael's case, an antelope.

Dashiell and Claudia straggled along. Claudia, age six, carried a troll doll by its shock of orange, wheaty hair, and she did not really understand what was happening; why the stealth, the need for solemnity, though she rarely questioned the authority of either Michael or Holly, who seemed to her as old as trees. As the youngest, she felt distinct from the others, even from Dashiell, who was only two years older. When she thought about Holly, she wanted to collapse and die, for Holly was so indestructibly female and beautiful, while Claudia herself was a crushable, fat, short-legged little thing, sexless and loveless.

After school Claudia often watched the four-thirty movie on channel seven, sitting alone in the den while the sky darkened outside and her brothers and sister went about their business elsewhere in the house. Movies had led her to believe, again and again, that when you became fully adult and grown, it was urgent that you find someone to love. In bed sometimes at night, Claudia embraced herself and kissed and licked her own hand, saying in a man's voice, the voice of an actor in the four-thirty movie, "I love you, woman, and I want to marry you."

She felt certain, even at her age, that it might be hard to find someone to marry her someday. She would have to pay him. Already, at age six, she was saving her money, stashing it neatly away in her hard white plastic Pillsbury Doughboy bank. Sometimes, on weekends, her parents would say, "Don't you ever want to spend your allowance, Claudia?"

"Claudia's cheap," Holly pronounced. Then she added, gratuitously, "I hate cheapness."

"I'm not cheap," Claudia said. "I have plans for my money."

Claudia Mellow saved her money quietly each week, spending nothing on herself, buying no chocolate, no Jolly Rancher watermelon stix, no little wax cola bottles whose single drop of liquid you were supposed to drink in a quick shot, your head flung back. She was parsimonious, she was a solitary nun, saving herself for the distant, swelling future.

Behind her on the stairs now came Dashiell, far more secretive than she was, and extremely contrary, walking along with one finger plugging a nostril. He knew what they were about to see, and he wanted no part of it. He tried to think of ways to get out of it, and as he thought, his finger continued to trawl. From the time he'd been born, Dashiell had seemed to be in a perpetual search for treasure of some kind. He spent entire days wandering around the Wontauket dump, sifting through old furniture and car parts. It was as though he was convinced that there was something extraordinary to be found somewhere, because this sobering life could not possibly be all there was. Or if it was—oh God, what an enormous letdown, what a tragedy.

Once, Dashiell's nose had bled for twenty-four hours and needed to be cauterized, a disturbing procedure involving a sizzling electric needle. He'd wept in the office of the GP, Dr. Enzelman, bright blood all over his small hands and face and the crisp paper scroll of the examining table, but afterward, on the way home in the car with his mother lecturing him, he had been unrepentant.

"Dash, you've got to stop this habit," his mother had said gently, though with obvious anxiety. "I'm worried that other people won't want to be around you, and that your friends will start to leave you out of games. You know, when I was growing up in Mount Arcadia—"

"I've heard this."

"No, you haven't heard this. Not this particular bit. When I was growing up, there was a little boy at our day school who had this very same habit. His name was William, and he just couldn't leave his nose alone. If memory serves, pretty soon he was ostracized in the school yard."

Dashiell had ignored her, not knowing what "ostracized" meant, but assuming it involved being tied up and perhaps even being beaten. He hunched down into the bucket seat of the Volvo and stared out at the expressway. His mother was a kind but sometimes overly emotional woman who liked to tell cautionary tales from her own Gothic, upstate childhood.

"Please look at me when I talk to you," she'd continued, and he'd turned his face to her with an expression of defiance, tilting his head up so that his nose—*his* nose, *his*—was front and center.

Dashiell felt defiant here on the stairs with his brother and sisters, too, except this time no one noticed or cared. If he resisted, he knew that his little sister Claudia would lord it over him forever. The moment she looked at the book herself, she would be pleased with the knowledge that she now possessed and that he still lacked. It wasn't only that he was afraid the book would disgust him—at age eight he had no doubt that it would—but also that he couldn't bear anything being imposed on him like an unwanted and sickening meal.

Out the large picture window on the landing just above the first floor of the house, they could all see the oil-spattered driveway with the station wagon missing. Their parents were indeed gone, having headed off to New York City, fifty-five miles westward along the Long Island Expressway. That was the thing about raising several children: If you waited long enough, eventually they formed their own colony and could largely take care of themselves, the older ones slapping bologna onto soft bread and handing it to the younger ones at approximately lunchtime, or else the older ones speaking in encrypted, deliberately stilted syntax over the shining heads of the younger ones.

Today, Michael shepherded the rest of them down the two

flights of front hall stairs and straight into the den, that autumn-
ally decorated room where over the years the whole family had
watched Jacques Cousteau specials (*"Eet eez deeficult to know
when zee white shark he weel attack,"* they would mimic), where
shy Claudia had sat alone on the kilim rug and chanted and
arranged her troll dolls in a circle like a druidic ritual, where Holly
had recently stood behind the drapes in experimental breath-to-
breath closeness with Adam Selig from Princeton Court, where
Michael had plowed through most of *Cat's Cradle* and *Great
Expectations,* where Dashiell, wanting to make a point, had hidden
behind the large Ming-like vase full of dried, crackling coins of
eucalyptus for hours and hours, singing quietly to himself, and
where late one night a few years earlier, after making love with
particular gusto and affection on the old brown ribbed velvet sofa,
the parents had hatched the idea for their book in the first place.

Now the children needed the natural world to disappear, the
parents to be gone, heading off onto the expressway, the mother
flipping down the passenger-side mirror that no man had ever
used, applying to her lips a light coat of pearly gloss from a little
pot, the father tapping a palm against the wheel to the beat of some
loosey-goosey radio jazz, the car conveying them far from the
house on Swarthmore Circle in Wontauket and off to the city,
where they would be well out of the range of their children's ferocious curiosity.

"Once we've seen it," Holly had said a few minutes earlier
when Michael announced his intention, "then we can never unsee
it. It will stay in our minds. Remember when we all saw the elec-
trocuted chipmunk? And then I had those dreams?"

"I remember." Her brother closed his eyes against the image,
the tiny racing-striped little body hanging from an electrical wire
in the yard. The dreams had come to Holly serially night after
night; she had cried at 3 A.M. and had been so terrified that their
mother, awakened from her own sleep, had given Holly a slug of
NyQuil so she would calm down. "But seeing it didn't ruin you,"

Michael added. "You're still you." His sister absorbed this thought, nodding slowly. Her eyelashes were *white*, he noticed. She herself wasn't earthly; she herself was a mermaid.

"So then what, Michael?" she asked. "Are we supposed to tell them we've seen it?"

"Why would we tell them?" he said. "They'd only want to discuss it. They always want to discuss everything. Anyway, do you tell them anything about yourself anymore?" Holly thought for a moment, and she had to admit that no, she didn't, they knew nothing about her, and that was the way she liked it.

The parents were right now on their way to a packed auditorium at the New School in Manhattan, where they would be delivering the first of many, many lectures that they would give over time in which they discussed the genesis of the book, the research they'd done, the process of trying out sexual acts and writing about them. They would talk about what it had been like posing for the artist John Sunstein's drawings: The mother would say how she'd been embarrassed at first, because she wasn't an exhibitionist at all, but Sunstein had turned out to be a quiet, affable young man in his twenties with long, light brown hair and buffalo sandals, both professional and respectful, and after a while she came to look forward to the sessions. "You both look wonderful," the artist would say to them, and then he'd disappear behind his easel and she would forget about him for the rest of the time.

"It was very peaceful, posing for him," she'd tell the audience.

They would also speak knowledgeably about Chinese erotic art and the teachings of *The Kama Sutra*, some of which they had incorporated into their work. And they would talk about the new position they'd invented, and how exciting it had been first to create it and then to refine it. "All that practicing," the father would say. "It was grueling!" Then there would be laughter, followed by questions from the wound-up audience, endless questions, everyone wanting to ask or add something even if they really had nothing to say.

Right now the parents were hurtling forward in the family car, the Volvo whose very name was itself suggestive of sex. But then again, everything was, once you realized it: a Volvo, the way you licked away your own sweat from above your lip. The world itself buzzed and bloomed into something living and carnal made of dirt, sand, water, and restless humans who filled the air with the plaintive and often indistinguishable sounds of pain and arousal.

The book was called *Pleasuring: One Couple's Journey to Fulfillment.* The title, when the children had first heard it and begun to understand it, was so incontestably mortifying that it threatened to stunt them forever, leaving them locked in time and in a steadfast refusal to enter the adult world with its harrowing demands on your day, your energy, your finances, your body. In the den now they gathered around the book, Holly and Michael in front, controlling the rate and rhythm of page-turn, Dashiell and Claudia on either side, the whole group of them, at first glance, like an advertisement for homeschooling.

"Here we go," said Michael as Holly turned the first page, and everyone made vague sounds: a trumpet introducing royalty, a snort, a snicker, a summoned kid-belch, followed by violent shushing. The front cover, aside from the title, held nothing much to frighten or excite them. It was a classic shade of white, and shiny, with a simple drawing of a rumpled white bed, that was all, the covers thrown back as though they wouldn't be needed here, and you knew why. It was a couple's bed, a man-woman bed, and so far they could tolerate this knowledge. The title was written out in curly gold letters, hovering in the air above the empty bed like the residue of a dream. So far, so good. Inside the book there was plenty of leisurely text, including an introduction by an academic named L. Thomas Slocum from the University of Illinois at Champaign-Urbana.

"Slocum," said Holly with contempt. "What a name."

"What?" said Michael, uncomprehending.

"Slocum. *Slow-cum?*" she said again.

"Oh. Yeah. Right," he said, finally nodding.

L. Thomas Slocum's prefatory remarks put the Mellows' enterprise in a social context, pronouncing the book brave and beautiful, and "exactly what is needed in times like these," and then after that came the opening chapter, "Sexual Intercourse: First Things First," which opened with a breathtakingly detailed description accompanied by a full-color drawing, the first of many.

It was them. Them. The parents. Lying on the creased sheets of the same large white bed from the cover of the book, him on top of her, both of them smiling and relaxed, their bodies fused together like the soldered parts of a single piece of machinery.

"Well, fuck me, Jesus," said Holly, who had lately taken to saying such phrases. In the Wontauket Mall on weekends with her friends, a group of girls standing in front of Blooberries or Stuff n' Nonsense and pretending to look covetously at halter tops but in fact glancing with smoldering disdain at the fleet of boys who skulked through the cavernous space, she only spoke this way for effect, but now she needed to say it, needed to respond out loud or else she feared she might split apart along some invisible seam that ran down the sides of her body.

Beside her, Dashiell looked away, furious at being here, muttering to himself, and then he quickly looked back. He went through a series of these repetitions, loathing his older brother for doing this to him, when all he had wanted today was to be lost inside the delicate, invented melodies that wafted through him. Instead, he was forced to sit here, looking at these pages, and he felt his face heat up, and he hated his entire life for the way it caged him inside it, and he vowed to show everyone, to *show* them, though he didn't really have anything to show. Meanwhile, his eyes kept drifting irrevocably back to the book, pulled there as if he'd been placed under a spell. *Yes, master*, he thought, but who exactly was the master: His brother? His sister Holly? His parents, with their outrageous openness? It was impossible to tell, and so he just let himself look and look, wishing someone would wake him up and set him free.

Beside him, little Claudia emitted giggling shrieks. She thought of herself and her future husband lying in bed at night, and for the first time ever she wondered if she really wanted to spend her money on this after all. What was the point? So that your back would arch and your teeth would bare? It was horrible; there was no other way to view it. Tomorrow she would spend all her money on candy, on those miniature cola bottles and Dum Dum lollipops, and those orange marshmallows that were shaped like peanuts but for some reason tasted like banana, and on anything else she could find at the little candy store that she'd been snubbing for months now. She wanted nothing to do with what her parents did in bed. She had been wrong all this time. Love wasn't for her; it wasn't what she thought it was.

In the den now, Claudia began to slap the side of her own face, saying, "Call an ambulance! Call a policeman!"

"Oh, just be quiet over there," said Michael lightly. Neither of the older children could bear any distraction right now. It was as though they were cramming for an urgent life exam, taking in everything that they possibly could and holding on to it for future reference.

Like all the illustrations in the book, this first one was pen and ink and shaded with lightly tinted pastel hues by that shy artist John Sunstein, who had already done a famous Rolling Stones album cover. Here he rendered the parents in all their humanness, and he drew them engaged in sexual practices both common and obscure, Western and Eastern, ancient and modern, freehand and apparatus-aided. No journalist had publicly come out and written that these pictures were actually *meant* to be the parents, and Sunstein had in fact tactfully altered the hair in both cases, changing the mother's Irish setter–red hue to something more neutrally brown, and turning the father, who in real life had a thick, dark beard and mustache, into someone clean-shaven but woolly-headed. But what did any of it matter? Everyone knew it was them. Everyone. The parents' own parents, elderly and fragile from bone loss and arrhythmia, knew. The family physician, Dr. Enzelman, knew. The mailman and the librarian and the neighbors on Swarthmore Circle and Princeton Court and Cornell Avenue knew. The children's teachers knew. The *children* knew. The hair alterations in the drawings were the equivalent of a poor disguise worn by criminals who unconsciously long to be caught and punished.

I would recognize my mother's body anywhere, Holly Mellow thought, for she and her mother used to undress in front of each other, though for the past year or so Holly couldn't bear it. In the changing room at Lord & Taylor in the mall, back before she became so self-conscious, they would slip off their blouses and jeans, standing there together in a space the size of a voting booth, with its straight pin–studded carpet and saloon doors; this female world in which henlike older women with eyeglasses on beaded chains and Kleenex tucked unaccountably into cleavage patrolled the corridor a few feet away, calling out, "How you ladies doin'?"

And at home, in the second-floor bathroom, they had once stood side by side, bare-chested, as the mother showed her daughter how to perform a breast self-exam.

"I learned how to do it from a diagram in *Ms.* magazine. And you should know how to do it too, Holly, because Grammy Jean had a radical. *With* lymph node involvement," her mother had cryptically explained as she lifted one arm up in a salute and brought her other arm across her own chest, fingers playing with sprightliness on the surface of the breast as though it were a harpsichord.

But here, now, in the pages of a book, the mother's breasts were available for the entire world to appraise, sloping slightly down to the sides of her chest as she lay on her back with the father astride her. Bodies, the children quickly understood, were one thing to view in isolation from other bodies, but when they were observed together, interconnecting in those ways that bodies could, then nothing could prepare you for that sight. Your eyes were simply unready.

On page after page, their mother and father gave themselves to each other in all kinds of ways. They had apparently assumed these positions in John Sunstein's studio, and perhaps they had also assumed them countless times in the house while the children slept with the vaporizer snuffling, or fed the unresponsive sea monkeys, or smoked a joint, or else ran a hand down the interiors of their own pajama bottoms, softly cupping their genitals as if protecting them from the future stresses and burdens they would by necessity endure. There was no way out, they were starting to realize; you just headed toward it all as though you were rushing to an extremely dangerous but thrilling war.

Michael glanced over at Holly; her fair, dotted skin was now universally flushed red—even the tips of her ears seemed to be aflame. She had a flexible, gymnastic body, and it was possible for him to imagine her arching up on a bed in a year or two, being fucked by a faceless boy in some spectacularly gymnastic way. But what could it possibly feel like to be fucked? He was incapable of imagining it, for you had to see yourself as hollow, receptive, and he was neither of these things. His sister's image tenaciously stayed with him now. *No. No. Stop. Don't think about her like that,* Michael thought.

The page had been turned during his brief, dreamy lapse, and now the mother and father were doing something involving scarves attached to the mother's wrists and ankles.

"They should be lovingly tied," read the prose, and as the children stared at the illustration, Dashiell thought: *Oh no, my mom's being . . . ostracized!*

All the children imagined the parents on a bed that had been set up in that New York City studio where they'd gone a couple of times a week over a period of months, "to work with the artist," they'd said, and none of the children had ever inquired as to exactly what that work entailed. Instead, they had often just looked up, bored and unconcerned, and let themselves be kissed good-bye. They'd said yes, we'll take care of lunch; yes, we know the Rinzlers' number in an emergency; yes yes, we'll be fine. And then they'd returned to their own states of self-absorption. But if they'd known then what they knew now, would they have tried to stop the parents? Maybe they could have barred the front door, keeping the parents captive in the house. Maybe they could have said, *Don't do this, for it will change everything.*

And it did change everything eventually, it did.

But for now, in the first flush of the book's grand success, its quick leap from money-maker to phenomenon, the parents were without either prescience or remorse. They were a good-looking woman and man in excellent shape for ages thirty-nine and forty, respectively. The father's unruly dark hair and beard gave him a slightly Satanic but artistic look, though in fact he was quite gentle and hardly an artist. He was thoughtful and playful and an excellent listener. He nodded his head slowly while the children talked, and he stroked his beard, and he remembered the names of their teachers. All told, he was an inordinately kind father who made banana pancakes on Sundays and taught his children how to sing "Norwegian Wood" in Pig Latin and how to whistle using two fingers. He wore turtlenecks, particularly black ones, and a thick, hand-tooled leather belt with a large square buckle of the sort you might find on a Pilgrim's shoe. While he loved his children thoroughly and sentimentally, this was *nothing* compared with the way he loved his wife, and all the children knew it, for the force of it was so strong that everyone could feel it as it traveled the house.

"Your mother," their father said once as they all sat at dinner in a seafood restaurant, "even looks incredible in a lobster bib. Just look at her. Winner of Ms. Sexy Lobster Bib of 1972."

"Oh, stop it now, you're being stupid," she said, waving a hand, her mouth bright with butter, as if to highlight this part of her that was particularly erotic to him. But he would never be able to pick a particular part; as far as he was concerned, the whole thing just *worked.*

It wasn't that the children felt ignored, for their father did turn his attention to them, too, and their mother never seemed entirely comfortable inside their father's gaze. At times she seemed as though she were irritated and trying to flutter away. It was a mating dance the two of them did: the worship followed by the pleased, proud, squirming response.

"Look at your mother," he instructed them. "See how graceful she is with a pair of chopsticks." Or "Look at your mother. She is an amazing woman." Or "Look at your mother. She is the most interesting person I've ever known."

So they looked. They looked across restaurant tables, across supermarket aisles, across the den at night, and across the kitchen, where their mother stood at the sink, tearing apart a head of lettuce under a column of water. Her deep red hair, pale skin, and large breasts rendered her vulnerable, motherly, welcoming, but also, apparently, seriously desirable. She was louder than he was, moodier and more dramatic, prone to tears that filled her blue eyes and made them look luminous. Her nose grew red quickly when she cried, complementing her hair, giving her the look of a fetching drunken Irishwoman with a deep, guarded secret.

"I know your father gets carried away," their mother sometimes said to them when he was not around. "But he's a very expressive man, which is a pretty unusual thing."

Certainly none of their friends' parents seemed to be so actively in love with each other. Most mothers and fathers coexisted like boarders in a rooming house, sharing the same space, trying not to aggravate each other, but essentially living separate lives, one involved with spreadsheets and the home office, the other involved with the children. The Mellows were different, and the children had long ago recognized this with a certain pride and unhappiness.

Their parents exercised every day at a time when exercise was not yet in fashion, performing the Canadian Royal Air Force's recommended count of sit-ups and push-ups each morning, keeping their abdomens from softening to that dreaded pocked-dough consistency that indicated surrender. Here, they were flaunting their self-preservation. In one drawing, their mother—"the woman," the children preferred to think of her—crouched on the bed, slightly bored, angling her head back as though to see what all the fuss was behind her, what "the man" was doing, as though she really had no idea, as though he might be back there folding a map. In another, she sat above him with her head raised, the segments of her throat carefully delineated by John Sunstein, who several years earlier had been the most stellar student his teacher had ever seen in his anatomical drawing class at the Cooper Union School of Art. The mother's eyes were shut, ostensibly because the pleasure was simply too great to absorb with them open, or perhaps because she knew her children would soon be seeing this picture, and she didn't really want to make eye contact with them.

"This can't be happening," Holly said as she flipped through.

"Well, it is," said Michael. "Obviously. So deal with it." Immediately he was sorry for the tone he'd taken with the sister whose trust and love he needed now even more than usual. He'd been the one to cause her to need to deal with it, though she would have had to deal with it on her own anyway. There was no way that she would have allowed the book to stay unread in that house. Like him, she would have had to know.

"I am dealing. *Obviously*. But are they totally sick? Whose parents do this?" she asked.

"Ours," he said. He needed to seem slightly unaffected now. He needed to seem casual, as though he wasn't to blame for having seen it, and, even more to the point, for having pushed it on the others.

All the action in the drawings seemed to take place during the daytime, the white pages serving as a sunlit or floodlit background. This was no bout of nighttime fucking; in the nighttime, specifics would likely be lost. Someone might touch someone else and the sensation would be wonderful but fleeting, and that combination of pressure and exactness could never be replicated. But on white paper, the white sheets of a bed let nothing be lost. A man's hand found a woman's nipple in just such a way, the thumb and index finger cradling it the way a photographer might reduce a shot to its essentials, leaving everything extraneous out of the circle. A woman pushed herself against a man, the surfaces of their bodies forming some kind of human grassland.

The man and woman in *Pleasuring* were presentable, very much so, though everything they enacted—every movement, every finger insinuating itself into folds, every cock tip, every hand, foot, abdomen, spine, opening, clavicle, swirl of hair, dew-bead of sweat, mouth pushing into giving flesh, silent scream, garter, handcuff, flowing purple scarf, stiletto heel on naked leg— was a new source of astonishment to their children, a series of faster and faster ball-peen hammer strikes, not all of them unpleasurable, some of them painful in the exquisite way that lifting the crisp little edge of a knee-scab is painful, and some of them arousing, though the younger children didn't even know they were aroused, for the sensation hadn't been defined for them yet.

The younger ones just felt ramped-up, heightened, the way they felt when they chased someone across the blacktop playground at school, or when they stayed awake until midnight on New Year's, or when they swam all day in the water at Jones Beach and then emerged, dripping, lips blue and scalps burning, inevitably wanting more, though their mother and father always told them *Enough.*

None of the four children could stop looking at the book; they had all been given orchestra seats for the primal scene, and now the heavy maroon curtain had gone up on the mysteries of love, which no child on earth has the privilege or the right to see.

Can I try that with Adam Selig? Holly wanted to know.

She would find out the answer sooner than she might have imagined.

God, I hate them, thought Michael.

He would learn to keep it in.

If I grab the book and take it to the Wontauket dump, will it disappear? thought Dashiell.

Sorry, no. The book would have many lives over the years. Nothing could kill it.

I will live a life alone, with my trolls, thought Claudia.

For a long time, some modified version of that vow would be true.

For this is what they do in bed, the children now knew. This is why the door gets locked sometimes at night. This is who your parents are, this is why you're not allowed in, this is who the world suddenly knows them as, this is what it's like to be human, to want, to be fully grown in America in 1975, to be in possession of body parts that move and react individually and startlingly; this is what it's like to be *them,* to be your parents, so don't turn away, keep your eyes popped wide, all four of you Mellow children, even the youngest one, six years old and overwhelmed with excitement and horror, for it's already too late now, the pictures may be pen and ink but they're anything but soft, and they will stay with you always, like that chipmunk in the yard that was frizzled in death and yet still clinging to a wire, for this is what it's like to cling to each other, a man and woman holding on tight, this is what it's like to be them, this is what it's like, and the most unbelievable part of it is that one day, this is what it will be like to be you.

Chapter Two

SEXUAL UNHAPPINESS was its own city, with windows blazing long into the night, and inside them, men and women delicately or tediously or angrily sat up in bed and discussed what had gone wrong, who was to blame, how to "get back on track," whether to try again tonight or just to give in to how tired they felt, how beaten down. Inside one of those windows, on the twenty-third floor of a high-rise fortress on Amsterdam Avenue, Michael Mellow was making love with Thea Herlihy, his girlfriend of two years. At age forty-one, he was an ardent, focused man, and though he was putting all his effort into it, this bout of sex was interminable. He just could not finish. Still, Michael felt the need to continue, to wear them both out with his diligence, sanding them down to a pile of fine shavings, a pyramid of human dust, before he could admit that once again he had failed at this simplest of human tasks.

It wasn't his fault, he knew; it was the antidepressant he'd been taking, and he supposed he ought to switch to another one, but it took time for a new drug to build up in your blood, and he couldn't bear the idea of returning to that earlier state of gloom. He had gone on his first antidepressant six months earlier, having become distracted at work, ineffably worried in the quiet, artful offices of Dimension D-Net. Though Michael Mellow was considered a self-effacing but authentic software genius there, he had found himself suddenly and surprisingly indifferent to the siren-song of the desktop monitor and the oval maple lake of the conference-room table. Indiscriminate images floated through his head, all of them given equal, anxious weight: Islamic terrorists blowing up the entire city; a gaffe he'd made at lunch by making fun of Scientology, when it turned out an important investor at the table was a longtime follower.

At the recommendation of a friend, Michael went to see a psychopharm guy named Snell who prescribed an SSRI that flushed his brain with the serotonin for which it begged. But that first drug had left him feeling coked up and manic in the middle of the night when he was supposed to sleep. He'd go online at 2 A.M. and stay for hours, sending out emails to his brother up in Providence, his younger sister in her walk-up in the East Village, his mother in her house upstate in Saratoga Springs, his father in the condo in Florida, and even his needy coworker Rufus, who lived God knew where, probably under the desk in his office, and who wrote right back to him regardless of what time it was.

Snell switched Michael to a new drug, whose name was Endeva, a disturbing name that was almost a word but not quite. The near-word implied that if you took this drug, you would start to become involved in "endeavors." Or, at the very least, "endevas." The latest generation of antidepressants had names that sounded like cars, like things you would want to be inside. What would happen, Michael wondered, when they ran out of all the hopeful, expensive names? What would they name the next generation of SSRIs? Torpitor? Minion? Fazzle? Three months into Endeva, life did in fact have meaning once again, but sex lacked an ending. He felt ashamed each time this happened, as though he'd been caught cheating on a test or found to possess the remnant of a dorsal fin.

Michael hovered above Thea now, looking down at her in the dim light of the halogen lamp whose switch he'd earlier nudged with his toe so it gave the room a warm, jack-o'-lantern kind of light, something conducive to love, and, he hoped, to orgasm. For the irony of the situation hadn't been lost on him: For the past month or so, he, Michael Mellow, the son of those forever-famous sex Mellows, couldn't finish what he'd begun, couldn't finish the sex act, couldn't, to put it bluntly, have an orgasm, a fact that both embarrassed him and made him feel reflexively ironic. Neither of those states was any good; embarrassment froze you over, and irony only gave you a running commentary, a little soft-shoe patter to accompany your failures and make you feel that somehow they didn't matter, even when they did.

And this one did. In the pumpkin light of the bedroom, angled into Thea Herlihy, he saw that her arms were now thrown above her head, as if in surrender, her fingers digging into the dough of a goose-down pillow. As he pushed in and then receded and pushed in again, he felt waves of excitement that rose and fell each time his head met the slate gray cushion of the headboard, thudding against it like a boxer doing rhythmic practice feints into a sandbag. "*Nnng,*" he heard himself say, and was self-conscious about the sound of his voice in this sparse, modern bedroom, which always seemed to echo during arguments or sex. "*Nnng,*" he kept saying. It sounded like a Vietnamese name: no vowels.

Thea's eyes fluttered open and then shut. She was discreetly checking, he realized, to see how close he was, and whether he was possibly going to finish up at any time in the near future. She didn't want him to see that she was doing this, but it was too late, he'd already seen, and now their eyes met in an awful moment of awareness that momentarily broke the rhythm, stopping it for a second like a skipped heartbeat. Now neither of them knew what to do, how to proceed. *Think,* he told himself, *think.*

"You okay down there?" he asked, and tried out a smile.

"Yup. You okay up there?"

"Sure," he said. "I'm just being leisurely. Taking a little stroll."

He stroked Thea's forehead, pushing back a few strands of hair that had fallen in her eyes. She looked preoccupied, he suddenly saw, but as if in a sudden change of plans, she drew him down to her and kissed his mouth hard, and then everything started up again. In a few moments Thea made her own quiet noises low in her throat and Michael had to wonder whether this was caused by arousal, or else simply done in order to speed up the process, like a growth hormone dropped in so that he would become more excited and *finish* already, and this could be over with, and they could lie side by side and talk about work, and her rehearsals, and his travel itinerary for tomorrow, and the latest news from their friends and from the world at large, which was what Thea really seemed to want to do.

It had been going on too long tonight, as had been the case for weeks now. At first, this evening, they'd had a good dinner that they'd cooked together in their miniature New York kitchen, using ingredients that Thea had picked up at Fairway on her way home from the theatre: tagliatelle, olive oil, slightly bruised basil, pecorino. They stood shoulder to shoulder, hands moving in bowls and drawers, and as they did, they sang that ancient Carly Simon and James Taylor duet "Mockingbird," his voice so deep, hers so sweetly and correspondingly high.

"Mock," he sang.

"Yeah."

"ing."

"Yeah."

"bird."

"Yeah."

And on and on. He was pleased she knew the song, for she was twenty-eight years old and it was well before her time. It was slightly before his time, too, and he'd had contempt for easy-listening songs like that back when he was younger, but who knew that one day he'd be standing in a tiny kitchen making dinner with his girlfriend, and he'd want some quick and snappy thing to sing with her, and it wouldn't turn out to be by Pink Floyd or Yes or any of the other bands he'd studied with Talmudic intensity when he was a boy, and whose songs he sang only when he was positive he was alone.

During dinner in the dining alcove, looking out across the avenue and the Hudson River and the distant strand of lights, eating off the lemon-colored plates they'd picked out when they first moved in together, Michael and Thea were entirely without tension. And even later, after he'd been online for a little while—first with his sister Claudia and then with Rufus from the office—he was still content. When they finally got into bed at 10:30, both of their bodies were the right temperature and texture, easily made responsive and excited. After kissing and touching and tumbling around a little, Michael ran a hand between Thea's legs and she reacted in her usual way, the contemplative quiet first, then a kind of shivering, and it was all good, it was all exciting, and she tightened both legs around his hand and craned her neck away from him, toward the window, as though she were shy and didn't want him to see her face as it contorted with its thrust-forward F.D.R. jaw.

Then she'd gasped and loosened her grip on his poor big hand, saving it from being crushed, and that was that. Michael's penis remained huge and waiting, almost *ticking,* it seemed to him, but he didn't mind, he was hardly in danger of coming. She touched it lightly, idly, while they shared a warmish glass of sink water and sang another couple bars of "Mockingbird," and then after a few minutes he put the glass down on the night table and they resumed their lovemaking.

Then, in that new phase, there was sudden tension: a question between them that would have to be answered one way or another. He moved on top of her and went inside her quickly, and the sensation of being enclosed and held in place was as pleasing as ever, but despite the fact that he said "Oh I love you, Thea," and she said "I love you too," right back, with feeling, it seemed as though she could have been anybody and he could have been anybody. For some reason, he pictured them as two indifferent people in a foreign hotel room. She might have been an illiterate prostitute and he a businessman—that was about how much love really passed between them at that moment in time.

His voice was thick with concentration, aiming for the gratification that was out of reach in the middle distance, the target on which his brain and all the separate muscles in his long arms and legs were focused. His penis wasn't going to collapse, but nothing would happen, he would never ejaculate, never ever. It was just no good, he couldn't go anywhere with this. "*Nnng*" became a battle cry of frustration and then panic, preverbal, encompassing.

Then, finally, he decided it was time to quit. He wasn't enjoying this now, and she probably wasn't either. It was like watching a wonderful movie and suddenly realizing that you're bored, that it's not wonderful anymore, that you're restless and want out. *Welcome to the city of sexual unhappiness,* he thought, *here is your apartment.* He stopped moving and just looked at Thea, shaking his head.

"You're stopping?" Thea said.

"Is that all right with you?"

"Sure."

"It's just not going anywhere again," he said. Michael held the base of his penis between two fingers and carefully started to slip himself out. He was aware of a little clicking and popping sound as he left her body, as though there were oiled metal parts stored in there, bolts and braces and wing nuts.

"I thought you were actually pretty close," Thea said.

"No, I wasn't. Sorry."

"Oh. I can never tell if you're close or not. Men. It's a great mystery until the moment it happens."

"No mystery here," Michael said, all the while thinking that the real mystery was women, who could fake their way through sex and no one would ever know the difference. He wondered for a moment if she had ever faked an orgasm with him, and became suspicious that she had. "I just can't do it anymore," he told her. "I'm sorry."

They lay looking into each other's eyes, and she appeared untroubled by his failure. "You don't have to say you're sorry," she said. "I'm not upset or anything."

"Well, *I* am. Just call me L. Thomas Slocum." He suddenly envisioned his sister's freckly adolescent face, glowing brightly before him, and he felt slightly heartened.

"What?" said Thea.

"Nothing," said Michael. "Not important."

This particular achievement, in recent weeks, had become so elusive that it had gathered steam in its brief absence, becoming in Michael's mind the prize of prizes, the thing that surpassed all memories of previous orgasms, those countless, brainless events that had occurred in this bedroom and others before it: in the cluttered backseat of a used silver Hyundai he'd once owned; on a soft, rotting dock in Maine; on a terrace during his junior year in Rome; in a girlfriend's father's streamlined RV in a Michigan parking lot; solo in a silky damp sleeping bag under the stars in his childhood backyard, while staring up at the impressionistic freckling of Orion and Cygnus and both dippers but seeing none of it, so lost was he in the profound and trembling moment. Those orgasms were careless, easy; if only he'd known then what he knew now: that pleasure was not endlessly available to anyone, that joy would be snipped away in small confetti-pieces as you got older, that just because you could dream up a female image that inflated your entire body with want, this did not mean it would always bring you satisfaction.

The days of the assumed orgasm were over. Tonight he'd foolishly gotten into bed with Thea Herlihy, the woman he loved, as though it might finally happen the way it was supposed to. Even though, for the past month, sex with her had become what it had been tonight: impossible, or at least impossible to finish. But it had seemed symbolically important to try once again, for in the morning he'd go off to the office as usual, and then at the end of the day he'd take a car to the airport, where he would fly off on his trip, and it would be nearly a week before he and Thea would sleep in a bed together again.

Michael was going to Naples, Florida, specifically to the gated community of Laughing Woods, an Indianesque name for a surprisingly nonugly series of condominiums where his father, Paul Mellow, lived with his third wife Elisa, or was it Elise? Michael still wasn't sure. He was going because his mother had asked him to, and Michael almost always deferred to her, this sixty-seven-year-old dynamo who made batches of translucent red- and green-pepper jelly each Christmas and taught a course in human sexuality to freshmen at Skidmore College, during which she famously put a condom on a banana—although obviously these freshmen could have clothed that banana in latex with their eyes closed. Despite the embarrassment factor, which of course had always been there when it came to his parents, Roz Mellow was his *mother,* and though she could be manipulative and emotional, she'd been good to him, and he had to try to help her.

Almost two years from now, *Pleasuring: One Couple's Journey to Fulfillment* would celebrate its thirtieth anniversary, and the original publisher had proposed reissuing the book. There had apparently been a fierce in-house debate about it before the Mellows had been contacted. Surely, said one of the older editors, the book was a fossil, a scarab that revealed traces of a lost civilization known for its moments of intimacy, of privacy, long before it had all been lost forever to the roaring eruption of electronic porn, with its nonstop availability, sites with names like *pussylicker.com* and *fuckbuddies.com* and *orgasm.org,* all of which someone, somewhere, proudly *took credit* for designing, and its wet pink moronic graphics that drew the eye to the glow of the screen night after night after wasted night.

"That's exactly why we need the reissue," countered a young and surprisingly ardent Chinese-American editor named Jennifer Wing, whose rise in the company had been swift. "We need," she said at a Monday morning editorial meeting, "to remind people of the lost world of love."

What was considered graphic back in 1975, what was considered shocking—those simple images of a man and a woman in a white bed—were rendered almost moving over time because of their unmistakable intimacy. After all, it was the same man and woman in all the pictures; there they were, those two, shaggy and sweet, imperfect but dedicated, always fired up when they were together, always ready for something new, always returning to the same white bed.

"So what if the book is a fossil?" said Jennifer Wing to the other sleepy and still wet-haired Monday morning editors. (She herself had been up since dawn rehearsing her talking points with her boyfriend.) That could be an added bonus commercially; it could make readers yearn for what no longer exists. In order to keep the book relevant, though, to keep it "cutting edge," a phrase that a suspiciously celibate senior editor named Marge Fenner used without a whiff of embarrassment, everyone agreed that there would need to be a new introduction and several chapters that would take into account, among other things, the imperative for safe sex and, more obliquely, the idea of "good lovemaking in an age of terrorism." (*What did that mean?* Michael had wondered: *Wrapping your penis in duct tape?*) Such caution would have been unimaginable, unnecessary, a futuristic nightmare dreamed up by some sci-fi nutball back in the creaky year of 1975.

There would have to be a new set of illustrations for the reissue, too, Jennifer Wing had said when she first telephoned Roz Mellow. Those old drawings were almost ridiculous now, particularly the long, tangled head of hair that the artist had given to Paul and the crushed white vinyl go-go boots that Roz had worn in one drawing that accompanied a brief text about fetishism. There would be new models posing, an up-to-date young man and woman with strategic piercings and a slightly mussed and sardonic look about them—a sexy, skinny couple who were somewhat appealingly disaffected, but who hadn't made the trajectory from love and lust into coldness and contempt for each other, the way the Mellows had over time.

It was this contempt that had made Paul Mellow say no. No, he said, he didn't want the book back in print again; no, he wanted nothing to do with his ex-wife Roz, nothing to do with that time in their lives. He had once loved her to distraction, had thrown his entire self into loving her, as all the children well knew, and look where it had gotten him. Besides, he said, he didn't need the money that the reissue would bring; his wife Elise/Elisa had her own inheritance, which took care of the upkeep of the Laughing Woods condominium and allowed Paul to do little more than contribute essays to journals and psychology magazines. Paul was also well aware of how much Roz wanted the book to appear again, how much she missed the talk shows and the sexuality panels with their academic imprimaturs and the articles in weekly news-magazines that would show photos of the young and burnished and vigorous Mellows, and then show them *old*, him with his paunch and the beard that used to be black and devilish but was lately gray and faintly, disturbingly Amish, and this made him say no with even more conviction.

"Go see your father," Roz had said on the phone to her son Michael in desperation a few weeks earlier. "Show him the new plans for the book that Jennifer Wing sent me, the new introduc-tion, the layout. It looks so jazzy. Maybe he'll change his mind. He won't listen to me, God knows."

"He's in Florida. I can't just pick up and go," said Michael. He started to ask her why she hadn't tried to get one of his siblings to go instead, but then he stopped himself, for he knew the answer. Holly was barely *in* the family anymore, but instead was a strange hologram living with her creepy doctor husband and their child

Buddy out in L.A. This was her decision, made over time, and no one in the family entirely understood it. She needed to be separate from them, and perhaps then she could feel okay. So Holly wasn't an option. And Dashiell wasn't very nice to their mother, though he spoke to her often enough. Which left Claudia, who would definitely have gone to Florida if asked, though she wouldn't have had any effect on their father whatsoever, for she wasn't a very persuasive person. Claudia was kind and very obedient, practically subservient, which never really made sense to Michael, for she was idiosyncratic, too, and surely she had some backbone, didn't she? No, in relation to their parents, she didn't. She was the only one of the children who still lived alone and who hadn't settled into a full-fledged career, and because of this she was the most invested in their parents' lives.

Silence peppered and stuttered Michael's phone conversation with his mother. She exhaled loud and long, and at one point she choked up for a moment or two. By the time the call ended, he had told her okay, okay, I'll go there, I'll talk to Dad for you, don't worry about it, Mom. His mother must have known that he would cave. It wasn't only that she was so insistent—she was certainly that, and always had been. But it was also that most grown men had a soft spot when it came to their fathers. Most grown men, it seemed to Michael, turned into patsies, big babies in bonnets with stubble, *pushovers*, whenever their fathers' names were invoked. Roz Mellow knew this, and though she didn't know some of the specifics about her older son's adult, private life—his depression and his frustrating sex problems in particular—she knew he would go.

Frustration was a fairly recent sensation for Michael Mellow; he was used to getting things, and in the urban life he lived, he rarely had to wait for what he wanted. Oh, there were waits for public transportation each morning and evening and for your coffee to be announced like royalty as it arrived on the pickup counter at Starbucks, but these were merely components of the common dance, the trivial crush and stretch of the city life you'd chosen. If you didn't like this life, you could always live like the rest of the country, taking your pick among big landlocked states where there was no waiting of any kind.

But waiting endlessly to have an orgasm was mortifying and intolerable. Somewhere along the way, the fast build of excitement Michael had taken for granted during sex was replaced by a neutral state, then an unexciting one, and then it felt as though he were sawing away at a piece of wood that just *would not* fall off. Finally he would give up, go into the bathroom, and stare at his vaguely anaphylactic penis with the baleful, disapproving look of a parent with a balky child.

"Look, it doesn't matter," Thea reminded him now in bed.

"Yes it does."

"You can beat yourself up about it if you want, but to me it really, really doesn't matter," she went on, and then she sat up and switched on the gooseneck lamp on her night table, picking up the Xeroxed script of the play she was rehearsing, which was based on Freud's famous patient Dora, herself a chronic depressive who was a collection of complaints, a sexual disaster. "I don't see why you get so worked up over this," Thea went on.

"Because it's become a chronic thing."

"Why don't you get them to switch your drug? They come out with new ones every day, don't they?"

"I already got switched once," Michael said. "It's a real pain to go off it and start something else. It takes weeks to build up in your blood. And anyway, this one is working."

It seemed to him that his inability to have an orgasm anymore gave Thea some mean little burst of pleasure. But this interpretation made no sense, for Thea loved him. Still, she seemed to grow inordinately relaxed in the presence of his dissatisfaction. Her voice took on a certain lilt. She said things like, "Oh well," and "It doesn't matter, Michael," and he believed it; for her, it didn't matter at all.

Thea Herlihy was one of those women who had solutions to a

variety of problems, and when occasionally she had no solution, she became at first philosophical and then cheerfully indifferent. She herself could have an orgasm in about three minutes, if you provided her with a vigorous little clitoral rubdown and a few slightly sinister suggestions of things you might do to her. Thea had an even temper, which was accompanied by a kind of androgyny, which made her seem more complex than perhaps she was. She looked French, and brave but wounded, though really she was from Marblehead, Massachusetts ("Mobblehead," she still pronounced it), and she had never been particularly traumatized during her twenty-eight years. Her dark blonde hair was cut like Mia Farrow's in *Rosemary's Baby*, and she wore pencil-legged jeans that came down to the middle of her calf, and men's shirts in Easter shades of pink and yellow, which no man he knew would ever wear. Her eyeglasses were bewilderingly expensive; it was her one indulgence in an otherwise fairly frugal life.

She was an actress who worked often and possessed an Equity card, but who hadn't yet made it big. She took parts in plays that paid almost nothing, but still she slogged on, earning a name for herself in a marginal universe of cold little theatres in the far west 20s of Manhattan, where actors bundled themselves in woolly layers on stages that were just bare platforms, and valiantly rehearsed their Sam Shepard or David Mamet, little puffs of condensation coming out of their mouths as they barked their terse and elliptical lines. Because of her haircut, Thea had played Joan of Arc more than once, and though she didn't yet know it, the Dora play *Hysterical Girl* would open and close as quick as a clam, and within the next few months Thea would be cast in a successful regional children's production of *Peter Pan*, and end up staying in the play—in the green tunic and tights and Tyrolean hat, fully wired for flying—for the better part of a year.

Michael had seen Thea in every production she'd been in since they'd met, bringing her wet paper-wrapped lilies and freesia from Korean delis and waiting in a corner of the communal dressing room while she spoke in actors' shorthand with the other cast members, or sat before a cracked mirror with a tub of cold cream. Offstage she wore no face paint of any kind. In bed with him she never left streaks of makeup on the sheets, as other women had done before her. There was a physical purity and grace to her, the kind of quality people associate with actresses, dancers, and young grade-school teachers.

"I'm going to go for a walk," he said now, not really knowing what else to do with himself. A body in motion tended to stay in motion; he was churning, unfinished. Maybe he'd get a hamburger at the 24-hour coffee shop around the corner. Maybe he'd just walk.

"Oh, what for? It's late," she said. "And it's cold."

He hesitated, and then realized she was right, it would do him no real good to go out. It was January, snowless but brutal outside. A street cleaner rolled along Amsterdam Avenue, leaving behind a wet slug-trail that immediately froze over, and while ten years earlier there might have been a knot of teenaged boys sharing a joint on a corner even in this weather, they'd been scared off by a crack-down mayor, and so they were off in their own homes now, smoking individual joints in their bedrooms with the windows wide, night air pouring in. Michael thought back to himself as a teenager, as a child, and it was like thinking about a death, for that person with the waves of black hair and endlessly replenishing orgasms had certainly disappeared. An abduction had taken place in the night, seemingly noiseless.

The truth was that if you paid attention to it, the sound of childhood ending was a terrible thing. If you were one of those supernaturally gifted people and could actually *hear* it, you would know that it was similar to glass shattering, or a body falling and hitting a surface, expecting that surface to be the accommodating body of a mother or father who would break the fall, but finding, instead, only the hard, hot sidewalk of the rest of life. These sounds were right now being made everywhere, Michael knew—children disappearing, as if through violence, and a troop of awkward but somehow authoritative adults replacing them. The world was packed with these new people who were granted permission to drink, and vote, and drive, and argue, and matter, and sometimes, if they were particularly unlucky or perhaps *lucky*, to grieve for things that had happened a very long time ago.

At age forty-one, Michael Mellow remembered almost everything that had ever happened to him, both before and after he had changed from that thin, brainy boy with prominent ribs and longish dark hair into a handsome, too tall, often worried, antidepressant-addled, non-ejaculating man. His grown face was creased in the forehead like a shar-pei's, and his clipped hair had gray tossed in with the black. At Dimension D-Net, though he was considered brilliant, he was also seen as not particularly ambitious, which puzzled some of his colleagues, who didn't grasp the subtleties of being considered golden your whole life, and how it sometimes bestowed upon people a certain paralytic despair.

It glazed you early, this goldenness, or else it never glazed you at all. Michael Mellow had always been intelligent and directed, preternaturally good at standardized tests and at getting smart, sexy girls to go out with him, and at impressing heads of personnel. The woman who interviewed him at Dimension D-Net had immediately written in a red Sharpie across his application, "Steve: HIRE." And though Michael's childhood had of course ended, soon the firm became a consoling parent, a flatterer who took care of his needs. There were bonuses each year. There were dinners in hushed, icy restaurants, where diners were encouraged to put together their own meals, comprised of various dissonant elements: grasses, seeds, the meat of innocent birds. He was celebrated by the company for being original, free-thinking, for being himself, just the way his mother and father had occasionally celebrated him long, long ago, when they weren't too busy celebrating each other.

"Go to sleep, Michael," Thea said, leaning over to kiss his cheek.

"You'll be wrecked tomorrow. You've got a big day. First work, and then your flight. Are you packed, even?"

"I can do it in the morning."

"Sweetie, you won't have time."

Thea wasn't worried about his sexual failure and despair, but she was worried that he would not have time to pack. What kind of sense did that make? To avoid any more discussion about it now, he got out of bed and began to pack a few items in the small leather carry-on bag that Thea had given him for his last birthday. He would only be gone for one week, and he didn't need to take much with him. Michael Mellow dug deep into the bottom of a drawer and pulled up a black Speedo swimsuit, which he flung into the bag with frustration, though it landed so silently that she didn't appear to notice.

All those years ago, when he was the boy he no longer was, when he'd brought his brother and sisters downstairs to look at their parents' book for the first time, to look at it and enter its world as he had done the day before, he was unprepared for the lifelong effects of looking. That November day in 1975, after *Pleasuring* was read by the children in one sitting and then snapped shut and returned to the shelf between the impassioned vegetarian cookbook and the handsome volume on golden retrievers, the four Mellow children had quickly dispersed. Over time Michael had learned what each of them had done that day.

He himself had walked outside coatless, heading into the woods, as the children called the place at the edge of the property, which had none of the qualities of real woods: no overgrowth, no underbrush, no fallen, rotted logs. There were just immature trees there with tentative, grasping roots, and the soft, once-fragrant cocoa mulch that had been spread by three men from Garden World. He walked and walked through these nominal woods, eventually emerging out the other side into the place where the

Mellow property ended and the service road off the expressway began.

"New York City 55 Miles," a sign read in reflective, wet letters, and his parents were out on the expressway, heading into the city, or perhaps they'd already arrived in the city, where today they would speak about their "work," their beloved opus, to two hundred paying listeners. Apparently no one could ever get enough of sex; it needed to be replenished again and again, filled up like a bucket in a well. It wasn't enough for people simply to *have sex* with each other, they also had to examine pictures of it, and read about it, and hear it described in agonizing and exhilarating detail.

He had decided that he would go to that auditorium, sit down in a plush seat, and then, during the Q & A, he'd raise his hand and shout, *"How do you think this makes me feel?"* His throat almost closed up as he thought about making a scene, for he'd never made a scene in his life. No one ever thought about how it felt to be Paul and Roz Mellow's children, he realized, how it felt to have your parents display their bodies, their preferences, their most private selves. When you leafed through those delicate drawings of the naked and entwined couple, you could only imagine them childless, floating on a disembodied bed as private and isolated as an outlying planet. But they had children, all right, and Michael wanted everyone to know.

He stepped out onto the service road and walked until he came to the expressway, and then he stuck out a thumb. A succession of big American cars went by, and finally a burgundy Seville cruised to a stop. The driver, he saw with a sinking heart as he opened the door, was Elaine Gamble ("We're not the Gambles/'cause we'd be covered with brambles"), the woman who lived down the street and whose twenty-three-year-old son Stu was missing in action in the Mekong Delta, having been drafted back in 1970 even though, people said, he could probably have gotten out of it like almost everyone else they knew. But no, no, Stu Gamble had said he wanted to go. He'd been a gun enthusiast, a reader of *Arms* magazine, an owner of a Glock, model 17. So he'd gone, and he'd been captured by the Vietcong and probably shot, and now his mother was nearly dead herself, or wished she were.

Mrs. Gamble had black hair that was kept up in a kind of fixed meringue; on her thin wrist she wore a 24-karat gold POW/MIA bracelet with a clasp that only opened with a special key when the person who had been missing, and whose name was etched on the side—in this case, Stu Gamble—was returned home. Her bracelet hand held a cigarette, and the carpeted burgundy interior of the Seville stank with the absorbed weight of all the cigarettes she'd begun to smoke since the army had paid a call to her house one day in their own enormous sedan, black with darkened windows.

"Hi, Michael," she said. "So where are you headed?"

"New York City," he mumbled.

Rumor was that Elaine Gamble had gone insane after Stu was declared MIA, drinking heavily and systematically calling up her son's former high school teachers late at night to say that they should have given him better grades, that he had deserved to make the honor society, and that he was probably dead, and that there was "no school in the afterlife."

"Do me a favor, Michael," Elaine Gamble said now. "I'll take you to the city, but I need to stop off at King Kullen first. Be a good kid and run in there for me, would you?"

He just looked at her for a moment, trying to temper his anger at having been lured in and now told it wasn't going to be as simple as he'd been led to believe. *Oh please just take me to the city,* he wanted to say. *Just take me there.* But she was pathetic and couldn't be spoken to harshly, and he was a kid, a boy, and he had no rights in front of this woman, and so he had to submit. The shopping list she reeled off was surprisingly long: "I'll need V8. And a package of Stouffer's French bread pizzas. Oh, and a frozen vegetable too for when I don't feel like cooking. Which is basically every day, so corn niblets if you would be so kind, or French-cut green beans. A six-pack of Tab. A carton of Larks unfiltered. Oh wait, they won't sell that to you. Maybe a gallon of Dolly Madison instead."

Then she was done, and she nodded at him tersely, as though he was supposed to have instantly remembered all of these items. What she didn't know, Michael thought as he entered the supermarket, clutching Mrs. Gamble's twenty, was that he was the kind of person who *could* in fact remember all those items. His memory had always been extraordinary, keeping him at the top of his class in all subjects and making life itself endlessly and sometimes involuntarily memorable. So Mrs. Gamble's V8 and her green beans were locked in there beside the names of all the rivers of Europe, and the process of egg osmosis, and the drawing of a woman, who totally resembled his mother, performing fellatio ("from the Latin word *fellare*, meaning 'to suck,'" said the book) on a blissful man who looked like a clean-shaven version of his father.

Once inside the supermarket he roughly grabbed all the items in his arms, and then brought them back to Mrs. Gamble in an armful of paper sacks. She was asleep when he reached the car, her head flung back against the seat, and he saw for the first time that she wore only a yellow nightgown under her parka and house slippers on her feet, and he realized that if she hadn't run into him today, she would certainly have entered the supermarket dressed for bed.

Thoughts of his own suffering, his own mortification at the hands of his parents, seemed self-indulgent in the presence of the genuine article. They sat together in complete silence. There was no more question of whether she would take him into New York City today; he knew she wouldn't. She'd apparently forgotten all about it, and he couldn't bear to remind her. Having marched through the supermarket aisles and then returned to the car of this torn-up woman, he saw that there was nothing for either of them to do but go back to their separate houses, and so they did, and in a way he was relieved.

Michael entered the front door of his house and soon disappeared into the deep blue funk of his room, where he would spend much of his time until high school graduation in four years. The younger set of siblings had by now joined forces in the kitchen, Claudia with her trolls and Dashiell with nothing but a song in his head and a desire to sit on his beanbag chair and sing it. But his little sister wouldn't let him; she was all pepped up now, wanting to play.

"I know. Let's do horsie," she suggested. It felt necessary to her, because even though she no longer wanted a husband, even though she now knew exactly what a husband and wife might do to each other, and how *awful* that would be, she had to do something with her restless, antsy, thick little body.

"I don't do horsie," Dashiell said with derision. "Daddy does."

"You could do it, Dash," Claudia said coyly. "You're bigger than me."

As though he wouldn't recognize this for the desperate flattery it was! But she looked so eager, and there wasn't anything else to do, so Dashiell got down on all fours on the white mock-brick kitchen floor, and let his sister climb onto his back.

"Go, horsie, go!" she cried. And then, in afterthought, she said, "On Donner! On Blister!"

"*What?*" her brother said, craning his head around, but she slapped him lightly, saying that horsies don't talk and that he should just *ride*.

Dashiell carried his little sister around and around that kitchen, feeling the weight of her body on his spine, not yet knowing that throughout his life he would experience himself as the misunderstood slave to other people, yet would not be able to resist them. He stirred with resentment now, made some typical horse-sounds, the loose-lipped equine spluttering he'd heard on cartoons but had never witnessed in real life, for he'd never seen a horse up close. He would have been too afraid of its shuddering skin and articulated flanks and enormous, unknowable opaque eyes. Dashiell had seen nothing of the world, really, except the bit of it he'd seen today in that book. Suddenly he went into overdrive, like a horse that's just been bitten on the side by a blue-bottle fly, and he began galloping across the floor, not caring if he dropped his passenger with a thud, in fact almost hoping he would.

"Whoa!" Claudia shouted from above him, but he didn't listen. And even so, she held on tighter than she'd thought possible, her legs pushing against her brother in fear and pleasure. Her hands jerked on the back of his hair and on the collar of his stretchy blue shirt, and her eyes closed shut, for even at her age she was able to intuit that closed eyes would enhance the game of horsie, and give the illusion that it would never end.

Holly, meanwhile, was up in her bedroom. Earlier, she had gone into the kitchen in desperate search of something to eat, and in the walk-in pantry she found an unopened box of Yodels, which seemed at that moment a gift from God. She took the box upstairs, closed her door, shoved an 8-track cartridge into its deck, sat on her bed, and systematically began to eat through the box. The lava-flow of macerated chocolate was soothing, and she turned the music up as loud as it would go because she knew that music had a way of warding off thinking entirely. By the middle of the afternoon, Holly Mellow had eaten six Yodels and listened to a loop of Led Zeppelin over and over, then lain bloated and stupefied on her bed, and finally called Adam Selig on the telephone to say, "So. What are you doing?"

"Nothing," he'd answered, for this was in the script for a lazy, potentially sexy boy like him, his upper lip slightly shadowed, the edges of his brown hair touching the collar of his velour shirt with its brass-ring zipper pull. "What are *you* doing?" Adam asked her from his own bed, one-sixth of a mile away along the network of shaded streets. His bed was nut-brown and old and narrow, and above it on the wall hung various black-light posters of tigers and women.

"Nothing," Holly said, sinking down into her bed. She wouldn't tell him about looking at her parents' book; she didn't want to talk about it, or think about it anymore today. "Bored out of my fucking brain pan," she added. "Fucking weekend."

"No shit, milady," Adam Selig said, nodding as though she could see him. "You have Hellinger?"

"Yeah. Third period. You?"

"Fifth. She give you that assignment?"

"Yeah."

And then both of them, pointlessly, snickered, their laughter covering the lameness of the assignment, the passive helplessness of their own lives. Their conversation continued apace, patched together with pauses. There was silence and breathing, a dialogue between two sets of lungs, and in the background of the Seligs' house a woman could be heard screaming words that sounded like ". . . dishwasher . . . forks and knives . . . the *bottom*! I said *the bottom*!"

"So," Holly said after a moment. "You want to come over?"

Within twelve minutes, Adam Selig was ringing the doorbell on Swarthmore Circle. No one answered, and so he just let himself in. Holly Mellow's house was empty of parents, unlike his own; right now, in the kitchen over on Princeton Court, Adele Selig stood in a bathrobe trying to pry a fork from the motor of the dishwasher. But in here the coast was clear, and Adam walked upstairs to the pink temple of a bedroom, where the remnants of the game of Life lay abandoned on the carpet, and where, improbably, this blonde and pink confection of a girl sat on her bed, waiting for him.

The path from telephone call to bed-sitting to body-touching was remarkably linear. They had already had a nominal conversation on the telephone, and so they didn't need to attempt too much more of that in person. Instead they nodded together to the emphatic bass of the music, and Adam scooted close beside her on the bed, and she turned her face to his. Her breath, chocolate-driven, and then her tongue, were offered in the slightly dispassionate way of people who are new to sex, but just the presence of that tongue was enough to create an *über*-boner in this boy whose Saturday was supposed to have been spent manipulating a three-ring binder.

Without even thinking it through, his hand went from Huk-a-Poo blouse to brassiere-cup to breast, and then from the click of silver Levi-snap to bikini panties which, had he actually seen them, would have been revealed to be decorated with a faded repetition of Roadrunners chasing Tweety Birds around and around from subnavel to ass.

"Oh, that is so, so nice," Adam Selig sighed in an angelic voice he hadn't known he possessed.

By 5 P.M. that day, with Adam sent back to his own home and the music turned off, the Mellow children found that they needed one another's company. Without any prearrangement they slowly and separately drifted into the kitchen, where the older ones filled a pot with water and took out two boxes of Kraft macaroni and cheese dinner. Holly poured the curved, cooked widgets of pasta into an enormous colander, and the water surged into the sink, sending up a wave of steam from which she recoiled, although in her teenagerdom and desire to cleanse herself, she suddenly realized that this was like a minifacial, and so she leaned over the sink, letting her pores open.

They all sat down together under the yellow light in the kitchen with the silhouettes of a few dead bugs speckling the inside of the dome, and none of them mentioned the book. It was almost as if they'd forgotten about it, so deeply had they taken it into their bodies and into their growing, replicating, breathing tissue. Instead, Dashiell lightly swiped at his nose and Holly scolded him, and Claudia began to cry in her tiny, rusty little way, and Michael said they'd all better eat their dinner, "or else."

"Or else what?" Dashiell asked. There wasn't a thing his older brother could say in response that could remotely be considered honest.

"Or else nothing," Michael admitted, and the children ate.

* * *

Now, on the day he was to leave New York City to visit his father in Florida, Michael Mellow sat behind his teak desk at Dimension D-Net and impassively looked into the grid of numbers and letters that filled his computer screen. The current project was a hunger initiative in Kenya; the last one had targeted the poorest population in Appalachia. The founders of DDN—Seth and Zachary Dibbler, "the twins," as they were commonly referred to, for they had been born minutes apart and tangled up in umbilici—had accidentally become great believers in doing good works. A confluence of events had led them to discover a few years earlier that the supply chain software they'd developed for Lady Gillette razors could actually be modified to help expedite shipments of food to starving populations. Because there was so much hunger in so many different zones of the world, the software was forever being reimagined, and Michael's work as VP of biz dev was never-ending, like hunger itself.

This was a corporate job that only felt soulless; actually, friends had often pointed out to Michael that it wasn't soulless at all. Sometimes it was hard for him to see the difference, for here, as in every other office building in New York City and Chicago and Los Angeles and industrial parks throughout the land, a waterfall pounded in the lobby and off to the side was an atrium where foliage, bribed and confused into thinking this was a rain forest, grew extravagantly. When he arrived at the Strode Building each morning and pushed through the revolving door, he was first met by the bold whack of water on jagged rock, and then by the sonorous, boomed hello of the armed guard Mohammed, and then he stepped into an elevator that rushed him upward far too fast, as though what he was going to do in those offices was an emergency. As Michael walked from the elevator into the corridors of DDN, he still felt stupidly impressed, as though he'd never seen the place before. DDN had "gone all out." They had "spared no expense." The rounded walls were covered in Japanese paper that had a rough, nubbed texture to it, as though made from oat. The lights were punched into the ceiling, and each office had its own individual Laarnen sound system so that employees could listen to music that might inspire them. Music enhanced ideas, the twins maintained in pamphlets about their company, and no one argued with this point, for the employees at DDN were largely productive and content, their salaries soaring, their need to do good continually satisfied.

Michael walked silently down the soft carpeted hallway, greeted by two male coworkers, one with chumminess, the other with a kind of modulated paranoia. The three women he met on his way said variations on "Morning, Michael," the first two greetings spoken with evident warmth and the third, by Deb from sales, with unaccountable irritation. What had he done to her? What had he possibly done? There was relief to be had by the time he arrived at his office. The space was immaculate; swirls of nap were still apparent in the ochre carpet from where it had been vacuumed in the middle of the night by a cleaning staff he would never meet. He slid a Mahler CD into the vertical sandwich of glass that made up the sound system, and for a brief moment he remembered how long ago when the marriage was about to fall apart, his father used to listen to Mahler all night long. He wondered if his father still listened to Mahler. He'd find out tonight, perhaps, when he landed in Florida and was taken into his father's home.

Michael suddenly became aware of a lurking figure in his doorway. It was Rufus Webb, product manager, twenty-six years old and agitated, his eyes bagged from no sleep, his private life an empty container. Rufus lived for his work, and he emailed Michael whenever they weren't together, whenever they had a brief break from office life, and the two men would engage in a volley of words. Michael had found, lately, since his sexual problems with Thea had begun, that he didn't mind the obsessiveness of his coworker, and the way Rufus was slowly dragging Michael into it as well. "Into my *Webb*," said Rufus, as he'd surely said to many people before.

"You're really going away?" Rufus asked now with undisguised anxiety.

"Yes."

"When exactly?"

"End of today. You know that. I'm taking a week. Lot of vacation saved up."

"Oh. Right." Rufus shifted from foot to foot in the doorway. "I hope I can keep on top of things without you," he said glumly.

"Of course you can."

"I'll email you about the changes."

"No. Don't. Please please don't," Michael said. "I need a little time to myself, Rufus. Family business. You understand."

Rufus Webb's eyes glassed out briefly; no, he did not understand, he could not understand, he had no family, it was an incomprehensible concept to him; he had been born in a solar pod on Zoron. "Don't forget, the twins are coming in two weeks," Rufus hissed quietly, ominously, before turning and making his exit.

The twins. Michael's mouth went dry. No one liked to say the twins' actual names aloud; it was like the way observant Jews were supposed to write G-d instead of God, Michael thought, for the full name was so powerful and daunting it should not even be written. The twins lived in Maui, in a wood-and-glass house they shared near a dormant volcano, and while they sat in that house attached to computers and headphones and Blackberries, overseeing the workings of their company in New York, it was as though they were sitting here in the offices, so present were they in all daily business. They were short, balding men in their early thirties, slightly malformed, and with a connoisseur's interest in marijuana.

Nothing in the twins' demeanor would suggest that they should be feared and lionized, yet their employees did anyway. Even Michael did. It was not just because they were so rich, but because they were rich men who devoted their lives to causes. And for this they were to be both feared and lionized, for it was a stance to which anyone who had been hired by DDN inevitably aspired: rich. Rich *and* good. You were reminded of the Beatles. You were reminded of ideals you thought you'd lost during the crazy, grabby dream of the 1980s and into the 1990s.

Michael had been part of that, too, making a lot of money in a start-up that had soon failed, living briefly with a fast-talking woman from L.A. named Alison Berman, who was obsessed with the stock market and started day-trading instead of going to her job as a financial officer at a bank. Sometimes Michael would come home and she wouldn't even look up from the screen to say hello. Her eyes never seemed to *blink* when she was in front of the computer. She sat there long into the evening, eating lo mein from a take-out container, noodles hanging doggishly for a moment from her mouth if something had caught her attention on the screen before she had a chance to chew. That relationship had ended, thank God; that whole time had ended, and he'd been alone for a while, and jobless.

After Michael had begun working for DDN in 1998, his mother had sent him an article from *Contemporary Psychology* magazine saying that people who worked for good causes suffered far less depression than those who didn't. "FYI," she'd written on a stickie that she'd attached to the cover. But apparently he was not one of those people. The Endeva was working, but only marginally, and he was an ejaculatory nonstarter, and he did not know how to make any of it better.

Impulsively now, Michael picked up the telephone and tapped in his own number. Thea answered right away, her voice fogged, and he realized he had woken her up. It was 9:23 A.M. "Hey you," he said. "Good morning."

"Hey." She yawned and covered the mouthpiece.

"Too late, I heard you," he said. "What a life you lead. Total luxury."

"I wish," said Thea. "But I have to get up now anyway."

They each reminded the other of the chronology of their day: her rehearsal for the Dora play, his in-office Bento-box lunch with the CTO, her improv class, then, finally, his 6 P.M. flight.

"Well, then, have a good trip, Michael," she said.

"Thanks. I think it's good that I'm going there. Maybe I can get my father to change his mind. Make my mother happy."

"Yeah. Listen, I wanted to tell you. Don't feel bad, okay?" Thea suddenly said. "I mean last night and all. In bed. Because I don't feel bad," she reminded him, as if he'd possibly forgotten.

Halfway to the airport later that afternoon, sitting in the backseat of a town car with the aggressive waterfalls and the indoor foliage of the city receding behind him, and with JFK and then a condominium in Florida waiting somewhere ahead, Michael Mellow realized that he'd forgotten to pack his Endeva.

Oh shit, oh shit, he thought, and he frantically called Thea from the car but of course she didn't answer, for she was off at the theatre. He tried to figure out the best way to remedy this. Who could he call? The pharmacy, that was who; he could have them contact his father's pharmacy in Florida, and the new prescription would be waiting for him when he got there. He wouldn't even have to miss a day of the drug. But he didn't want to involve his father in this; he didn't want Paul Mellow to know he was taking Endeva, and to say to Michael with truckloads of empathy, "So tell me what's wrong."

Michael thought about how hard he'd tried in bed last night with Thea; even thinking about it now was excruciating. The drug kept him fairly happy but totally unfinished—and how could you really be happy when you were unfinished? One canceled out the other. Even now, his brain was being remodeled by the pale green, diamond-shaped tablet he'd downed that morning with his tall latte. And even now, if the most exciting woman in the world were to slide into the car beside him, unzip his fly, and put her head in his lap, he would be unable to finish the thing. The *job.* DDN was his day job, and this was his night job.

So no. *No.* Maybe forgetting to pack the Endeva was a sign, telling him to stop scrambling his brain with those endlessly spinning isomers. He would go off the drug cold turkey. He knew that was supposed to be a bad idea and that there were side effects—dizziness and the shakes and the sweats—but somehow he didn't care. He was full of pioneer energy now. He'd go to Florida, and he'd get his father to agree to what his mother wanted, and soon Michael would be different, and he would return to New York and to his bed and to the fragrant, waiting body of Thea Herlihy, and he would finish what he'd begun.

Chapter Three

CLAUDIA MELLOW was driving a white rental car out of the city—white because almost all rental cars were white, as if to be more recognizable for what they really were: slightly illegitimate and *off* in some basic way. Which was pretty much how she felt, heading along the Long Island Expressway at one in the afternoon on this bright winter day, the car back-loaded with rented cameras and cables and dollies. Traffic was light, for the L.I.E. was a commuter road, and the commuters were settled into their city offices by now, their children installed in the large, colorfully adorned classrooms of their suburban schools.

She turned the heater on high and the air came in harshly, smelling of cooked plastic, but soon the warmth relaxed her, softened her rigid stance behind the wheel. Driving did not come naturally to Claudia Mellow; she had a license, but almost never had cause to drive. It all returned to her surprisingly easily, the sluggish passivity mixed with vigilance. She was going back to Wontauket to shoot a movie, though she knew she had no real business doing so. Her equipment was lying across the red upholstery of

the Nissan Maxima and filling the carpeted trunk; its presence in
the car gave her a kind of authority, the way equipment always
did. If you wrapped yourself in the trailing vines of wires and
cables, then you seemed somehow connected to the world at large.

Claudia was a film student, one of many in the city. Film students were everywhere now, not just here but in smaller cities, too,
all of which now boasted their own film "academies." These schools
sprang up wherever classrooms were available and equipment was
rentable and a handful of a certain kind of film-school graduate—
who now did industrials or commercials or made independent films
or had sold a screenplay—were available to teach a class in the
afternoon or evening. The students were a mixed, sloppy lot, their
ages ranging from right out of college to the mid-fifties. Classes
were available for a weekend, four weeks, eight weeks, a semester,
or an entire year; the programs were so expensive that they tended
to attract a certain kind of soft trust-fund type, someone with no
clearly delineated goals for his or her own life.

At age thirty-four, Claudia watched movies as often as she
could, sometimes in clusters, roaming from theater to theater in a
multiplex and ducking out one set of double doors and into
another. It was simply a continuation of the interest that had
started during the four-thirty movie as a child. It never really mattered to her if she'd missed the beginning of a film because she
knew she could always catch up. Narratives were not that diverse
or complicated, except in superficial ways; movies essentially gave
you the same sensation, dipping you into a liquid coating of darkness and forcing you to watch the screen, for there was nothing
else around you to compete for your attention.

When video stores began to open everywhere around America,
Claudia took out multiple memberships in her neighborhood. She
was forgetful and would invariably incur late fees, but it didn't
matter to her. The fees were a small slap on the hand for being the
kind of person who needed a continual dose of movies in order to
make life flow by.

She had some money that her parents had put into an account many years ago, and now she was finally spending it on film-school tuition. Her parents had given all the children this money when they were still married; they had sat everyone down in the den, a foreshadowing of the divorce conversation that would one day follow. "We want you to know," their father had begun, "that we are putting some money in trust for each of you."

Claudia didn't know what he was talking about, what "in trust" meant, but Holly had nodded and coolly asked, "When can I get it?" Years later, Holly would rant to her sister and brothers that it was "sex money, I mean, fucking *blood* money," but she'd accepted it anyway; all of them had. So the money from the book, which had pulled and stretched and altered the family, was now going into the pockets of the New York branch of the Metro Film Academy, in which Claudia had enrolled for one semester. Thirteen weeks for a 16mm-film class, and it was costing her thousands of dollars, not even including the rental of the Arriflex camera.

She'd worked in jobs of marginal interest for the past few years, having been a typist at a law firm at night, and a dog walker, and, most recently, an assistant to the publicist Marnie Lembad at the PR firm Kline Lembad, until Marnie had shouted and called her "a stupid, fat cunt" in front of everyone after Claudia had forgotten to give her a telephone message from an important agent.

"No I'm not," Claudia had said bravely and unwisely. "You're the cunt." There were vague muffled gasps from the hallway, where people were huddled, indiscreetly listening.

"Just leave," Marnie Lembad said, waving her long white hand. "Just get out." And so Claudia did. As she passed the staff of Kline Lembad—everyone too frightened and awed to offer more than a fleeting look of telepathic sympathy—she had felt horrified at herself, and she had gone straight home and put on the DVD of *The Godfather*, then gotten into bed and watched it through to the end, and followed it up with *The Godfather Part II*, crying intermittently over the loss of her job and how unmoored she was in the universe, as well as over the terrible thing that had been said to her. For she wasn't stupid, and she wasn't a cunt. But it was the fairly reasonable accusation of fatness that disturbed her.

At five foot one, Claudia Mellow wasn't exactly heavy, but appeared too solid. She imagined that her body looked like a garbage bag full of leaves. Small, loosely filled, her legs very short, as though she were one of those little dogs that the Queen of England favored. Her breasts, too, were quite big for such a small, squat body. They overhung too far, like buck teeth. Buck tits, she had always thought about herself, and sometimes she wondered if in fact she had some sort of genetic condition that no one had ever noticed, something really obscure, perhaps called Poorly Assembled X.

Claudia's body broke every aesthetic rule. Short, thick, big-breasted, *strange*, that was what she was. The redemption existed in her face, for she was in possession of beautiful blue eyes, fair, unblemished skin, and dark waves of brown hair. If that head had been on another body, everything would have been different. But men, and boys before them, understood that a woman was a composite thing, a package of brains, face, and body, and as a result, most of them stayed away. The men she'd gone out with had often had something wrong with them. Clifford Zelman, several years older than she was, had been a Thalidomide baby, with one arm tapering off to a slender stump. But he'd been mean to her, too, asking Claudia in bed whether or not she'd ever thought about having her breasts reduced. Another man named Andy Meyers had recently been released from low-level psychiatric care, though he seemed perfectly normal, if a little melancholy. Depression ran in his family like a river, he said. He and his father and sister had all received electro-convulsive therapy before they were twenty-one. In college, Claudia had slept with several different men, two of whom had turned out to be gay, and who, she thought in retrospect, had been attempting to employ her in their quest to verify their sexuality. Yes, it had been verified.

Instead of being a lover, Claudia Mellow was a friend, and a good one, too. Many people counted on her and confided in her in ways that made them say, afterward, "I don't know why I told you that. I've never told it to anyone before." She had her own secrets, of course, though her sense of shame was so profound that it almost always kept her from revealing too much. It was her soft-edged, indistinct quality that Claudia was certain separated her from everyone around her. And this, she was convinced, could be tracked right back to her childhood, to the moment when her father mounted her mother in the pages of a book.

People always wanted to hear about that time, that strange experience, and usually she was willing to say a few things to them about it. Over time she formulated a canned response, which she used again and again, something along the lines of: *Well, it was pretty intense. I guess it embarrassed me. It embarrassed my brothers and my sister, too. But we got through it.* And then she tried to change the subject, to train the attention back toward the other person, which invariably the other person wanted anyway. She was relieved when she could listen again.

As a child, Claudia had been the kind of girl whom teachers liked to have around. She'd clapped erasers fiercely for her kinder-garten teacher, Ms. Pernak, whom she had loved, back when teach-ers used erasers and blackboards. She was a Mellow, a famous Mellow, and most of the teachers had felt sorry for her, poor funny-looking little duck, having to go through childhood living under the vast wing of her parents' sex life.

School had saved her from their sex life and from the uproar that sprang up around it. On the night that her father found out that his wife was ending their marriage, he had taken all the chil-dren for a wild car ride. Claudia, not understanding any of the specifics yet but still somehow understanding the essence of what was happening, had sat in the very back of the station wagon and closed her eyes. *Think of school,* she told herself. *Think of school.* As though it were a temple, a place of quiet worship. Her family was fracturing in ways that made no sense, but school was still there for her, day after day, and the teachers looked after her tenderly.

And this was how, so many years later, Claudia had come to choose the subject for her student film. It was to be called *K Through 6,* and it would be a documentary about the teachers she'd had in elementary school in Wontauket. She would find out what had happened to them, and what they had thought about their students, and about teaching in general, and about their own lives over the decades that had passed. Claudia had looked them up on the Internet and had then contacted the ones she'd been able to locate, and each of them had agreed to be interviewed on-camera. None of them seemed particularly surprised that Claudia wanted to come interview them. Two were still teaching at the school, three had retired, and two more, she learned from the others, were dead. Today she would be filming the first of them, Ms. Pernak, and she felt a certain anxiety and excitement at the prospect, not only because she'd never made a movie before and didn't know what she was doing, but also because she had no idea of what she would find.

Claudia pulled her white car onto the Wontauket exit and headed into the heart of the town. She drove in broad circles, checking out the main drag dispassionately, the new nail salons and old stationery stores and the Brunckhorst deli, where macaroni salad sat for years in metal tubs. The car passed the Wontauket dump, where Dashiell used to dig, and on whose periphery Claudia and Dashiell played hiding and tagging games in a frenzy, unattended for an entire day, back in the time when parents could risk letting their children out of sight.

"I can't believe you're going to make a movie in Wontauket," Dashiell had emailed her the week before. Though he was always frantic at the campaign office in Rhode Island, their emails were fairly constant. Ordinarily Dashiell was kind and praised Claudia's meek steps out into the world, but when she wrote that she was going out to Wontauket to shoot a student film, he had written back, "I don't know why you'd want to do that. I'd never go back."

"Really?" she wrote. "Not even to see how it's changed?"

"No way," he responded. "Let it change without me. I'm done with that place."

Claudia had been done with it too, but now, suddenly, she wasn't. She didn't have to be at the elementary school until four today, and there was time to kill, and the only way to spend it would be to go take a look at the house. Claudia hadn't known the prospect would make her so anxious. She pressed the search function on the radio, quickly located one of those "smooth jazz" stations, with its honey-dripping female DJs and noodling guitar riffs. She tried to let the insipid music lull her, and all the while she looked around and noted that the chicken take-out place, Pluck of the Draw, had survived the years of her absence, its aromatic grease still being released through a furred vent, and that so had the Clothes Pony, where Claudia had gone with her mother to buy an ugly orange dress for the band concert in seventh grade. She'd been third flute, nothing special.

Claudia took a right and plunged back into the neighborhood of collegiate streets, where the house sat waiting. Here were Amherst Drive and Bryn Mawr Avenue and Wellesley Lane; here were Princeton Court and Grinnell Way, which had always puzzled Wontauket residents who had never heard of that college, for it was all the way out in Nowhere, Iowa, unlike the other, East Coast jewel boxes, which were meant to inspire envy. The trees in the neighborhood were massive, and what had appeared brittle and young and anemic back then had now been filled in, as though a child had diligently worked a green crayon across an enormous page.

She turned onto Swarthmore Circle and fastidiously parallel-parked across the street from the house, shut off the jazz and the engine. There it was, almost unrecognizable now, though still it evoked some feeling of being unnerved and vulnerable. The cedar shingles and rough brick had been whitewashed, and the front door was turquoise and gaudy, with geometric shapes gouged into the wood and a big brass knocker. The mailbox at the curb read "Gupta," which at first was surprising, for she remembered that the house had been sold to a family named Feng. It seemed odd to Claudia that the Fengs would have sold the house so soon. The reason that Roz Mellow had eventually sold the place was because her marriage was long over and the last child, Claudia, was going off to college. The Fengs hadn't seemed the type of couple to get divorced or even uproot themselves; both of them were tiny and deferential, and they had served Claudia and her mother a thermos of green tea and a bag of Brach's hard candies to seal the deal.

That year, 1986, was the height of pan-Asiafication in Wontauket. The suburb had gone from blond kids on banana-seat Schwinns to an oasis of darker ones who, as time passed, traveled on more evolved vehicles: dirt bikes, skateboards, electric scooters, and eventually longboards, those land-kayaks rolling along suburban tar. Claudia sat for a few moments in the car, just looking at the house and the peaceful street, which many years ago had absorbed the celebrity and scandal of her parents, and then the end of the Mellow marriage, all done in public, all done so everyone could see it and have an opinion. The ordinary had replaced the unusual, and the individual and collective sorrows of the Mellow family, formerly of 8 Swarthmore Circle, had been pulled into the atmosphere and dispersed over time.

She would have liked to email Dashiell right now and tell him it was okay, he could come back here, it wouldn't be as bad as he thought. She almost wanted to write to all of them and find some excuse to bring them here. But none of them would ever come. Holly was Holly—disconnected from the others, fucked-up, out of commission, essentially useless to the family, for reasons that Claudia had not been able to name, without resorting to a kind of babble that involved generic words like "damage," "inadequacy," and "anger," specifically the "unresolved" kind. And Michael was so preoccupied. She thought about him now, off in Florida with their father and Elise. She pictured Paul Mellow in shorts and sandals, his beard a mix of curling white and gray, his eyes still kind and alert and wounded. It was difficult to imagine Michael relaxing down there with him, for Michael didn't relax; it wasn't in his uptight nature. So what was he *doing* down there? Though he had supposedly gone to Florida for only one week, two weeks had already gone by, and there he stayed.

"I'm fine," Michael had told his sister when she telephoned him at the condominium a few days earlier. She'd felt the need for a phone call so that she could actually hear his voice and gauge how he sounded. She decided that he sounded very strange.

"Are you sure?" she asked him.

"Of course I'm sure. Why wouldn't I be? Did someone say something about me?"

"Don't get paranoid. I was just wondering, that's all. I thought you were only staying a week."

"Yes, well, that was the plan," he said. "But then the week went by and Dad hadn't changed his mind about the book yet, and basically I thought, oh what the hell, I'll stay here. Why not? It's really nice. I got a little leave from work. No big deal."

It was unlike Michael to leave work for a minute. The story got stranger and stranger. "Thea thinks it's fine," said Michael. "And I think it's very productive that I'm here. Dad and I are working things out. Mom will be pleased." Then he'd quickly gotten off the phone.

Claudia saw that someone was at the blue mailbox down the street now, opening it and depositing letters. It was a woman wearing a down vest and thick woolen headband, and she paused for a moment, looking in Claudia's direction, and then approached the car. It was Elaine Gamble; the formerly pretty, crazy Elaine Gamble, whose son had gone missing in Vietnam, was now a senior citizen, her hair a silvery gray. Alone, childless, divorced, she had stayed on in her own house diagonally across the street from the

Mellows'/Fengs'/Guptas' house, and here she was, scrawnier, fairer, less wild-eyed than she used to be, as though time could even take care of the problem of incessant thoughts about a son, dead in a misbegotten war.

Claudia opened the car door and stood to meet her. "Claudia Mellow? Is that you?" Mrs. Gamble asked.

"It's me," Claudia said, trying to smile, and in one fluid movement the woman swept her up into her arms mother-style, though they'd never been nearly as affectionate back when the Mellows lived on Swarthmore. Elaine Gamble had been too stunned and disturbed back then. Now she was somehow sanded down, smoother, as though she'd been listening to nothing but that jazz station.

"Well, what in the world are you doing here?" the woman asked. "And at this time of year?"

"Actually, I'm making a little film," Claudia said, at first with pride, and then embarrassment. The equipment poking up from the back seat of the Maxima seemed to give her away, the spindly tripod and lights and the handheld Arriflex and the Nagra, all of which she would have to clumsily manage today without a crew, without help. She was on her own here, alone, and it had all been her choice, but when asked to explain herself, she couldn't. Something must have brought her back here—a very strong wind, maybe?

"Well, isn't that just great," said Mrs. Gamble. "I don't think we've ever had a movie shot on this block. The last time the cameras were here was, well, with your mother and father."

"Oh. Right." There was silence. Claudia didn't know what else to say now. *Is Stu still missing in Southeast Asia, or did they find his remains?* She wasn't good in social moments like these.

"I work at the library part-time," Mrs. Gamble offered. "There's a group of us ladies who've lived here forever. I get first pick of all the seven-day express books. That's a plus; all the juicy novels. And you—you're a filmmaker."

"No," Claudia said sharply. "Not really. This is my first

attempt." She noticed, all of a sudden, that Elaine Gamble's wrist was exposed and that she wasn't wearing her old POW/MIA bracelet. Finally, she must have had it cut off or pried open. Claudia blinked and felt an unaccountable disorientation, and so she tried to smile.

"Well, good luck to you," said Mrs. Gamble. "And tell your mom hello. And your dad, too. And that sweet brother of yours, that Michael, say hello from me. I always liked him."

She turned to leave, and Claudia called after her, "Mrs. Gamble?" The woman turned around. "Who are the Guptas?"

"Pardon?" said Mrs. Gamble.

"The Guptas. Who live in the house now?"

"I don't really know them, but they're a husband and wife with grown children. They're Indian. *Indian*-Indian. Obviously. They own Bombay Café, the restaurant downtown."

"What happened to the Fengs?" asked Claudia.

Mrs. Gamble squinted. "Oh yes, the Chinese. They moved out long ago. Went back to China, I believe, or maybe it was just to Queens. I'm embarrassed to admit I can't really recall."

Then she was off with a shy, quick wave, hurrying back into her house. Claudia looked over at the Guptas' house, which was dark inside and without a car in the driveway. What did the rooms look like? She wanted to go in and see what was there now, what had been dismantled, what no longer existed. Maybe, before she finished the shoot in a few weeks, she would return to the house and see if she could find a way to get inside. But now it was time to drive off to the school to meet Ms. Pernak.

School had been wonderful because her teachers, particularly Ms. Pernak, had wanted to protect her from her *parents,* she had once realized, those exhibitionists, those pornographers, though surely at least a few of the teachers owned a copy of *Pleasuring.* "Why do you choose to live in the suburbs?" an interviewer had once asked Paul and Roz, and they'd answered that they wanted to give their children a life of "open spaces." It didn't matter to them that their neighbors might not be as sophisticated as people in the city. But only twenty minutes away by car, in a town less affluent and open-minded, candlelight marches were held in 1975 in front of the public library, and the marchers demanded that *Pleasuring* be banned, even though they hadn't bothered to learn that the library had already removed the book from its collection. But the temptation of a march, with torches held aloft and a late-night claiming of suburban streets, was too great for angry village parents who had dreams of witch-burning and barnstorming in their heads, as though their own fierce response would drown out the sounds of two people making love.

Claudia's teachers presented themselves as being above the scandal, the gossip, and even being above sex itself. Some of the younger ones unconsciously began to dress less like women and more like the children they taught. If you looked back at class pictures from that time you would see twenty-six-year-old teachers in tartan plaid and flat shoes and even with the occasional pigtails hanging loosely from either side of the head.

Claudia parked the car now in the near-empty lot at Felice P. Bolander Elementary. No one even remembered the woman whose name was gouged into a granite slab on the tan brick side of a building. She had died in 1965, in the era of space flights and molded gelatin desserts. Felice P. Bolander, Claudia had once heard, had been a librarian in the school district back then, recommending her favorite children's authors to whoever would listen, until cancer felled her at age thirty-seven. There were no yearly mammograms back then to detect the lump that stayed suspended in her breast like a small chunk of fruit in one of those gelatin desserts.

Someone on the board of superintendents had felt sentimental about the pale woman who used to stand copies of *Blueberries for Sal* and *The Yearling* up on the library table and actually *polish* their transparent plastic covers with a chamois cloth. So a few years later, when the ground was broken for the new elementary school, it was named after her. Eventually, the people who had known Felice P. Bolander began to retire, or move away, or die, and the new crops of yearly children thought of her not as a person but as a name, and then not really as a name but as a word. Where do you go to school? *Bolander.*

Claudia dragged her Arriflex and Nagra and the rest of the equipment piece by piece from the backseat and trunk of the car. Her hands were unsteady as she lifted the cameras onto the carpeted wooden plank, and wound up the coils of rubber so they wouldn't drag under the wheels.

Inside the building, there were sounds of chairs being moved and papers being collated. There was a distant clang of gym equipment, or was it cafeteria trays, and Claudia stood still in the hallway with her burden of equipment, surprised at the lack of security in this age of Columbine, and finally she just walked on through, a giant in a strange, small land.

A man appeared from the AV room and stood looking at her for a moment. Small, bony-faced, lightbulb-headed, yes, yes, he was Mr. Corcoran, who ran the media center then and forever after. "Can I help you?" he asked.

"Mr. Corcoran? I used to go here? Claudia Mellow?" she said, all questions, waiting for the lightbulb to in fact light up, which it did momentarily.

"Yes, Claudia, right. We wondered what became of all of you," he said.

"Well," Claudia said stiffly, "I wondered what became of all of *you.*"

"Me?"

"Not you in particular. My teachers, I mean. K through six."

"You're making some sort of film?" Mr. Corcoran asked. "That's heavy-duty equipment there. You should see what we've got in here." He motioned with his head toward the AV room, and to be polite she let him take her inside to show her all the innovations, the taxpayer money that had been spent on media since she was a child. The room was filled with metal stands on which sat state-of-the-art video cameras and slide projectors and DVD players and monitors.

"Very impressive," she said.

He nodded. "We should use this stuff to make a movie about *you*. About all the kids who've graduated, and what they've done with their lives." He paused. "I didn't ask you," he said. "What exactly *have* you done?"

At which point something inside Claudia tightened and squinted; she didn't want to talk about her own adult life and its shapelessness and disappointments. K through six was a perfect bracket of time; that was where she wanted to be. "Oh, I've been in women's prison," she heard herself say. He stared at her for a moment, so she quickly put him out of his misery. "Only kidding," she added.

"Very good, very good, you had me there," said Mr. Corcoran.

Claudia found the kindergarten classroom by some sort of interior compass, and there was Ms. Pernak, just as she'd said during their brief but friendly telephone conversation, except she was a little different, as though she were Ms. Pernak's *aunt*. She was still big and broad-shouldered, but her hair was short now, frosted. She wore a blazer adorned with a glittering pin. There was no teacher's desk in the classroom—those had been done away with years ago, and the Socratic method, even the K through six version, had been abandoned, along with any semblance of unchallenged authority. The teacher never had time to sit, anyway; she wandered the room during the day, crouching, kneeling, tying, fixing, drying, wiping, saving, changing, imploring.

Ms. Pernak was different, but still she was the same. The teachers stayed in place, and you, the student, moved on through life, racking up achievements, creating a new body of friends and work and a block of hard, bright status. And if you were ever in need of a slug of cheap gratification, you could always visit your old teachers and they might say: *Look at you. You've turned out splendidly.*

But here was Claudia Mellow now, age thirty-four and not entirely splendid. She was almost exactly as she had been in kindergarten, still short and somewhat stocky and unfinished but touchingly appealing to most people who met her. It was as though she was not fully baked, was still damp in the middle where you stuck in the toothpick to check for doneness. She felt uncertain as she lingered in the doorway, not quite in the room, not quite out. No matter what she did with her life, how she grew and altered over time, she was still *Claudia*, the insecure but affectionate youngest child of two parents for whom children were a serious responsibility, and sex was bliss. Her teacher called her in.

A little while later, sitting at a cluster of pushed-together desks, Claudia held the camera with a shaking, loopy hand, and at first she'd actually forgotten to remove the lens cap, a mistake that she rectified with a "whoops" and a quick mime of shooting herself in the head with a pistol.

"Take your time, take your time," Ms. Pernak said.

"Okay. Thank you. Sorry about this." Claudia dropped a light meter, which bounced off the leg of a chair and went skidding off. She chased it down and then returned, red-faced and muttering but determined. She pressed a button and there was a whirring sound. The film started rolling.

"I guess I wanted to start by asking you what you've learned, teaching here for so many years," Claudia said.

"What I've learned?"

"Yes."

Doreen Pernak tried to answer as best she could, and while she spoke, Claudia was a one-man band with all her equipment, steadying the camera on her shoulder, keeping a finger on the microphone, taking pauses to adjust lights and check cables. She was as insecure and determined as always. All those stories about how teachers molded young minds weren't exactly true. An awkward girl tended, eventually, to be an awkward woman.

"What do you remember most from those years?" she asked.

"Let me see," said her teacher. "Well, I remember a lot of things. It was a happy time, I think. The 1970s. You know. Everyone was so much more hopeful than they are now, I guess. I don't even know why that was so, because we were still in Vietnam, and the economy was bad, but the children seemed more innocent to me. And when I would come here each day, it was like returning to that innocence."

In the middle of filming, the door to the classroom opened, and two young women burst right in, both of them with winter coats on, laughing. "Yo, Doreen!" one said. "Get your coat on, wench. It's happy hour, and we're going to get hammered!" Then they realized that Doreen was not alone, and the woman clapped a hand over her mouth.

"Oh God," she said. "We didn't know . . ."

"It's okay. I'm only in here shooting my Academy Award–winning role," said Doreen Pernak.

Introductions were made all around, and the teachers, both of them fresh-faced and lively and younger than Claudia, retreated with further apologies. They were part of a whole new generation of teachers, modern, jazzy, armed with methodology that hadn't even been dreamed up when Claudia was a child. "If you finish up soon," the first one said, "feel free to join us, okay? Both of you."

When they were gone, Claudia Mellow lowered the ungainly camera, placing it with a dull thud on the surface of the desks, and she looked at her teacher with an expression of lopsided intensity. "I guess I also wanted to ask," she said, "what do you remember about *me*? I mean, this isn't for the film exactly, it's just for my own curiosity."

What she might have said was this: Ms. Pernak, elementary school was my Xanadu. Nothing has felt as safe or as comfortable or as pleasurable since then, not college, not men, not work, not anything. And now I'm here in this body I don't like, trying to figure out what to do, renting an incredibly expensive Arriflex and Nagra and trying to operate them just the way I've been trying to operate this body of mine, to make it move and thrive and be out there in the world, but it's too hard, it won't work the way it's supposed to.

Doreen Pernak cleared her throat and fiddled with the cat pin on her blazer. "I remember what a tough time you had at home," she began, "what with your parents and all. And I remember how much you loved school. And how much you wanted to please me. And that you did."

Both women sat there for a quiet moment in the classroom, recalling another afternoon twenty-eight years earlier when they had stood together in that same room and clapped erasers, clouding the air with white and pink and yellow dust, knowing that even though these weren't clouds of mystery, they were close enough.

When the sky took on the coloration that, in childhood, had indicated dinner and homework and the slow march toward bed, Claudia Mellow left Bolander and drove back through the town. Ms. Pernak had been as thoughtful and patient as always, and yet there was something *boring* about her that Claudia hadn't noticed when she was young. Perhaps children want the adults who take care of them to be slightly boring, she thought; God knew, her own parents rarely were. They were endlessly interesting, at least to other people. But Doreen Pernak wore a cat pin with green eyes shining out from the matte finish of a 14-karat gold circle, and it seemed like the kind of gift that an entire class of parents would chip in to buy a teacher. And this would dictate the teacher's personal aesthetic. It could have been worse; she could have been forced to wear rigatoni earrings.

Now Claudia planned to head back home to her fifth-floor walk-up studio on 7th Street in the East Village, where the heat came on only sporadically, as if following some internal rhythm. She lived alone and mostly liked it, but there were times when it was difficult to go back to that coldish room and its smells and textures and piles of things. This was one of those times, and she drove her white car around Wontauket once more, circling it all again, passing the Carvel where her father had taken the kids during his famous car ride, and the bank where she'd opened her first passbook savings account at age seven and the teller had called her "ma'am." And then she drove back to Swarthmore Circle, understanding that she had planned to return to the house in darkness all along.

She parked right in front this time, a bold move on such a quiet street. Now, at night, the house was lit. There was excitement at seeing that—seeing a golden stripe of lamplight coming from the picture window, not from the living room proper but from deeper inside the house. She sat in the car and looked, listening to that numbing jazz, and then, as if sleepwalking back into her own childhood, Claudia unbuckled her seat belt and opened the door. Quiet, she was so quiet, so unassuming. So many years of virtual invisibility had given her the idea that she literally *was* invisible, and it was that sense of herself that allowed her to unfold her body from the Maxima and walk silently across the dark front lawn of the house she used to live in. She walked up to the very edge of the front window, shielded her eyes, and looked inside. Some sort of gauzy beige curtains misted the glass. She could see something brown in the near distance—a couch, maybe—and could vaguely make out a shape, then two, moving together and melding into one larger shape, then separating like amoebas. She stood and watched the shapes, and one of them peeled away from the other, moved out of view. Then there was a sound nearby, and she realized it came from outside, and Claudia turned in the darkness on the front lawn, and to her horror she found herself facing an Indian man in his sixties. *Gupta.*

"Just what are you doing?" he said, his voice tight and alarmed. He was a small, compact, bald man in an open dress shirt, hugging himself in the cold.

"I was looking," she said, aware for the first time that she had no real business here, and that he had a right to be angry and frightened. "I'm very sorry," she said.

"I could call the police," Gupta told her without much conviction.

"I used to live here," Claudia said to him, hoping that would explain everything. His face relaxed slightly; he rubbed his head. "Is this true?" he asked.

"Yes. I lived here until 1986. This is where I grew up." He kept looking at her so hard, and finally she said, "The door to the downstairs bathroom always used to stick. Maybe it still does."

Something shifted inside him. Yes, apparently the door still stuck; it had to be forced.

"And you want to see the house now?" he said. "Is that it? At nighttime, without asking? Without telephoning?"

"Well, no, I didn't think I was going to be able to come inside. I was just going to look, really quick, through the window."

Mr. Gupta turned abruptly and started walking back to the house. "Well, come on, then," he said over his shoulder. "It's freezing out here."

She followed him in. Walking up the three steps into the house, her legs knew exactly how high to lift as she ascended. The concrete steps were shallower than you would expect; only a seasoned pro could know precisely how to walk here, and that was what she was. She'd ascended and descended these steps thousands and thousands of times, never once thinking: Will this be my last time? Yet eventually there had been a last time, and by then so much had happened, and most of the family had already moved out, so that she had felt saturated in the house and all it represented, and was perfectly willing to let it go.

Claudia walked through the open door with Mr. Gupta and into the front hall. Once this had been all wood and white walls and photographs; now the walls were darker, an off-yellow color that made you feel that someone's grandparents lived here. They entered the living room, where the carpeting was beige and a sectional sofa was broken up into right angles, and Claudia saw that the blurred shape she'd seen through the glass was a young Indian man of about her age, dressed in jeans and a U. Penn sweatshirt, and who, except for his full head of black hair, was a ringer for Mr. Gupta. They were father and son, both of them short, intense, a little odd looking, with slightly bulbous noses and wide eyes.

"This is David," Mr. Gupta said. Then he nodded to Claudia and said, "The young lady lived in this house once. You'll show her around?"

David looked searchingly at his father, attempting to find the code in his words and decipher it, but apparently there was no code, for Mr. Gupta simply left the room. The telephone rang a moment later, and Claudia heard Mr. Gupta striding upstairs, and then the sound of a door opening. Gupta the Younger looked at Claudia for a moment with displeasure; he didn't want to show her around, not at all.

"It's okay," she said. "I didn't ask to come in. You don't have to do this."

"My father asked me to," he said flatly. "It's all right. You lived here when, exactly?"

She told him the dates and he nodded. Neither father nor son had real trouble believing her; they couldn't imagine why anyone would want to look around this house if there wasn't a legitimate reason. She didn't seem like a burglar, though of course she could have been casing the joint, she supposed. But from the little she had already seen here, there was not much of interest to see, or steal. The furniture was minimal; perfunctory attention had been paid to decor. The house felt like the inside of a large, clean box.

They walked through the kitchen, which was also spotless, though the oak table that had once sat beneath the round light fixture had been replaced by a metal folding table and folding chairs. David Gupta seemed to sense Claudia's surprise or disapproval, which she'd tried to hide, for he said, "My parents are very slow to decorate. I offered to drive them to Ikea, but my mother said she doesn't want her house looking Swedish, whatever that means. Then we didn't discuss it again because she went to help take care of her sister in Karachi who has cancer. So I don't know if they'll ever furnish this place."

"Please," Claudia said. "It looks very nice. Look, I'm here for a minute, and then I'll go. This is really awkward."

"No," he said. "You might as well see the rest."

They toured the first floor, peering into the den, whose recessed bookshelves, which had once been stuffed to the gills, were sparsely filled. Now books alternated with small pieces of pottery, and there were wide-open spaces where nothing at all sat on the shelves, as though a family was in the process of moving in, or moving out. "My parents have almost no time to read," David said, his voice becoming more apologetic, even slightly frantic. "They would if they could."

That was when Claudia realized that he did not live here with them, but was just visiting. All of this was theirs, distinguishable from his. She wondered where *he* lived, and for a moment her thoughts tentatively landed on his home, his life, but she could not provide details, and she had no reason to try to imagine them, anyway. He offered to take her upstairs, and how could she refuse this? Up they went, David Gupta leading the way past pale green walls, underneath which the Mellow children's ancient height marks were scratched. On the second floor, they went into the parents' open bedroom and quickly backed out, for Mr. Gupta was sitting on the bed, talking on the telephone. In that quick moment, Claudia saw that the Guptas' bed was high and austere, and that behind it on the unscuffed, undented wall was a shelf that contained a few knickknacks, including several Indian elephants of jade and bronze. There was no reason for her to have been astonished; what did she think, that after all this time some remnant of her parents would still be left behind?

"Let's go up," David said.

"Of course," said Claudia, following him up to the third floor. "Ah. The children's floor," she found herself whispering.

He stopped briefly on the landing and said, "What?"

"This is where we all lived. The children."

"It's also where my sisters and I stay whenever we visit," he said. The rooms were neat now; no sea monkeys and geckos lived here. There was Michael's room, now a guest room with a day bed; there was Dashiell's room, now loaded with cartons that said "Major Grey's Chutney" on the side; and Holly's room, which currently held a StairMaster and a Tunturi stationary bike, as well as a set of skis leaning against a wall. *Indians on skis,* Claudia thought, and she imagined the Gupta family schussing downhill in matching traditional garb.

Finally David took her into what had once been her own room, which turned out to be the room where he was staying. The bed was made, as if in a hurry, and there were a few books stacked on the night table and a filled-in acrostic from the newspaper. A piece of luggage lay open on the foot of the bed. One nautical print hung on a wall.

"This was my room," Claudia said, and she heard how plaintive that sounded, and she felt flooded, light, nauseated. It was as though there were some recovered memory here, the kind women were always having on talk shows, under hypnosis or merely under the care of a kindly, motherish type of quack therapist. It was as though *something* had happened in this room, instead of *nothing.* In fact, she knew exactly what had happened in this room, and what had not. She wasn't the one who'd had sex in this house; everyone else in her family had done that, but not her. Across the hall, Holly and Adam Selig had humped each other, doglike. If you'd stood outside and placed your ear against the door, as Claudia had done, you could hear repeated sounds of wet mouths sliding together, and the noises of *interiority,* the sounds of desire whipped up as if by a rabble-rouser within the human body.

But in this little room, this nunnery, Claudia had been intimate with no one except her troll dolls. She'd lain in the bed that used to be here, the bed with the rattan headboard. The walls were covered with posters, and the floor had had a carpet she'd chosen herself, an oatmeal grain shot through with purple. It had been her place, most intensely hers, and it had rarely occurred to her that one day she'd have to leave it, that the carpeting would be uprooted, revealing a stained wooden floor beneath. That one day, she would have to give up the enclosure of her room and go out there into the world, for which she, alone among her siblings, was so woefully unprepared.

Here in the room, she thought she might not be able to breathe. Was it her, or was there no air here? "I think I'm going to faint," she said.

"Oh. Oh no. Well here, come sit down," David Gupta said, and he led her over to the bed. "Put your head between your knees," he said, the only thing that anybody ever knew to say in such a moment, and she did as told, feeling the blood bathe the lining of her skull. David Gupta knelt in front of her on the now-blue carpet. She could see his face, staring so closely at her, his eyes wide with concern, or maybe irritation. He didn't need this, after all. Who was she, this interloper, this sad girl who didn't belong here or anywhere, really?

"I should go," Claudia said, and she tried to stand up, but David placed a hand on her shoulder.

"No, no," he said. "It's too soon."

"I'm fine," she told him.

"You know, when I got my medical degree from Heidelberg," he said, smiling, "the first thing they always told us was 'never let the patient stand up too quickly.'"

"Oh really?" she said.

"Yes. Absolutely. And the next thing they told us was 'always wait one hour after eating before you go for a swim.'" His face was so close, and the plunge into forced intimacy was so unexpected. "You got overwhelmed here," he said. "It happens."

"Apparently. I was feeling fine, and then . . . whoosh!"

"Are you any better now?" he asked, and she slowly lifted her head and realized that yes, she was better. The light in the room seemed brighter, and the floor wasn't undulating. The room was just a room. Yes, she'd lived here once, but you would never know. She looked around anew.

"I had a lot of trolls," Claudia said. "They were everywhere in this room. Troll dolls, I mean. I had hundreds. The place was totally overrun with them."

"With the strange hair," David Gupta said. "Yes, I've seen those. I had Matchbox cars. I lined them up and rearranged them all the time. I should have become a parking attendant. It's obviously where my aptitude lay."

For a moment she imagined them as parallel creatures, both of them slow to enter life, both of them in a house belonging to parents. There was no real reason to think he was like her; the only reason to think so was because she suddenly wished they were similar. The wish surprised her, coming on as suddenly as her dizziness had.

"So what job did you end up with?" she asked. "You're not really a doctor, are you?"

He told her that he was an intellectual property lawyer. He worked in Philadelphia, where he lived, and where he'd gone to both college and law school. Hence the Penn sweatshirt. He was back here now for one week to help his father with some legal matters involving the family restaurant. He expected to be back and forth over the next few weeks. "Oh," she said. "Right, the Indian place downtown. I saw it."

"It's a little Pakistani, too. We're Paki on my mother's side. But we just tell people Indian."

"I love Indian food," she said. "My neighborhood's filled with those restaurants."

"The East Village? I've always wanted to live there. You're lucky."

"Not really," she said. "You should see my apartment." By which she meant: You should see my life, its parameters, its limitations, the way it encloses me. He asked her a little about herself, and she told him about classes, her film, and the movie she was shooting.

"Give me your email," David said suddenly. "Maybe we'll be out here at the same time—me for the restaurant and you for your movie. You could come to Bombay Café. You'll need to eat, right?"

Claudia was startled and pleased, trying to parse his words and figure out whether they were perfunctory or charitable or simply impulsive and unanalyzed and perhaps genuine. She exchanged email addresses with him on scraps of paper; everyone's pockets and bags and wallets seemed to be filled with these linty slips, and if no action was taken shortly after receipt of such a slip, the address would become a faded hieroglyphic, a key to someone who would soon become forgotten, and lost forever. The exchange of email addresses was routine now, even between people who knew they would probably never hear from each other again. But she wrote hers down, and he wrote his down, and there was a slightly awkward moment in which they traded, and then Claudia slowly stood. He watched her to make sure she didn't keel over in the middle of his bedroom.

They walked together back into the hallway, where, in the distance one level below, they could hear the thrum of his father's voice. She thought of Mr. Gupta in that thoroughly transformed room, sitting on the edge of the bed, talking on the telephone to his wife, who was off on another continent. Even all the way up here on the third floor, his voice came through. The sounds of parents traveled through walls, traveled up stairs, were inescapable. Wherever you went on earth, you could hear them.

Chapter Four

"TRY THE CHICKEN, it's got pine nuts," Paul Mellow told his son Michael as they sat in the window of a restaurant, and at once he heard the unwanted undercurrent of a magnanimous chuckle that had been planted deep in his vocal cords the moment his first wife gave birth to this man sitting across from him, their first son. The chuckle had never left. Paul Mellow wanted to be a good father, and good fathers were easygoing, so he said, "Try the chicken, it's got pine nuts," and, "Save room for the dolce de leche cake," even though neither of them was really hungry, for it was just noon on a January day in Naples, Florida, and they'd eaten a heavy, gleaming, egg-and-butter breakfast less than four hours earlier. They had been up since seven, two men jogging together on the dewy track that ringed the cluster of bleached-pine Laughing Woods condominiums. Michael was wired, lean, jangly, wanting to be in motion. His father was thicker, gray-bearded, still handsome but softened, forever struggling to catch up. After the jog they'd showered in adjacent stalls at the condominium's sparkling gym, pumping the fragrant turquoise gel soap from the wall, then taken a small motorboat out, catching and releasing the occasional undistinguished fish, and then they'd returned to the condo by noon, where Elise, predictably, was still asleep, her head on the special pillow she'd bought from a TV infomercial that testified to its miraculous effects. The pillow was stuffed with raw Japanese red rice and supposedly offered a better, richer night's sleep. Apparently, this was truth in advertising, for Elise slept and slept.

She kept different hours from Paul, out at her part-time social work job three days a week, while he stayed home trying to write articles for *Modern Maturity* and the *AARP* magazine and was interviewed once in a while by representatives from the Council on Aging, for whom he was soon to travel to Miami to deliver a talk called "Sex After Seventy." There weren't all that many hours in the day during which his and Elise's lives really intersected. This, as it turned out, wasn't a bad thing, particularly now, with Michael here in town. He'd come only for a week, which had turned into two. With his son on the premises, Paul felt suddenly happy, nostalgic, resurrected, as though Michael had lifted him up by his belt loops and forced him to engage in ways he hadn't done in a very long time.

Florida leveled you. It didn't matter who you were. In the beginning you were besotted with the enormous high-colored flowers that looked like they had faces, and by the sauna atmosphere and grilled fish and abundance of citrus and pastel clothes and geniality of everyone you met, who like you had removed themselves from the din and clack of urban life, saying they'd had enough. But after a while you became a little aimless, dreaming at night of subways and coffee shops that stayed open until morning, and of black people, whom you never saw down here. You started to want something more for yourself but knew that that was impossible.

It wasn't that your mind had to shut down; Laughing Woods itself, with its array of adult education classes held on the premises, was like a miniature School of Athens. "School of Naples," Paul had joked to Bart Dombler next door, but the retired anesthesiologist had just blinked and said, "Pardon?"

Once a week, Paul and Elise went down to the Gathering Room in the C building for their class in American poetry. They were now reading Emily Dickinson, which Elise loved, and sometimes recited quietly to herself when she thought he wasn't listening. Long ago, Paul seemed to recall, Roz had loved Emily Dickinson too, but he had barely listened when she'd read a poem aloud. Instead, he'd been distracted by looking at her, moved somehow by the sight of Roz reading poetry, yet he was unable to concentrate on the words themselves.

Yoga classes were also available here, and Szechwan cookery, and an under-enrolled class in political theory, offered by a retired Haverford professor who lived alone in the B building and didn't seem to know what to do with himself all day. Paul, feeling a little sorry for the man, had attended one of the sessions, at which he'd been given Xeroxed handouts of Marx and Engels from a thick, optimistic stack.

Everyone in Laughing Woods, Paul was certain, felt this double-barreled awareness of loss and disappointment. Some of them felt it all the time. He wished he could turn to one of his neighbors and say, "Do you feel it too?" But he couldn't even say it to Elise, for she was the one who had asked that they move down here in the first place. When she wasn't working with Spanish-speaking families in desperate need of her services or sleeping in bed, she liked to paint. Her artwork wasn't very accomplished, but it was lively and heartfelt and she enjoyed doing it. In New York she would have had no luck, but here in Naples she had been part of a group show, held in an airy gallery. The local newspaper not only reviewed the show but also ran photographs and interviews with the painters. Elise had sold a few paintings, too, and if you happened to wander into another apartment in the complex you might see one of Elise's "lost girl" series hanging over a sofa, immediately recognizable by the muddy greens and golds, and by her difficulty in painting symmetrical eyes.

She herself was entirely symmetrical, though she had one of those faces that, months after they'd gotten married, Paul had begun to see everywhere. Eventually he realized it was because she'd had her nose fixed in college, and that many people had such a nose. The slender nose with its little button at the end, coupled with her hair permed into a tangle of loose curls that fell in her eyes, gave Elise the accidental look of a poodle. When she dressed up for the evening and wore the chocolate brown lipstick she favored, she reminded him specifically of a dancing poodle in a circus. What a terrible thing to think about the woman you had married! But he still loved her, was attracted to her as well. It was just that she had become, or he had realized she had always been, a little dull, though he supposed that he was dull as well, age sixty-eight and still wanting love to exist in a pure column of light, still convinced that it could.

Michael was having troubles with love too. After dinner on the second night of his visit, sitting together in the living room while Elise puttered around elsewhere in the condo, Michael had admitted to his father that things weren't going well at home. He wouldn't give any specifics about his love troubles, except to say that he and his girlfriend Thea needed a little time apart, so it was really a good thing that he'd come down to Florida.

But Paul saw that his son looked shaky and sweaty, and he was in the habit of jiggling his leg while talking. What the hell was wrong with him? If Paul didn't know any better, he would have thought his son was a drug addict. But of course Michael hated drugs and always had; he was constitutionally unfit for them, and decades earlier, on the occasions when teenaged Michael had seen his parents share a joint, he'd ostentatiously waved his hand in the air and coughed prudishly, letting them know that the smoke offended him.

So it wasn't drugs. It was just trouble, love trouble. Yesterday, while the two men were playing nine holes at Hilldale, Michael had given him a little more to go on. He had told Paul that things with his girlfriend Thea were difficult because she seemed not to care about his well-being. "What exactly do you mean?" Paul asked. "Give me specifics."

"I can't," said his son.

Neither of them was a golfer, but the day was quiet and the air lightly lifted the hair on your forearms as you stood perfecting your stance, worrying your iron slightly back and forth, setting up the shot that would end up no good anyway, no matter what you did.

"Well, I'm sorry things are hard for you," Paul said. He kept his eye on the ball and didn't look up at Michael's unhappy face; long ago he'd read that the best way for two men to talk to each other was while they were doing something active—and didn't actually have to make eye contact and then feel threatened and retreat into their groundhog holes.

All of a sudden there was a chirping sound, and Paul looked up at his son, who said, "One sec, Dad," and then reached into the pocket of his trousers and pulled out his PDA. Paul watched as Michael punched some keys and squinted at the tiny screen. "Oh, crap," said Michael. "It never stops."

"Thea?"

"No. My job. There's this guy there, Rufus. He can't do anything without me. He's totally dependent, and he's freaking out at work. The twins are coming, the twins are coming. That's all he talks about."

"The twins, eh? They're coming to the office?"

"Yeah. Tomorrow. I reassured him that I'd be there, but I'm not, obviously. Just a second, Dad, okay?" And Michael tapped out a response to the message, then returned the PDA to his pocket. It would ring off and on throughout the remainder of his visit, during golf games and meals and moments of quiet conversation, and always Michael would respond. His son would never be free of work, or of worry, would never be able to just *relax*.

"Forgive my bluntness," said Paul. "But what you were saying before, about your girlfriend. The problem is sexual, am I right?"

"No. Yes. Yeah. Yeah, it is," said Michael, and he swung the golf club, knocking the ball loose and sloppy into the middle distance. "I can't believe I'm telling you this."

"Why not?" said his father. "I know one or two things, right?"

"Yeah, you're the sex god, Dad. I always forget that."

"I'm not the sex god. I'm not *a* sex god. I'm nothing like that," Paul said. "Your mother saw to that."

"I was kidding."

Paul found himself blushing, as if a thickset sixty-eight-year-old man with a gray beard and bifocals could in fact be sexually powerful, could knock the socks off women in a serious fashion, the way he once had. And actually, a sixty-eight-year-old man *could* do that. *He* could do it, Paul felt certain, if the circumstances were right. The woman would have to make an effort, though. He couldn't ask Elise to, for what could he say: Can you turn your poodle eyes on me with admiration—no, with worship, please? Can you bring your quivering, hand-shy self into my lap and touch me and stroke me and remind me of why we married each other?

Just as Michael could not say to Thea, a woman his father had met just twice: Can you forget about yourself for a moment and make it about me?

Through their problems with women, father and son were bonded now, they were tight. They finished their golf game and rode the cart back to the clubhouse. Stay here forever, Paul wanted to tell Michael. Stay here as long as you want and recuperate from Thea and the stresses of DDN and urban life here in our peach-colored guest room in Naples, Florida, and forget about that actress in New York, who will never give you anything other than grief. Stay here with me, he thought, because I'm your father, and as you may have noticed, I'm unhappy too.

Miraculously last week, as if reading Paul's mind, Michael had asked if he could stay a little longer. He was vague about how much longer, and Paul didn't want to press him. Elise was less than thrilled at the news, though she hid her feelings from Michael entirely. But in furtive whispered asides, she said to Paul, "Just wondering. No pressure, but any idea when he's taking off?"

And Paul shushed her and said, "Whenever he wants. He's my kid, and I'm lucky he's here so long." But of course Paul worried, too. What did it mean that Michael didn't want to leave? And now the twins were coming tomorrow to the New York office; wasn't that supposed to be a momentous event? Hadn't Michael told him, in the past, that whenever the twins arrived, all the employees had to rally around them, to show spirit and brilliance and teamwork and *vision*? Michael seemed unconcerned about being absent, so Paul didn't press it. He was so excited at the prospect of his son staying a little longer that he didn't want to say anything that might change his mind.

As far as Paul was concerned, it had been two great weeks of long, free-associative talks and golf games and jogs and arterially disastrous man-meals, through much of which Elise slept peacefully on her pillow stuffed with rice. And now, here in the restaurant at lunchtime, the ongoing conversation would continue, Paul hoped. It wasn't that he liked to see Michael so vulnerable—it worried him to see his competent and intelligent son seem so lost—but he knew that a vulnerable son felt closer to you.

"So, you and Thea . . ." Paul began, when their entrées arrived on enormous plates. Michael had ordered the chicken, as Paul had suggested. It was a breast the size of a man's shoe, and it had been sprinkled with the advertised pine nuts and calligraphically swirled with a red pepper reduction, whatever that meant. The chefs down here went wild with pent-up artistry. As the waiter receded into the almost silent restaurant, Paul delicately broached the subject of Thea again, by which he would be broaching the subject of Elise as well, and he knew it.

The subject was women, their women, and how it was that one

of them had a woman who didn't love him enough, and the other had a woman who did love him enough, but only during the brief times when she was awake, and even then, he had trouble loving *her*. So the subject was why men and women could not be in concert with each other. *Oh God,* Paul thought as he miserably poked at his own meal and heard himself speak, *I sound like one of those courses they offer down here: "'Male-Female Communication— An Inexact Science,' taught by Dr. Nancy Gould in the Gathering Room of the C building, Wednesday nights from 7 to 9. Wine, cheese, and stimulating discussion will be served."*

"Dad, I don't want to talk about Thea now," Michael said. "I don't want to talk about that anymore. You've been really good on the subject. I'll deal with it when I get home. I'll work it out with her."

"You will?"

"Yes. But now I want to talk about the book again."

Paul shut his eyes. "Oh, come on," he said, and his voice in that one second had gone completely flat, nearly dead, the way it always did whenever Michael, or anyone for that matter, tried to talk about *Pleasuring*.

"Like I've said to you, this reissue, it's not a bad idea," Michael said. "It'll bring in money. That's always a good thing. And attention."

"I don't need attention," Paul said.

"Maybe Mom does."

"That's not my business, Michael, is it? What your mother wants now, at age sixty-seven, is something she can discuss with her current husband, not with me."

Paul could immediately see how his reply slapped against the grown son of divorce and reminded him that estranged parents were ugly, grotesque, burying entire lives beneath the ground as if they had never existed, and as if the fact that children had been born from that union were beside the point. It was a real talent to bury an ex-wife deep into the bottom of the mind. Paul had been able to do that very well with the wife who had come right after Roz and before Elise, and whose name was, semicoincidentally, Elisa. He and Elisa had been married for less than a year, in 1980, and she was now forgotten, as surely as if she'd never even existed.

Elisa had been a mistake from the start, though he'd once been attracted to her laugh, and her leotards, and how she wore her shiny dark hair pulled back into a knot in an attempt to look like one of George Balanchine's women. In reality she was a fledgling sex researcher whose own ideas about sexuality were derivative. Elisa wrote a book called *Bloodbonds: Loss of Virginity and Female Identity*, for which she interviewed dozens of virgins and dozens of nonvirgins about their experiences or lack thereof, and for which, in the end, she could not find a publisher. No one had liked her, not the children, not Paul's friends, no one, and yet he'd insisted that she was right for him, she was it for him, she'd be the one to get him over the hump in his life that was Roz.

Roz, the first.

Roz, the one he would always think of as his wife. These women who came afterward, they became second wife and third wife, but never simply *wife*. Elisa and then Elise were wives, the ones who came later, the ones who had missed all the things that had happened before them.

"I can't have the book in print again," he said tightly to his son in the restaurant.

"You don't want to give Mom the pleasure," said Michael. He pushed away his plate elaborately. "I'm not hungry," he announced. "I hate this chicken."

"Don't be a child," said Paul, and it was an absurd comment, for if Michael wasn't going to be a child here, in front of his father, then where? From the outside, they appeared to be just two men at different stages of life, one ascending, the other starting a shaky spiral downward. His son knew the truth about him, knew it like a visionary, or like a psychoanalyst.

Paul didn't want to give Roz one thing. Even thinking about

the way he used to hold her against his chest created a tide of unbearable sensation. The second wife Elisa had been wiped away, his skin was clean of her, but Roz hung around like an apparition, and he had to defend against her, prevent her from staying for an eternity. He would not be seen with her in print again, not ever. Michael was correct; he would not give her the pleasure.

Now a shadow darkened the midday table, and looking up he found himself facing Elise, she of the hundred-year nap. "There you guys are," she said. "I looked on the golf course, but you weren't there. I wish you'd told me you were coming here. I love this place. Michael, I see you got the chicken. Isn't it good?"

She was fully dressed in a lime-colored linen outfit, and if you hadn't known she had been asleep only moments earlier, you could never have guessed. She smelled clean and limey, as though she'd chosen a scent to match her clothing. No sleep creases lined her face; she was carefully composed even now, in a way that Paul and Michael were not, and never would be.

Paul realized how sorry he was to see her here. His own wife, and her presence sank his heart. "Here, I'll pull up a chair for you," Paul said, starting to stand, but two waiters, who had nothing much else to do, were already on the job, producing a high-backed chair, a place setting, and a menu.

"What have you been talking about?" Elise asked, looking from Paul to Michael, and back again.

"Oh, the usual suspects," Paul said. "Life, love, birth, death," and because he felt so guilty about his disappointment at seeing Elise conscious and ambulatory, he reached out and took her hand in his.

Early on in his first marriage, Paul Mellow had boasted to friends at a dinner party that if you really want to get to know the woman you will marry, then you should begin your relationship as analyst and patient. For this was how Roz and Paul Mellow had met, forty-five years earlier, in January 1958, at the Ava Schussler Psychoanalytic Institute on East 36th Street in New York. The Institute occupied a surprisingly shabby town house in the middle of the block. You entered through the front and found yourself in a yellowed antechamber with a spectacularly ugly set of chairs. There the patients sat, lining the walls like people in a subway car who were conscientiously ignoring one another. In the beginning, Paul, age twenty-three, a clean-shaven, eager new candidate, was also one of those patients. The Institute accepted students without medical degrees; Paul was working on a PhD in psychology from NYU, and that was acceptable to the screening committee, though like all candidates in the program, he would have to undergo a classical analysis himself while attending classes.

The Institute's eponymous director was a woman in her eighties who had personally hit a kind of dazzling analytic trifecta, having been analyzed by Carl Rogers, Melanie Klein, and, very briefly, by Freud himself. At least this was how the story went. Ava Schussler was, to most people, a terrifying figure with her ice-white hair and gnarled cherrywood walking stick, and yet she was also apparently a gifted analyst whose grateful former patients sent her presents of potted plants and fudge and orchestra seats for *Oklahoma!*

"To me, Melanie Klein always represented the approving mother," Mrs. Schussler would say at a reception following someone's lecture, with a gaggle of young, nodding analysts sitting nearby, preferably on the thin rug or on a scatter of low ottomans. She always spoke slowly, punctuating sentences with sighs or long *umms*, as though she were extemporizing. "And Freud, he was . . . well, oh . . . I guess I made him out to be the short-tempered father. Sometimes I would be late to an appointment, and I could almost *see* his anger in the air as I entered his consulting room at Berggasse *neunzehn*, though naturally he suppressed it, for it would have been an interference. And I guess that I," she added after a moment, chuckling lightly, "am the eternal daughter." In reality she seemed like no one's daughter, but instead like someone's imperious, irritating, ultimately shunned grandmother.

One night Paul dreamed that he and Ava Schussler herself were dueling. The battle took place between her cherrywood cane and his penis, both instruments clanging loudly, as if made not of knotted wood or fibrous muscle, but of steel. He knew enough to be wary of her, yet he was also excited to be in her presence. Having spent far too much time applying electrodes to mice in a laboratory during graduate school and helping a professor conduct sodium-pentothal experiments on volunteers from Riker's Island, the correctional facility for men, he was restless and trying to give his life some shape. Psychoanalysis was still in vogue, a lasting craze in a long line of American crazes—the whalebone corset, New England Transcendentalism, the jitterbug, anti-Communism, and so on—and to Paul the idea of entering his own analysis, and later managing those of other people, seemed a compelling way to spend his life.

He had come from a neat row house in Queens, from a set of parents—a pipe fitter and a housewife—who were earnest, kind, and unwaveringly literal people who said grace around the dinner table, almost never read books, had no insight into the self, and certainly meant well, but when he was a child, had often told their exasperatingly questioning son, "You think too much." *Yes*. That must be the problem; he thought too much! It made sense, even as he was offended by the sentiment, as if the mind were there to simply lie around like a piece of liver in a pan. Year after year he thought about his parents' remark, reminding himself of it so that he would never forget what his problem was and why he felt alone much of the time.

As a brainy boy he attracted similar girls, and they always wanted to sit endlessly at a varnished library table and work out elaborate outlines for school papers they were jointly writing. The girls were decidedly unerotic, like Adele Flick with her shadowed upper lip and furred forearms, or Susan Masterson, whose features seemed to have been manually pushed into the thick flesh of her face. Or else they were sexually unapproachable, like the dark-haired beauty Margaret Paymer, who did physics problems in her head, and who, for four years, had been writing "an epic poem about seafarers," but who was apparently saving herself for the equally brilliant, as-yet-faceless man she would someday marry.

Sometimes Paul would notice a claque of fast, easy, hungry girls lurking on a street corner, and he understood that they weren't virgins, and it infuriated him that he had no access to their accessibility. Their hair was piled on their head, their breasts were forced upward and outward through some miracle of cloth and wire, and their bodies, he knew, were pale and hot and endlessly calisthenic. But they would never want him, for though he was good-looking enough, he was too cautious, too smart, too mild, too everything, and so he stayed on his own, waiting for the time when he would get what he wanted. It would happen someday, he knew; he simply had to believe this, or else there was no point to life. He lay in bed at night, fantasizing about sexy girls and women of all kinds, big chesty ones, small shy ones, older ones with entire résumés of sexual experience. The only quality these phantom women had in common was their willingness, their eagerness, their *desperation* to have intercourse with him, and as a result, Paul's bedroom at night was a festival of masturbation.

Later, in college and even in graduate school, he began to find women to sleep with who were both attractive and bright, and though sex was certainly exciting and in fact a great relief after all this time, none of the women were willing to go deeply enough into the world of the bed, to try things that he could only vaguely imagine, but which he longed to make real. No, these women wanted straight-up fucking, the kind they'd read about. You could kiss them first, you could touch their breasts, but then they expected you to perform right away, as though they'd read a manual in which this was described. He couldn't help but feel disappointed, for he wanted to linger, to be daring, to use his mouth, to move about, to doodle his way through lovemaking with a sense of leisure and discovery. Once, when he tried to keep the lights on during sex, Cynthia Brancato, a student at NYU's dental school, looked at him with furor, the small panes of her own sharp, perfect teeth showing. How dare he try to see her during the sex act! She wanted only shadows and muted colors, with the outlines of body parts occasionally rising up for attention in the darkness.

One day when Paul was a graduate student working part-time at the lab, attaching electrodes to quivering mice, it occurred to him that he could find a way to "think too much" professionally, while wading waist-deep in the river of sex and sexuality, a place that no woman would yet let him go. He would train to become a psychoanalyst, spending his days sitting in a chair and applying traditional Freudian principles to the ramble of words uttered by the person lying nearby. He'd always enjoyed reading Freud's case histories, the torment of those patients laid out for all to see. All people were tormented, though usually not to the point of the Wolf-Man or poor Dora with her unproductive coughs and fear and trembling. If he was lucky, he would meet an exciting female analyst-in-training who would want to have all kinds of sex, in all kinds of positions, perhaps with the lights on, and certainly without shame. They would be vocal together, and adventurous, and equal in their shared mission.

Yes, Mom and Pop, I think too much, he imagined himself admitting to his parents, but here is what I've decided to do about it, and in his vision he was much older, wearing a three-piece suit and a watch fob; he had sophistication and could finally justify his absorption in thought. Actually, he knew in some deep and sheepish way, the truth was that he had never exactly thought too much—he had just thought too much about himself. But as a psychoanalyst, he would train his eye away from the inside of its lid, and instead he would focus on other people's hidden worlds and longings and failures.

When he first began his training, his parents presented him with a gift: a set of books, The Standard Edition of the Complete

Psychological Works of Sigmund Freud, with baby blue covers and crisp, uncut pages. Inside the first volume, his father had written, "To our Son who Makes us Prouder than He'll ever Know. With Affection From your Mother and your Father." He was moved to tears when they shyly presented the books to him one night in their living room. How had they known what to get him, and even where to buy it?

For the first few months at the Schussler Institute, Paul Mellow attended weekly classes, wrote papers, and began an analysis with one of the senior analysts, a Dr. Sherman Long, whose unwavering, gentle paternalism was a tonic to all his male patients who hadn't gotten enough of their fathers, those distracted, unyielding men, those actuaries and patent lawyers and pipe fitters. Paul would rest his head against the burnt-orange hide of the analytic couch in Long's office and speak so bitterly about his own father that after a couple of years of this there was no bitterness left, only a small, thin, sucked-on lozenge of regret.

This was what most men arrived at eventually in their analyses, Paul began to realize as he compared notes with a few of the other young analytic candidates, all of whom, to his dismay, were men. The group of them would have breakfast once a week at the Murray Hill Coffee Shop on Lexington and 39th, where above the clatter of plates and china and shouted egg orders, they talked about their analysts and their fathers and their dreams and their progress. Though the details and locales were always different, there was homogeneity to the experience of being a son: it seemed to mean wanting more than you were given. And this, he'd learned so far in life, was also the experience of being a lover. Why didn't women want to go the distance, to taste everything and try everything? Why were they always hesitant when push came to shove? Four times a week, Paul dutifully recounted his bedroom dissatisfactions to Dr. Long.

"Marie, yes, Marie . . ." Long once said thoughtfully, stroking the edges of his mustache, after Paul had mentioned a former girlfriend. "Forgive me, Paul. Was she the one who gagged uncontrollably when she attempted to orally gratify you, or the one whose mother had lupus?"

The conversations he had with his analyst had never seemed to go deeply enough—not unlike sex. Later on, after being sent on his way by Dr. Long, pronounced by him "an interesting, still somewhat conflicted young man who will make a fine analyst," he realized that he alone seemed to want something more than what was available. Almost everyone else accepted the limitations of dialogue, of bodies in motion together, of being mortal. It was depressing to find this everywhere he looked, but still Paul slogged on during dates with unsatisfying women, and, now, with the two analytic patients he had recently begun treating.

One of the patients was a handsome homosexual teenager named Ricky Lukins who looked about thirty-five, and the other was a thirty-five-year-old reference librarian named Miss Fowler, who looked about sixty, and who spoke at length about how she lived in fear of the cataloging system being changed. "And all my good work, gone down the drain," she said mournfully, as though it had actually happened.

Paul worried about his interpretations, fretting to his supervisor, Dr. Marty Stengel, about whether they were good enough, original enough, or whether, in fact, they were perhaps *wrong*. The work was intermittently interesting and deadly, like all jobs, he supposed. Other people's interior lives could be compelling, but there were occasionally times when Paul had to suppress the desire to stand up during a session and say, "You said *what* to her? Now you've ruined everything!"

Still, he tried hard to be attentive and insightful and consistent; it would never have occurred to him, in those early days, that he was the kind of person who could commit a serious transgression. But he was; oh, he was.

In the winter, Paul Mellow arrived at the Institute one day in a snowstorm, unwrapping a snow-crusted muffler from his frozen, red face. He was to meet a new patient that morning, and there in the waiting room he found himself looking into her warm, young, radiant, intelligent face. Her name was Rosalyn Woodman ("Roz, if you don't mind," she'd said when they shook hands). Upon absorbing her beauty, he practically began to shout at her to come inside this very minute.

Paul Mellow was Roz Woodman's analyst for only seven months. Throughout that time, the analyst tried his best to remain neutral, to listen "with evenly hovering attention," as Freud had suggested. But as he listened, and glanced at the rise and fall of her chest and rib cage as she breathed, and as he took in the full power of her beautiful skin, sympathetic nature, palpable intellect, and the plaintiveness of her desire to make something of her life, he became frustrated by the need for distance.

"I never really relax completely," she said. "I never try to have an experience for experience's sake. I'm always thinking about how things seem to the outside world, and not how they feel to me. I don't know why it's like that, but it is."

Paul scrawled in his notebook, trying to catch her words, to preserve them for himself, like a little treat he could take out later when no one was around. For what she was saying seemed to exist on a track that ran parallel to his own unhappiness. "I don't want to be afraid of things," she went on. "I don't want to be held back all the time, but I keep noticing that I hold myself back anyway, and don't realize it before it's too late. I think it might be related to being female. I'm pretty certain that *you've* never experienced anything even remotely like this."

Paul bit down gently on his tongue to keep from admitting the truth to her. It was his job here to be quiet, to shut up, to not impose, to not try to fill in a moment of silence just because it was there. *Learn to work with the silence,* he told himself. *Let her speak or not speak. Keep yourself out of it.*

Paul sat bathing in that silence, keeping himself still, and steady, listening so hard to Roz Woodman's words that he realized his teeth were clenched in concentration, as though, through her speech, he might get *more* of her. Countertransference was common, he knew, and in the beginning he tentatively discussed the matter with Dr. Stengel, making sure to dissemble enough so that his feelings appeared to be limited to sensations of protectiveness toward his lovely and sensitive patient.

"I just want to help her so much; she seems so fragile," Paul told Stengel. "She had a very unusual, difficult childhood. I guess, what with her history and all, she brings out these fatherly feelings of countertransference in me."

This was all an elaborate way to conceal the fact that he was falling in love with his patient. It wasn't just her beauty, although that was certainly a big part of it. Her story *got* to him—the emotional neglect she'd experienced as a little girl, growing up on the grounds of the psychiatric hospital that her father ran, as well as the shocking sexual attack she'd suffered when she was nine. But Paul was also troubled and stirred by Roz's adult relationships—how unfulfilled she was in love, just like him, and how she wanted more from people, from the world, from *sex*.

She'd recently had a boyfriend named Carl Mendelson, a law student who liked to get very drunk and screw her in the backseat of his car. The boyfriend was large, impassive, angry, and though she experienced very little pleasure with him, she'd stayed with him for a year. She'd closed her eyes as he pumped away at her, and cried a little after he left her apartment without so much as a kiss or a tender word. *Jesus Christ, she and I are the same,* Paul thought. *We're the same.* It was so painful to think that just when he'd finally found someone who seemed so similar, she was untouchable. He could never tell her what he wanted her to know: that she was breathtaking, exciting, a wonder. That he wanted to *taste* her. To bury his head between her heavy breasts and then lower it into her lap and lick her and kiss her and stay there for as long as she would have him, the light blazing, the whole world lit up and blazing and in flames all around them.

It seemed to him that life had had a way of picking Roz Wood-man up like a house or a car in a tornado and plunking her down wherever it felt like. This wasn't fair; she was a red-haired beauty of a girl who was studying fashion design, and whose intelligence was far-reaching, yet she was hobbled by a low-level depression that was as present as a pilot light. Paul admired her wavy hair, her skirt that spread out all around her in a half-pinwheel as she lay on his couch in the tiny room beneath a cheap print of *Christina's World* that some unimaginative analyst had placed over the couch. She wore a thick black patent leather belt that cinched a waist so narrow it *begged* a man to try to put both hands around it, finger-tips meeting in back. He admired the brave associations she made, and the way her voice thickened when she was about to cry. Oh, it was a terrific combination, so what was he supposed to do?

Nothing. Absolutely nothing. He was hamstrung. He was doomed.

Paul went to see gangster movies and musical-comedy fluff on weekends to distract himself, and he threw himself into his clinical reading, trying to puzzle out his young patient Ricky's omnipresent need to seduce shady older men, diamond traders, and high-end bookies, but nothing helped. During the week, when Paul could see Roz again, he was uncomplicatedly happy, yet he knew that all this sensation could lead to nothing. She would be his patient, and he her analyst, and she would never find out the extent of what he felt for her. Still, the happiness he experienced being in her presence in his small, hot office served to blur the enormous sadness at knowing she would never be his.

Then something happened. It was the end of that first July, and Paul was about to leave for his requisite August holiday—though really, he was in training and hardly deserved such a break, much less wanted one. Roz had been in the middle of talking at the time. She usually talked easily, without much coaxing. She was saying something about her roommate Vivian, who also wanted to go into fashion design, though Vivian's illustrations were terrible, "like clothes for undernourished secretaries," Roz said, which made him laugh.

"Well, undernourished secretaries have to wear something, don't they?" he'd replied, pointlessly. She'd laughed too, and then he'd laughed again, and there was a long, awkward silence.

Finally, Paul said, "So. What's going on in there?"

"Nothing," she said.

"Nothing? Really?"

"Well, maybe it's not nothing," said Roz. "But it's very embarrassing to talk about. I don't know that I can say it."

"Take your time."

"The thing is," she went on, "I have to admit something I've known for a while. Something that's been bothering me. No, not exactly bothering me, because it's kind of exciting, but more like preoccupying me. My roommate Vivian says I should say something, so here it is. I have these feelings about you. Strong feelings. It's kind of come out of the blue."

Paul allowed a careful silence, before saying magnanimously, "Everyone has feelings toward their analyst. You know that the basis of a good analysis is the transference. You put on to me all the feelings and thoughts that you've had about other people in the past. It's quite natural."

"I know all that," she said. "But this is something else. Something different. I don't think it's just the transference. I think it's real. I think it's about you as a person. You as a man, and what I imagine you'd be really like, you know, to be involved with. To sleep with. To have as my lover." And then she began to cry. Her admission, followed by these tears, made Paul want to burst apart in pleasure, or weep himself from the star-crossed quality of it all. He gazed at *Christina's World* over the couch; even the crippled, faceless girl in that field in the middle of nowhere made him want to cry now.

What he said to her, when he could finally speak, was, "And how does that make you feel?"

"I already told you," she said. "Terribly embarrassed."

"Yes. Yes. Right. You did tell me."

The clock showed that it was more than time to stop. Out in the waiting room sat Miss Fowler and her interior cataloging system. So Paul stood up and nodded formally at Roz Woodman, ushering her out the door, his expression poker-faced, his body clenched tight. During Miss Fowler's session, he could barely stay in his chair. Miss Fowler was saying something about her Grandma Lou and a bowl of Brazil nuts that she always kept on her table before she died. The nuts were shaped like wooden shoes. They made Miss Fowler think about Holland, a place she'd never been, and which she doubted she would ever visit in her entire life. "Even if I went to Holland, I'd still be myself," she said bitterly. "Still good old me, the lady who people have to remind themselves to send a Christmas card to each year."

Maybe, Paul began to think, *he was meant to be Roz Woodman's lover*. The stars were in alignment. They both felt the same way about each other. If he were to tell her he was in love with her, then what would that do? Maybe it would cause her to stand and embrace him, and for him to be flooded with the relief he'd been waiting to feel his entire life. She'd feel it too! Gone would be her cold psychiatrist father, her useless mother, that child molester Warren Keyes who had touched her when she was a girl. Gone would be Paul's own history, his clueless but well-meaning parents, his own unhappiness. Gone would be the withholding that they had each had to do throughout their lives. *Whoosh!* Both of them would start from scratch.

"Don't do it," his friend Bob Darling warned him at the Murray Hill Coffee Shop. The two men were the first to arrive for the weekly group breakfast. "Ava Schussler and her henchmen will destroy you. They'll eat you up and spit you out in little unrecognizable pieces."

"I know, I know," said Paul, and he put his head in his hands.

"Still," Darling continued thoughtfully, "that girl *is* a pretty nice piece of sirloin. I've seen her in the waiting room. Red hair. Bet she's got a muff to match it."

"Shut your filthy mouth," said Paul, and he became frightened that if he didn't act, then maybe Bob Darling would. He pictured Darling waiting outside the building for Roz to emerge, then striking up a conversation with her about the weather, and even taking her to dinner.

No. No. Paul couldn't allow this to happen. *He* would take her to dinner; that was what he would do. And so, in the middle of Roz Woodman's next analytic hour, while she hesitantly continued to explore her powerful "feelings" for him, he abruptly cut in during a pause in her monologue and asked her if she thought she might want to go out with him that night to Mr. Lo's Noodle Parlor in Chinatown.

There was quiet for a moment. "Dinner?" she said in a confused voice. "Is that allowed?"

"No," he said. "It's not."

Silence. "Oh," she said. "Then I don't know. I just don't know."

"I understand," he said. "This isn't appropriate. I've momentarily stepped out of my role here. I'm sorry, I'm really sorry."

"You don't have to be," Roz said. "Look," she went on, "I have to think. This is so strange. I'm confused."

"I am too," he said. "The blind leading the blind."

They both laughed a little to relax themselves, and there was no use in trying to return to being patient and analyst. Apparently, in one fell swoop, that was over; it could never be recovered, and she knew it, and they would both have to mourn it separately. She sat up on the couch and turned to face him.

"Well," she said, "I should go."

"All right."

"And about dinner . . . I'm just not sure yet. I might be there, but I can't promise anything."

She left the room without another word, and Paul Mellow sat in his chair for a few more minutes, feeling his face burn and understanding that he'd done something serious, even appalling. She could report him; she'd be well within her rights. He'd crossed a line, jumped a fence, changed the course of his life and hers.

That night, in the dark recesses of Mr. Lo's Noodle Parlor on Elizabeth Street, he sat alone at a table and regretted what he'd done to his patient and to himself. He checked his watch. She wasn't going to come; he'd lost her forever. He'd lost his career, lost everything. He'd have to turn himself in anyway, he decided. It was the right thing to do.

But just when he'd gotten comfortable with this moral decision, the tiny bell over the restaurant door chimed, and there she was, pushing her way inside, heading right toward him. Psychoanalytic theory had many things to say about misery, but surprisingly few about joy. And this *was* joy, he knew, as Roz Woodman took her seat across from him in the fragrant room. A waitress handed her a laminated red menu, but she didn't even look at it. For a while Paul and Roz just smiled stupidly at each other, and then they joked about the strangeness of their predicament, and finally they talked about themselves. He had a great deal to fill her in on, for she knew nothing about him.

Later, after the soup course and the lacquered duck and the perfect, salty mound of shrimp fried rice, after the orange sherbet and cup after cup of strong black tea, he accompanied her to her apartment on the Upper West Side. The roommate, she assured him, was out.

In her narrow bedroom they stood facing each other, and then they embraced for the first time. Their faces were close; her breath was a little curdled, he realized, as though she were very anxious, which of course she was, and he was touched by this, not repelled. They stayed there for a few seconds, like characters in a movie who have just been through some ordeal together.

"Is this okay?" he asked.

"Yes," Roz said into his shirt. "I think this is what I want."

"You think?"

"Yes. I mean, it is."

"Because it has to be mutual," he said, somehow justifying the transgression, making it seem less inappropriate if he could ascertain that she felt exactly the way he did.

"I know," she said.

"I can't be your analyst anymore," he told her regretfully, and then Roz Woodman began to laugh.

"It's all right," she said. "No offense, but you weren't all that good."

This hurt him, but it was true—she was a girl who said things that were true. He wasn't a very good analyst; he'd tried, but it hadn't worked out. Even if he hadn't fallen in love with Roz Woodman, this would have been the case. But as he faced the fact of his limitations, he became less upset that his professional life was about to fall apart. He'd find something else to do; he could work in a lab again, with mice. Now he and Roz touched and kissed, and the sensation was crackling and keen. Then he sat on the bed while she stood, and he opened her blouse and lowered his mouth to her breast, a place he'd been waiting to go. His tongue encircled the nipple, felt it bunch and harden, and soon he thought he would go wild if he didn't do something more with his mouth, his hands, his penis, the bulk of his entire self.

"God please let me fuck you," he said, the awful words coming from his mouth in a rush, and she told him yes, yes, do that, do everything. Let's not be shy with each other, there's no point to that. We know what we want from each other, and now we need to find out if we can really get it.

So they were in agreement, two schemers with a crackpot plan. Roz lay down on the bed and first his mouth went between her legs, that woodsy place that men ached toward, as if trying to get back to a forest for a ritual they all knew how to enact, and she was whispering and he was muttering; they were chattering together like crickets. And then, in one swift movement, he threw himself fully upon her like someone flinging himself onto a coffin as it is lowered into the earth.

His newborn career ended within days. It was that snake Bob Darling who reported him, Bob Darling who could tell, by looking at Paul's elated face, what had occurred. This happiness had eaten away at Bob Darling and sent him into Mrs. Schussler's office, where Paul would have gone on his own, anyway. Mrs. Schussler herself hastily arranged a tribunal that included herself plus Sherman Long, Marty Stengel, and a pointy-featured female analyst named Wanda Grink. Throughout the proceedings, held on a Monday morning in Mrs. Schussler's office, Paul hung his head and stared at his hands, though the shame he felt was beaten through with a kind of goofy pride. It was corrupt to love a patient, that was incontrovertibly true, but it was also, in this case, unavoidable, for Roz Woodman was as delicious as birthday cake, which was not something he could tell these people.

All he could think about, as he stared at the hawk-faced old Ava Schussler and her colleagues, was that none of them could possibly understand love, or sex, or unfettered gratification. Even Sherman Long, who'd tried hard to be a good analyst, a jolly father, had always seemed too slack-bellied and convivial to understand sexual and emotional need. Marty Stengel was basically an oaf; everyone thought so. About Wanda Grink, Paul had no particular opinion, though an unfair one could have been formed within moments, if he'd given it any thought. The radiator in the office shrilled and banged. There was someone trapped in there and trying to get out, some fledgling analyst who had once been on trial in this very room, the way Paul was now.

"I love her," Paul explained to the panel in a strangled, besotted voice. "I simply love her. I know it's a violation. I know it goes against everything I've been taught here. But it's love. There it is, the real thing. What else can I tell you?"

"Your so-called love, it is immaterial," said Mrs. Schussler sharply.

Paul looked up, making eye contact with Mrs. Schussler, and then, suddenly, he asked her, "Did you ever even meet him?"

"Pardon?"

"Freud," he went on, and he was unstoppable now. "In Vienna. Was he really your analyst, or did you maybe just bump into him once, say, in a butcher's shop, buying lamb chops, and the rest was a delusion?"

The expression that came over the old woman's face then was so disturbing that he was afraid she was having a stroke. He didn't want to be around for what might happen next, the falling on the floor, the yelling, the recriminations, and so he just gathered his things in a loose armful and got out of there. He couldn't bring himself to come back the next day to collect the set of books his mother and father had given him, and though it always caused him pain to think about, he never found out what became of them.

For a long time, Paul and Roz proved that firing squad of analysts dead wrong. Their love affair had lasted, turning into a marriage. All of the analysts, once so powerful and full of absolute opinions, were dead, but Paul and Roz lived on. Eventually their bodies graced the pages of a notorious book, interwoven, aglow, endlessly game for anything, on display for others to see and envy and imitate.

One night, in November 1975, right after the book had appeared and taken off like a shot, Paul and Roz Mellow were driving home after a lecture they had given at the New School. As he drove the car, Paul thought back to that crabbed panel of analysts and wished they were alive right now so that they could see what he and Roz had made of themselves. He wished that they could see the drawings of him in bed with his beautiful wife. There wasn't an analyst among them, he felt sure, who would not have been jealous of the freedom he'd found.

His own children, perhaps, had already seen the book. He hoped they had, not so they would be jealous or frightened or, God knows, stimulated, but just so they would *know*. Because knowing things was better than not knowing them: this was the mantra of psychoanalysis, and though he had long been excommunicated, it was an idea that he still believed.

Beside him in the Volvo, on the way home from that lecture, sat Roz. In silence they drove through the city streets and the tunnel with its staccato line of lights, then onto the expressway going eastward; worn out and yawning, Paul hunched his shoulders against the night. In the close quarters of the green Volvo station wagon he could detect the tang of wine on her breath and a trace element of garlic. This was merely an observation, with no opinion attached; they'd been too physically close for too long a time to have the occasional drift of wine or garlic or anything else really matter. Always she was a source of wonder, a creature, a mythical beast who loved him, and who made him continually marvel at her beauty and the concentrated essence of her femaleness. Soon, now, in the darkness of the car, Roz dropped off to sleep, her perfume making his nostrils widen and then contract, her hair flying up slightly through some sort of electricity that hummed around her.

Paul pulled off the road at the Wontauket exit close to midnight, and as they turned onto Swarthmore Circle with its arch of trees and recently tarred surface, its clutch of unmistakably suburban but somehow vaguely noble houses, he turned to her.

"Hey there, this is it," he whispered. "Ye Olde Homestead."

Together they went into the house, enduring the excruciatingly protracted moment of late-night key-in-lock, until the doorknob turned and they stood dumbly in the front hallway like vaguely lost campers consulting a compass. All was silent. A small light had been left on in the living room, and Paul and Roz went up to their own pristine floor, where they briefly dropped coats and bags and lecture notes, and then continued on up to the third floor.

All of the children were now asleep, little Claudia in her bed, a ghastly blue-haired troll beside her on the pillow. In the next room, Dashiell slept on a beanbag chair in the corner. This chair was practically breaded with hamster hair, but he never minded.

"Should we just leave him there?" Roz asked, looking down at their small, curled son.

"Sure. No need to wake him. He looks wiped out," said Paul.

Next they visited the rooms where the teenagers slept; Holly with her hair spread out on the pillow, as though the surface were water and she had been set afloat, which in a way she had. Michael, on the other side of the wall, slept with his mouth half-open, as if he were amazed about something, but really it was just adenoids. He was a mouth breather and always had been, though in adulthood his mouth would close.

All four children looked exactly the same as they had that morning, before they'd looked through the book together. What the parents couldn't know was that throughout the day, the children had been rapidly and frantically changing. By the time Paul and Roz Mellow had returned home late that night, their four offspring were different, though this wouldn't be apparent for quite a while, and even then, it could only be seen in subtle ways. The book was responsible for that interior hosing of chemicals, the yogic stretching and pulling of the double helix. Together, by nightfall, the four Mellow children would have shed thousands of old cells, unknowingly sloughing them off and replacing them with newer, in some cases *vulgar*, ones: cells whose mitochondria contained buried commands that went far beyond "do homework" and "be kind to slow child in class," and went instead into the territory of "be dominated" and "touch this" and "tell no one."

Pleasuring: One Couple's Journey to Fulfillment had, on that day in November 1975, stimulated cell death and growth all at once, a combination slaughterhouse and labor floor. In a short period of time the four Mellow children, "the kids," their parents still thought of them back then, picturing an undifferentiated mass of heads and elbows, needy, cranky, but nonetheless heartbreakingly *theirs*, became overloaded with thoughts of sex and of undraped body parts. Earlier, while Paul and Roz Mellow had driven along the Long Island Expressway toward the city, making excellent time, cruising seat belt–free, air-bag innocent, thinking not of the possibility of a car crash or even, particularly, of sex, their children, as they knew them, were disappearing.

Their parents, of course, knew none of this yet. They witnessed only the sweetness and blandness of their greatly loved children in sleep, and they mutually enjoyed a moment of silent parental contemplation, feeling the tidal pull toward these people they'd managed to create through four distinct acts of love. Always, over and over, year after year, parents marvel at the idea of this as though they had never thought of it before.

Paul and Roz were calm, quiet, emotional about their children, satisfied with how the day had gone, the turnout at the lecture, the sales of the book at the reception, and, for that matter, the prospect of enormous sales in the future, both here and around the world, much of which seemed to want and need the lessons that *Pleasuring* had to teach. They were both pleased with the liveliness of the dinner that had been held in their honor after the lecture today, and then the easy ride back to the home, the hearth, the children. All was well, they thought, all was well, and for now that was incontestably true.

"Let's go to bed," Paul Mellow told his wife, and they descended.

Chapter Five

DASHIELL FOUND the lump in his neck when he was shaving, and what astonished him was that he hadn't found it sooner, for by the time his fingers happened upon it that morning as he angled his chin in the mirror and drew the razor northward, the thing was enormous, a monster setting up shop inside him. When he found the lump, his fingers pulled away as though they'd touched something hot, and then, magnetically, they returned to the surface of his skin, delicately palpating, touching with the tenderness of a lover, though the thing they were touching deserved no tenderness. He touched it on all sides, ascertaining its circumference, its bold rotundity, its discrete marble hardness, as though it were a prize stuck inside a cake in France for a lucky child to find.

The lucky child would dig up the prize and say, "*Voilà, maman!*" The unlucky man in Providence, Rhode Island, found the lump and thought, *Oh, fuck*, because right away he feared he was facing death in the form of something hard, a gift you hadn't asked for, stuck deep in the soft cake of your body and waiting to be found.

What had he been thinking all those other times he'd stood there shaving with this thing lodged inside him? That his neck certainly had a kind of interesting *roundness* to it on the side? How had he missed it before? It was like the way babies behaved when they dropped something on the floor; for some reason they often couldn't see it even when it was in front of them. Apparently Dashiell had been a baby all this time, happily missing the truth, shaving himself back to babydom, to a time when his face was clean and poreless, and no tiny dots of stubble showed through like printer's errors. Shaving had always provided him with a rhapsodic state in which he let his thoughts bump around like a boat lightly banging against a dock, and those thoughts were rarely practical or of this world. They were faraway, unlinked, certainly having no relevance to the idea of mortality. He liked to shave; it was the one time in the day when he felt it was possible to start over, to have another crack at the perfection he'd lacked the day before, and the day before that.

But today there would be no perfection, for here was the neck lump, solid, nonnegotiable. He felt that something was likely very wrong, and his razor-hand jerked upward and he nicked himself on the throat, and then he cried out sharply as the blood began to flow. By the time he'd grabbed the styptic pencil from the cabinet and scribbled furiously up and down his skin, blood had run all over the basin.

Tom, who was in bed shooting out mass emails to the entire campaign staff from his laptop, heard the whole thing and came running in. "Jesus!" he said. "Jesus, Dashiell, what did you do?" With all that blood everywhere, it looked like a suicide scene. But Tom Amlin was a calm man, calmer than Dashiell, and he quickly managed to ascertain that this was merely a shaving accident of epic proportions.

The following day they sat together in the waiting room of their mutual internist, young Dr. Adam Forest, he of the rock jaw and fifty-percent-gay-male practice, he of the tiny rectangular-framed eyeglasses and excellent haircut. In that waiting room, Dashiell's anxiety came back full strength, but because Tom was there, it never had a chance to foam up over the surface and become unmanageable. This had been how, at age fourteen, Dashiell had first understood he was homosexual: When he was with men or boys, various kinds of anxiety became so much more manageable. Whatever the problem was, the presence of a male could make it better: school, sex, money, despair, job, future, politics, parents— even the imagined, glowing lip of the abyss.

He was seeing the positive effect of a man now, that thready, hopeful light that emanated outward. When Dashiell had to separate from Tom briefly for the physical exam, he felt the loss. Sitting in his boxers on the examining table paper, having the surface of his entire body navigated by Dr. Forest (an experience that, under other circumstances, would have been mildly and secretly exciting), he couldn't help but feel that death was in the room with them, sitting off to the side on a stool like a physician's assistant. Dr. Forest was scouring Dashiell for other swollen nodes, and when he found a few of them—scattered casually and deeply in Dashiell's groin and under one arm, embedded in flesh beneath the thick shock of hair—the doctor stroked his strong chin thoughtfully like Clark Kent in a journalistic quandary and said, "Dashiell, I'd like to do a biopsy."

"What is it you suspect?" asked the patient, now diminished, now shrunken with fear. Dashiell was HIV-negative, of that he was sure. How he'd managed to escape HIV was something he had never understood, for in the 1980s he had had plenty of unprotected sex with men who were possibly carriers, all before the news about AIDS came crashing down. But miraculously, when he had himself tested at the Gay Men's Health Center, he'd come out negative. He'd been so convinced he was sick, back then, that when it was time to appear for the results, he'd brought a handful of fresh tissues with him, neatly folded in his pocket. The idea of a stranger, a volunteer counselor no less, pushing a box of Kleenex at him after relaying some life-crushing news was unbearable. He wouldn't want that stranger's tissues. He would want to be given *good* news, and nothing else. Anything more—a tissue, a shoulder, an Altoid, the name of a therapist who specialized in an HIV-positive clientele—would have been grotesque.

But today, all these years later, Dr. Forest was not saying such a thing; he was preparing a needle for a biopsy. He was buzzing his nurse and saying that he would need to cancel his next patient.

"Can I call Tom in?" Dashiell asked in the smallest voice.

"Of course," said Dr. Forest.

The three men, all of them strong-bodied and muscled, filled the small examining room, and though Dr. Forest wore an extra layer of white, poly-blend professionalism, still he was one of them in every way. Tom held Dashiell's hand while the needle was pushed into the side of his neck, a place where needles so clearly *should not go*. Dashiell thought of how once, on the street in New York, two black teenagers had shouted at him that he was a "faggot" who put his "dick where it don't belong."

He was a small man, five foot seven, tightly constructed and doelike. He did put his dick where it maybe didn't belong but where, in the heat of love, it ached to belong. *You would do this for me?* he used to think when he went to bed with a new man and there was the wordless maneuvering toward sex, for it seemed to mean an unspoken trust was there, even between two people who had only exchanged the barest of words in a bar. Sometimes, sensing the desire in the other man, watching it reveal itself in such a way that the man was rendered exposed, Dashiell would think, *I would do this for you.*

But of course, no one ever did anything only for the other person; this wasn't saintly behavior, this was open-mouthed, joyous fucking, the tense, anticipatory, counterintuitive preamble and then the flowering, the depths of unwinding that spread like sonar through the body, radiating outward conically until the waves left your body and entered the atmosphere.

The needle in the neck, now, this would never turn a corner into pleasure; it hurt like a crucifixion, even though a local anesthetic had been injected first. There was a burning pain as the drug went in, and then a thicker, more wrenching pain as the needle attempted to aspirate something, anything, from Dashiell's ungenerous lump. The liquid it managed to procure was clouded, bloody. Dr. Forest turned away from Dashiell to bag and seal the specimen, and his mouth was a straight, dry line.

The news, a few days later, was bad, though not, Tom reminded him, the worst. Cancer, yes, Hodgkin's disease specifically; treatable through chemotherapy and radiation, which meant that Dashiell would be sickened for a while.

"You'll feel pretty lousy," Dr. Forest said over the phone. "You'll think it will never end, but it will, I promise you. This is like a dark cloud, and then it will lift. Hodgkin's is very curable." An oncologist was already on the case; Dr. Forest was signing off.

In bed that first night after the diagnosis, Dashiell took stock. "Very curable," he murmured, lying on his back.

"Yes, and that's *good*," Tom said. "If you in your twisted way manage to find another interpretation of Forest's remark, then you're insane."

"I did think of another way," Dashiell admitted, "but I guess I'll keep it to myself."

"Thank you," said Tom.

They lay next to each other in similar pale blue pajamas, arms by their sides, like toy soldiers in a box. "What about the campaign?" Dashiell asked after a moment. "This is an extremely bad time to have Hodgkin's disease."

"It's always a bad time," said Tom. "But there's so many people on the case, we can all cover."

"And anyway, who was *Hodgkin*?" asked Dashiell. "I mean, who *was* he, getting this disease named after him? A scientist, I guess, but American? British?"

"No, no, Dash, you've got it wrong," said Tom. "*Hodgkins* are these little mythical creatures. Small and furry and persistent, kind of like swollen lymph nodes. They were rejects from *The Lord of the Rings*. Tolkien said, 'Nah, they'll just confuse things. I think I'll take them out.'"

Dashiell was relieved that there could still be joking here between them, that it hadn't ended with the sudden wind of this bad news. He shifted in the bed, tried to become comfortable, but found it impossible. Still, he was aware of feeling oddly well, which was disconcerting, considering what his well-seeming body concealed. "If Wyman doesn't get elected," he said, "it'll basically be my fault."

"I love that kind of vanity, Dash. Look, if Wyman doesn't get elected, it's because people don't like him, and not because the public didn't get to hear your magnificent words flowing from his lips."

"Trish's speeches are shit."

"True."

They both laughed meanly, thinking about Wyman's other speechwriter, a twenty-five-year-old horsy girl named Trish Leggett, who had somehow won a place in Robert Wyman's senatorial campaign by writing a sample stump speech for him that Wyman had loved and used all over the state, just because of a phrase she'd put in about "the extraordinary soul dressed in the clothes of the humble"—about how average citizens of this country had risen up as one against terrorism. Trish Leggett was hard-pressed to find real-life examples that postdated the destruction of the World Trade Center, and so she relied heavily on generalized imagery, picked up during a brief stint as a poetry student at the University of Iowa Writers' Workshop. She was green in the world of speechwriting, but still a visible threat to Dashiell, who had been a political speechwriter for years now, and a good one, having worked for several different candidates: a city councilman, two mayors, and now, most excitingly, a potential United States senator.

It was in this capacity that he'd met Tom Amlin six years earlier. Both were attending a New York City convention of the gay organization Log Cabin Republicans. Dashiell was living in Boston at the time and Tom had just relocated from L.A. to Providence to work in the office of then city councilman Robert Wyman, the so-called Kennedy Republican, called this only by people who knew him, and mostly because he had unusually large teeth.

The convention was held at the Helmsley Plaza, with its hangar-size lobby and glass elevator that ferried masses of festive gay Republicans to and from the sky. Some of these LCRs acted as though they'd never been in a glass elevator before, hooting and clapping as the car rushed upward. They were like *Shriners*, Dashiell thought.

On the first night of the convention, at the meet-and-greet, the glass elevator opened and the LCRs spilled out into the ballroom, and there they were, the businessmen, the pastel polo shirts, the occasional lesbian, the swath of fringe that cut across the American GOP. Their voices were deep and droney, like the voices you could hear in the bar car on a commuter train. *Wulf, lub, guf, yub*, all of it punctuated by the meaty laughter they freely gave out into any room. It was likely that many of them were boring, but somehow Dashiell found himself slightly excited by their potential dullness.

At the entrance of the ballroom was a table covered with name tags, and he found his tag and put it on, while beside him a tall, rangy man with silver hair and a good suit seemed to be having trouble peeling his own tag from its backing. "Fuck," the man muttered quietly, and Dashiell offered to help him.

"Here," he said, quickly taking apart the two pieces of paper and slapping the name tag onto the man's chest, taking note, in that moment, of the way it felt when his hand met the lapel of the man's jacket, so close to the man's chest, to his heart. When he took away his palm, he read the words: "Tom Amlin—L.A.—I Mean Providence."

The men shook hands; there was nothing between them, no

electric anything, but that was fine, or anyway it would have to be. Dashiell was young then, just thirty, and it slightly bothered him that he was not one of the youngest members at this convention. There were guys in their early twenties here, and even an entire contingency from Harvard, still undergraduates but already single-mindedly conservative and totally out. The Harvard Weenies, as Tom would come to call them, stood in a cluster by the punch bowl, effete and slightly sneering, like a fraternity for the characters in *Brideshead Revisited.*

On the other side of the room stood the most unlikely group to be here: the transvestites, a handful of men in conservative dresses or skirt sets and makeup, so way out there, so much more feminized than the lesbians in their dress-for-success monkey suits. The trannies, with their colorful wigs and perfume, treated this all as a game, as performance art. One of them, hovering at more than six feet tall and wearing a yellow dress with little blue cornflowers all over it, had a sash with a variety of antique GOP buttons dotting it: "Re-Elect Nixon." "Vote Goldwater." "Go Dole." She looked to Dashiell like a demented Girl Scout leader, and it made him feel, for a moment, that he was on Mars, that he needed a drink from a cool, clear Martian stream.

Tom Amlin, standing right in front of Dashiell, was forty, a lifetime older than he was. That decade was the one in which you proved yourself, and Amlin had already done that. As they stood at the bar with their drinks, Dashiell said, "What's with your name tag? 'L.A.—I Mean Providence'?"

"I just moved east," the man told him. "It used to be great to say I was from L.A. It meant something. Now I have to say Providence and I immediately have an inferiority complex. Even though moving was actually a good thing for me. And it's a nice city; I like it there. You'd like it."

He talked about City Councilman Robert Wyman, what a terrific man he was, so brainy and direct, lacking the slimy snake-oil quality you sometimes saw in the GOP, which put off a lot of potential swing voters, particularly suburban women. And Dashiell told Tom about his speechwriting jobs, how he was often hired at the last minute to punch up someone else's terrible speech, how he'd often crossed party lines if his services were needed and the pay was good enough.

Tom Amlin observed him for a moment, looking displeased. "You're a mercenary, then," he said, and though Dashiell said no, no, that wasn't the case at all, Amlin patiently walked him through a kind of concentrated Republican manifesto, a long, teacherly but amazingly not boring narrative that aimed to remind Dashiell of what being a Republican stood for, and being a Democrat did not. "Small government," was repeated frequently. "Even *smaller* government. Fiscal independence. Growth. Wealth. And *that's* compassion, that's taking care of our nation's people, not some leftover, failed Carterian plan."

"*Carterian?* What? You mean Cartesian?" Dashiell asked.

"No. Like Jimmy Carter."

Dashiell blinked. "That's a real word?"

"Nah. I just made it up," said Tom Amlin.

That night, after sitting beside Tom at a prime-rib dinner with superstars of the GOP shoulder to shoulder on the dais and lots of table-pounding (the Harvard Weenies pounded hardest and did that fist-in-the-air woofing that seemed to Dashiell one step away from brown shirts and jackboots) and a bid by one of the trannies for the LCRs to embrace "inclusiveness," and then a few unexpectedly moving and personal political speeches, the evening broke up and a large group of them ended up at a club called Speed on West 18th Street that had been recommended in their welcome handout.

The music at Speed was bad but sufficiently loud, and Tom and Dashiell pulled off their jackets and ties and scream-talked at each other, pressed very close together by necessity. Finally, when it seemed pointless to continue this nondialogue, Tom Amlin, this superior man, this man who reminded Dashiell in a way of his brother Michael—elite, older, dark, educated, and so fucking smart—sat back on a bar stool, his legs open slightly, and pulled Dashiell toward him. Neither of them was drunk; it was disturbing sometimes, the first time, if you weren't drunk and you had to confront the purity of your own desire.

Something about the gesture was so exciting that it was sickening, too. Tom Amlin braced a big hand against Dashiell's back, and Dashiell thought of the white dress shirts they both wore, the accommodation to male conservatism, the Brooks Brothers crispness and order they shared, as though the two of them *were* in fact the Brooks Brothers—an incestuous, identical pair. In the GOP dream, though, order happened naturally, not through watching and governing but through rights, and without the embarrassing, cry-on-my shoulder of preferential treatment.

You were on your own here in America, but it wasn't a wilderness anymore, it was a great country, and you were free to live as you wanted, to make money, to pull yourself up. You were free, in a bar called Speed, to press yourself upon a man you had just met and kiss him with an open mouth. In a strange way, if you really thought about it, this was what being a Republican stood for.

Asleep, now, in the bed they shared, six years having passed since the Log Cabin convention and the awakening of an inordinately mutual love, Tom Amlin and Dashiell Mellow had begun to resemble each other. Dashiell no longer looked perennially young or entirely fawnlike, nor Tom like an older teacher to this precocious student. Their crispness had dissipated. Dashiell had been aged by the usual wear and tear of life, and, more recently, by his illness. A couple of weeks of chemotherapy and radiation had taken him for all he was worth. He felt as if he'd been knocked against the side of a building. His mouth now had scattered sores; his eyes were recessed from dehydration; his hair had started to fall out and so he'd quickly gone to the barber and had gotten one of those shaved homo-heads that he'd never liked, for they reminded him of the kind of people who *beat up* homosexuals.

Tom, with his silvery hair a little whiter, looked healthy but very weary now. He used to be a runner, jogging every day past the gates of Brown University and down College Hill, then back up again, but he was too busy managing Robert Wyman's campaign and taking care of Dashiell, and so his own body had begun to show signs of slack.

They slept facing each other, and when Dashiell opened his eyes and saw that it was only 7 A.M., and realized that he was nauseated from the drugs and might have to vomit, he tried to suppress the feeling, pressing on his thumb pad, as a nurse who had a side interest in holistic medicine at Rhode Island Hospital had taught him, digging deep into the flesh and finding the acupressure trigger that would quiet the churning. Amazingly, it seemed to help. The nausea calmed down, lost interest in pursuing him. Dashiell was feeling proud of himself for outfoxing it when the telephone rang, and caller ID indicated that it was his mother on the line.

Don't take it. That's what Tom would have said, if he'd woken up in time to offer an opinion. For ever since Dashiell had gotten sick a few weeks ago, his family had been making their presence known all the time. His father and Michael called continuously, chiming in from separate telephone extensions and interrupting each other. Michael, throughout his life an overly serious, measured person, here sounded hyper, his voice coming out in a rush.

"Hey, I can come up, Dash, I can leave Dad and come right up," Michael said. "Or wait, no, Dad can come with me. Whatever you want."

"I don't want anything, thanks," Dashiell said. "I'm fine. I've got Tom." He paused a moment. "Are *you* okay, Michael?" he asked.

"What do you mean?"

"I don't know," Dashiell said. "You're still down in Florida. And you sound sort of . . . speedy or something."

"I'm fine," Michael said abruptly. So both brothers were fine.

Their father sounded the same as always: warm, thoughtful, slightly melancholic. "You know I'm there for you," Paul Mellow said, and Dashiell felt stirred by this because it was who his father was: "You know I'm there for you." And though it rarely translated into anything tangible anymore, the sentence seemed to represent a kind of shared father-son dream of intimacy.

Claudia had called several times too since the diagnosis, and she was sometimes tearful on the phone and Dashiell felt compelled to make her feel better, because she was the youngest of all of them and had always been a little fragile. She was the only one who still had no real career, who'd never lived with anyone, who was still alone. She'd been having a flurry of emails with some man she'd met recently at the house in Wontauket, of all places, and Dashiell told her he was glad about that, but in truth he didn't know what to think, if anything. This was similar to how he felt about her foray into film school: Until it materialized into something tangible, it was almost as though he didn't *believe* her, as though she were spinning a life, or a story of a life, out of air. Dashiell felt the impulse to protect Claudia, but he never really pitied her; she was too good for that.

During these phone calls there would occasionally be moments of phlegmy crying, which would drive Dashiell crazy, causing him to say, "Claudia, get a grip. *Claudia.* Now, listen to me, Claudia. I am going to be fine. Really. Fine."

When she stopped crying, she was specific in her offers of help: "So if you want me to come and sit with you while you're throwing up or whatever," she said, "I'm happy to do it. I've just been making this stupid student film about my teachers, and believe me, the world can wait to see it."

Holly, who apparently had been contacted by Claudia, had telephoned Dashiell once from her outpost in Los Angeles, saying she was sorry he was sick, and did he know anything about the wheat gluten–cancer connection? "Because, you know, it might have caused it," she said. He stiffly told her no, as far as he knew it wasn't linked to diet. She said she'd send him a book about it, which had never arrived, surprise surprise, and which he wouldn't have read anyway, so it was just as well. He hadn't heard from her again, and probably wouldn't for months or even years. You never knew, with Holly. Once she'd been such a brooding presence, but it was as though she'd used up all her authority, burning through it when she was young and then simply wandering off, having lost interest.

It was Dashiell's mother who had now become difficult to manage. Her constant calls unnerved him. She wanted to see him, she wanted to go with him when he went for his treatment, she probably wanted to throw herself in front of the pinpoint of radiation and say, "Take me instead." He'd always felt constrained around her; he didn't want her to know him deeply, he'd once realized.

He picked up the ringing phone; it was what you had to do when you were a son. "Hey, Mom," he said.

"Dash, did I wake you?"

"Nope."

"Are you all right?"

"Not great."

"Can I please come up there? I won't drive you crazy. I won't even stay with you and Tom. I'll stay at the Biltmore. They have good rates."

"There's no need, Mom, really," he said. "I would feel like I had to entertain you or something."

"But you wouldn't!" she said. "You know you wouldn't."

"I know," he said, "but I'd still feel like I did. It's the way I am. And look, Mom, I've got everything I need here with Tom."

There was silence, and an intake of breath, and he realized that this remark had hurt her. The self-contained gay son was a force to reckon with. Sometimes he needed nothing from you. Never, really, had Dashiell wanted much of anything from his mother.

She'd always made him uncomfortable, watching over him all the time. He remembered when he was a little boy and his frequent nosebleeds had created a need for weekly visits to Dr. Enzelman. He could still feel the agony of those car rides, with his mother's lectures about picking his nose and what it might do to his life if he kept it up. The essence of her argument seemed to be that no one would love him. But really, wasn't picking your nose just another way of touching yourself, of *pleasuring* yourself, in a sense? And what was wrong with that? Nothing, she would have had to say; pleasuring yourself is more than fine, it's wonderful, it's a necessity, everyone should do it.

But he hadn't been able to confront her back then; she was an unassailable figure, so maternal and giving and pretty, and he knew that his father would come rushing to her defense if Dashiell dared to criticize her. "Your mother tries so hard," he would have said. "Just look at her." Together they would have had to look at Roz, seeing her vulnerable nobility, her blue eyes already watering, and Dashiell would have backed down. She cried a lot, and Claudia cried a lot too. Why did women cry so much? What were you supposed to do? There was no way to respond, and he wished they were more like him. Private, interior, closed corporations.

Secretiveness had always been Dashiell's primary mode in life. After the four Mellow children had first read through *Pleasuring*, Dashiell had gone back to the book again and again. He was certain the others did, too, but he never saw any of them do it. Sometimes he would creep into the den when no one was around. He'd pull the book down, along with a couple of other oversize books from the shelf, particularly the one with all the photographs of golden retrievers, which was so large it could quickly swallow up *Pleasuring* within its covers if someone wandered in and said, *Hey, what's that you're reading, Dash?*

He learned a great deal from *Pleasuring* over the years, and eventually, when he got to be old enough, he was distraught by what he learned. The only mention of homosexual love came in a brief section on anal sex, which Dashiell had read again and again. According to his parents, there was a hierarchy of human orifices, and the anus was at the bottom, literally and figuratively, a stingy bit player, used once in a while for variety, but mostly unloved:

> Though the gays by default do go gaga over this decidedly tricky way of expressing sexual desire, we're a wee bit puzzled when we hear singing accolades from our own camp. Sure, an intense sexual experience can be had this way, as we well know. But it almost seems to us that there's a sadomasochistic component here. Why go to such lengths more than once in a blue moon when the real thing is just around the corner? If you and your partner are adventurers, however, and do wish to try a Lewis & Clark–style exploration (or should we say Louisa & Clark?) by pleasuring each other in this more difficult and potentially injurious way, then be sure to have the appropriate lubrication handy. We recommend . . .
>
> *(Pleasuring, p. 183)*

"The gays"! "A wee bit puzzled"! "Our own camp"! The tone here, unlike almost anywhere else in the book, was hostile and preening. "We're not afraid of the human body," his mother had said in a 1975 television interview on *Ken London's Night Owl*, and the suave young interviewer with the wide lapels and Prince Valiant haircut had nodded and replied, "Obviously."

But my homo human body, Dashiell had felt certain when he first read this passage for real meaning, *is something that they can't deal with*. He didn't have the nerve to bring it up or to criticize them openly, though. He was fourteen then, alive with something that wasn't just anger and boyish irritation. Ham Kleeman, the older brother of a boy at school named Nick, had recently stopped him in the cafeteria and said, "You're Nick's friend, right? You were over at our house."

Dashiell had been startled, for it was unheard of for a twelfth grader to talk to a ninth grader, or for one even to have been aware of the members of his own brother's social circle. So what if he'd been to the Kleemans' house; what kind of older brother noticed such a thing? It was only younger brothers who paid attention to their older brothers' lives, watching each move as though trying to be a quick study, to pick up everything they could. It hadn't been fun keeping an eye on Michael, though, for he and his friends, back when they were in high school, were as square-headed and straight-up as they came: Model UN without actually being Model UN. They were an intense knot of boys who were either Westinghouse Science Award semifinalists or oboists dragooned to perform in local productions of *Peter and the Wolf*. They were brainy, sarcastic, and unsexy with their acrylic sweaters and *har-har* sarcastic laughter, their fried foods and correspondent patches of acne. Only Michael stood out among them, was attractive in a way that his little brother could not see at the time, because the built-in sun shield against incestuous desire was working.

But Dashiell's friend Nick's outgoing older brother Ham was something entirely different. Everyone knew him; he was nicknamed Ham because over the years he had played the lead in virtually every play put on at Felice P. Bolander Elementary, then at East Street Junior High School, and finally at Wontauket High. Ham had, appropriately, once played Hamlet at a drama camp he attended in Stockbridge, Massachusetts, but most of the parts he was given were genial singing leads. *The Music Man* suited him fine; his Harold Hill, according to the *Wontauket Ledger*, was "masterful," which was pretty much the same thing they said about his Nathan Detroit and his King of Siam.

But when Ham Kleeman approached Dashiell Mellow in the cafeteria and asked when he was coming to the house again, he took on another persona entirely; he seemed in that moment predatory, dominant—interesting. So Dashiell made sure to hang around Nick a little more that week at school, even though Nick was deeply into an unrelenting Dungeons & Dragons phase. On Friday afternoon, the three boys were all at the Kleeman house alone, and after it was ascertained that Nick was lost in a babbling ether of blackguards, dwarven defenders, loremasters, and shadow-dancers, Dashiell crept up to the attic room, where Ham had his lair. Indian curtains draped the windows, posters of sports figures hung on the slanted wall, and on a day bed in the corner of the gloom lay Ham himself, absently playing a harmonica. He looked not at all surprised to see his brother's friend.

"Come over here," he said, and Dashiell walked to the bed. Ham's mouth was slightly swollen and ridged from the harmonica, which he tossed onto the bed. His blond hair was wavy and soft, and he looked at Dashiell and then said, "Take down your pants."

Dashiell was unsurprised; Ham was the one who seemed surprised when Dashiell obeyed so quickly, unbuckling his belt and dropping his jeans and then his Hanes briefs to reveal his big, springing penis, a marvel for a fourteen year old, by anyone's standard.

"Would you fuckin' look at that? Big things come in small packages," said Ham Kleeman, pleased with his own wit, and he scooted forward and grabbed Dashiell lightly by it, pulling him toward the bed. The tug didn't hurt at all. It was as though Dashiell had been waiting forever for an older boy to pull him like this, to grab hold of his dick like he was uprooting a carrot from the earth. *The Carrot Seed* was a book Dashiell's mother had read to him when he was little. "It won't come up, it won't come up," the large-headed little boy in the book had complained, waiting for his carrot to sprout up from the dark and boring earth.

Then one day it came up.

So when he fully understood his long-separated parents, who would both be accepting and no-nonsense when Dashiell officially came out in college, had clearly disdained gay people back in their book, which claimed to be the sex manual for everyman and everywoman, he subtly turned from them further. Annoyance with his mother became something worse: a secret dislike. His father was mostly spared. It was difficult to remain angry at Paul because he was so level and gentle, and for some reason Dashiell needed his father to pay attention to him. But he resisted giving in; he held fast, kept to himself, kept his secrets, and, over a long arc of time, he turned away from his parents.

In turning from them, Dashiell became different from them and from anyone he knew. It was as though he had to give it all up, to cast off this old, soft, boyish self who was the second youngest in the family, the almost-baby, the one with nonsense songs in his head. He became more difficult to read. He withdrew. And in 1993, in an act that was as profound and secretive as the long-ago day in the attic room when an older boy pulled him onto the bed, Dashiell Mellow became a registered Republican.

It was cold on this early Sunday morning on College Hill in Providence, and the only people out were the occasional Brown students looking for cigarettes or coffee to help them recover from a night of campus debauchery. They walked in couples or trios, scarves around necks, hands dug into pockets. There was laughter; they were young and didn't yet know that things might happen to them that they couldn't manage. Dashiell, dressed in a thick down coat, his bald head tucked into the turtle collar, ducked into Store 24 on Thayer Street for some groceries needed at home. He didn't want to make Tom go out; Tom was still sleeping, exhausted from being a caretaker. Dashiell had been sick three times in the night, and all three times Tom had stayed up with him.

Dashiell had just gotten off the phone with his mother, having convinced her that he didn't need her at all, that he and Tom could manage. "Michael is still in Florida with your father," she'd said at the end, thinking he might be interested in other Mellow family news.

"I know that. They've been calling a lot. Why's he taking so long?" Dashiell asked. "It was supposed to be a week. Now it's been, what, *three*?"

"He was supposed to get your father to agree to the book, then come home. He'd better get him to do it *soon*. The publisher has to get cracking." She paused. "Maybe you could say something."

"*Mom*." Dashiell's voice was sharp with her, suddenly. "I'm sick here. Did you forget that?" She hadn't forgotten, of course, but she was also wrapped up in her insistence on putting this book back into print. "I need to go shopping now," he said to her.

"All right," she'd said, retreating, wounded, and once again he was reminded of why she always made him so mad; that combination of hypersensitivity and pushiness—what could you do with it?

In the frozen foods aisle of Store 24, as the frost curled from the standing glass cases and Dashiell pulled forth a few packages of Tabatchnick's soups, if only for their soothing name, he suddenly found himself facing the speechwriter Trish Leggett.

"Oh my God, Dashiell," Trish said, and she hugged her own purchases to her bosom. "Look at you."

She hadn't seen him since he'd gotten sick or since he'd had his head shaved. She was a pretty blonde woman wearing a velvet hair band and a down vest, and she observed this wretched bald and ashen man with a kind of sympathy infused with horror that was unbearable if you were on the receiving end of it. He could only stand there, looking bad, looking sick, waiting to see what she would say. Would she speak of his "extraordinary soul dressed in the clothes of the humble"? Would she speak of "pillars of goodness"? But all she said, again, was "Look at you."

"Yes, look at me," he finally managed. "I look like shit, I know that, Trish."

"It's just that you had such nice hair," she said before she could stop herself. "I don't know what I'd do if I lost my hair. . . ." And here her voice dropped off, as if she'd just realized this was a terrible thing to say to someone. "I'm sorry, I didn't mean that," she tried desperately.

"Don't worry about it," he said.

"You know, there are all these incredible drugs now, aren't there? Those protease inhibitors? My cousin Mitchell takes them around the clock. You can live a full life, you can."

He stared at her, letting the freezer door fall shut with a sucking sound. "What?" he said.

"With AIDS," she explained.

"Trish, who said I had AIDS?"

She began to fidget with her groceries, moving them from arm to arm. "They said you were sick. In the office. Obviously. Tom came in, and *he* said you were sick, and that we could send you cards and so forth. I hope you got them. And I guess I just assumed you were one of those really late cases. Oh, God, I am mortified. You mean, you don't have AIDS, Dashiell?"

Several seconds passed before he could answer her. "No, just plain old Hodgkin's disease," he said. "It's totally unrelated to my faggotiness." His voice came out louder and harsher than he'd meant it to be. So all of them at Wyman's lively, buzzing, round-the-clock downtown campaign office thought that he, Dashiell Mellow, was sick with AIDS, and this misunderstanding was simply because he was gay. Robert Wyman *himself* probably thought Dashiell had AIDS. Tom hadn't disabused them of this fact because he probably didn't know that this was what they thought. These days everyone used shorthand and discreet terminology: Dashiell was "sick." He was "being treated." He would be "out for a while." In the world of Republican politics, a gay man with a sickness was apparently a gay man with AIDS, and though he'd never known this before, now he did.

"I didn't mean to offend you," Trish Leggett tried, and she seemed so distraught that she was actually crying. Jesus Christ, another crying woman! He couldn't stand to see the brightness of her eyes or hear the new vibrato that rippled through her speaking voice; it reminded him of his mother, which wasn't fair and made him seem suspiciously misogynist, he knew, as though he thought all women were the same.

"Look, I've got to go," was all he'd give her, and he turned around and carried his armful of groceries to the counter, dumping it onto the belt with a vengeance. *Oh fuck. Oh fuck.* People would think what they wanted; you couldn't control them, couldn't make them see you the way you needed to be seen. *I have no control,* he thought, and he paid with a shaking hand and got out of Store 24 as fast as he could, away from that crying woman who would write up a storm of speeches and eventually be invited to work in the White House, while Dashiell would languish at home with his bald head and his frozen soups and a body that was studded with darkness and uncertainty.

Chapter Six

EVERY FALL, when Professor Rosalyn Mellow taught Introduction to Human Sexuality in a large, sloping room filled with
freshmen, she couldn't help but be reminded of the auditoriums
that she and Paul used to fill. There had been a certain thrill and
tang then, too, as though the entire room of two hundred and fifty
people had wished they could all leave together and go some-
place dark to engage in mass sex. Couples sat close together, arms
entwined, listening, talking back, wanting to find a way in.

But now it was a different world, a different life entirely. At
age sixty-seven, Roz Mellow had a smudged but still definitive
sexuality about her. Although technically she was a grandmother,
Roz wasn't someone who looked grandmotherly-comical teaching
the ways of the flesh. Her own body was rounder and more opu-
lent, if of course more *fallen* than when she was young, and her
hair, which had lost some of its luster over time, now bore expensive, dark color that gave it the look of highly polished Colonial
furniture. Roz still spent money on her clothes, too, though each
winter the punitive upstate weather made it pointless for anyone

to dress well, for you were always forced to zip up into some enormous down cocoon if you wanted to step outside your door. And when you came indoors again, that coat would have created such a field of static on the surface of your clothes that all fabrics clung and pulled on you, and your hair, beneath its Nanook hood or hat, stood in discrete strands away from your head. Still, Roz tried as best she could to look good, and she certainly was one of the more attractive faculty members at Skidmore College—an older woman with beautiful milky skin, lovely dark red hair, and a generous body that looked like it would be warm to the touch.

Several male colleagues in the Psych department desired her, and the fact that once, twenty-eight years earlier, she had coauthored an international best-seller that featured graphic illustrations of her making love with her husband at the time added to the appeal. But over the years, as she'd stayed on at Skidmore and made a life for herself in this college town, with its summer ballet season and racetrack crowd, attending faculty meetings and bringing hummus and pita points to potluck dinners for the outgoing department chairman, and once even taking a perilous toboggan ride down a hill of ice with her students, there was a grudging acceptance of her as someone who was, if not exactly like everyone else, then at least was *of* them. Always, there would be a certain amount of bitterness in her midst, for Roz Mellow had no doctorate or even a master's, just her ancient, irrelevant undergraduate degree from the Fashion Institute of Technology, while the rest of them had worked slavishly for their PhDs and had then desperately grasped for available teaching jobs. Yes, yes, they knew; it was her "field work" that had landed her this easy job and then greased the way to tenure; it was her 1970s sexual pioneering that had brought her from the noise and clatter of that era to here, a perfectly nice liberal arts college thirty minutes north of Albany along the Hudson River. She had been *around* while a majority of them had not, but it all leveled out in the end. Both she and they had ended up doing their grocery shopping at the Foodtown off I-87, salting their driveways each winter, and sitting, as they were all doing right now, around a long rectangular table for the Friday afternoon faculty meeting, yawning discreetly as the minutes from last week's meeting were read.

The fact that Roz had been *around* was more significant to her at this point than it was to them. She couldn't forget about her prior life, though it had collapsed; she had collapsed it, in fact, had taken a pin and stuck it in. Still it occupied her mind, especially at moments like this one, when she was both so antsy and so anguished that she feared she might fall face-forward onto the table with a loud hollow sound and a quiet whimper. The personal problems that preoccupied her were vast, and she wished more than anything that she could go outside into the frozen air and have a smoke. That would make her feel better. She wished she could be anywhere but here.

Today, the acting chairman of the department, Dr. Deanna Stegman, was talking about the new Computer Learning Center on the second floor of the revamped library, and how all faculty members were required to take an evening course there in order to help acquaint their students with the software they would be using to help them with statistics and graphing.

"And I mean all of you," Stegman said meaningfully, looking around the room, trying not to stop at any one person in a duck-duck-goose way, though really, everyone understood that this last comment was for the benefit of Roz Mellow. The comment meant: *Even if your job description has you standing at a podium each fall saying "fellatio" and "cunnilingus" without blinking, and also has you inching a Trojan-Enz with spermicide onto a Chiquita banana, don't think that you're exempt. Because you're not. You're one of us now. You're not special anymore.*

Simon Post raised a hand. "I'd like to say, Deanna, that I think it's a really good idea. Some of us only *think* we're computer literate, when in fact our seven year olds know more about writing code and about Linux than we do."

"Speak for yourself, Post," said Donald Mosher, and all the academic psychologists and statisticians laughed a little, though it wasn't funny at all; they were just high on the monster box of Krispy Kreme doughnuts that the department secretary, Celeste, had placed in the center of the table. The only doughnuts left in the box were two slightly misshapen plains. The surface was dotted with crumbs, as was Donald Mosher's thick brush of a mustache. Even Roz had eaten a jelly doughnut, released briefly from her terror about Dashiell and her anger at Paul by the doughnut's predictable scent and its squirt of sweetness and pectin.

Finally it was 4 P.M., time for the meeting to end, even though legitimately it could have ended half an hour earlier. The faculty drifted out into the hall, and Roz walked with her one close friend here, a Southerner of fifty-eight named Constance Coffey, who specialized in forensic psychology. Haunted-looking students in Gothwear left over from high school often clustered around Constance's office to show her their papers on the tragedy at Columbine and what it said about nihilism and young people today. Young people today, Constance had once complained to Roz, slightly drunk on Saratoga Slings at a Christmas party, had no rights to the word "nihilism." Unlike the youth of the '60s, these kids hadn't earned it. They knew nothing about history, Constance railed; they knew very little about anything.

"Roz, how is Dashiell?" Constance asked now as they headed outside into the cold. "I've been so concerned."

"Oh, I don't know," Roz told her friend. "Doing all right, I suppose, but he doesn't want any of us there." She felt as though she might cry from talking about it, saying the words aloud. "He's always been like that. At least he *talks* to me, unlike my oldest, so I guess I should be grateful." She sighed and clutched herself tighter in the wind.

"He still needs you," said Constance. "It doesn't matter what he says."

"Well, I doubt that. But thank you for saying it," said Roz, and she began to feel irritated with Constance, who didn't know Dash, who didn't know what it was like inside the Mellow family.

"Is your ex-husband involved with the whole medical situation?" Constance asked. They were headed down the path to the parking lot now; the tall lights had just come on, pale violet in the deepening afternoon.

"Yes," Roz said. "That's not one of his failings."

Constance looked at her for a moment. "You're still angry with him about the book thing?"

Roz nodded. "He still refuses to let it be published. He just wants to hurt me, Con, because *I* was the one who left *him*. If it was the other way around, I guess he'd still have his pride or something. But I mean, can you *believe* it? We're talking about something that happened twenty-some-odd years ago! Does it never end? Is it going to follow me to the grave? And pardon me, but he's remarried, too. Why hold a grudge so long, when the reissue would benefit both of us? Why not just grow up?"

Constance shook her head in sympathy. "It was a landmark, that book of yours. My ex-husband and I practically got twin hernias trying some of those positions. And that one you made up, the position that people were supposed to try after they had a fight?"

"'Electric Forgiveness.'"

"Yes, yes, that's it!"

"Whenever I hear that name we came up with," said Roz, "I want to hide."

"It was the seventies!" cried Constance. "Anyway, I guess we did it wrong or something, because—oh, this is so graphic—he kept popping right out! It was like a cork in a bottle." Both women started to laugh. "What you did was important, Roz," Constance went on. "That kind of sexual openness and tenderness about the whole thing. Nothing's *tender* now. No, wait, that's not entirely true. I look around the campus and I see these eighteen-year-old boys and girls leaning into each other like saplings. Needing each other. Inhaling each other. And *that's* tender. That's unspoiled. I want to say to them, 'Oh, you poor puppies, make love now like there's no tomorrow. Because soon enough you're going to see the grotesquerie and . . . and . . . the *leeringness* of the world.' I know that's not a word, but you know what I mean. God, Roz, the cheapness of everything! Everything's a quick feel. Nothing's hidden. The culture is so fucking ugly." She took a ragged breath. "Sorry for my raging diatribe," she said. "I was lecturing for an hour and a half this afternoon. I can't seem to stop. But I just want you to know how important your book was. You should make your ex-husband change his mind." The two women had reached the parking lot, where their ice-crackled cars sat side by side in coveted spots.

"I can't. He won't," said Roz. "I sent my oldest son Michael down there to convince him, and then Dash got sick and the whole conversation got *diverted,* of course."

"Look, at least you've got Jack," tried Constance.

"Yes, at least I've got Jack. He's been home cooking one of his soups today."

"His soups are excellent. I remember he made one with curry once. Senegalese chicken. In many ways you're a very lucky person," Constance said. "I've often thought that about you. That you're blessed. And I still do."

"Why exactly am I blessed?" Roz asked sharply. "My son has *cancer,* Constance, he's very sick."

Constance flushed. "I'm sorry, Roz, I didn't mean to be cavalier. I only meant because you have Jack. He's such a good guy." She shoved her hands deep into her coat pockets and cast her eyes downward.

"Oh, Con, I didn't mean to snap at you," said Roz. "I know what you meant. I'm just tightly wound. I'm basically falling apart here." Impulsively she put her arms around her friend.

Constance Coffey was divorced and somewhat pummeled by life. Her ex-husband had been a loudmouth from the Political Science department who embarrassed her at faculty parties, and it was her distinct pleasure that he had been denied tenure. But a single woman in a college town in upstate New York did not have many chances of meeting someone new. It was cold all winter, and you would sleep alone in your bed and perhaps lightly touch your own body in the morning before you had to get up and teach a class on homicidal personality types to your wild and sexual students. Constance had a tragic aspect to her, Roz felt, although it was entirely possible that this was only projection. It was just that Roz couldn't imagine a life without being touched. Not just a sexual touch; not even primarily a sexual touch. Just some kind of touching.

"Good-bye," the women sang out to each other in the parking lot. Good-bye, have a good weekend, enjoy the soup, try to get some rest, let's get together next week for drinks at the Parting Glass; let's drink to the new semester and to the defeat of the warmongering president in the next election. They climbed into their cars and closed the doors with synchronous thumps, and then left the lot at separate exits and headed to their homes, one dark, one all lit up.

But in a sudden change of mind, Roz kept driving. She drove right through town and kept going, heading out into the countryside, where the road narrowed as it climbed upward into the mountains. She knew this route well, had driven it many times since she and Jack had moved to Saratoga Springs. It was the same road she'd driven with her parents when she was a child, though back then it had been unpaved and lacking all these bright warning signs of deer that might leap into the path of your car, or the variety of sudden hairpin turns awaiting you. By the time she reached the front entrance of what was now the Mount Arcadia Yoga and Wellness Center, the sky was dark and Roz Mellow pulled her car into the parking lot, took out a pack of cigarettes, and began to smoke.

In the distance was the enormous mansion that was the center's main building. Roz rolled down her window to let the smoke out, and as she did, she could smell food. It was almost dinnertime, and inside the mansion a cook was probably preparing a dinner that made use of millet or quinoa or other, more obscure grains that the guests who paid a great deal of money to come here for a week-long stay seemed to like.

Often, when she was a girl, Roz had walked these grounds at twilight. For she had been born right here in 1936, on the property of what had then been the Mount Arcadia Hospital for the Insane. Her father, Phillip Woodman, was chief of psychiatry, and because of this, Roz grew accustomed to the sounds of misery before she went to sleep at night. She would lie in bed upstairs in her family's house, which was situated one hundred yards from the main building, and after lights-out she would hear shrieking and weeping as though animals were being slaughtered. *No, no, it's nothing like that*, her father assured her, coming into the bedroom. *These patients are in psychic anguish*, he said, *and no one is laying a hand on them.*

But every night the gates were padlocked at dusk by an aging groundskeeper, and those nighttime shrieks echoed through the surrounding hills, frightening the locals and waking the deer.

"Is anyone being beaten?" she asked her father before bed.

"No one is being beaten," he answered.

"Is anyone being whipped?"

"No one is being whipped."

"Slapped?"

"No one is being slapped, Roz."

"Throttled?"

"Where did you learn *that* word?" asked her father. And so it went, this bedtime ritual, and though many of the patients stayed up weeping and howling throughout the long night, she was able to sleep the fluent sleep of children. To the patients, this place was a hospital, a prison, but to her it was home.

During the Depression and throughout the Second World War, a small, elite population remained at Mount Arcadia, and these patients were Dr. Phillip Woodman's bread and butter. They were an unlikely assortment of men and women whose families had secret, inexplicable reserves of money, and who seemed untouched by dark times. Here was the nucleus of unassailably rich America: shrewd bankers who could afford to keep unbalanced, yammering wives confined to the mountaintop for as long as it took, sometimes forever.

Over the years, seeing the same faces in the windows of the hospital, the same figures in soft robes lumbering down the gravel footpath, Roz became comforted by how little anything changed. The faces were as familiar as those of relatives seen year after year at holiday dinners. There was Harry Beeman, a financier who had jumped from his fifteenth-floor office in the Bankers' Equity Building, only to bounce twice on the striped tarp of the building's awning, crushing several ribs and both legs. Now he limped through the halls of Mount Arcadia with a copy of *The Financial Times* in front of his face, muttering about bonds and interest rates as though they mattered to him. There was Mildred Vell, a society matron with milky cataracts and a delusion about being Eleanor Roosevelt, which none of the nurses really minded because it made Mildred a great help on the ward, always volunteering for some project or other. The core group of patients never grew worse, never seemed to get better, and never asked when they could leave. The world stayed stubbornly shut for these people, an aperture that let in no outside light.

The same was true, in a way, for the Woodman family. They seemed separated from the world, at least the world as it revealed itself through the large rosewood radio that sat in the living room. The war, when it began, took Phillip Woodman away from home for a period of months, but soon he was sent back, for a unit in his hospital had been designated a place of recovery for GIs with trauma disorder. Though the world outside Mount Arcadia had been shifting and convulsing, Roz Woodman felt very little of it.

Her family inhabited the large house across the lawn from the hospital, her mother and father taking as their bedroom the room that overlooked the road out front. Sometimes, especially in the daylight, it was almost possible for her to forget that she lived on the grounds of a psychiatric facility, and to imagine that she lived in a normal home, on a real street. But at night, when the howling started, she remembered.

Dr. Phillip Woodman was a big hit with the nurses and orderlies. He strode the shining halls of the hospital as though he had been running the place since birth. Even his memos were praised. ("Re: Hospital gowns. It has come to my attention that the dung-colored gowns worn by our patients are perhaps no good for morale. Might we find something with a bit more dash—perhaps peach or sky-blue?")

Roz's mother was less graceful in her role as the chief psychiatrist's wife. Before the Depression, her job had largely entailed standing in the middle of her kitchen, conferring with a mute Negro hospital cook about upcoming dinner parties at the house. She would wave her pale hands vaguely, opening drawers and pointing to spoons and knives, saying, "Now, there are the spoons. Oh, and the knives."

Both of Roz's parents were aimless, rolling around in this huge house together, anxious to populate the rooms with children. By the time their daughter was born, they were tired of seeing only mentally ill people, eager for an infant's simple and understandable cry. But when the obstetrician told Mrs. Woodman that she could bear no more children, her husband let his only daughter into his life in a way that no one, not even his wife, had been allowed.

Every few months Phillip Woodman took Roz on a whirlwind tour of the hospital: the dining room, which smelled perennially of fried flounder; the Occupational Therapy room, where dead-eyed patients pressed images of dogs and presidents onto copper sheeting; the solarium; the visitors' lounge. They breezed past doors with doctors' names stenciled onto the grain, and past doors with signs that read "Warning: Electricity in Use." These doors were always shut, and she longed to see what electricity looked like when it was "in use." And she also longed to see where the patients actually lived, where they showered and dressed and bathed. But the wards themselves, their heavy doors with chicken wire laced into the glass, were off-limits.

Roz was permitted to see hospital life only from a distance, watching as patients slogged through the halls in their dung-colored gowns and flannel robes. Once she made prolonged eye contact with a former naval officer whose face was blue with stubble, until she was whisked off into the nurses' lounge, where big-band music emanated from the radio, and she was given a handful of sourballs by a trio of fussing women.

Although Roz was allowed into the hospital only at her father's invitation, she was free to explore the grounds whenever she liked. With the sun sinking and the air aromatic with pine and earth and Salisbury steak, the whole place smelled like a summer camp. One day, at the rear entrance of the building, she saw deliverymen unloading drums of institutional disinfectant. As they rolled them up a ramp and into the service entrance, she could read the words "Whispering Pines," and even though the name referred to nothing more than a rancid fluid that would be swabbed across the floors and walls at dawn, it sounded like the perfect alias for the hospital, the ideal name for a splendid summer camp.

Whispering Pines, she whispered to herself as she stepped into the thicket that continued until the edges of the grounds, where it was held back by the iron fence. Vines flourished along that fence, wound around the spokes like a cat winding around a human leg; just as the patients sometimes wanted out, so did the vegetation. Everything grew frantically at the farthest reaches of the property. The most tangible signs of the times could be found there, at the edges of the land, where nobody had bothered to prune or clip or chop away at the excess. Sometimes a group of patients would sit on Adirondack chairs on the lawn, taking in a chilly hour of sun, and sometimes a nurse would take a patient on a supervised stroll, but only along the circular path closest to the hospital, and never into the woods. The woods were hers, at least for a while.

When Roz turned nine, her father implemented a program he called "Tea at the House." This involved inviting a promising patient to join him and her mother for afternoon tea in their living room. The patient was always someone at least a little bit appealing, someone who wouldn't make any sudden moves. Someone very close to health, who needed a bit of encouragement to get to the other side.

The first person invited to Tea at the House was a woman named Grace Allenby, a young mother who had had a nervous breakdown and was unable to complete any action, even dressing herself in the morning, without dissolving into hysterical, gulping sobs. At the hospital she had made a slow but admirable recovery. She came to Tea on the Friday before her husband was to bring her home, and Roz sat watching at the top of the stairs. Both Mrs. Allenby and Roz's mother were lovely-looking and uncertain, like the deer that occasionally made a wrong turn in the woods and wound up stunned and confused and frightened on the hospital lawn. The women shyly traded recipes, while Phillip Woodman sat between them, nodding with benevolence.

"What you want to do is this," Mrs. Allenby kept saying, and as she spoke she blinked rapidly, as if to remove a speck from her eye. "You take an egg and you beat it very hard in a bowl with a whisk. Then what you want to do is this. . . ." The living room smelled strongly of oolong tea, Dr. Woodman's favorite. He liked it because it was the closest thing to drinking pipe tobacco.

Roz eavesdropped on several Teas at the House over the year, and she came to understand that mental patients could be divided into two groups: those who wore their affliction outright like a bold political stance, and those who actively and industriously hid it.

Warren Keyes was of the second variety. He was a GI, a twenty-two-year-old former Harvard undergraduate who had been decorated for his flying missions in the war, and who had tried to kill himself with a razor blade the day he came home. Now he was close to leaving Mount Arcadia and finally returning to college. Over dinner, her parents discussed this boy who would be coming to Tea at the House the following day. "He's young," her father said, "and good-looking, in that Harvard way."

Warren Keyes registered in Roz's mind in that moment, was locked into place even before she had met him. Here was a Harvard man. That went over well with her father, who often fantasized about the privileged upbringing he himself had lacked.

The next afternoon at 4 P.M., Warren sat in the living room gripping the fragile handle of a teacup. He had trooped across the lawn with a squat nurse, who now sat in the foyer, dully knitting like Madame du Farge. Roz knew that he had been invited to the house as a reward for getting well, but casting a critical eye on him from the top of the stairs, even she could see that he was not well.

"Warren plans on returning to Harvard next semester," her father said. Her mother cooed a response. "Leverett House, isn't it?" her father went on.

"No, Adams," said Warren. His voice was relaxed, although his cup jitterbugged in its saucer.

Conversation pushed on about Harvard in general, football season, and New England weather, dipping only lightly and tentatively into the war and exactly how many missions he'd flown. At the end of the hour, Warren Keyes looked exhausted. Roz imagined that he would go back to his hospital bed and sleep for thirty-six hours straight, regaining his strength.

Breaking his own tradition but questioned by no one, Dr. Woodman invited Warren Keyes back for a second Tea at the House, and then a third. On his fourth tea, he was unaccompanied by the dour-faced nurse. Instead, he made a solo flight across the lawn, his coat-tails floating out behind him. That afternoon, Roz had been strategically sitting on the porch doing her homework before taking a walk in the woods. Her hair was sloppily bound up behind her head with elastic, and there was ink on her fingers, for she had not yet mastered the fountain pen. But even so, Warren Keyes climbed onto the porch and gave her a good hard look. Although it was not the first time she had seen Warren Keyes, it was the first time he saw her.

"I'm the daughter," Roz said. He nodded. "They're inside," she told him, inclining her head toward the screen door. Deep in the house, the teakettle shrilled.

"Do you like tea?" Warren asked. It was the kind of question that her father's colleagues often asked her when they came to dinner: well-meaning and uninteresting probings from people who had no idea of what to say to children, yet somehow, maddeningly, meant to be answered.

"I like it okay," she said.

"Your mother makes good tea," Warren said. "It's Chinese, you know."

Roz slid off the railing. "I have to go," she said.

His eyes widened slightly. "Where?" he asked.

And for some reason, she told him. She told him where she went every afternoon; she practically drew him a treasure map with an X. Later, she sat in the woods reading *The Red Badge of Courage*, and suddenly there was a parting of branches. Warren Keyes came through, stooped and stumbling. He had in his hand a familiar folded linen napkin with scalloped edges. He squatted down beside her, this handsome, ruined GI and Harvard student, and he opened the napkin, which contained three golden circles: her mother's butter cookies. She ate them silently, while Warren watched.

"So what's it like to live here?" he asked.

She shrugged. How she wanted to ask him a similar question: What was it like to live *there*, inside a hospital for the insane? What was it like to be insane? Did you *know* you were insane? Did you long to crawl out of your body? Did you actually see things—shapes and animals and flames frolicking across the walls of your room at night? But she couldn't bring herself to ask him anything at all. Light was draining from the patch of woods, and suddenly Warren said, "May I ask you something?"

"Yes," she said.

"Could I maybe touch you?" the boy asked.

She nodded solemnly, really believing, in that moment, that he was referring to her hand, or her arm. He wanted to touch her to see if she was real, the same way, years earlier, she herself had surreptitiously touched the bloodless face of her cousin's beloved china doll, who had been named Princess La Vanilla. He wanted to touch her in order to have the experience of touching someone who wasn't insane—someone who had a normal life and lived with her parents in a real house without bars on the windows.

Warren came closer, sliding across the dirt floor to where she sat with her book. "I won't hurt you," he said.

"I know," she said. When his hand came down on her shirt front, on one of her pre-breasts, those very slightly swollen nipples, she could not have been more shocked. She didn't know how to stop this, and she felt at once hurled out of her own realm and into his. "Wait," she said, but his hands were already moving freely above her clothes. He seemed not to have heard her. He sat in front of her, touching her breasts, her neck, her shoulders, and in fact he wasn't hurting her. So what was she upset about? She didn't know what to call this activity, this casual exploration. His face frightened Roz—the intense and worshipful expression on his features, as though he were kneeling and lighting candles. His mouth hung open, but his eyes were focused.

"I'm not hurting you," he kept repeating. "I'm not hurting you."

And all she could answer was, "No. You're not."

Roz closed her eyes so she wouldn't have to see his face. She closed them as if to block out strong sunlight. She felt herself grow dizzy, but she thought it would be worse if she fainted, because who knew what would happen then? She made herself stay conscious, and she felt each motion he made, the starfish movements of his fingers as they slipped beneath her blouse and headed downward.

He moved against her as if in a trance, and Roz felt like a wall, something for others to rub against; she was a cat-scratching post, a solid block. She felt his large hand inside her underwear, so out of place. The elastic waistband was pulled taut against his knuckles. Just that morning she had chosen the underwear from a drawer, where it lay with the others, ironed, white, floral, and touched only by her and by Lena, who did the Woodman family's laundry. No one else was meant to touch it, but now Warren's hand was trapped inside it, like an animal that had run into a tent.

Now one of his fingers was separating itself from the other fingers and pushing into her, sliding up into her body. She felt a shiver of pain, and then something that wasn't pain at all, but surprise. She sat straight up, and started to cry. His big finger, which had held on to her mother's teacup, which probably wore a Harvard ring sometimes, which had a flat fingernail that he trimmed in his cubicle in the hospital for the insane—if they let him have nail scissors—was deeply embedded in her, like something drilled into the ground to test for water or crude oil. Like a machine, a spike, testing the earth for vibrations or for moisture. The finger felt all these things, but she felt nothing.

After some endless time, Warren Keyes made a small sound like a lamb bleating or a hinge groaning open, and she knew that it was over. She sank back onto the surface of leaves, her body returning to itself, small, flexible, a skater's body, while Warren turned away from her, wiping his face and the front of his trousers with her mother's napkin.

In a quaking voice, he told Roz it was better if they left the woods separately, and, of course, if she told no one about what had happened. "There's nothing to tell, anyway," he added casually. "I didn't hurt you." And it was true; he hadn't hurt her in any discernible way.

She left first, walking slowly with book in hand, like a dreamy girl leaving an afternoon of reading, but when she reached the edge of the woods, where the lawn began, she broke into a run toward the lights of her house. Inside, she walked straight up the stairs, claiming she was ill and didn't want dinner. Her mother pressed a cool hand to her forehead, but Roz shrugged it off. There would be no more touching today; even the back of a familiar hand, prospecting for fever, was too much.

Weeks would pass, and she would notice her own shift in feeling almost as though she were charting the progress of a bruise, watching it go from black to blue to brown to yellow, until finally it was only a smudge, a small trace memory. She couldn't understand whether what had happened was something that Warren Keyes had actually wanted to have happen, or whether he'd been unable to stop himself because he was, as the name of the hospital announced, insane. Should she have felt furious, or should she have felt compassion, as her father would have? She was lost, not knowing, and after a while it became too late to ask anyone.

Time would separate her from the memory, and other things rose to replace it. She would grow up and meet men who would touch her when she wanted them to, but whose touch would be, to her, too rough and clumsy and charmless. She would want more from them, would want to coax the love and exploration out of their taciturn selves, but found herself unable to do so, for these men were mostly impassive and unyielding.

But eventually Roz would meet Paul Mellow, and she would talk to him about so many things, including her childhood and then, as if out of nowhere, about Warren Keyes, who sprang up before her like an apparition through the puzzling wonder that was known as free association. Warren Keyes, who had shoved a finger inside her and left her with a strange absence of sensation but a need for more of it, all the time. Eventually she would make love with Paul and would one day be convinced to pose with him for pictures of that love, as though such moments could be captured when still. But movement was everything, she knew; the way your body turned or clutched or curled when it was stroked or entered. A picture could never really show that, and neither could a whole book of pictures.

But she didn't know this yet; she couldn't imagine herself grown, or the mother of children—four of them no less. She was still a nine-year-old girl who had just been forcefully touched by a man in the woods of a mental hospital in the mountains of New York State. Roz would soon forget this day, or at least she would think she'd forgotten, until she went into psychoanalysis with Paul Mellow, and remembered. But that was still a long time from now.

On the night of the day that Warren Keyes touched her, Roz Woodman pushed up the window by her bed and poked her head out. From the hospital across the lawn, she heard the familiar crying and baying, and without thinking, she opened her mouth and softly joined the chorus. The sound came naturally, and she hung out that window howling quietly in a low, effortless voice, as though it were natural to her species.

The cell phone in Roz's bag on the car seat was ringing now, and it was her husband Jack on the line, wanting to know where she was, why she hadn't come home yet. "I went for a drive," she said, and the connection was crackled and unstable, for she was in the mountains.

"I can hear it," he said. "I know exactly where you are. Your usual place."

"Yes," she said. "My usual place."

"Well, don't get too sad, okay? Come home. I've got soup."

"All right," she said. "I'll come."

So she put out her cigarette in the ashtray, took another look around her at the place where she'd once lived, and then backed out of the parking lot to head for home. To be wanted, to have someone say *Come home*, as if you were a runaway, as if you were Lassie, and nothing would be all right until you set foot inside your house—this was what everyone hoped for. She worried that one day Jack would not say it or feel it—that he'd lose his desire but wouldn't have the heart to tell her. With Paul, she'd never had that worry. For she was so much younger then, and she was beautiful, and she held sway over him as though he'd been hypnotized in his sleep and had never come out of the trance.

Paul's overwhelming need for Roz, back in the beginning, was actually a source of power and pleasure. "Baby," Paul had called her. "Baby," he said in bed, and sometimes on the telephone. This was a circa-1958 affectation, an implied-hipster word that gave him a surge of independence each time he said it because it was so far removed from the milieu of Ava Schussler and her analytic compatriots. In his training up until then, "baby" had only been another word for infant. Now Paul Mellow had rescued the word and given it an additional, dirty quality.

"Baby," he said to Roz in bed in her apartment in the beginning when he arrived there most evenings.

She would have just come home from her apprenticeship to a midlevel fashion designer who called himself simply "Pierrot," but who was actually Canadian, not French, a fact that he told no one. Within a year Roz would see that she had no great aptitude for fashion, or even a real passion, and would quit her job and let Paul support them both. And not too much longer after that, of course, she would start having babies and would never look back.

Paul had a new job by then, having been forced out of Schussler; he was working in a lab again, this time not with mice but with pigeons, which to his surprise was even worse. Mice, he'd told Roz, were disgusting, but at least they had those liquidy, allergic-looking eyes and warm, quivering fur with a fragile puzzle of bone beneath it, and they gave off the vaguest notion of *pet*, and *cute*. Pigeons, however, made you think only of dirt and city filth. They brought out no kindness in you; their eyes were perfectly round and perfectly dark and devoid of emotion. The pigeons were a cageful of ciphers, stupid, pointy-faced, unwanted. When he held one in his hands it flapped to get away, and pecked him and struggled, but sometimes, Paul admitted, he thought about wringing its neck, just because he could. He never did, instead transferring the birds from cage to cage, adjusting their feeding schedules, and taking exhaustive notes on their eating patterns and mating behaviors. By the time Paul arrived at Roz's fifth-floor apartment in the evenings, he smelled birdy and sometimes had a stray feather in his hair, and she always felt sorry for him and gathered him to her.

Roz's fashion-student roommate Vivian was often cutting fabric in the next room; they could hear the sound of shears on material, lulling and rhythmic, not unlike sex itself, and when Roz and Paul lay down in the small bed together, Roz felt smoothed over, as though she herself were a large square of fabric.

It wasn't that she was exactly sexually attracted to Paul in the beginning; he was undeniably handsome, but he had a little too much hair on his head and on his face and sprouting out the end of his sleeves. He was also so kind and understanding; though these were good qualities for a psychoanalyst, they were less desirable for a lover, at least at first. The men she'd been to bed with had been brutish and sullen, in particular her law student boyfriend Carl Mendelson. The fact that Paul Mellow clearly didn't possess these traits was puzzling. She didn't know how to react to him at first, how to create her usual pattern of initial sexual excitement followed by disappointment and then self-pitying sorrow. In 1958, Paul Mellow was sturdy and black-haired with a large head, large hands, large feet, and large penis. It was as though everything that sprang from the main part of his body had grown inordinately. Carl Mendelson had been slightly rough with her, rolling her around the bed, and all the sensation had immediately rushed out of her, as though the stopper in a drain had been pulled. It was only during sex with Paul, who as her analyst had encouraged her to hold nothing back, that she could finally relax and enjoy herself, and feel everything more completely.

It was thrilling, actually, to be so close to a man. How different this was from her childhood spent on those mental hospital grounds. Now it was all about proximity. This was how, slowly and over time, the idea for *Pleasuring* came about. When you were that close to someone else, you tried to find various ways of expressing it. You tried verbally, using all kinds of words, saying *love* and *adore* and *no one else has ever*. And you also tried with your body, letting yourself be overtaken, or else overpowering the other person as though you might find a way never to let him escape you.

One night, when Roz and Paul were making love, she heard herself command Paul, *Fuck me*, and she realized that she'd forgotten that this was exactly what he was already doing; she'd been lost inside the act, and it was like listening to music and thinking, *I'd like to listen to some music now*, because you were so stimulated that you needed an influx of *new* stimulation, an overlay of something else. *Bring on the next thing*, you thought, *come on, come on, make it snappy*. His body was dark, strong, and his hair seemed patterned, fanning out delicately over his chest and narrowing into a funnel-shape as it went down to his groin.

Paul, ardent and worshipful and patient, had shown her how their two bodies could be gently arranged so that he could penetrate her from various directions, some of which seemed geometrically impossible until you tried them and found that they actually worked, after a fashion. One day he came home with a worn, paper-covered copy of *The Kama Sutra* and announced that here in his hands lay the future of Western sex. "The East understands," he said. "They always have. They're way beyond American suburbanites having missionary sex."

"We're not suburban," she said. *Not yet*, she should really have said, for fairly soon they too would fall prey to the green gold of the suburbs. In 1960, Roz gave birth to Holly in Mount Sinai Hospital on Fifth Avenue, followed two years later by Michael, at which point a house seemed necessary, and houses were in suburbs. By then, Paul was running an animal behavior lab, and between his salary and some money given to them by Roz's parents, there was enough for a down payment on a large house on a street called Swarthmore Circle in the commuter town of Wontauket.

But on this night in December 1958, Roz and Paul, still recent lovers and childless city-dwellers, sat in bed reading *The Kama Sutra.* "'There are four basic embraces,'" Paul read aloud.

"Four? I thought there were dozens."

"No, only four embraces, but dozens of positions," he said. "There's a difference. Listen. 'There's touching, piercing, rubbing, and pressing. When a man goes in front of a woman, or next to her, and touches her body with his, it's called the "touching embrace." But when a woman bends down and basically "pierces" a man with her breasts, it's called a "piercing embrace."'"

"Pierce? How can her breasts pierce him?" she asked. "Does she sharpen them?"

"I think it just refers to the fact that it's an individual body part connecting with skin. It's not just skin to skin. And then there's a 'rubbing embrace,' which is basically whole bodies being rubbed together. And then finally there's a 'pressing embrace,' where one person presses the other one's body against a wall or a pillar."

"Like you did the other night," Roz said. "After we came home from the lobster place."

"I did? I can't quite remember," said Paul, smiling. "Oh wait, wait, yes, it's coming back to me. I see a wall. A big white wall."

They both sat in happy silence for a moment, conjuring up the evening they'd spent at a Spanish restaurant that featured complete and inexpensive lobster dinners. Roz had had trouble getting the meat out, and Paul had taken over, cracking a thick-shelled claw easily, then reaching in with that tiny pitchfork and pulling out a long, tapered column of pink flesh with its vernix of white scum. He'd dipped it in the little butter pool and fed her. Later, when they had just arrived at home and he suddenly turned to her with an elliptical expression and quickly pushed against her, driving her toward the wall, the light switch unfortunately poking into her spine, and then lifted the edge of her gray skirt, Roz thought that lobster was definitely an aphrodisiac, or maybe melted butter was.

"But then there are other embraces," Paul continued now. "Listen to this one. 'When a man and woman are very much in love, and not thinking about anything upsetting or painful, they embrace each other as if they might enter into each other's body. It can either be with the man holding the woman on his lap, or with her sitting in front of him or on a bed. It is an embrace known as a "mixture of milk and water."'"

There were apparently subcategories in *The Kama Sutra* too, including the embrace of the thighs, the embrace of the jaghana (from the navel downward to the thighs), the embrace of the breasts, the embrace of the forehead. Even giving someone a shampoo could be considered an embrace, because it involved the deliberate and tender touching of the body. Positions weren't the only things included. Also listed in the book were the eight kinds of crying:

> The sound Him
> The thundering sound
> The cooing sound
> The weeping sound
> The sound Phut
> The sound Phat
> The sound Sut
> The sound Plat

What did any of this mean? It was mysterious, ineffably Oriental, fascinating, and it made Roz think of the time she had cried when she was in bed with Paul. It had happened the third time they slept together. He had entered her, was slowly moving in that leisurely way he had when he was just starting, and as he moved she realized, for the first time, exactly what she had done: She had become her analyst's lover, and all was irrevocable. He had thrown over everything for her, and the drama of the gesture was so strong that she'd forgotten to wonder whether it was a mistake or not. But then she looked at his face in the heart of sex, saw his eyes squinted up like those of a baby being born, and couldn't miss the drunkenness, the pride, the love he exuded, and it made her think that if he was so damn *happy*, then she ought to be, too.

Sex would save Paul Mellow, but she knew in that moment that in some way it could never save her, could never be as important to her as it was to him. Roz needed to push this idea aside at once, for here they were, bound together in a bed for good. But how could she do that?

The next thing she knew, Paul had stopped moving inside her and instead was asking with concern, "Roz? Why are you crying?"

In later weeks, they learned about the different kinds of kisses: the straight kiss, the bent kiss, the turned kiss, the pressed lips. Paul's mouth was soft and almost female, or at least the way she imagined a woman's mouth would feel, but above it were the grains of a mustache that wanted to grow no matter how often he shaved. By 1967, he would give up shaving forever and simply join the party, letting it grow like Jerry Garcia or Paul Bunyan.

The Kama Sutra was filled with very specific details that seemed quaintly specific and prim, and this was in such contrast with the actual experience of lovemaking—the freedom to choreograph as you saw fit. "'Once the wheel of love is set in motion,'" Paul read aloud to her, "'there is no order.'"

There was no order between them anymore; that had been assured the first moment he met her in the Chinese restaurant, looking up expectantly as she came in with the little bell jingling, and again the moment he kissed her in her overhot room. And through *The Kama Sutra*, they enacted a historical version of love, lying down on her bed in the "widely open position," Roz's head lowered, her body raised, lotion applied with Paul's slightly shaking hand. They moved through the "yawning position," and the "twining position," and the "mare's position," following the instructions as though they were children learning to play a new board game. Sometimes, as a favor to him, she picked up the book when Paul was asleep, so that by the time he awoke again she could casually say to him, "There's something called the 'crab's position.' We could try it."

Sex became an activity that she never took for granted or simply incorporated into their time together, like the other things they did: the meals she prepared, the movies they saw at the Waverly, the laundry they folded together on the pink and gray vibrating surfaces of the Laundromat on the corner of Seventh and Charles.

The Kama Sutra took them to India in the winter of 1966, a full two years before the Beatles arrived with their entourage. Later on, Paul would joke to friends that he and Roz had always been ahead of their time. They had been living in Wontauket for three years by now, and they had left their children Holly and Michael, ages six and four, with Paul's parents in Queens for a week. Holly had wept as they walked out the door, clinging to her father's leg and saying, "But Daddy, I *need* you." Michael, however, had just coolly looked up from some block structure he was building, and said, "Bring me something from the Taj Mahal." For already he knew the landmarks of the world.

During the day in India they traveled with the other tourists to temples and aromatic gardens and bazaars, navigating around the beggar children and cows and entire families camped in the middle of the road. Sometimes at night, they escaped the other tourists in the group if they could. They slipped away from the schoolteacher and her retired husband, the two nuns from Akron, the beautiful, tragic-seeming older woman whose name Roz inexplicably still remembered—*Mrs. Delgado*—and sat by themselves at a two-person table in a restaurant and ate chapatti that had just come out of the scalding oil. Alone, they could quietly say words to each other that were meant to arouse, to bring them into the sensibility they'd learned from studying *The Kama Sutra*.

To this day, Roz wasn't sure which of them had come up with the idea for *Pleasuring*. She still liked to think that it had been mutual, although even in the most mutual of orgasms, she understood, there was always someone who sent out a test shiver or wave or tremor that made the other person respond in kind, and one thing would lead to another, and soon the couple forgot where any of this had begun, because the only thing that mattered now was where it led. Most likely, though, it had been Paul's idea, for he was the one who would have been more authentically excited by it.

"If we write this thing together," Paul had said back in 1970, when they were sitting on the brown couch in the den in Wontauket, her feet in his lap, "then we'll have to include our own experiences, you know. The things we do together. The things we do to each other."

"Yes, of course," Roz had said. "That's the point, isn't it? It isn't some third-person Masters and Johnson exercise. It's us."

"Can you handle it?"

"Of course," she said.

"You won't care what people say?"

"No. I mean yes. Of course I will. But I'll get over it."

"We should be the illustrations," he'd said.

"Oh, right."

"No, Roz, I'm serious," Paul said. "It should be *us*. Us having sex all over the place. Why not? Are you embarrassed?"

"Yes, of course I'm embarrassed," she'd said, laughing, and he'd dragged her out of the den and over to the bathroom mirror, then closed the door and lifted her blouse. She was braless; this was 1970, after all, and breasts were swinging free like wrecking balls all over America.

"Look at yourself," he'd said. "Just look. You look so sexy. Those incredible breasts."

"No one wants to see them. They're starting to sag," she said.

"No they're not," he said. "I love your breasts, I just love them.

I love them equally, I don't play favorites." As if to prove his point, he kissed first one, then the other. "But even if they *were* starting to sag a little, which I repeat they're *not*, then so what? This has to be a book about real people, not idealized ones. This has to be incredibly human, so that every couple out there can relate to it."

The next day, when all the children were safely out of the house, Paul set up a tripod and camera with a timer, which loudly ticked away across the room as they arranged themselves in bed. The photographs were awful, which was no surprise to Roz. As far as she was concerned, she was all double chin and breast, and Paul was a shapeless Monet haystack of body hair. Everything unattractive was accentuated, and everything at all appealing seemed to have been airbrushed out. Their bodies, joined together in standard missionary sex, looked grotesque, their faces screwed up in pain and courage, as though the act in which they were partaking was excruciating and required a sort of personal heroism in order to endure it. The next series of photographs, in which Roz was on top, showed her looking mortified and involuntarily on display. Rising up above him, she was like a woman being carried on a rickshaw high above the action. Whatever was going on down there, she seemed not to know. Her breasts were pendulous and bovine; even a cow would have been ashamed.

"We have to destroy these," she'd said to Paul after they printed the pictures themselves in a makeshift darkroom set up in a bathroom.

"I hate to admit it, but I agree," he said, and they burned the photographs in the fireplace, as though their destruction also destroyed the actual fact of how Paul and Roz really looked while making love.

But it occurred to her that this was what practically all people on earth would look like if you captured them during sex. Everyone would possess a certain grotesque quotient, as though Diane Arbus herself had come to the bedroom and photographed them. Roz thought of the shots of aging nudists that Arbus had taken;

how homely and proud those people had been, sitting in their colony on metal folding chairs, those people who no one else would love except other nudists, those people who had needed an organization in order to be themselves.

To be captured most lovingly, lovemaking could not be entirely candid. They needed not a photographer but an artist, someone who could provide the essence of the acts and help to dissolve the parts that would not be exciting or beautiful or compelling to other people. *It would have to be us*, Roz thought, *and at the same time not us. It would have to be a better version of us, one that other people would want to see.*

They typed up a proposal for the book and sent it to a literary agent who was the brother of a behavioral scientist at Paul's lab. "Our book will be illustrated with drawings of the two of us engaged in lovemaking," they wrote. "Among these drawings will be one that shows the new sexual position that we have created." They went on to describe "Electric Forgiveness," which was the name of a position they'd come up with accidentally one night after a bitter argument about something that neither of them could remember anymore.

"The 'Electric Forgiveness' position is for couples who are trying to repair something," they wrote. "Whether because of anger or stress, lovers sometimes find themselves in need of a way to forgive each other and express calm reminders of their love and sexual connection. 'Electric Forgiveness' provides a means to that end."

The position itself was complicated and involved a certain degree of maneuvering and friction and discomfort before ultimate success; they described it in detail, along with many positions from *The Kama Sutra*, recast to be appreciated by American couples.

Their book, now called *Pleasuring: One Couple's Journey to Fulfillment*, was sold for $50,000, which was an extraordinary sum back then, and soon they were off into an art studio, in front of a total stranger, posing on a bed.

The publisher had conducted an intensive search for an artist.

Three finalists were chosen: a Japanese watercolorist who lived in Northern California and who had illustrated an expensive coffee table book on erotica of the Orient; a poker-faced woman who had worked in medical illustration for years, drawing bodies both healthy and corroded by cancer; and a recent graduate of the Cooper Union, whose work was shockingly lifelike, and who had been chosen a year earlier to illustrate a Rolling Stones album cover. People had sworn the painting was a photograph. Mick Jagger and the band had appeared plausibly sullen and entitled and sexual, lying on chaises on some Caribbean beach.

This Rolling Stones' artist, John Sunstein, was picked, and Roz and Paul informally met with him in a conference room at the publishing house. This was in May 1973. No one could talk about anything but Watergate, and Haldeman and Ehrlichman had resigned weeks earlier. But inside the studio everything was peaceful and free from headlines. John Sunstein was a shy young man, skinny in the manner of many young men, unchanged by anything he ate or drank, his stomach practically concave in his jeans and the old, pale striped Arrow shirts he favored. His hair was long, parted in the middle, and at the very darkest end of blond. He wore enormous work boots and a braided leather bracelet on one wrist. His face was wide and not really handsome, but definitely intelligent. He showed them his portfolio of drawings and paintings, and Roz understood why he'd been chosen: His work was careful and delicate and extremely detailed. The details, in fact, worried her; would he capture her failings, her imperfections, every crease, every irregularity?

"Don't worry," he said in his soft voice, though she hadn't expressed her fears aloud. "I'll make you look great. It won't be hard. You already look great, you both do."

But still she was embarrassed. The first day that Roz and Paul Mellow entered the studio on West 22nd Street to pose for him, she felt as though she would hyperventilate, and she had to sit on the closed toilet in the cold bathroom with her head between her knees. Paul stood over her. "It's not a big deal," he said. "You've undressed in front of other men before."

"But they were undressed too," Roz said. "Obviously."

"When he sees you," said Paul, "he is going to kiss the ground you walk on."

"That's ridiculous. The ground around me is already prekissed."

"What?" he said.

"By you," she said.

Paul smiled slightly. "Oh. Maybe so. Look, you want me to tell Sunstein to take off his clothes? He probably doesn't look bad, a young skinny guy like that."

"Very funny," she said. "He'd die of embarrassment, taking off his clothes. And so would I. God, we must look so old!"

"You're thirty-seven. The prime of your life. You're beautiful, Roz. And me, I still look okay, I hope," Paul said.

"Yes, you still look good," she said.

"So let's go out there," Paul said. "We'll just see what happens."

He handed her a bathrobe and she slipped it on. Then she stood slowly and let him lead her from the bathroom and back out into the large white room, where a bed was ready. There, in the middle of that sunlit room, she took off her robe while John Sunstein pretended to be uninterested. He seemed to be in no hurry at all. There was music playing on the stereo, something soft with medieval instruments and a female vocalist singing about being in love with a unicorn. John offered tea to Roz and Paul, who said no thank you, and then, when their clothes were off, the artist made a joke that maybe tea wasn't such a good idea after all.

"My insurance doesn't cover hot liquids," he said, and they all laughed a little, though Roz noticed the way laughter made her breasts shake a little, and so she promptly stopped.

The studio was located all the way west by the Hudson River, and sometimes during the day when they were posing, a barge would move past the uncurtained windows. Slowly she made her peace with being naked in front of a barge, in front of John Sunstein. She had never met a man as unobtrusive as he was. From the start he was barely there, barely a presence in the studio, quietly sitting and sketching, not feeling the need to contribute anything to a conversation that didn't really concern him.

"Is this what you were like with the Rolling Stones?" Paul asked on the first day, as he positioned himself beside Roz, their bodies lined up to match, notch to knob, like the carefully measured, discrete sections of a piece of cabinetry. "Move down a little, okay?" Paul said to Roz. She shifted, then they both waited.

"What in particular?" the artist asked.

"Quiet. Like a cat," said Paul.

"Well, pretty much," said Sunstein. "They talked so much, and they were always demanding things."

"What kinds of things?" Roz asked.

"Orange juice," Sunstein said. "Vitamins. Bee pollen. They didn't even seem to notice me after a while. Keith Richard did, once; he asked me for a smoke, but I didn't have any and he never said anything to me again."

"See, that's what I mean," said Paul. "You blend into the scenery. It's a great talent."

"I never thought about it before," John Sunstein said, and with evident relief at retreat he ducked back behind the easel.

That was perhaps the most extended conversation they had with him for months. Everything worked better if they treated him as not quite a person, and the artist understood this. At any rate, he did not seem all that interested in either of them. Once, when the Mellows were leaving the building, Roz noticed a young woman lurking out on the street. She wore a poncho and had long hair and a green minibike. When John came out a moment later, he climbed on the back of her bike, put his arms around her, and they rode off. He was young but not that young, and yet his singleness made him seem infinitely younger than they were.

Coupling aged you; it was an unavoidable side effect. You formed a couple in order to be in love, to stay away from loneliness, to forge a life instead of a series of days strung together one after another and punctuated by meals and movies and trips to the store. But no one told you that it would add age to you quickly, and that when you looked back on your wedding photographs you would be both moved and stunned into silence. This, at least, was what Roz sometimes felt when she thought of herself as Roz Woodman and then as Roz Mellow, and saw the division between the two lives: the leap, made by a very young girl, into a deep pool that, when she emerged, had turned her into someone different. No one had told her this would happen, that her girlishness would give way to the solid force of wifehood, motherhood. The choices available were all imperfect. If you chose to be with someone, you often wanted to be alone. If you chose to be alone, you often felt the unbearable need for another body—not necessarily for sex, but just to rub your foot, to sit across the table, to drop his things around the room in a way that was maddening but still served as a reminder that he was there.

And now, all these years later, her ex-husband Paul Mellow, once her collaborator, once so gentle and sensual and considerate, once so *wild* for her, had changed. His black beard was gray and dry as a shrub. His thick and muscular body was softened, and his boundless love for Roz had frozen over and transmogrified into love's opposite. He loathed her now. He flexed his rage by withholding permission to reissue their book. It wasn't just the money, which would be modest at first but then potentially big; it was the whole *snapping back to life,* the zest of being in the light, of being thought of again, and giving lectures—and not just to a room of open-mouthed, hungover, privileged nineteen year olds in North Face jackets. Roz had nearly forgotten how much she had enjoyed that attention, how sometimes she had liked it much more than sex.

She hadn't realized how much she longed for that attention again until the day last fall when the young editor Jennifer Wing had called to introduce herself, saying that the publisher would like very much to reprint the book. "I just want to tell you that

Pleasuring meant so much to my parents, and even—you're not going to believe this—my *grandparents*. I come from a pretty progressive family for Chinese Americans," Jennifer said. "They basically left the Hunan Province and never looked back. Me, I wasn't even born when your book came out, but now I really love it."

"Oh, well, great. I'm glad," Roz said uncertainly.

"We're planning a huge campaign, with entirely new, relevant sections. And new illustrations," said Jennifer. "We've got a great artist in mind. Someone young, like last time. It will give a youthful flavor to the book, introduce your work to an entirely new group of readers."

"We can't use the old drawings?"

"Sorry," said Jennifer Wing.

It all would have worked so well: the release of the book in an explosion of attention, the joy, the ease, the pleasure. It would have all been wonderful, but Paul said no. No, no, no way, *no*. He didn't want to go through that experience again. It was over; Roz had been the one to end it, and he didn't want to start it up again. She knew now that she ought to just give up, to realize that it didn't matter now anyway, because all she ought to care about was Dashiell getting better. And that *was* what she cared about most of all, but in a way the two desires had become joined together. Was she a bad person, a bad mother? She wanted to breathe life into Dashiell and into herself as well, because she suspected that she needed it, that without the book she would eventually be left with nothing.

Roz pulled her car into her driveway in Saratoga. The day had turned to night, and it was pitch black outside. The door to the house was unlocked; people rarely locked doors in this town. As soon as she walked through the front hall she was aware of the smell of Jack's cooking; it was immediately and clearly so much better than what was being prepared at the Mount Arcadia Yoga and Wellness Center. Cooking smells made you enter a house more quickly, going deeply and single-mindedly inside, tracking down the scent much the way that, in sex, you were drawn toward the locus of arousal, with its inexplicable, jungly imperative.

Roz walked directly into the kitchen now. Jack was at the stove, stirring and peering and adjusting spices. His head was bent over the burners, and she could see how thin his skein of hair was. While Paul's hair had thickened and blossomed with age, Jack's had thinned. Most of it would be gone in a few short years.

"I need your soup," she said to her husband.

"Well, you got it," he said, and he turned around to give her a kiss.

"I think I need it intravenously," Roz said. "It's all just so hard."

"I know," Jack said. "Any news from Dashiell?"

"No."

"From Paul, at least? Or Michael?"

"No."

"I'm sorry," he said. "You could use some good news."

Roz took off her coat and sat down at the table. Their old dog Ginger was underfoot but tired, barely moving, providing a footrest for these equally tired adults at the end of the day. Roz buried a foot in Ginger's blond fur and waited for Jack to bring over a bowl and a spoon. She felt, in a way, like her friend and colleague Constance Coffey, who came home each winter day to darkness and a low thermostat that would need to be raised, the heat clicking into gear as it prepared to tend to the climate needs of a solitary human.

Roz Mellow needed something else now, something more than soup, more than love itself. She thought she might have to cry, and then, all of a sudden, she did, surprising the dog, who raised its head from under the table to look, and surprising Jack, who replaced a pot lid and came over to her. It seemed to Roz, as she let him hold her, that by the time she was finished she had done all eight kinds of crying.

Chapter Seven

THE DIRECTOR of *Hysterical Girl* was a thin, lupine man named Arnie Nelson who, by his own admission, had been obsessed with Freud's case histories for much of his adult life. The chance to direct a play based on Freud's patient Dora brought out all of his nervous and excited energy, so that as he sat with the actors in a circle on the bare stage, one of his legs went jiggling and the fingers of his left hand played an invisible keyboard on the dusty black floor. Thea Herlihy was to be Dora, who had entered into treatment with Freud in Vienna in the year 1900, and for whom symptoms were like breathing—continual and necessary. Nelson had been walking Thea through the part for weeks now, giving her Xeroxed articles on the case study to read and helping her maintain an erect, corseted posture and a relentless, annoying cough, the kind that would have made people on a streetcar in Vienna's Ringstrasse send out angry glances at the unfortunate girl who insisted on making those sounds.

At night in bed, lying alone now that Michael was away on his never-ending visit with his father in Florida, Thea practiced her cough, as well as a particular kind of miserable moaning. Michael had been gone for an entire month now, and while he was gone his younger brother had gotten sick, bonding Michael to his father in some new, puzzling way. In his absence she found that she had much more freedom, a state she had been used to in her life, and which she realized she had missed. They had fallen from the heights of their initial love—a slow, unstated drop. How it had happened she didn't know. After he left she thought of him often in the beginning, and then less often later on. There were still times when Thea wished he were home so that they could be together, and she could try out her lines on him and see what he had to say about her interpretation of the character. Michael had read everything and had studied Freud's case studies in college, while Thea, who only had one year at the American Academy of Dramatic Arts doing scene studies, had read far less than she would have liked. She was undereducated and she knew it, and mostly when she was among her actor friends it didn't bother her, but now it did.

Hysterical Girl wasn't a particularly strong play, but the character of Dora was compelling, this frightened and repressed teenaged girl who was so riddled with coughs and gags and twitches and seizures that her father, in exasperation, finally took her to see Freud. What her father couldn't have predicted was that, over the course of her brief and truncated analysis, Dora would tell the doctor all about her father's affair with a young, pretty woman referred to in the case study as Frau K., a nurse who tended to Dora's syphilitic father, and whom Dora herself worshiped. When Dora revealed that her beloved Frau K.'s husband Herr K. had tried to kiss and fondle Dora almost as though she were a consolation prize, Freud offered an association between the complex sexual triangle and Dora's symptoms. Dora was so disturbed by Freud's unsparing interpretations that she abruptly broke off treatment, never to return. Forty years passed, and the unhappy girl became an unhappy old woman, and when the Second World War

began, Freud's former patient became, like him, just one more per-
secuted Jew, her misery drowned out among the miseries of others.

The idea, Thea Herlihy felt as she listened to Nelson talk about
his beloved Dora, was that the story contained the elements of a
tragedy. It was all about one woman's unfulfilled life, and the actors
nodded and spoke about Dora in ways that made them feel superior
to her, as though she were nothing like them; as though all of them
had masterly control over their own wishes and gravest fears.

"What's interesting to me," Nelson told the assembled cast, "is
that Dora's symptoms were basically a nineteenth-century phenomenon. We don't see neurasthenia anymore. It was very much
of its time. They say that every era gets the symptoms it deserves.
Like today, the beginning of the twenty-first century—what do
people have now?"

"Despair," said one actor.

"Terror," said another.

"Unrealistically high self-regard," said a woman, and everyone laughed briefly.

"Chronic fatigue?" asked Anne Freling, the actress who was
playing the part of Frau K.

"Yes, Anne, that's right," said Nelson. "Chronic fatigue. No one
is sure if it's real or not, right? Chronic fatigue, fibromyalgia—
these nebulous diseases might be symptoms of a terrible over-
scheduling in our lives, a drumbeat of activity and ambition.
Multitasking; isn't that what those women's magazines say we're
doing all the time?"

Before rehearsal ended for the day, Nelson said that he wanted
each of the cast members to learn everything they could about
the real-life case history and the characters involved. "Dora had a
very troubled family life," he said. "It's all there in the literature,
so please do your homework. I want these people to seem both
from another era and yet completely understandable to a contemporary audience. This is a play about sexuality and repression, and
these are timeless themes, people. Don't forget that."

The cast walked out in small groups, and Thea found herself beside Anne Freling. This was slightly awkward, for everyone held back from Anne; it was a phenomenon that had occurred naturally since the rehearsals had begun. The actress was the only one among them who was famous, having appeared for ten years in a television show about a group of twentyish friends who jointly and improbably inherit a Park Avenue apartment. When *Classic 6* went off the air to great fanfare three years earlier, a few members of the six-person cast tried to keep their television careers alive, but in most instances this was like starting a fire with damp twigs. They had all belonged in that absurdly enormous fantasy apartment-set each week, and nowhere else. Fairly soon they were extruded one by one from the tight and time-limited world of television fame.

But Anne Freling found a way to cope. Instead of appearing on commercials for pizza bites or calcium chews, like two of the other cast members, she went right to theatre. She was given parts in small, interesting plays, and whenever she appeared, the production was likely to be reviewed and taken seriously. Anne Freling was aloof, in her late thirties, blonde and wan, thinner than she should have been, and she was never without a bottle of Poland Spring water, all aspects that impressed the other actors as being somehow connected to success.

Walking out of the theatre, past the low-hanging lights and the scenery propped against walls, Anne gave a glance in Thea's general direction and said, "Coffee?" which Thea initially interpreted to mean that the actress wanted Thea to run out and fetch her a cup of coffee. But no, that couldn't be right. Quickly, Thea reinterpreted.

"Sure," she said after a beat, trying to conceal her wonder.

The two women sat in a diner called the Chelsea Delight; Thea, on a nervous whim, ordered rice pudding as well as coffee, and Anne Freling seemed amused.

"I haven't seen anyone order rice pudding," Anne said. "*Ever.* That's how long it's been."

"I had a hankering for it."

"And I haven't heard anyone use the word 'hankering.'"

"I'm a woman of surprises," said Thea, instantly jarred by the strangeness of her own remark, as though she were reading lines from a drawing-room comedy.

"I was thinking that maybe we should get together to practice," Anne said. "The scene where Dora and Frau K. meet for the first time, at the picnic? It seems kind of wooden to me."

Thea tried to appear only mildly interested in the suggestion, but the following week, when she appeared at Anne's apartment door one morning to rehearse, she was reminded of the first time she and Michael went out. They had gone to a Vietnamese restaurant downtown and drunk beer and eaten garlicky noodles in deep bowls, and told each other as many details as they could about themselves. He talked about his parents, God, those wild, oversexed parents, though when you met them individually they were just these really nice, suburban, sort of *old* people. It was so hard to imagine that once they'd been sexual forerunners, and it was even harder to imagine that Michael was the product of that marriage. For though he was attractive and strong and good in bed in the beginning, he was almost never spontaneous or free. In exchange she'd told him her own, much more mundane stories about life in Marblehead, Massachusetts, and her father the veterinarian. Afterward, they'd gone back to his high-rise apartment on Amsterdam Avenue, and she realized that she didn't know anyone else who lived as well as he did. All the hardscrabble actors' apartments she'd been in, and lived in, all the shares up in the Dominican enclave in Washington Heights, or else deep in the sooty belly of Brooklyn, in Fort Greene or Red Hook. This was entirely different, this pristine bachelor pad that Michael occupied, with its large, unopenable windows looking out over the city and the river, and its onyx kitchen counters and shining bathroom.

He was good-looking and smart and troubled and lonely, and

she knew, that first night, that he would want her embedded in his life, for he wouldn't come across women like her too often in the world of Dimension D-Net, where he worked. And she knew that she would want to be embedded in his life, too. After the sex, which was fun and exciting that first time, if not exactly up to the standards of *Pleasuring*, she'd slept better than she ever had in her entire life. Maybe it was the sheets, which were something like one-million-thread-count, or maybe it was Michael Mellow himself, who was like a large, soothing prayer stone beside her in bed. This was well before the depression, the Endeva, the sex problems that followed.

Anne Freling also had a good apartment, though very different from Michael's. It was off Gramercy Park, in an old doorman building, with flowery moldings and a fireplace made of delicately veined rose marble. Thea wasn't proud of this fact that she was rapidly learning about herself—that money and its trappings attracted her—but as she walked through Anne's foyer and down a step into the sunken living room (just the word "sunken" sounded rich) she felt as though she were sleepwalking toward something inevitable. Anne had made her money on *Classic 6*, and there was a scatter of photographs in her living room of the former cast members, all of them trapped in a hopeful time, before they would disappear from view and become ordinary civilians again.

The two women sat on the low white couch and rehearsed the picnic scene, and Anne was right; there was something about being away from the chilly, naked theatre, the other actors, and the ambling collection of crew members that gave the scene an intimacy it had previously lacked. Now each line of dialogue hovered, isolated, in the room, and anything that came out flat or false could be immediately recognized.

Dora and Frau K. had been very close friends; Freud had written about bisexuality after treating his troubled young patient. All of the women in that time and place, Thea had learned, were stuffed into muslin and starched cotton and forced to sit ramrod-straight and plait their hair or pull it back off their faces with fish oil. There were shoes that laced up with a hundred eyelets, and corsets that required a special hook to open. Women were all in it together back then, as opposed to now, when one woman's experience could differ so greatly from another's that you never knew who you were talking to.

Thea Herlihy had nothing in common with Anne Freling. The former television actress seemed confident and slightly irritated. She regularly visited a chiropractor for unresolved neck issues, was divorced and wealthy, and had time on her hands. Thea was younger, more cheerful, had never been successful, had never made any money, and, until Michael had gone away to Naples, Florida, last month, hadn't been alone in two years.

But Michael was away now, and Thea could almost pretend to herself that her life was not all that different from Anne's. Without Michael around she was available for private rehearsals during the day and perhaps in the evening, and she was not required to explain herself and her movements. While at first Thea had been annoyed by his protracted visit to his father, she started to realize that her annoyance was manufactured, a product of some atavistic place in which women were eternally angry at men for their thoughtless behavior. Vaguely she had an image of her own mother standing in the doorway of the house in Marblehead, waiting with quiet righteousness as her father came into the house a solid hour late for dinner. Though his veterinarian's excuses were always good—a horse was foaling, a schnauzer had been hit by a car—her mother was practically on fire with being wounded, with being *right*, holding out a Pyrex casserole of green beans as if to say, *See? See?* as though he might be able to tell, simply by looking at the casserole, that it was ice cold.

It wasn't that Michael made many demands on Thea, but she kept being aware that she was relieved with him gone. Sex had become difficult, yes, if only because there was now an actual sexual problem between them, something that needed to be solved, and every time they slept together the problem came along, lumbering and enormous. She was twenty-eight years old; this was too young to deal with someone's sexual problems. She tried to bring him to orgasm again and again, all the while feeling a kind of anxiety and desire for things to hurry along to their conclusion. Aware of how difficult it was for him to have an orgasm, she seemed to be forcing it, yanking on his penis as though it were an object stuck in a drain.

His unhappiness made her despondent, too, for she didn't want him to be miserable like this, but still she had to admit that if it was completely up to her, they wouldn't have sex again until this issue was out of the picture. Why have sex if there was a *problem* with it? Wasn't the whole point of sex its freedom and abandon and ease? That two bodies could come together as *bodies* and not worry about all the neurotic hollows of the psyche? Apparently, no. Apparently problems crept into sex, too, and if you loved the other person, as Thea loved Michael, then you had to work them through, whatever that meant. You had to keep yanking on a penis until it unstuck itself, until the man it was attached to was able to lose himself in pleasure, and both of you could sigh with relief and settle down to sleep.

Michael was a better person than she was, for if the roles had been reversed, he would never feel impatient with her. She had a fantasy that when he returned from Florida his skin would have a golden tan, he would smell of coconut oil, and they would fall upon each other in a pileup of lust, and he would ejaculate in about two seconds, and they could share a pint of mocha chip and joke around long into the night before sleep. His sexual problems would have been mysteriously worked out somehow while he was gone, as though spending time with one's father could cure difficulties in the bedroom, not to mention larger difficulties.

Such as, that she no longer loved him as much as she once had.

She had written him a letter, trying to broach these matters in a way that wasn't inflammatory. She referred to "the problem," as well as her own "distancing mechanism." The letter seemed like a manual for an appliance of some sort: technical, devoid of lyricism. It said nothing much, but it sent him an obscure warning: *If you think things between us are fine, then you are mistaken.*

He called from Florida in response to the letter but did not seem very upset by it. "I know what you mean," he said. "We'll figure it out." As though the appliance were broken, or needed another part, but it wasn't the most urgent of tasks.

Something had changed, they both saw, had frayed over time, had been there even before he went away. Maybe it was the fact that he had gotten depressed and needed to take Endeva. Or maybe he had gotten depressed and needed to take Endeva *because* there had been a subtle shift in her love for him. Maybe he had sensed it, but had never been brave enough to mention it to her.

"Let's run through the scene again," Anne Freling was saying, and Thea was grateful to think only about late-nineteenth-century Austria and Freudian principles and, most of all, of having the total, rapt attention of Anne Freling. "Dora was obsessed with Frau K.," Anne said. "She worshiped her, and so did her father. And Frau K. obviously got off on being so loved by the two of them. Who wouldn't? God, it's like being on TV. People love you and they don't even know you. They build up this idea of you, you know? And then it becomes fixed in their heads, and nothing can change it." Anne had a tight smile as she spoke, as if to demonstrate her own courage at having once been important, at least in the world of television, and then losing that importance.

When the rehearsal was done, Anne offered Thea lunch, bringing a collection of take-out menus from a drawer. They both chose *salades nicoises,* which Anne paid for, handing money to the delivery boy, who immediately ducked back out into the hallway, looking terrified. Anne inspired terror in anyone she was with; Thea felt a little bit of the spillover, and it wasn't unpleasant.

They sat at a big oak table in the living room eating lunch

from round tinfoil containers, spitting out their pointy olive pits. Anne served bottles of water, which, Thea noted, she guzzled as though she'd been in the desert for months. Back on the couch after lunch as the rehearsal continued, Thea felt emboldened by the food, even a little bit high. She found herself joking with Anne, making wisecracks about "poor, clueless Dora," and about "that sexpot, Frau K."

"Now, now," said Anne. "Dora was manipulative, you know. That was the whole point of such an illness. It gave the sufferer something that she wanted, and that she didn't know how to get any other way."

"I wouldn't know how to be manipulative," Thea said, deadpan, and Anne laughed with a little bark.

"Oh, right!" she said. "That's not what I've heard."

"What? Where have you ever heard something about me?" Thea asked.

"I read about you in a magazine. *Failed Experimental Theatre Monthly.* You were on the cover."

Now Thea whooped a little, excited by the idea that this actress had hidden reserves of wit. "Yes, I remember that cover," Thea said, feeling herself getting worked up further. "It was a picture of me in *The Bald Soprano.*"

"You really look a lot better with hair," said Anne Freling. And then, before there was an unrecoverable pause and a shift to some new, different moment, Anne reached out a hand and placed it on Thea's hair. She let her fingers play with the hair, as though testing it for texture and thickness.

When Anne came forward and kissed Thea, she thought of the scene from another angle, as though it were in fact a *scene,* something watched by others, something that would be commented on afterward during the critique.

"I think the women were both very hot," someone would say.

"I wanted to see them *do* it," an actor would add. "I mean, really do it. Clothes off on that couch."

Yes, the clothes would come off, in two similar little piles, but there would be no audience for this. Anne crawled across her the way a cat might, with the lightest paws, and Thea found herself pinned down, looking up. Anne's hair swung in her face, and Thea could detect the various components of female *clean*: the soap, the lotion, the scent on wrists and neck, released full-force in moments of stress or heat.

It's too bad the imaginary audience isn't here, Thea thought, *because this is so amazingly aesthetic.* That was the thing about two good-looking women having sex. At first you could almost die from the delicacy, from the long wrists, yoga-bred bodies, and subtle flashes of thin gold chain or ear-stud or pearl-gloss pedicure. Sex between two women now seemed to her like an exclusive club, and in order to join it you would need to look like this, and admire yourself and the other person, and feel a great relief that no one else was allowed in.

Thea couldn't help but feel: *Sorry, Michael, this is not for you.*

Or maybe it was more like: *Sorry, Michael, I am not for you.*

She felt the regret and the acceptance of her own infidelity only secondarily, for how could it not be eclipsed under the cat-weight of Anne Freling, and the idea of touching her? Lost in this, Thea somehow became sure that Michael would understand. He would have to, really, because she wouldn't be able to stop doing this, she would want to go to bed with Anne whenever she could. Making love with another woman was an intoxicant, an inhalation of all the surface scent until you came to what was below it, the liquid center—unapologetic, vivid—and found to your astonishment that you wanted that, too.

You couldn't help but be aware of the absence of a penis, that great bluff presence, that thing that always arrived at some point, making its presence known. That thing that did not work well, in Michael's case, and so you needed to stop and be encouraging and decent and kind. But there was no need for kindness now, the subtle shift to the maternal, in which the beautiful woman comforted the big, muscled, frustrated man. It was as though Anne wouldn't give her the opportunity to pause and regret or pause and shift the tone they'd already established. They were fully naked, both of them seemingly poreless, with matching skin tones the color of good stationery, with Anne cupping her hand between Thea's legs, and Thea aroused to distraction, pliant, open for Anne and Anne alone, emitting some sounds that were like sighs but more insistent, thinking how this was like the surprise ending to her life— except, of course, it was far too soon for this to be the end of her life at all. A single finger entered her; women had fingers, after all, and here they were in action. For a second she thought about Michael's parents' eye-popping sex book, which she and he had looked at when they first got together. There had been one particular drawing, a close-up of the father's hand on the mother, and this perhaps had been the most shocking drawing in the entire book, for a finger, used like that, was taken from the realm of the utilitarian, of hand-washing, vegetable-slicing, pen-holding, piano-playing, and on and on, into the realm of contact and exploration and, of course, pleasure.

Thea felt herself clench her jaw and curl her toes, and she was unable to stop herself from these familiar actions; they were encoded into her. Anne, too, responded similarly a little later, and Thea had the startling opportunity to imagine herself in orgasm, to see what Michael saw, and what those other men before him had seen. And as she saw, she was lifted further into a strange appreciation and shyness of the female body, that banshee with its throat sounds and wet center and locked jaw and tree-dweller toes. This was what she looked like too; how amazing to get that view.

But the orgasm that was brought on by Anne Freling was no different than any other with Michael or the handsome actors Thea had gone to bed with over the years; apparently there was a sameness to orgasms whether they were brought on by men or women. It was simply the volume that varied between experiences, the decibels of excitement, and then the recovery from it. Orgasm was such a basic, generic experience, and the one you had was just like the ones that other people were having everywhere in the world at this very moment. It was not unlike death, somehow, for no matter what kind of a life you'd led, there was that great sameness at the end. Making love with a woman, like a life itself, offered possibilities for mutual stirring and admiration and a kind of excitement that required no accommodation to differences. You could be *similar to*; you didn't have to *complement*. There was no *furred* against *hairless*, no stark contrast to marvel at. You didn't have to take care of the other person, and try to resolve their problems, although you could if you wanted to.

She suspected that Anne Freling was not troubled to the extent that Michael was. Anne had a clear, unworried brow; most of her needs were taken care of elsewhere, in the office of her chiropractor and at her yoga class held in a brutally heated room, and in a small workshop she still attended with the legendary nonagenarian acting teacher Senya Orloff, who wore those signature turbans.

Thea wondered if Anne would ever need anything from her, or if what they might do together would involve only mutual competence and gratification and physical admiration. If you let it be about more than that, then there was the possibility of dragdown closeness, the kind you already had with your women friends. The kind that men didn't understand. Men *did* things, and women talked, talked, talked. The idea of talking all the time with Anne Freling—complaining bitterly or confiding secrets and even crying—had the quality of a bad foreign film to it. Then she realized that today they'd talked surprisingly little.

Finally, Thea said, "I have to go." Neither of them wanted to linger on the white couch, which had become their bed. There would need to be some kind of transition now to getting up, getting dressed, acknowledging the sex and seeing how it appeared, as an idea, floating in the open air.

"All right then," Anne Freling said, and she smiled a little and asked Thea if she needed anything.

"Like what?"

"I don't know," said Anne. "A towel. A drink. Anything."

"No. I'm good."

They dressed, for some reason facing away from each other, then kissed on either cheek, as though in Europe and not in fact sudden lovers, and then without another word Thea left, hurrying out to Irving Place and passing Gramercy Park with its curved rails and clusterings of tiny leaves poking out from the frost and its throngs of nannies and young children in snowsuits who were entirely ignorant of love, and sex, and choosing someone, and so much else in life that was still waiting.

Back at home, there was a message on the machine from Michael. "Hey, Thea," he said. "I swear to God I still exist. My dad and I, and what's been happening with Dash, I think it's good that I stay at least—"

Thea clicked off the machine, already impatient, even though his message hadn't ended. She got the drift; she knew what he was telling her. It was the same thing he had said in other phone calls. He was there in Florida, he was staying there, he was not coming home just yet. She picked up the telephone and dialed Anne, whose telephone number she had memorized from the cast contact information sheet.

"It's me," Thea said, enjoying the new familiarity, and how at this moment in time she occupied the central place in Anne Freling's consciousness. Right now, she was front and center, and this was a position that was enjoyable, like having the lead in a play, even if almost no one went to see it. "I wanted to tell you that you don't have to feel weird about this or anything," Thea said. "Because I don't."

"Oh really?" said Anne.

"No."

"Well, that's good to know."

"I want to come back there," Thea said. "Can I come tonight? Can I do that?"

"Sure," said Anne. "We have all that research to do, isn't that what Nelson said? We're supposed to learn all about Dora's illness, and about her father, and about Frau K., and turn-of-the-century Austrian life in general. So we'd better get cracking."

And the two women laughed together.

Chapter Eight

CLAUDIA MELLOW returned to Wontauket several times over a period of weeks to film her old teachers, and on the fourth time, David Gupta accompanied her to her interview. They had been emailing each other intermittently since the day they'd met in the house on Swarthmore Circle and she'd nearly fainted in front of him. She had begun to believe, on and off during their exchanges, that David Gupta was flirting with her. Maybe he was, but if so, then surely he'd forgotten who she was in person; surely, in his imagination, he'd replaced her imperfect, squat, and breasty little self with someone better. It didn't even matter to Claudia that David wasn't poised or particularly handsome. She hadn't forgotten who *he* was; she could still picture his dark, questioning face close to hers as he knelt before her on the carpet in the bedroom where she'd once lived.

He had emailed her the day after they first met, inquiring as to whether she'd recovered from what he called her "recovered-memory Satanic ritual dizzy spell," and she'd promptly written back to say yes, she was completely fine, and then she'd assumed that that would be the end of him. But three days later another message from him was waiting. "One more thing," he had written. "Did you ever notice that the floor in your/my bedroom slants a little? It's like Van Gogh's *Room at Wontauket*." The emails picked up speed; she wrote him between film seminars and hours spent in the editing room, and now she was driving back to Wontauket to see the last of her elementary school teachers, and this time he would go with her.

It hadn't been her idea that David accompany her to the interview, but when he suggested that he come along and help her unload and carry her equipment, she said yes. Today the interview would be taking place away from Bolander Elementary; Claudia was going to visit the home of her second grade teacher, the once-stylish Mr. Ed Stanton, who back in 1977 had driven a silvery blue fiberglass Corvette and wore synthetic, sherbet-colored shirts that instantly conformed to the plains and valleys of his chest. He'd also worn a large handlebar mustache then, and as a graduation gift that year the children had chipped in and bought him a red leather mustache-grooming kit. He'd been openly moved by the gift, sitting on the edge of his desk and turning it over and over in his hands.

"I'll never forget you boys and girls," he'd finally said, and some of the girls had started to cry.

Claudia remembered being one of those crying girls, and she knew then that time did not pause, not even for someone as cool and amazing as Mr. Stanton. As a heartthrob, this had been his brief and shining moment; fairly soon, or at least sooner than anyone could have expected, the tight shirts would have to go, the car would prove potentially ridiculous if not dangerous, and the grooming kit would be rendered useless, for he would brutally sever his mustache from the skin above his lip, revealing a philtrum as naked and vulnerable as anyone's.

Mr. Stanton lived in the less affluent section of town, where the houses on their fractions of acres stood side by side in defiant sameness. The Wontauket dump was located nearby, this pit of legendary but as yet unprovable toxicity that was often picketed by local concerned mothers. She thought for a horrified moment of Dashiell's illness and wondered briefly if it might have been caused by exposure to the dump all those decades ago. She pictured her brother—small, solid—trotting around the periphery of the dump, picking through other people's castoffs.

Yesterday Dashiell had called to tell her that his Hodgkin's had suddenly started resisting chemotherapy. He was slated for a peripheral stem cell transplant in the next few days—a bone marrow transplant using his own, cleaned marrow. The news came spilling out, so much more chilling over the phone than it would have been in one of his usual emails. Claudia was shocked and overcome, and had palpitations and needed to lie down while she spoke to him.

"Oh, Dash," she'd said. "Let me come up there this time, okay? Please. Don't be like this. I mean, it's just *me*."

But no, he said; he still would not let Claudia or any of the family come up to Rhode Island. Right now he was being prepped for his transplant, given rounds of tests and sitting in boredom and anxiety in several different impersonal hospital waiting rooms. Tom was there with him, he reminded Claudia; he was hardly alone.

So she would not go up to Rhode Island, but would instead worry from afar, while trying to find a way to concentrate on her incoherent botch of a student film, which, all these weeks later, still seemed to have no coherence to it. Instead, it was just a mass of teachers speaking into the camera. Claudia didn't even know what to ask them, so she had just let them talk. In one interview, the school fire alarm kept going off and her sixth grade teacher, elderly Mrs. Rook, had cast her eyes off-camera and repeatedly murmured that "someone ought to do something about that." But no one did, and the alarm punctuated her words every few moments until Claudia could barely stand it.

Here now, directly in the vaporous path of the Wontauket dump, sat Mr. Stanton's small blue ranch house. Her teacher came out onto the porch when Claudia and David arrived in the rental car, and he waved to them lightly. "He looks so different," Claudia said under her breath, still sitting with the engine idling, as though she might decide to make a break for it.

"Different *bad,* I guess you mean," said David, and Claudia said yes, definitely, different bad. Mr. Stanton had warned her over the telephone that he'd had a stroke a few years earlier. Though he was mostly recovered now, his face appeared to be half-happy and half-sad, which struck Claudia as the way her own face ought to appear if she were to honestly present herself to the world. *Half-happy* would be for the times when she was alone and content and unpressured. But in the world at large, Claudia was *half-sad,* wandering around and timidly entering places where she did not speak the language, forced through the narrow, shape-changing pastry-tube of adult life. It was too fast, too strident, too demanding. Whenever she experienced a moment of true intimacy—if a friend confided in her, as they often did, about an abortion or a love affair or its violent end—Claudia felt afterward that she needed to take some time to be silent and still.

She felt this same way after she slept with somebody for the first time. After the man had gone home, she would be relieved. Sometimes she'd get back into bed and watch a Tracy–Hepburn movie, the fast dialogue soothing her like a clicking, distant rhythm. Now, at age thirty-four, Claudia felt as though she had to engage much more with other people or else she feared they would think, *Why is that woman always alone? Why doesn't she have a boyfriend? Why is she such a stupid, fat cunt?*

In meeting David Gupta through the strange bond of their shared house, she had not in fact found her soul mate, her other half. He'd never really lived in the house, for his parents had bought it long after he was fully grown. His own childhood home had been in a suburb of Buffalo, with an entirely different set of associations and memories. David had a sturdiness about him that she didn't really understand, but was still appealing, as though he were a human tool kit who would know what Claudia might need at different points in time: when he should be quiet, when to laugh, when to offer his help—like now, as they sat in her car in front of Mr. Stanton's house. He didn't even know her and still he was here with her.

There had been a stilted but mutually pleased exchange of hellos when she picked him up at the house today in yet another of her rental cars filled with equipment. For all he knew, she was a brilliant filmmaker, an *auteur*. Coming with her today might have been like helping François Truffaut carry his equipment around France in 1960, and for the rest of your life you could say, "Remember *Jules et Jim*? I carried that camera." But amazingly David Gupta seemed to have no expectations; he had come all the way back from Philadelphia for the weekend to stay at his parents' house and see her, and he was cheerfully sitting beside her in the car, pleased to be even fleetingly involved in a project that had nothing to do with him, and that he might never see completed.

Men like David seemed to exist as concentrated kernels of goodness in the world, or at least they'd decided that this would be how they would present themselves. Usually, Claudia thought, such men were not particularly handsome, and so instead they became cheerful and benign. In his sweatshirt, pressed jeans, down jacket, and Adidas, David looked ordinary; the only thing about him that stood out was the fact that he was Pakistani. His dark skin looked soft and somehow broken in.

They sat in the rental car, a little formal, looking through the windshield at Claudia's old teacher with his half-fallen face, this man who had been a 1970s Mr. Chips with his Corvette and his cassette tapes of the Who and his love of the boys and girls who surrounded him like apostles—and an as-yet-unknown vulnerability in the brain that would eventually and with no warning cut off blood flow one day, leaving him with an arm that hung loosely and a face that could never express any of the things that he felt so deeply as he stood looking at his old student, his former favorite.

David said to Claudia, "So, are you ready?" and she said yes, she was, and they began to unload the car.

The house was tidy and tight, like the living quarters on a boat. It appeared overly clean, and its upkeep was clearly maintained by a maid. No wife graced the premises; Mr. Stanton had been divorced for a long time, and Claudia surmised from the absence of framed photographs that he had no children. She took a seat on the sofa and accepted an offer of Pepperidge Farm Chessmen cookies that had been laid out on a plate. She bit into a cookie and looked around the room for an outlet in which to plug her equipment.

"Strange," said Mr. Stanton. "This house is very ... outlet challenged. I never noticed that before." Soon all three of them were poking around the living room, moving chairs and couches and end tables. "Here's one," her teacher muttered, "but it's all full up. No room at the inn." Finally a solution was reached; an extension cord would be run into the living room from the small bathroom right beside it. Mr. Stanton dragged the cord with him, and Claudia and David sat watching as it unwound like a slowly waking snake, pulled taut across the green carpet. In a moment they both heard a crash, and then "Goddammit!" They sprang from their chairs and crowded into the bathroom to find Mr. Stanton on the floor.

"I'm sorry," he said. "I lost my balance. That happens to me a lot."

She watched as David held out both hands to Mr. Stanton and pulled him straight up; her teacher wobbled a little as he righted himself. "Are you all right now?" David Gupta asked.

"Yes, thank you."

"Okay. Good. You really took a tumble." David helped him out of the bathroom and back into the living room. "Do you have any-one helping you?" he asked. "I mean, day to day?"

"No. Just the cleaning woman."

"You know, my parents live nearby, on Swarthmore," David said. "Maybe my mother knows someone who could come in once in a while. I bet she does."

Claudia observed the way he spoke to Mr. Stanton and was struck by, almost confused by, the helpfulness, the strength. In con-trast it made her feel like Mr. Stanton's second grade Claudia, who had sat and cried at the prospect of losing her beloved teacher. She *had* lost him; each year, a new teacher was found and then lost, but in the bracket of time from September to June, the current teacher swooped down and rescued any child who was in need of it. Inevitably, year after year, Claudia was one of those children. She had gotten used to the role, hadn't even thought to give it up because it fit her well, and she suspected that it always would.

Bombay Café, when they arrived, was crowded but subdued, with waiters moving swiftly among the tables. David's father Mr. Gupta circulated the room discreetly, making sure the patrons had what they needed. Claudia recognized no one from the old days in Won-tauket. Most of the families from back then had folded up their tents, and these new ones, these hopeful, chattering people spoon-ing lamb korma and raita onto their plates on a Friday night after work, had replaced them.

"Do you need to help your father with anything?" she'd asked David at the start of the meal, seeing Mr. Gupta's anxious expres-sion, but David assured her that no, his father was on top of the sit-uation and needed no help.

"He wants me to relax and enjoy myself tonight," David said. "He's always worried that I work too hard and that I'll have a crack-up or something."

"Why would he think that?"

David played with the silverware in front of him. "I got very stressed out last year when I was working around the clock on a brief, and I had an anxiety attack that felt exactly like a heart attack. I was positive I was about to die. A friend of mine took me to the emergency room in Philly, but they did an EKG and told me my heart was fine, I was just under too much stress." He shrugged. "Which of course was true. It's gotten better now, but I still tend to work too much, and to not sleep very much at night. It's as if I don't really know how to shut off. There's no one around to tell me to, and so basically I forget."

"I always know how to shut off," Claudia said, imagining herself in front of a movie screen, the shadows darting around with the sole purpose of distracting her.

Over their many-course vegetarian *thali* dinner, David and Claudia swapped details from their lives and small things that they'd noticed over the course of the afternoon with Mr. Stanton. They discussed the rapid passage of time and what it did to people you hadn't seen, and how the unfairness of life was on display almost everywhere, shifting shape freely to fit the form of, say, a former teacher who needed to grip a Koosh Ball in his hand to strengthen it and who fell when he went into the bathroom to stuff a plug into a socket.

"I wanted to do this film because elementary school was a time when I was happy," Claudia said. "I didn't mean for it to have all this *pathos*. But here it is."

"Where's the pathos? In the teachers? Why is that, exactly?"

"Because they're still here and we've all moved on."

David shook his head. "They're not 'all still here' in the way you mean it. School isn't everything to them the way I think it was to you. Their lives are bigger than that, I hope. They have their secrets. Their affairs. Their travels, their families. I don't mean to insult you, Claudia, and I'm sure your film will be very good, but what makes you think that your life is so much more expansive than theirs? I don't even really know what 'moving on' means.

Who 'moves on,' really? I'd have to say that the pathos is a little more generalized than you think. We've all got it in our lives."

He was right, of course, and she looked away, ashamed. "I know. I was being really reductive," she said to him. "And I apologize. But when Mr. Stanton started talking about the last day he ever taught a class," said Claudia, "and how he didn't know it would be his last day because he didn't yet know he was going to have a stroke on the way to his house—I started to feel that I should never have come here and filmed him, or any of these people."

"What did you think they were going to tell you?"

"I don't know. Funny stories about the 1970s. People really like hearing about that time. It seems so long ago already. Those smiley-face buttons. 'Have a nice day.' The clothes that everyone wore. The way our parents looked. Well, at least the way mine did," she added.

"What's that mean?"

He had no idea who her parents were, perhaps had never even heard of them. "They wrote a book," she began, and after she mentioned the name, he lit up with recognition almost immediately.

"Yes, yes, I remember that book," he said, and he popped the remnant of a vegetable samosa into his mouth and chewed excitedly. "Oh, that's amazing, your parents, huh? That must have been quite an experience."

"Oh, I guess so," she said. But then something made her keep talking. "In the beginning, I was too young to understand what it was," she told him, "but my brothers and sister were freaked out by it. Later on, when I got a little older, I realized what was happening. That that book I'd looked at, other people could see too. I realized that this wasn't the only copy in the world; that there were others, in all kinds of languages. And that millions of people around the world were seeing pictures of my parents screwing each other. And, basically, that there was really no good that could come out of that."

"Maybe not for you. But other people got a lot from that book," said David. "I was always hearing how it changed a lot of people's sex lives. It basically woke them up."

"Oh, that's what they say," said Claudia. "But I've never seen sex change anyone's life. At least not personally."

"But they invented that position, right?"

Everything had turned, suddenly, and Claudia had gone from the surprisingly easy back-and-forth with this new person to a stilted conversation about the last thing in the world she wanted to talk about. She became aware of a nasal Indian female wailing from the speakers in the restaurant, and the rapid clicking of finger cymbals.

"Right," she said. "It apparently came out of that mishmash of research they'd done. They borrowed ideas from *The Kama Sutra*—I mean, they basically stole them—and also from Chinese erotica. It was supposed to represent a feeling of excitement and, well, letting go of anger or something. I remember once, on TV, I think it was on *Ken London's Night Owl*, they said it was a good position to use after times of great emotional upheaval. Well, it didn't work out for them. Obviously."

"Why obviously?"

"My mother left my father," Claudia said. "Two years after the book came out."

"Oh. That must have been a shock."

"To me, yes. To my father too. She fell in love with someone else, but I only realized that later on. I mean, nobody told me then. Anyway, it's a whole long story."

"I'd like to hear it," said David.

"My father went crazy," Claudia said. "He was so deeply in love with my mother; she was his ideal. She was this, she was that, and he couldn't believe that she would leave him. He took us off in the car the night that she told him, and he drove us around and around the town. We kept going past the stretch of stores right here, where your restaurant is. We went around and around, and when I looked out the window it was like the backdrop on some low-rent TV show where people are driving in a car and they keep passing the same tree, the same cow. The whole ride was very, very strange."

"I guess you must have been scared," said David.

"Yeah, I was. I sat way in the back of the station wagon. We had this family song we always sang, and for some reason my father started singing it. I guess it was meant to be ironic, because obviously we weren't going to be a family anymore. And he was crying so hard I remember thinking that they should have windshield wipers for people who cry when they're driving. Little wipers for my dad's aviator glasses. Nothing bad happened that night, though. We all just ended up getting Carvel, even my father, and then going home. A week or so later he moved out. My mother stayed in the house because all of us kids were still at home. So we saw my father every weekend, but he was different. Angry and depressed, I guess. One by one, my siblings left home, and finally, when I went away to college, my mother sold the house. She got everything she wanted, but he didn't. He's never gotten over the fact that she left him." Claudia paused. "Why am I telling you this?" she asked. "Usually people confess things to *me*. I have no idea why I said all of this to you. My apologies."

He was looking at her with interest, and she thought that he was being hoodwinked by her face, the features that were pleasing to the eye, the hair that she was able to bring to a high shine with ease. But if they were to stand together he would be reminded of her squat dumpiness, and he wouldn't want to touch her. She imagined touching him, though, putting her hand on the soft, pale material of his shirt, peeling it back to reveal the complementary dark surface of his chest. Men's bare chests seemed *brave* to her, reminded her of young warriors.

David broke a wedge of nan into a few smaller pieces. "I don't mind at all," he said. "It's really interesting. Look, this may be too personal, but I wonder if you've ever tried it."

"Tried what?"

"The position."

She stared at him. He obviously didn't know her at all. What did he imagine, that she'd had dozens of lovers with whom she had celebrated the freedom of sexuality, of being female, human, alive? "Of course not," she said. "Why would I?"

"I don't know," said David, and then he shrugged and tried to smile. "Just to see?"

Later, with the rental car in the school parking lot, they sat on the merry-go-round at Bolander Elementary, letting the frozen metal disk slowly spin, so close to the ground. Once it had been thrilling when this thing was set in motion; now, though, the combined weight of the two adults made the process seem like the failed liftoff of a spaceship. But they needed motion between them, some sort of movement to help continue the conversation even after all the Indian food had been eaten. First they had walked around town, but it had appeared as deserted as a place with a curfew; there was no nightlife in Wontauket and never had been. Almost anything that happened after dark happened in the home.

"Are you freezing?" David asked her as they slowly spun.

"I'm okay," she said. "It's not too bad."

"The town where I grew up," said David, "was always cold. We were just north of Buffalo, and we wore these big ugly gray-and-orange parkas all fall and winter and even into the spring. But there was some sense of pride in the cold because we'd always heard how hot it was in Pakistan, where the cousins lived. Whenever we were freezing and would complain about the weather, my father would say, 'Your cousin Partha is probably sweating buckets right now. You should think of yourself as fortunate.' I heard about my cousin Partha my entire life. He was born one month before me, and he did everything perfectly. He was brilliant at mathematics—almost solved Fermat's Last Theorem at sixteen. Of course, nothing comes out the way it's supposed to, does it, because today Partha is a carpenter living on the Pakistan border and involved with corrupt political activities."

"As opposed to you?"

"Yeah, I'm way not-corrupt. I'm the least corrupt intellectual property lawyer in the world."

As the metal disk spun he told her about his job. His law firm, he said, was currently involved in a case that concerned the author of a little-known book about birth order and its psychological implications, which had been published in the 1950s. The author was suing another author, who had recently published a similar book that was currently on the best-seller list.

"Our client is the original author, Hubbard Elwell," David said. "He's eighty-five years old and indignant that his ideas have been stolen. But ideas are difficult because they're not concrete. They're not things. You can't hold them up as 'Exhibit A.' Writing is concrete, though. And this motivational speaker, this slick guy named 'Dr.' Don Ardsley—and believe me, he's got a doctorate in something fake like 'life coaching'—who's written the new book and is making a lot of money off it, he hasn't stolen our client's writing, exactly. The words are different. But *all* the concepts behind them are similar to Elwell's. I think we have a fairly strong case, but a judge will have to decide."

"So do you believe in the whole birth order thing?" she asked.

"Actually, I do," David said. "I mean, it's a little bit like astrology, I guess, but it seems to hold up in a lot of cases. My own family, for instance, my sisters and I, we're classic. I'm the youngest."

"Me too," said Claudia.

"Hey, what do you know. How many are you?"

"Four."

"So tell me about the others in order," David said. "And I'll make some conjectures. Who comes right before you?"

"That's Dashiell," she said simply, and as she did, she remembered her brother's latest news. She thought of him in isolation in the hospital, and something must have crossed her own face because David tilted his head slightly.

"What is it?" he asked.

"My brother's really sick," she said quickly. She hadn't wanted to talk about it, particularly about the information she'd learned only yesterday, but here it was, and she couldn't go back. "He has Hodgkin's disease," Claudia said, "and it was supposed to be okay, but now he has to have a stem cell transplant."

"I'm sorry."

"I really love him," said Claudia, and she felt herself start to fray. "We're only two years apart. You should see him, he's really good-looking, totally handsome and buff. He's small, but he's got this amazing physique, lean and graceful. You'd never think we were related."

David stared at her. "Why do you say something like that?" he asked. "You're so pretty."

"Ah, you mean my face," she said bitterly. "My good old face."

"What do you mean? As opposed to your body?"

"Yes," she said, looking away slightly.

"I don't know that I was just thinking of your face. I was thinking of *you*. You aren't . . . unscrewable. You can't just screw off the head. It isn't in pieces. I'm sure you're very . . ." He suddenly laughed and looked away.

"What? What were you going to say?" she asked. "Tell me."

"It was accidentally kind of crude," David said. "I was going to say I'm sure you're very . . . *screwable*. Oh God, let me shoot myself now."

So the moment was interrupted with a little laughing, and the thoughts of poor Dashiell began to recede. She was silently apologetic as she pictured a hospital bed drifting away from her, moving quickly out of reach. Claudia had often felt that her three older siblings thought of their younger sister as an eternal baby, and she was perceptive enough to understand that this was a valuable asset in life. It kept you ageless, perhaps immortal. As you got older and older, there would always be someone older than you, always someone more decrepit, closer to death.

Now she thought about Dashiell dying before she did, and she just couldn't stand it. The bed came rushing back toward her, and he was still on it, but this time he was clay-colored, impassive. She'd never really thought of any of them dying, actually, because their parents were so powerful and they, the children, were always *the children,* so much so that they carried a banner of childhood with them their entire lives. Their fully sexual parents kept them from growing up completely. No, it was more than that. Her parents would have been upset to know this, but they'd kept her from having sex. Sex was their territory. The children would have to try something else. Maybe model airplanes? Tournament bridge? T'ai-chi, maybe? Yes, t'ai-chi—they could choose the loose-flowing, turtle-slow movements of limbs in space instead of the frenetic rubbing and pushing toward ecstasy that had once been her parents' stock-in-trade.

"If you still want to hear about it," David Gupta said, "being the youngest can be particularly hard. Because the *formerly* youngest one—that would be your brother who's sick? When you came along he might have gotten very threatened. He'd always been the baby. But he also would have realized that there was someone new to be the scapegoat. So he would've made you feel that you were too young to be a companion to the others. That you weren't good enough. So you probably went off into your own little world. And now I should just shut up here," David said. "You have more important things on your mind, and this probably doesn't describe you at all. Pay no attention to me."

But Claudia was already picturing herself in the role of fourth-born, youngest, watching movies in the den after school, ignored by the others, never taken fully seriously. Her troll dolls had been her mainstay, and she had sat in the middle of them, arranging them as she saw fit. They were naked, those dolls, and once in a while she would put one on top of another just to see how it felt to watch them. But it had felt like nothing, like a marriage of tan plastic, and so she would pull them apart and return them to their circle, their endless ring in which no one was the youngest, the oldest, the most knowledgeable, the least beautiful, the favorite, the disappointment.

On the way back to the car, walking across the spongy black rubber panels that had been laid over the school playground, David Gupta linked his arm through Claudia Mellow's, causing her to turn to him in surprise, only slightly inflected by disingenuousness, for this, everyone knew, was the prelude to whatever was to come. Even if it hadn't happened to you this way before, you'd been around long enough to know that this was how it was sometimes done. One person stepped forward bravely from his or her square of shyness and interlocked an arm through the other person's arm, or perhaps lifted a hand to graze a cheek.

They stopped at the edge of the playground, with its silhouetted equipment creating a backdrop of, if not romance, then at least beauty, for all was silvered and removed from childhood, swing-chains glimmering. *There are no children here,* she thought as David Gupta stepped forward and kissed her with the assuredness of someone who understands that he won't be rejected. The kiss had been earned during the exchange of emails, over the course of the afternoon with Mr. Stanton, and during dinner at Bombay Café. And it was earned here, too, in the nighttime playground of Felice P. Bolander Elementary.

His mouth was too wet, she thought, and she was sorry, wishing that the kiss was different from other ones, so different as to ease her sexual frozenness of all these years and change the legend so that it now read: I used to be uncomfortable with myself as a sexual being, until I met a man I could love. And now I love sex, and love him, and everything that came before was just vamping as I waited for my life to begin.

But she couldn't say that, and so she stood with her face moving lightly against his, their mouths open together, and it was a little too wet, yes, but somehow she liked it. Then his hand found its way to her breasts, and she felt her back straighten, for now he would begin to discover who she was, what was wrong with her, how the pieces of her body fit together so imperfectly that he would have no use for it whatsoever. Already she mourned the loss of him, the way he would not want to continue with her, the kind voice he would use when he told her, later, that this couldn't go anywhere.

She imagined his hand getting caught in the alley between her breasts, or perhaps underneath a breast. When she was verging on adolescence, she and her friends would take the "pencil test" to see if they needed to wear a bra. They would place a pencil horizontally beneath a breast, and if it stayed there, a bra was necessary, and it would be purchased that weekend at the mall. Claudia's friends had joked that she could keep a *pencil case* there, and perhaps a sharpener, too, and maybe a three-ring binder and even a book bag.

But, of course, there were plenty of men who loved getting lost in a landscape of breasts and who felt themselves go weak at the idea of submitting to the sheer acreage of it all. David didn't seem to be going weak and senseless now, nor was he recoiling from her. He apparently liked what he was touching, and he drew back to see her and smile at her as his hand traced the outline of both breasts, and it forced Claudia to forget her own horror for a moment, to forget her long, unscrolling list of imperfections. Her body, she had realized once when she was an adolescent, resembled one of her troll dolls. Yes, she was a troll, and she had gravitated toward those interchangeable creatures because she saw herself in them. *You are my people.*

"Claudia, I love the way you look," David said, as if in answer to a question she could never bear to ask him.

No you don't, she wanted to say, but if she said this, he would say right back to her, *Yes I do,* and his voice would be forceful and he would have the last word. He rearranged himself against her and touched her and kissed her again, and Claudia became aware that even though she was uncomfortable, she was making an unbidden dove-sound that was unnerving to her, particularly as it was the only sound in the night, unless you counted the distant, ambient static of traffic on the expressway.

A short while later she was one of the people on that expressway, merging her little car into the flow, almost forgetting for a moment which was the gas and which was the brake and slowing down infinitesimally before she overcompensated by roaring forward into the press of cars, joining them gracelessly, but somehow safely. She was so anxious after they had kissed and said good-bye and she had driven him back to Swarthmore Circle that she didn't know what to do with herself. For an hour now she would have to sit buckled into this car, though her legs seemed to need to move, to dance an independent dance from the rest of her. She wanted a box of jawbreakers, would have liked biting down hard, feeling the resistance and improbable give of rocks being crushed inside her head.

It was as though she'd been kissing David Gupta for hours, or days, a marathon of kissing in which they had somehow worked out in advance every small thing that might go wrong between them, and how to set it right. She didn't listen to music now, although the crescent edge of a CD poked out of its slot, ready to be slid in. Instead, she lowered the window a few inches, heard the mix of car noise and night noise, and thought about a wet mouth, a flock of red taillights, and the city fifty-five miles up ahead, where one day she would take him.

Chapter Nine

CLAUDIA CALLED again, saying, "Hi, it's me. I need to tell you something. Things are kind of bad." Then she made an awful croaking sound, a bitten-off sob, and vaguely Holly recalled that her sister had often cried as a child, and that the rest of the family had learned not to take these episodes too seriously, but instead to incorporate them into the atmosphere of any given meal or vacation or gathering.

Ordinarily, the sisters spoke perhaps once a year; all three siblings and both parents stayed in touch with Holly in this unofficial, annual, ritualistic way, being sure to contact her now and then so that she couldn't accuse them of freezing her out of their lives. Frankly, Holly Leeming knew she was a big pain in the ass, a difficult sister and daughter who had deliberately walked off the edge of the family map, and though she regretted it at times, here she was, far away in Topanga Canyon, recovered from the worst of everything but still not *one of them*.

"What's wrong?" she asked Claudia now. "Dashiell again?"

Holly had been told of his illness weeks earlier, and she'd even telephoned him once herself. But she'd become too depressed and inarticulate by the news to call for a follow-up, so her sister was following up for her. It was ten in the morning here in L.A., and Holly and the baby were sitting in the nursery, on the plush, plum-colored carpet that was so stain-resistant that all spilled juice and ground Honey Grahams immediately seemed to fly up and away from the fiber. Holly held the cordless phone against her shoulder and gave Buddy a big plastic hand mirror, which he eagerly took from her to stare at himself for a while with the blunt interest and absence of vanity common to all babies and perhaps no other group on earth.

"He's worse. He needs a stem cell transplant."

"A transplant from *me*?" said Holly. "Oh shit, Claudia, I don't know, I don't know. I'm really not good with things like that."

"Relax," Claudia said. "I actually didn't mean from you. They're using his own cells. They clean them and put them back in or something. It's done all the time."

"Oh," said Holly, guilty, sulking.

Here now was the punishment for extracting yourself from the bosom of your family. True, you avoided all the sand traps of holidays and the ongoing petty melodramas that most grown children were forced to enact, but you were also denied the most basic knowledge about the rest of your family until everyone else had been told. In short, you were always the last to know, and when they finally told you, they made sure to twist the knife.

Someone might call and say: In case you care, Mom went crazy and started shooting people with an Uzi in a mall.

Or: Oh, by the way, Dad was in a head-on collision and he's brain-dead.

Or, as Michael had actually said a few months ago: They want to reissue the book.

That one had been bad enough; Holly hadn't wanted to hear the follow-up, the back-and-forth bickering that was surely taking place between her parents. *Leave me out of it,* she'd said to Michael. *I don't know why you even called me.*

But she couldn't say such a thing to Claudia now about Dashiell being sick. In truth, when Claudia called and gave her this information, Holly primarily felt the sting of shock that accompanies anything that can truly be considered news, or, more specifically, bad news. But beyond that, the human feeling that was supposed to flood her now simply didn't. Dashiell was so much younger than she was, and she'd never really known him well. By the time he became old enough to be interesting, Holly was an adolescent, and all she wanted then was to be away from the family.

She knew he was gay, and also, astoundingly, that he was a Republican, which she absolutely couldn't deal with and couldn't begin to understand on any level. But no one had seen fit to call before today and say he had gotten much sicker. This, Claudia insisted, was because they hadn't known how serious it was. Cure rates were high with Hodgkin's, they said, and he had responded immediately to the initial drugs and the radiation, and he had been expected to be fine again, to bounce right back, but instead he'd gotten worse. He was a short, handsome, fine-featured man—a *boy*, Holly still thought whenever she actually did think of him. It was true that the idea of Dashiell being really, really sick didn't even seem possible. But here it was.

"Well, I'm sorry," she said to Claudia.

"You're sorry?"

"Yes, as a matter of fact I am. He's my brother."

"Theoretically," said Claudia.

"No, *actually*," said Holly. "So don't fuck with me, Claudia, okay?"

"I just thought you'd want to know," said Claudia. "But all right, so I also felt like acknowledging your . . . *absence*, okay? That's why I said 'theoretically.' I mean, you only called him once all these weeks, okay? You told him you'd send him some healing book or something, and you never did. It was the thought that counted, right? But no, it's more than thoughts that he needs."

"All right, fine," Holly said.

There was a grudging moratorium. Claudia rattled off a few facts: Dashiell had been admitted to Rhode Island Hospital this morning, he'd receive some drugs first, and then he'd have to be in isolation. He wasn't allowing any of them to come visit because he had his boyfriend Tom there with him, and he'd be too sick anyway, but if Holly wanted to send a card that might be nice.

"He'd know you were thinking of him, at least," Claudia said. "Even if you're not."

The mirror that Buddy had been looking into was now covered in strings and smears of saliva, Holly noticed. The baby, who was actively teething, had apparently been gnawing on it the whole time Holly was on the phone. Then he'd lost interest, had waddled over to the mesh safety gate, and was now trying to pry the suction cups from the wall that separated the nursery from the hallway and the steep stairs-of-death beyond.

"Go," he said to his mother. *"Go!"*

"Claudia," Holly said into the phone, "I have to go."

"I'm sure you do," her sister said.

"Oh, fuck you."

"No, fuck you. I call to tell you something really bad, really upsetting, and as usual you still can't get outside yourself long enough to act like a normal person."

"That is so unfair," Holly said. And then she added, truthfully, "Buddy needs me."

This seemed to soften her sister. Though Claudia sometimes took a certain guarded, testy tone with her during her annual phone calls, as a way to lightly punish Holly for ceasing to be much of a sister, and for hurting their parents so badly, she wasn't an angry person, really. "All right," Claudia finally said. "So go to him, if you have to."

"In a sec." Holly wanted to find some way to stall her, for the *fuck you* exchange suddenly seemed excessive and nasty. Claudia was allowed to be angry; Holly would just have to suck it up, and not complain. Now she tried to work her way back into a normal conversation, even briefly. "So how's everybody else?" Holly asked. "Anything else I ought to know?"

"They're okay. Weird but okay. Michael's still down there with Dad and Elise, if you can believe it. He's moved in there, basically."

"What? Why?"

"Who knows why. Male bonding. *Something*. And Mom and Jack are okay, though Mom's obsessed with this book thing. Getting it back in print. You should see her."

"It was the highlight of her life," said Holly, and then she added, "but not mine."

"Not mine either."

Good. *Rapprochement*. A sisterly moment after the hard insults and cursing each other out. The annual telephone call was like a family newsletter containing all the information that anyone needed to know about these six people who had once lived together and never would do so again. There was a pause, as both of them considered how to continue.

"How's the baby?" Claudia asked.

"Fine. Fine. He's great."

"I sent him something last spring for his birthday. A bunch of books, ones that I liked when I was little. *Goodnight Moon*, I think, and some others. Did you ever get them?"

"Yes, I did. I meant to tell you. Thanks."

Claudia, who had no children, couldn't possibly know that at this point in time *Goodnight Moon* was such a cliché, such a staple in every young family's household that it was like buying someone a copy of the telephone book.

"You're welcome. And Marcus, how's he?"

"Fine. Working all the time."

"*Go*," the baby said again. "Mom, want to go."

"That's my cue," said Holly, and she and Claudia said good-bye. They would speak again when the next bad thing happened, whatever it was.

That night, Holly couldn't sleep at all. She did in fact think about her brother; she had gone on the Internet after Marcus got home and was spending a couple of minutes playing with Buddy. She wanted to find out some information about Dashiell's sickness and its survival rates. At first she kept spelling the disease "Hodgekins," and then she tried "Hotchkins," and finally she noticed that the search engine was asking her a question: "Do you mean *Hodgkin's* and *survival rates*?" it asked, and she could hear the snideness in the computer's tone, the recognition that she, the searcher, hadn't gone to college, hadn't gotten herself educated in the way that her three siblings had. "Do you mean *Hodgkin's* and *survival*, you loser, you slut, you druggie fuck-up, you failure, you empty, hollow piece of nothing?"

"What are you doing?" Marcus asked, appearing in the doorway with the baby in his arms. Translation: What are you doing when you know it's time for me to give the baby back to you?

"Nothing," she said, and she put the computer into sleep mode and never remembered to look up "Hodgkin's" and "survival rates" again. Because as far as she was concerned, Dashiell would survive. He would live on and on because he was young and strong and transplants were amazing, they basically reconstituted people, and Holly didn't have a dark enough imagination to envision any other outcome, and because any other outcome would be unbearable, even with this thick lack of feeling that separated her from them.

But that night in bed, she found that once again she couldn't sleep. This happened to her periodically, and it usually heralded the beginning of a weeks-long period of cluster-insomnia, in which sleep was a holy grail that she could not locate, and that she might have to spend the rest of her life in search of.

It sometimes seemed to Holly Leeming that she hadn't slept in three decades. Even now, she could be found wandering the L.A. house at three in the morning, as though her lactating breasts had awakened her with the urgency of dual smoke alarms, pulling her from her warm bed. But in fact Buddy never nursed in the middle of the night, and hadn't in ages. He still nursed during the day, which was fairly unusual among the circle of L.A. mothers and babies she'd met in a Babycize class when Buddy was just a few weeks old. One by one their babies had been weaned, but not hers. One by one the women had gone back to their studio jobs or their decorating jobs or their jobless days of driving the freeways and having lunch with friends. Holly proudly stayed put, freezing the moment, not doing much except be with Buddy, who was such a pleasure. She was proud of how long he'd gone on her milk, as though this was an endurance contest and he, among all the other babies, had won.

But here she was, wide awake, without a baby to feed, and her sleeplessness needed to be cured or else she would start thinking about Dashiell, and her other siblings, and her parents, and about loneliness, and about death, and about the fact that the universe was much bigger than we could ever imagine, and far more terrifying and violent. Holly Leeming walked into Buddy's peaceful room and stood over the crib, looking in and humming to herself, pretending that she was unaware of what she was doing when in fact she was quite aware.

She wanted him to keep her company.

Her humming became louder, a flat, slightly minor-key version of the theme from *Barney*, which was really just a rip-off of "This Old Man," and the tune reached out to him and dragged him up from sleep, as if from the bottom of a pond. Buddy stirred and blinked his eyes but only partially awoke. His big blond curlicued head, like always, was wet with perspiration, and after she had lifted him swiftly from the crib and settled him against her in the white rocking chair, he executed a graceful transition from sleep to breast, as though it were perfectly natural, at nineteen months of age, for him to find himself with someone's nipple in his mouth in the middle of the night, without having asked for it first.

She sat with his wet head against her and let him drain first one breast and then the other, and she thought of how impossible sleep was for her, what an effort, a feat, and how easy it was for Marcus, a fact that maddened her. Why did *he* get to fall into unconsciousness so easily? Who had died and made *him* King of Sleep?

Sometimes at night Holly would lightly poke an elbow into her husband's gut in order to wake him up so that they could have one of those middle-of-the-night conversations she needed from time to time, not because they were interesting but because they were soothing. She was the one who needed the breast; she was the one who, when her eyes opened at 3 or 4 A.M.—or when they never closed in the first place—needed to find solace.

Once in a while, Holly initiated sex for just this reason. Of course Marcus was delighted at being awakened by the soft mouth of his wife on his cock; he never knew that in those moments she was using him for comfort rather than excitement. Even the most excited rhythm is of course *rhythmic,* and therefore calming. It was possible, she knew, to be excited as well as calm. Sex had given her both of those qualities since she was fifteen.

Poor, doomed Adam Selig, that goofy boy from Princeton Court in Wontauket. On a Friday night in May 1977, a year and a half after he had first come over to the Mellows' house and rolled on top of her and tasted her chocolate breath and pushed his hand down her Looney Tunes underpants, Adam Selig had gone to an amusement park that was set up for one weekend each summer in the parking lot of the JCPenney. Holly had been there that night too, although by then she and Adam Selig no longer spoke. There had been no real breakup, just a general drift and mutual loss of interest. She was with her coterie of dumb mall compatriots, and he was with two boys with whom he rode dirt bikes at a nearby construction site on weekends. Tonight he and the dirt-bike boys went for a ride on the Trabant, an attraction of uncertain lineage. The name made it sound German, or maybe French, and mysterious in its own way—a far cry from the garden-variety roller coaster or the Spider with its eight spiky arms that dangled children and teenagers over the roof of JCPenney and let them look down upon this town in which they lived, and maybe let them realize for the first time that it wasn't exactly a metropolis.

But on this particular night, the Trabant came loose from its mooring, reared up into the sky above the makeshift amusement park, and flung the six people on it (it was never a very popular ride) to their instant, juddering deaths. For months the local newspaper referred to the lawsuits, the grief, the Baltimore-based carnival company, Port-a-Carn Entertainments, that was ruined by this tragedy, and, of course, the famous Trabant Six, whose faces would forever form a gallery of lost souls. Side by side they would remain: three teenaged boys, a school janitor, a mildly retarded girl named Candy and her mother. With the exception of Adam Selig and his dirt-bike friends Tony Spee and Chris Canetti, there was nothing to join them all but this slightly embarrassing death.

Holly Leeming thought of Adam Selig fairly often after all these years. She marveled at how he, the first boy who had touched and aroused her with an almost accidental, intuitive talent, had been killed while she had been spared. By some peculiar stroke of fate, she had poured drugs into her body year after year and still lived. The years had hardened her and leathered her up so that she was practically crocodilian, but to her amazement she found that she was constitutionally sound, and that through some accident of Mellow and Woodman genetics she was able to go on and on.

In summer 1977, shortly after the carnival tragedy—though not, she was sure, because of it—Holly began her descent. At first she couldn't sleep at night but simply got up and wandered the Wontauket house. Her parents were sometimes awake, those hipster night owls; her father might be listening to the stereo in the den with enormous headphones clamped to his head and his bare foot tapping on the coffee table. He would pull off the phones and say, "Hey, kid, why are you awake?"

Or else it might be her mother, sitting in the kitchen and talking quietly into the telephone in the middle of the night. Though her parents were united physically in every one of those drawings in their book, by late summer 1977 they were rarely together at home, and they seemed to operate in entirely different corners of the house.

Something was up. Something was brewing. Something was terribly wrong and perhaps always had been, but only now, with the startling clarity that late adolescence brings you, she was able to see, or at least to infer, something desperately important.

Her mother no longer loved her father. Her mother loved someone else.

One night Holly found Roz Mellow hunched at the kitchen table at 2 A.M., the cord around her arm like a series of bracelets, and she was talking into the receiver with a great sense of urgency, her voice hushed and throaty. Holly heard, ". . . but no . . . I want to . . . I don't think . . . I do . . . I know . . . I know . . . I know . . ." And then Roz looked up and saw her daughter, and appeared stricken, *found out*, as though Holly had shined an enormous spotlight on her during a prison break. Roz Mellow, scaling the electric fence, said something into the receiver and then hung up.

"Who was that?" Holly asked.

"No one. Just a friend."

"Oh, right. Like I'm supposed to fucking believe that?"

"Please don't speak that way," said her mother. "I know you can't understand this, but my life is complicated. I try to be a good mother, to keep things stable here at home, to give you kids a normal life. I try and try. I don't know how much longer I can keep it up, Holly, I just don't know." That was when Holly realized her father was standing in the kitchen doorway. Husband and wife exchanged looks, then he silently backed away. "I don't really need this kind of shit," said Roz Mellow.

"Please don't speak that way," Holly mimicked, and then regretted it, for she saw how upset her mother was. Roz Mellow, whose face was moment by moment being loosed from its beauty even while her daughter's face signed on to beauty for the long run, began to cry. She cried hard at the kitchen table, all the surfaces gleaming around her, the cabinets and fixtures and the five-speed Sunbeam blender brushed bright in the strange light of the middle of the night and the nearly adult child's awareness of a mother's pain.

"Oh, Mom, don't cry, please don't, okay?" Holly asked, and she realized that she couldn't bear to witness this. It was too fucked up, too inexplicable. Wasn't it bad enough that her parents had displayed their incredible horniness, their togetherness? Now they had to display, at least for her, in the middle of the night, their separateness. The marriage was going to end, she understood; there was nothing that could keep it together. When your father sat listening to the gloom of Mahler or breakable Billie Holiday in the den, and your mother urgently whispered to someone on the phone in the kitchen, there was no going back. All the sex in the world could not alter this. Love broken stayed broken, unrepaired. Or if someone did try to repair it, you would forever see the spot where the soldering iron had applied its adhesive silver. The *weakness*. The place that must not be jarred or touched or stirred up again, for if that happened then there would be another break along the exact same fault line. But this time it would be cleaner, irreparable, final.

Roz Mellow could not stop crying. She would cry and cry, and one day after that marathon of crying, both parents would sit the children down in the den and tell them they were getting a divorce. Michael and Holly were entirely dead-eyed and unresponsive during the talk; this was no surprise to them, obviously, but the younger ones looked as though it were a bolt from the blue. Their mother reassured them that none of them would have to leave the house, because she would keep living there with them and their father would take a place nearby, where they could visit him whenever they wanted to.

No one asked: Why is this happening?

Holly, age seventeen, wandered out more and more into the night, seeing it not as a time of day, but as a place. Night was a town, a more exotic version of this for-shit suburb in which she lived. And at night, too, you could meet the kind of people you could never meet during daylight hours. It was night when she met a guy who was called Hojo because of his combination of red hair and perennial turquoise jacket, and he was the first one who ended up staying awake with her into the hours before the sun poked up over the top of the Stride Rite and the town library and the forever-marked JCPenney. She'd met him in a cluster of people at the train station at 1 A.M.

All of the marginal figures popped out like ghouls after dark. Some, like Holly Mellow, were from the richer part of town, but more likely they were from the tract houses and the garden apartments and even from a town or two away. They were teenaged or in their twenties; occasionally they allowed an older man into the group as a kind of paterfamilias figure, but usually his function was to provide a car and a stream of quality drugs.

Holly eventually moved out for good, into an apartment in Hoboken at first, and then various other places. But she spent the next year or so coming back and forth to this town, staying up all night with a variety of companions, all of whom had been destructive and inappropriate and essentially awful for her, the kind of cohort you shrug off like bad fashions as the eras collapse and pass, only to replace them with new, equally bad ones.

Hojo must have had a real name at some point, but if so she never knew it, for he was one of those people who would have liked the idea of wrapping himself in grungy mystery and sitting for hours in the company of a bitter, privileged girl like Holly Mellow, who had gone so far afield of her previous, cushy life that her trajectory didn't even track. He would have liked the idea of going far afield *with* her, of pulling her into an alley or a gutter or a literal field for a while, the kind of place where people who called themselves simply "Hojo" and had no employment and no shape to their days tended to congregate. So she had gone there with him and stayed for a period of months, becoming just another apparition, a lost girl in jeans and a running jacket that had once been a vivid salmon color and eventually ended up the color of smoke.

Over the years she became one of those people whose name is on the short-term lease of an apartment where no one knows their neighbors, where the doors slam and shudder all night long. She never got around to fully furnishing any of the apartments she lived in, for just when she started thinking it was time to get a futon with an actual frame, she would decide to leave. She'd visit friends, dropping in unannounced.

Once in her mid-twenties she happened to be in New York City, and night came and she realized she had nowhere to go. She was high, and it was raining, so she ducked into a phone booth—back in the time when phone booths existed on corners in New York—and called Information for her brother Michael's number. He'd just graduated summa cum laude from Princeton and was sharing an apartment on Riverside Drive and 102nd with two friends. It was a Saturday night, and Holly had no reason to think he would be at home, but he was. Soon she was standing in the doorway of his long-halled, dark apartment, and he let her in.

She was so high, and she sat in his living room and cried about how awful everything was for her, and how badly she'd fucked up her relationships with men, and how sex had held so much early promise, but in the end it was only a disappointment. Didn't he agree? But Michael hadn't said too much. He seemed overwhelmed by her. In the background, his roommates came and went, knocking back beers and making evening plans. Finally it was time for bed, and Michael gave her the mattress in his small bedroom while he lay on the floor beside it, wrapped in a green blanket their mother had long ago, and improbably, crocheted. In the morning, Holly awoke with a thudding headache. She felt something heavy and opened her eyes to find herself face-to-face with her brother, who was fast asleep. He was pushed up against the mattress where she lay, his arm flung across her. In his sleep he had instinctively come as close as he could without actually being on the mattress too. Their faces were inches apart, though on different levels, and she looked at him, really looked at him, seeing that his brow had gotten creased over time, and that he was indisputably a man at twenty-two, and that he had a beautiful mouth, and that he was very handsome. She wished she could do something for him, but of course he didn't need a thing from her, he would be fine, he had graduated "summa," which apparently was a big deal. Doors would swing wide for him throughout life, and women would drop with a thud beside him in bed. He would be all right, he didn't need her at all. They had once been twinned, joined together by proximity of age, yet always she had been the suffering one, and he had known that and accepted it; he'd even seemed impressed by it when they were young, as though a beautiful teenage girl's unhappiness was a thing of awe. He silently admired her, and she accepted this quietly, pleased to have him there. Then, when she waltzed away from home in that haze of rage-at-parents and self-pity, he tolerated her absence. He asked her occasionally, at first, "Why did you have to *disappear?*" She had no real answer, of course, and both of them understood it was partly in her nature to leave the family, and that really, in the end, it wasn't such a surprise that she had done this.

After that night in Michael's apartment on Riverside Drive, Holly would return to her drifting, directionless life, and they wouldn't see each other again for more than a year. She'd embarrassed herself, blubbering so hard in front of him and his roommates, snot-nosed, red-eyed, high. It was a good thing she was going.

Holly carefully lifted her brother's long arm from around her back and climbed off the mattress. "Think of me, Michael," she whispered into his ear before she left, but he didn't stir.

Over the years, Holly continued to float in and out of apartments, other people's lives, U.S. cities. She stayed afloat through the money she already had, the money she earned dealing pot, and the occasional day jobs she took. But what kept her alive, she always felt, was some kind of ingenuity on her part, the X-factor that you either had or you didn't. Maybe its presence was genetic, but no one really understood. Something, though, had made her different from everyone in her family; something had plucked her away from them but had also kept her going over the decades. An engine. An instinct. She'd had long bad stretches from time to time, of course, and when she was younger had been knocked flat from depression and cocaine and a daily influx of pot. But even though she'd gone into recovery, she'd gotten out of it, too. Holly had never collapsed completely, but instead she always kept on traveling, moving, seething, thinking, keeping herself alive, remembering to eat protein and to drink enough water, to pay the electric bill and to have her teeth cleaned every year, and to wear some kind of coat when the weather changed.

Holly had a perpetual restlessness about her, and once, after reading a magazine article, she became convinced she had adult ADD, though she'd never been diagnosed. "See, what we're doing is self-medicating," a friend said one time when they were chopping up some crunchy cocaine into a fine sand, rolling dollar bills into tight tubes, then lowering their heads reverently. "We're treating our emotional problems ourselves."

Sitting in a studio apartment in Waterbury, Connecticut, or Holyoke, Massachusetts, in a room with shag carpeting and maybe a mattress, smoking dope and watching the snow fall or the rain pour or the sun brighten the streaked windows, Holly always made sure to listen to music, for if you were going to sit around and get stoned in an empty apartment, one hand dangling and unmoving in a bag of chips like a fish hook waiting in the water for action, then you were going to need music. Without music, you might have to confront what you'd done to your life, how you'd made a hash of it and essentially ensured that nothing good could come of it as long as you were in charge.

Late one night when she was still in high school, Holly and Hojo had sat side by side on the green wooden bench of the Wontauket railroad station, and he'd wept against her as he told her about his childhood spent in the St. Anthony's Boys' Home of Ronkonkoma. The nuns there had beaten the boys with mops and forced them to drink the mop water. The story was so unbearable that Holly pressed him against her harder and, later that night, hidden behind a row of billboards at the train station advertising *A Chorus Line* and *The Ice Capades,* she knelt down and unbuckled his pants. She was happy to do this for him. He was so grateful, and his eyes partly rolled up into his head, which pleased Holly and caused her to feel a swoop of sensation. That swoop would dip down upon her from time to time over the next few years, but she became aware of its incremental lessening. And none of these experiences—not Hojo or any of the men who followed—came close to the sweet depths of sex with Adam Selig in her bedroom. That early, nearly unmanageable excitement was gone, and she wanted it back. How could she get it? Where was the fulfillment? Where was the journey her parents had written about? Over time Holly Mellow looked and looked, like someone frantically searching the globe to find a person who no longer exists. It occurred to her that she'd been sucker-punched, made to believe that such early intensity could be repeated in countless ways as you lived your life. She'd thrown over a chance to be educated and normal, choosing instead the pursuit of rapidly fading sensation. Once you started down that path, it was hard to change. Even if you wanted to, people would always see you in a certain light.

At least, along the way, she was almost never alone. There were lovers, friends, people who were simply there. One companion in the early days had been a girl named Joanne Mikulski, a dealer of every drug to come down the pike, and what a pike it was, welcoming the panoply of powders, whippets, capsules, and buds that were so bountiful then. Once, the fall after her parents separated, Holly had been picked up by the police in the band shell of a Huntington park. They had put her in a squad car late at night with her blood saturated in THC and methamphetamine, and for some reason she asked them to take her to her father's house. They agreed, handing her over to her mournful father, who embraced her, and who seemed that night, with his longish hair and beard in need of a trim, to appear slightly lost himself, as though a willful daughter could deflate even the most powerful and sexual of fathers. But later it occurred to her that he might not have been lost because of her actions at all, but because of his own sorry life: the wife he had loved, who now loved someone else.

He took his daughter inside that night and looked at her in the light of the front hall. Her pupils were dilated to the size of olives. What a wreck she was! He shook his head and said, "My little girl. Just look at you."

It was the opposite of the way he'd always instructed them to look at their mother, and she felt ashamed of herself, for she was a disgrace, an exemplar of adolescent fuck-up. This is who you do not want your child to be. *Just look at you,* he'd said, but he spoke without love and adoration, and only with a kind of resigned acceptance of the failure that was Holly.

Neither he nor Roz seemed to have much sway over their older daughter, for the tug toward the world was sharper and stronger in her than they could possibly contend with. Roz, too, had been pulled toward the world. Her marriage hadn't been enough for her, or it had been too much.

Once, they had all liked being a family. For a long, long time they had been a fairly good one, taking vacations together, sitting down to meals, and, no, the parents hadn't been terrible; even after *Pleasuring* was published, they came to school plays and teacher conferences between interviews and lectures. They tried. But they were an embarrassment to their older daughter, and adolescence was just too hard, being a *person* was just too hard, and then the divorce happened. One day that same year, Roz Mellow pulled the Volvo into the driveway and found that Holly was not there.

She was off, first with Hojo and then with Joanne Mikulski, who had one canine tooth the color of a corn niblet. Then, a while later, she was off with Danny Jett and those girls she'd met in the city, and then she was off in the city itself, up in Spanish Harlem where a bartender she met in a dance club inexplicably insisted on calling her "Rosalita." Over the years, Holly Mellow, beautiful Holly Mellow, the most gorgeous one in the family and the haughtiest, too, simply gave up her status as daughter, deciding it didn't "work" for her anymore. She gave it up, and she left them. They relinquished their claim on her, had long agreed to return her to the world, where she told them she belonged.

Except the thing was, at age forty-three, she didn't belong to the world anymore. She had retreated from it, but it was too late to go back to her original family; they were completely different now, and she would have been the worst kind of hypocrite, and anyway, she had her own family. The house on Swarthmore was gone, the marriage was gone, even the children were unrecognizable in their fully grown selves—Dashiell a fucking *Republican*, Michael so tightly wound and corporate and unhappy, and Claudia just a vague, and vaguely artistic, loser.

But it wasn't as though Holly should talk. Until recently, she'd had nothing much to show for herself at this age except, improbably, the beauty that she'd carried with her throughout her life like a little treasure you kept in your shoe, guarding it as you traveled. And then, in a late-life burst of fertility, she'd been fortunate enough to have a baby, and he had changed everything in one bloody instant of birth, turning what had previously been a dissolute life, then an obedient life spent beside Marcus Leeming, into something indescribable. She now had purpose.

The baby, whose name was Ross (a dull name but Marcus had insisted, after his dead father) but whom everyone called Buddy, was now nineteen months old. For the past year and a half, Holly had been as immersed in him as anyone could be in another person, and for nearly a year before that, she'd been entirely immersed in the pregnancy itself, reading those books that offered advice about nausea and folic acid and genetic testing and labor itself, that sickening stew of pain, Pitocin, ice chips, and continual begging for reprieve.

Marcus was a doctor, though not the kind that could be of any use during pregnancy. He was an orthopedic surgeon, and his clients included pro-football players and old women with hip fractures. His practice was full, and he was a thin, gangly man with long hair that he still wore in a little ponytail, if only to remind himself that once, before medical school and the internship and the residency, he'd been a renegade. Long ago, when he was a teenager in Oregon, he'd been in a rock band that had played frequently in the Portland area. They were good, not great, he told Holly, which also described his own academic career—the reason he was rejected by every American medical school he applied to. Getting his medical education "offshore" had been at first humiliating and then wonderful, he said, for by the time he came back to the States to begin an internship in a hospital, he was far calmer than his stateside counterparts, psychologically much more able to cope with the daily assault of hospital life. She wasn't sure that what he exuded was calm; it seemed mixed with a kind of tense wariness that was notable to her from the start.

They had met in 1995 at a party in Malibu that had lasted all night, and she, who at that point in time was living in the hills in Silverlake, selling pot out of the garage apartment she rented in a red-roofed mission-style house, had drifted to the party in a caravan of friends, one of whom actually knew the party's host. When she first saw him, Holly was sitting out on the bleached deck looking at the ocean and thinking about committing suicide. The thoughts of suicide came unbidden, as they had done occasionally throughout her life. Usually they occurred when she was at her most aimless, in a car with people she didn't really know, lying stoned beside someone unfamiliar, or at a big party of strangers, like this one in Malibu. Out on the deck of this house on stilts, she imagined the entire house being washed away in a storm; she pictured herself as just a tiny head bobbing in the water, and then she thought of the relief she would feel as she swallowed a mouthful of it and went under for the last time. Her hair would swirl around her head; a tiny starfish might be found lodged in her throat. No one would know who she was.

She was smoking a cigarette when the tall, bony man with the ponytail came out onto the deck. There was no one else outside because the night was chilly for Malibu at this time of year, and everyone else seemed to want to stay in where the fire was burning in the room-size fireplace. A former rock musician was singing an acoustic version of his one hit, "Try Me," and everyone was joining in on the chorus. "*Try* me . . ." the guests sang, "and if you don't like me then re*turn* me . . ."

"They sound like shit," Ponytail said, standing beside her at the wooden rail, and she nodded. "You shouldn't smoke," he added.

"Who says?"

"The surgeon general."

"Well, tell him to tell me personally," Holly said, thinking: *You asshole.* Back then she thought most people were assholes; it was satisfying to be able to categorize someone quickly.

"Look," he said, "I'm a physician. We're trained to think this way. It's a knee-jerk thing by now. But we're all hypocrites. My partners and I—we've got an orthopedic practice—and among us there's not a sin we haven't committed."

Holly looked at him with interest now; the idea of suicide was put away in that instant, just like an unfinished book you close before sleep. She was tired and lonely and had been up in her apartment since dawn stuffing sensimillia buds into those miniature Ziploc bags, all the while being kept company by a neurotic ex-prostitute named Rita, who resembled a blaxploitation star who'd died not too long before. Rita had recently decided to enter the marijuana trade, but she liked to tell stories about the halcyon days in "the life"; she spoke of johns and cash flow and STDs, including a particularly woeful tale of chlamydia that ended up in botched laparoscopic surgery in a free clinic in Venice Beach.

In Malibu, with the ocean blurry and loud just beyond this deck and a houseful of rich people and their friends singing around someone's unplugged Fender Stratocaster, Holly took comfort from the tall orthopedic surgeon beside her. She realized that she didn't know anyone who was a doctor; her life was populated by people like herself who hadn't gone to college but who had a natural smarts about them.

A doctor. She gave Ponytail a weak but genuine smile.

"What's your name?" he asked, and when she told him, he said the inevitable: "Mellow? Maybe it's a common name, but any relation to the sex book Mellows?"

And she had to confess; she hated this moment whenever it happened. "Yeah," she said, "my mother and father wrote *Fucking: One Couple's Story of How to Do It and Why.*"

There was a brief pause, and then Ponytail smiled slowly. "That's funny," he said. "You're funny."

She listened to him reminisce about what the book had meant to him, how he had used it, what he had learned from it, and on and on. Throughout his monologue she looked away, trying to convey her discomfort and boredom all at once, but people almost never picked up on it. Usually they were so taken by their own little leaf-storm of memory about the book that they became lost in the telling, and Marcus Leeming was no exception.

Later on, when the party was over and the guests were wobbling to their cars, she wobbled to his. Her friends didn't question this; they barely remembered that she'd come with them. Instead, they were stuffing someone new into the backseat, and soon they would be barreling along the Pacific Coast, heading for home, or at least someone's home.

In Marcus's rented house he tried to show her what he had learned from her parents' book. Though very thin, he was quite strong, with a sheeting of pale, blondish hair. At first she didn't feel much with him except a kind of slightly annoying and lulling friction, but finally he seemed to understand that in her opinion the sex—like most sex she'd had in recent years—was inert, static, would never happen again unless he did something about it. So he brought out a tiny bottle of pharmaceutical-grade cocaine and they quickly snuffled it up, and everything was temporarily fixed. The friction became simply rhythm, and she heard her own breath coming faster and louder, as though she were being chased by a young woman, herself, down a long road. When, weeks later, she saw him in his blue-green scrubs about to go into the OR, she would think that the opacity of the outfit was about right. For who knew who he was underneath? His own past was still only partly filled in; she didn't really want to know it all.

It was too late to take on anyone else's past; she had her own, and that was too much. She had never thought that you could marry someone you didn't really know, and who didn't really know you, but now she not only knew you could do that, she was *going* to do that. Marriage would imply *movement* in her life and would give everyone the idea that she, Holly Mellow, was passing through the same channels that most people passed through. Marriage would break up time and provide constancy. There would be one house, one other person. She knew that sex was not what her parents' book had insisted it was. Surely her *parents* no longer thought it was. Marriage came with irony attached to it, but this in itself had a sharp and pungent appeal to Holly.

It was as though she carried within her formerly druggie, pissed-off self a 1950s notion of marriage: If you were a woman who did nothing, who *had* nothing meaningful, then you could marry a doctor. His name would become your own, and thank God for that, because then you could lose that telltale Mellow tag once and for all. Even his medical degree (though from St. Martinus University on Curaçao) would be your own. You could erase yourself, letting the edges that were *you*, for better or worse, become blunted and blurred and eventually lost to you, like the names of people you had known during your drug years and could now no longer retrieve.

It wasn't that Marcus Leeming cleaned up Holly Mellow's act, but simply that in his presence she had the desire to clean up her own act, for she understood that otherwise, this wouldn't work at all. As it was, he barely tolerated her slacker, finish-nothing attitude, her lack of ambition, her slovenliness. In those first weeks, she confessed all her wrongdoings to him—the laundry list was extensive and tried his patience and what he thought he could stand. He sat back against his couch in his living room, listening with a falsely friendly smile.

She told her future husband about 1991, the year she spent staying on in Minnesota after leaving Recovery House. Like recent college graduates whose best years occur in the embrace of the campus, Holly Mellow and a few others had taken an apartment only two miles away from the facility they'd lived in together, and they proceeded to find jobs for themselves at local ice-cream parlors and bookstores. Holly worked the counter at I Can't Believe It's Yogurt, lifting levers and feeling the pressure and hearing the hum as she let soft-serve snake out into little Styrofoam cups. Her hands and clothes smelled continually of yogurt midspoil, and whenever she or one of the other employees would complain to one another about this or anything else, the other one would say, archly, "I can't believe it!" Sarcasm ran high in that small, bright store. Because she was older than thirty at the time, she was the oldest employee there. The manager, who was only twenty-three, was incredulous that she didn't want to climb the employment ladder, rising at least to the rung of assistant manager, but she assured him she did not. The work was just too boring. And besides, she had the money from her trust fund, which had allowed her this long, serpentine, dissolute life, and she supposed she ought to be grateful, but she was not.

During all those years, when she barely spoke to her parents, she still took their money, removing it silently, so silently from her bank account via ATMs all over America, signing checks and paying for food and dope and vodka and rent and gas and record albums and later on CDs, not really thinking about her mother and father, who had made it possible for her to acquire these things. Her mother and father, who had made it possible for her to live.

Even now, at age forty-three, with her drug days over, she seethed like a teenager over the wrongs that had been done to her, and, sometimes, the wrongs she had done to others. She pictured her mother crying in the kitchen in the middle of the night. She pictured her father wandering the house and stroking his beard, perplexed and mournful. She saw her parents going at it like monkeys, telling the universe that sex was a pleasure, a thrill unlike any other, a view that she'd shared for about a minute when she was a teenager, and which became harder to support as she aged, and as men aged too, everyone seeming to flatten against the beds they lay in, exhausted and angry in addition to being aroused. She saw her brothers and her little sister, all of them as wide-eyed and innocent as children in a painting on black velvet, though in this case their eyes were wide not from wonder but from what they'd *seen*.

It was fair to break from your parents in the beginning or the middle of your life; she had enough reason. They had mortified her, they had ignored her, they had humiliated her. And life had been waiting, like a convenient getaway car. She was seething still, as she sat here in the white rocking chair with the baby. Holly Leeming's husband had swept into her life, getting extra credit from her because of his ponytail and his medical degree, the combination of which was impressive and relieving all at once. *Someone to watch over me,* she had thought. Someone who had a little power and could give her a life that might feel permanent in a way that nothing had felt since she'd sat with her brothers and sister in a little tribe on the pink carpet of her bedroom. She'd spun the slow, clicking spinner of the game of Life and it had landed on mortgage, marriage, a family. Holly Leeming, amazingly, had all of that. The past was fucking old hat. The present, while it didn't really possess the unmistakable taste of reality, was in fact real, and upon her.

She was a wealthy wife in a large house in Topanga Canyon, still pretty though vaguely battered-looking, the skin around her eyes and mouth bearing the telltale parched pull of a former smoker. Her hair remained blonde and luxurious, and her body was freckly and tanned and lithe as always. Holly had become a mother after age forty; the nurse in her OB's office had given her a pamphlet that featured various gray-haired women holding newborns on the cover. Her own baby was against her now, flesh against flesh, and the light was starting to tint the nursery window. Buddy Leeming was coming fully awake, lifting his head up from her left breast and looking at her quizzically, like someone coming out of a drug stupor to ask: Who am I? Where am I?

"Mom?" he said.

"Hi, Buddy boy," she said. "Hi, sweet bean."

Now Buddy was reaching out to the arm of the rocking chair, running his fat hand along the curve of white wood. "Go," he said. "Go down. Go down, Mom. Now."

But all she wanted to do was sit here with him, stealing a little more mother-baby time before the light came fully into the room and Marcus woke up in a surgeon's sour mood, and she had to fall back into this suburban L.A. married life as though it was where she really ought to be. Holly thought of Dashiell and his illness, and she thought of her parents, first entwined and then separated forever. She thought of her brother Michael, who'd always looked at her with such longing, which she'd known about forever but had consistently ignored, because what could she do about it? What could she do for him? They'd been breathlessly close, those two, a duo, and now they were nothing. His life was almost unknown to her: the time at Princeton, the corporate world he inhabited, the woman he loved, the money he spent. She'd let him go, along with all the others. Holly thought of the entire Mellow family first as one big object, then as a collection of separate, broken-off pieces. God, life was wild and sad. It sometimes seemed to be like some whirling laser show you went to see at midnight. There you were, all fucked up as you sat in your theater seat, your head back, your mouth slightly open in awe.

"Go *down*," Buddy said now, more insistent this time.

But she couldn't let him go down, she wasn't ready and she wasn't sure when she ever would be. Holly Leeming took her baby's head and moved it back to her breast, planting it there. His eyes looked up at her, as if to say: *What the fuck?*

But she was resolute, unapologetic, and she slipped her nipple back into his mouth and waited a long moment for him to latch on again, which she knew he would, for he was good-natured and didn't want to make trouble, and it was just as easy to be here, in the small, warm room with her, as it was to be out there in the world.

Chapter Ten

JUST BEYOND the semicircle of hospital rooms, a corresponding semicircle of nurses manned a large, curved dashboard of controls, and in the middle of a sequence of hallucinations Dashiell Mellow imagined that he was on a spaceship, lifting off from Earth. "Going somewhere better," he said in a dry voice.

"What's that?" asked the night nurse, a gentle blob in a yellow gown and mask, who was just passing through to check on his meds and make some notes on his chart.

"Going somewhere better," he repeated, though even now he was losing the conviction of those words. What *did* he mean? He struggled to remember why he'd said that, but found that he couldn't.

"Oh no, you'll be fine," said the nurse. "The medical care is excellent here, believe me. My brother-in-law had a triple bypass six weeks ago, and he's already back at work." Then she patted his blanket with one Latex hand and swished out on silent shoes.

The spaceship lifted up over Providence, Rhode Island, carrying its cargo of passengers, all of whom were in isolation and too weak and sick to peer down through the windows at the city they were leaving. Dashiell, though, managed to sit up and look outside. As the spaceship went up, he saw the roof of the house where he and Tom lived, the wrought-iron gates of Brown University, and in the middle of a park he saw a statue of Roger Williams, founder of Rhode Island, wearing one of those three-corner hats, boots, and a waistcoat. Roger Williams looked up at the spaceship and, with all the effort he could muster, waved a bronze arm as the thing lumbered higher and higher into the night sky. Dashiell would have waved back, but his own arm felt as though it were made of bronze and was unliftable. He turned his heavy head to the side and closed his eyes, going for a ride, unsure of how long it would take before he got there.

By the time the morning came, Tom was sitting in the single chair beside the bed. He too wore a yellow gown and mask, though beneath it Dashiell could see the cuffs and collar of his one really good suit, the black Armani that had cost so much money that the two men had had to figure out their expenses for the month before they decided it was okay for him to buy it. But in his position he needed to look authoritative and well dressed. Ever since the advent of Bill Clinton, Democrats had had a lock on fashion, and the Republicans had given them a wide berth; for every slim, Italian-suited liberal, there were three bad toupee- and checkered-poly-blend conservatives peppering the landscape. Something needed to be done about this. It was gay Republicans to the rescue, Tom had felt, and Dashiell had agreed that he ought to buy the suit. Besides, Tom looked so good in it that Dashiell sometimes felt improbably proud when they walked down the street together, as though he wanted everyone to know: This is my boyfriend. Look at him and *weep*.

This morning, though, in the somber, dim light of the unit, in which all the patients were soon to be recipients of stem cell transplants, there was no sexual heat to speak of, and behind the face mask, Tom Amlin's eyes looked terrified.

"Dashiell? Are you awake?" The yellow patch of cloth was sucked slightly into the concavity that implied a mouth.

"Yes. Just," he said.

"They say you're doing really well so far. I spoke to the nurses, and also to Dr. Chang and Dr. Balakian."

"Really? How can they tell?" Dashiell realized, with a great measure of relief, that the hallucinations had subsided. He was not in outer space; he was not on any sort of spacecraft; no orderlies floated past in antigravity, carrying trays. He was earthbound, intact, or at least as intact as someone could be whose cancer was advancing.

The peripheral stem cells, which had been collected directly from Dashiell's bone marrow, would, after he finished this new round of chemotherapy, be returned to him in a cleaner, purer state. His own immune system would be turned off, a sudden blackout that would leave him vulnerable to anything: to a careless nurse sneezing and sending out an invisible spider-thread of snot, then touching the edge of a magazine that Dashiell might soon pick up, to the vent under the window that seemed to have a soft accretion of mold on it, much to Dashiell's disturbance. But he didn't want to say anything about the vent because he was too tired to complain, and because he feared it would make him seem like a difficult patient.

"They say you're tolerating the new drugs really well," Tom said. "That's what I mean."

"Oh."

"Listen, Dash." Tom shifted and crossed his legs. Even his shining black shoes were covered in stretchy yellow slippers. "I have to travel for the campaign."

"I know."

"Yeah, but I mean basically, *now*. Just a few days here and there, back and forth. I'll be in and out. There's really no choice. Wyman's numbers are down farther and they want me out there. He's getting a lot of heat because in interviews he was all for the war in

Iraq—not that he was actually in a position to *vote* on it—and now things are not going so well. Soldiers dying every day. You know about that mother?"

"What mother?"

"Mary Ann McCullough, I think her name is. She's from Paw-tucket, and her kid was blown up last week in Fallujah. So she's going after Wyman, of all people, like he was somehow responsible, even though he's still just a candidate. She follows him around to campaign stops and photo-ops armed with these giant pictures of her son and these pictures of his coffin draped in a flag. She's even got his first grade picture turned into a *billboard,* and underneath it are the words "My Boy Died in a Phony War," or something like that. So she's been haunting Wyman, and the RNC wants us to control these events more tightly. I can't really trust anyone else to run the show; everything's getting out of hand. It will all fall apart without me."

Dashiell couldn't even imagine what to say. He felt dizzy, and he wondered briefly if he really *were* in space, and if Tom was there with him. They weren't the Brooks Brothers anymore—they were Neil Armstrong and Buzz Aldrin, heading for a walk on the moon. Because how could Tom say such a thing; how could he leave him *now,* of all times, while his own body had been strafed of marrow and infection-fighting cells and lay waiting for the savior marrow and new cells to come riding in and make everything okay? Dashiell had barely enough energy even to move his head, but he swiveled his eyes over to Tom and fixed on him what he hoped was an evil stare. More likely, though, he just looked hangdog-sick.

He saw, in that moment, that Tom was deeply upset, too, and that clearly he did not take any of this at all lightly. "I know, you hate me," Tom said quietly. "I mean, who would do such a thing? But they're *making* me, Dash. I heard right down from the RNC. The big guns of the GOP are basically offering me the following options: I can either go on the road with Wyman right now, all around the state, putting out fires, and if I do a good job then I'll probably keep rising and I'll be able to cover whatever your insurance won't. Or I can quit now, and be blackballed in the Republican party of Rhode Island forever, not to mention *nationally*, and then I don't know how we're going to pay all your medical bills."

"They wouldn't do that to you," said Dashiell.

"Try them."

Both men sat and looked at the port catheter in Dashiell's chest, into which doggedly dripped cyclophosphamide, melphalan, and etoposide. The expense of his illness was something they could barely think about. With Dashiell unable to work, it all fell on Tom, the unrecognized spouse. Still, they managed their lives side by side. They were two men who loved each other and still got really turned on looking at each other coming out of the shower in the morning. Two men who knew how to make each other happy just joking around or talking all night about politics or sprawled across the bed in the glorious freedom that belonged to the well.

God, that freedom was lost, Dashiell thought, for beds were now places to lie still in, to raise the head or lower the foot. Beds were motorized. They had a thick urine-protector that you could feel even beneath the sheet. This was a far cry from the bed at home, the low bed where sometimes Dashiell lay diagonally, completely naked and hard, waiting for Tom to come into the room and be surprised. And Tom would leap on him like a kid jumping into water, and they would both feel the symmetry of skin, the wonderful rub of parts that even to this day reminded Dashiell of Boy Scouts, trying to make a fire with two sticks. You could feel boyish and scoutlike in bed. Tom Amlin threw off his bureaucratic style, his power and influence and dogma, and became just a really adorable, sexy boyfriend in a bed. Everything was there that they needed: little candles, music, a tub of something vanilla-scented called Luv Butter that Tom had bought as a joke but had been depleted with surprising alacrity, and, of course, their two strong and willing selves.

Dashiell had left that bed and traded down, way down, for this one, which included an interminable poison drip and no guarantees that anything good would come of this. Sometimes the transplant killed you before you had a chance to see if it would have even worked. "All right," Dashiell said to the man in yellow, whose body was hidden from view in a hospital burka as if a punishment for some obscure sin.

But Tom was not done. "So the thing is," he went on, "I called your mother."

If Dashiell could have yanked the tubes from his chest in protest he would have, but the news only further flattened him against the bed. "No," he said. "Why did you do that?"

"Someone needs to be with you while you're here, to be your advocate."

"Claudia, then. She's offered."

Tom shook his head. "No, I don't think so. From what you've said about her and from what I've seen myself of her, I don't think she could do a forceful enough job. And look, your mother really, really wants to do it; you already know that. She's coming the day after tomorrow."

By the time plates of scrod were wheeled in to the patients in the transplant unit at Rhode Island Hospital on Wednesday evening, Tom Amlin was standing in one of the waterfront mansions in Newport, drinking champagne from a ludicrously tall flute. The mansion was filled with heavy-donor buzz and the pleasure that came with feeling that you were close to the nucleus of power, or at least projected power. The hospital unit, meanwhile, was quiet and humming; there was the occasional click of a fork and knife against a Chinet plate and the sound of someone softly crying. Dashiell raised the head of his bed a little higher to try to get a look through the window of his door into the window of the door across the hall, but he saw nothing.

It was into this sleepy evening environment that his yellow-clad mother came. Dashiell looked up as she strode to the head of the bed, and he said, "Mom."

To her credit, she didn't cry and she didn't make any loud, startling noises. She simply stood there, suited up for the visit, and she reached out and held his hand in her own gloved one. "Dashiell, hi," she said. "I'm glad you let me come."

He didn't argue; this wasn't the time and he wouldn't have done a good job at it, anyway. Her presence had been foisted on him the way the nodes of cancer had, and in both cases he had no vote. But he found that he didn't feel angry at seeing her here. Maybe he was getting soft, getting sentimental, but he found her demeanor appropriate, even potentially helpful. Right away Dashiell was impressed with his mother's lack of hesitation.

"Are you feeling totally rotten?" she asked.

"Not yet," he told her.

Over the next days, as he descended slowly through the levels of hell, Roz Mellow was there with him, not exactly a Beatrice to his Dante, but more like a sidekick. She descended too, though she was able to do it enclosed in some kind of magical glass casing, free from the pain all around her, not so much to save herself, but in order to be strong for him. There were jobs she needed to do: nurses who had to be told and retold with greater emphasis and eventually anger that Dashiell was nauseated and needed an antiemetic *right now;* doctors who had to be summoned; nutritionists who needed to be advised about what he could eat and what didn't stay down. Dashiell saw all the insistence and fervor and drama he'd always seen in her now put to good use. And he thought that she would have liked to have his pain, to take it from him and apply it to herself. Was this what mothers did? He'd never thought about that much when he was a boy. He'd been wrapped up in himself the way children are, but not because he thought he was so great, the way Michael clearly always thought of himself, and the way Holly seemed to think of herself too, back when she was a beautiful, arrogant girl. Back when she held sway over the younger ones. Dashiell actually thought of himself as a *criminal*, and in dream after dream throughout his childhood he was continually apprehended by the police and carted off to jail. In one particularly memorable dream, his parents come into his room before dinner and say to him, *Son, the police are on to you. They will be here in an hour.*

But what have I done?

You know what you've done. There's no time to go into it. Here, we've put together some food and clothing and a little money for you. Take it and leave now, before they get here. Head out to the expressway and keep going.

But I'm just a kid.

Yes, we know that, says his mother, starting to cry. *And we will never be able to see you grow up, because you can never, ever come home again or they will find you.*

We would rather you have a life of freedom, says his father, *than one spent in prison. Take care of yourself.*

And then they hug him tightly and let go of him, and they hand him a little hobo stick packed with his things. He slings it over his shoulder and heads outside. It's early evening, and all around the neighborhood are other families, other kids, and Dashiell thinks to himself, *Why do I have to go away when they all get to stay? What is it I've done again? What's the terrible crime?* But he can never remember, and off he goes, tears streaming down his face, and his parents wave good-bye from behind the screen door, and he will never see them again.

As if to make his own dreams more sensible, Dashiell started stealing a few items when he was twelve. In the record store downtown he'd stolen cassette tapes of the Velvet Underground and a compilation of the Doors' greatest hits, slipping them quickly into his windbreaker and praying that there wasn't some metallic strip inside them that would make an alarm go off as he left. When he walked out the door of the store he felt a surge of anxiety so powerful that it almost sounded like an alarm, and he was tempted to break into a run. *But no, steady, steady,* he insisted to himself, *there is no alarm, there is only silence, and you are fine.*

He was never caught, though once, when she was briefly home, Holly walked by his room when he was playing a purloined tape, and he was sure she knew. There was a kind of mirth in her expression, but she never said a word to him about it, and he couldn't bear to ask. He would never find out exactly how much she knew back then, and now, as a grown man, he felt a need to know. But maybe it was just a need to be young again, under the control of a powerful, sultry sister who would one day become diminished to an extent he still found shocking.

For no particular reason, Dashiell grew out of the desire to take things that weren't his. His parents gave him a decent allowance, and he took pride in laying out cash for cassette tapes and other sundries. But he understood, when he turned fourteen and started fooling around with Ham Kleeman, the perennial musical-comedy lead, that he wasn't done with guilt yet, or it wasn't done with him.

One night it was dark out and he was late for dinner, and when he left the Kleemans' and came through the door of his own house and looked at his divorced mother, she knew, and he knew that she knew.

"Where have you been?" she asked.

"Out," he said, borrowing an answer that Holly had used often.

"Well, all right then," Roz had finally said uncertainly. "Go wash up."

He washed and he washed. He stood in the tiny downstairs bathroom with its basket of clove and dried flecks of tangerine peel and its never-laundered little hand towels, and he thought of what he'd just been doing up in Ham's attic room with the door bolted. Initially, Ham had put on the album from *Pippin,* and he had even sung along lightly with one of the songs.

"'Everything has its season,'" Ham had begun in his premature baritone, a hand reaching out and yanking Dashiell's shirt up over his head. "'Everything has its time,'" Ham went on, undoing the button-fly jeans with eager fingers. "'Show me a reason and I'll soon show you a rhyme . . .'"

Then Dashiell had interrupted, saying, "If you keep this record on, I will have to shoot you." Ham had simply laughed and changed the record to something he knew Dashiell would like: the drone of boy rock, with its mournfulness and electric keyboards. "Here," Ham said as the album began, "is this better?"

"Much. Thank you."

Then they'd wrestled lightly on the bed and, surprise surprise, it had turned into sex. Ham was very efficient with his hands and all else; after trying and failing to make it as an actor for a year after college, Ham Kleeman had gone to medical school and was now, apparently, an endocrinologist in New Jersey. Ham took Dashiell's penis in his mouth with very little preamble; they were just boys, these two, and they did not know anything about kissing or cuddling or hugging. They had no book to learn from. Dashiell always came back to the fact, astounded all over again, that *Pleasuring,* for all its extravagant explanations, did not say one word that was meant for male couples. Not one word.

"Not one word," Dashiell blurted out to his mother now.

"Honey? What's that?"

She leaned over the bed, and he became aware that she'd been there for hours and hours, perhaps all day, for the light was different and the bustle of the hospital was suddenly different, even the fractional amount of bustle that found its way here into the unit whose isolated patients became less and less animated with each passing day. Meal carts still were trundled through, but no one could eat anymore. Soon, all nutrients would be given through tubes; soon, scrod and chicken and ice cream would be the topography of someone else's landscape, not theirs.

"Why," he asked, "didn't you put men in the book?"

"Men? There was plenty about men."

"Men on men," he persevered.

"Oh. That again. We've talked about that." She sighed. "And

you know, I was defensive about it in the past, but I've come to see that you're probably right. It *was* a mistake. We wrote about our own experience. We weren't gay men. We were so ignorant of everything, Dash. We thought only about ourselves in a bed. We couldn't imagine other people's experiences. I'm really sorry."

Even through the fog, he was startled by her apology. "Oh," he said. "Well, okay."

"It's okay?" she said.

"Yes," he said. "It is."

And then she was not allowed in for a while, not allowed anywhere near him, for his body was missing its essential soup of immunity, and anything could have killed him, it seemed, even an apology.

It was two days later, but it might have been twenty, or thirty, or an entire lifetime later, with Dashiell a futurist Van Winkle figure in bed with a long beard, that his mother returned, and a few others came to visit him as well. First there was Tom, who was home briefly from the road. Now he was here again in his gown, and Dashiell could see that he had been crying. *I must look like shit*, he thought, and then Tom said, "No, you don't," and Dashiell realized that he'd spoken aloud once again without knowing it.

Tom came and went, saying he loved Dashiell, and then he came back, and this time he actually brought a gowned and masked U.S. senatorial candidate Robert Wyman with him. A few of the nurses stood in a proud ring around the bed, but Dashiell became aware of his mother's sudden absence, as though she couldn't bear to be in the presence of a powerful Republican, as though she might spit on him or something.

"How are you doing, guy?" Wyman asked.

Guy. No, he didn't think Dashiell's name was Guy. He *knew* his name; Dashiell had written speeches for him. His words had poured from Robert Wyman's mouth. Guy was what a man called another man in a moment of drama, when words would fail, when tenderness would have been embarrassing, when other people were listening, when there was no way to express anything with any kind of eloquence, so the best bet was to reduce the world to its sparest elements. Two men in a room: How are you doing, guy?

And to Dashiell's amazement, he found himself able to briefly rally, slide upward in the bed a little, and reach out a hand so that Wyman could shake it. This man was the master of the handshake, and Dashiell felt the inadequacy of his own cold, frail hand; the hand of the sick embraced by the gloved hand of the living, the hearty, the man who would be king, and though probably he was imagining this, it felt as though power passed from palm to palm, entering Dashiell through the skin. That was what he thought, anyway, and he tried to explain it to someone, but the next thing he knew, the person in yellow standing over the bed was none other than Trish Leggett, the zealous speechwriter who in Dashiell's absence had written speeches for Robert Wyman at a fever pitch, staying up all night in her one-bedroom Benefit Street apartment that looked out over original street lamps and cobblestones.

"Dashiell? It's me, Trish," she said, and as she leaned down closer he could smell Neutrogena soap through her mask. She always seemed like someone who had just that very moment stepped from a shower.

"Hi," he said. "Is Wyman gone?"

"What? Oh yes. Hours ago," she said. "He had to give a speech at a battered women's shelter in Kingston."

"He shook my hand," Dashiell said. "There was power there."

Trish paused. "Yes," she said. "He's very powerful. I know what you mean. You can actually feel it sometimes." She played with the edge of his hospital blanket for a moment, and then she said, "Dashiell, I know the road is hard."

"What?"

"The road you're on. But keep a steady pace. For there's a farm-house up ahead, and a light is burning in the window, and they're waiting for you."

Dashiell blinked. Because she was wearing a mask, he couldn't

really tell what she had meant by this; her eyes seemed to be filling with tears, much as they'd done when he'd run into her in
Store 24, and she'd thought he had AIDS. Then it occurred to him
that she was saying words that were meant to give him faith, and
optimism, and hope. This was her sick-person speech! This was it!
She was forming the words for the first time right now, and she
was already editing them in her head. Though he could not know
this, eventually she would use these very words in a speech that
President Bush would deliver at a naval base. It would be about
Iraq, and about having hope even in the face of immense suffering. But for now it was simply her latest combination of words
designed to elicit a swift response.

Dashiell thought about what she'd said. Who exactly, he wondered, were *they*? Who were the people who were waiting for him?

"I don't know any farmers," he said.

"What?"

"In the farmhouse."

"It's a *metaphor*," Trish said gently.

"I know that. But for what? For what?"

It was as though she didn't want to say, for she backed up
slowly, starting to leave the room without telling him. But he had
to know. Did she mean that the farmer and perhaps his wife were
the embodiments of *death*? Or were they there to *save* him, to
take him inside and give him a bowl of warm broth and a feather
bed to sleep in? He had to know; he absolutely had to know, for he
had convinced himself that she knew the answer to this.

"Trish, come back," Dashiell said, but his voice was barely a
whisper, and the room was dark. It was nighttime; the visitors were
gone, and he was alone. Distantly, the nurses shuffled around in
the hall, and someone in another room was crying, and someone
else was coughing, and still another person was retching; he was
able to separate out these strands from one another so that the
whole of human misery here in this unit was not just one writhing
mass.

Then, with all the energy he'd ever possessed, and with the new infusion of it that he'd received from Robert Wyman's hand, Dashiell sat up in bed. The port that delivered the drugs to him was attached to a bag that hung from a hook on a pole, and he was flummoxed by the different tubes that sprouted from his chest, and so instead of disconnecting himself completely he just grabbed hold of the pole, using it like a crutch, leaning against the shaky metal as he took a few steps across the dark, shining linoleum. His chest ached, and he was wearing only a pale green hospital gown, but still he walked, tilting forward into the hall past the nurses' station, where three nurses were in a football huddle, none of them looking at him, all of them intent as they gave their attention to something in the middle of them, which happened to be a box of Godiva chocolates that another patient's family had brought. "It says that this one's praline," he heard one of them say. "And this one's nougat."

Out of the transplant unit he went, pushing through the doors and into the vestibule, where the light was brighter and where the bank of elevators was. One came right away, and Dashiell went downstairs and wound up in the lobby, which at this time of night was dead. The gift shop was locked, but he could see the things pressing against the glass from inside, the collection of shiny synthetic stuffed animals and jumbo find-a-word omnibuses, none of which had ever saved a single person's life. He stepped onto the rubber mat of the front door of the building, and the electric eye saw him and permitted egress.

So then he was outside in the cold winter air of Providence, Rhode Island, and up ahead he could make out the receding form of Trish Leggett, as she wound her way along the sidewalk that bordered the parking lot and started walking toward her car.

"Trish, wait!" Dashiell called as he pushed his pole along. God, the wind was cold; it shot a column of air up his flapping gown. Trish didn't hear him, and he had to keep walking, heading forward, his feet in their terry cloth slippers on the sidewalk, going past the Emergency sign, and the fleet of idling ambulances, and the cluster of residents laughing and joking like students, their stethoscopes bouncing as they walked. If they saw him they didn't show it, and on he went, leaving the gates of the hospital and heading on to the boulevard. It must have been ten o'clock at night, maybe later, and the trees were enormous and black, and the wind became something you just had to get used to, which was pretty much like anything in life: like sex, actually, for in the beginning it hadn't felt natural to do it with anyone but yourself. You had to break away from that solitude, from the grip of the hand with which you held yourself in the dark, the distinctly unpowerful hand that wasn't Robert Wyman's, that was just the hand of a boy, nothing more, curling around something that you were only now acknowledging was your own, was *yours*, belonged to no one else.

Sex was joyous, his parents had said in their book, and they rode each other with the unwavering assuredness of heterosexuals at the top of their game. Sex does not need to be shameful or conducted in dark, soundproof rooms that were havens for the furtive. But sex was for men and women only; it was not for two women and it was not for two men, and he'd learned that the moment he'd opened the book for the first time in November 1975 and stared at all those drawings, one after the other. There wasn't a way in, there was no picture that could have been him, for he would never do those things to a woman, never, ever, and in some way he knew it even then. But he had no alternative yet, no way to convert the images so they suited him, and instead he sank back into his anger and his sneaky life of secrets, of cassette tapes tucked inside his jacket with their price stickers still on, of longing, and wanting what he couldn't have, and being single-minded in his desire to obtain it.

But now, walking along the side of the road in Providence with the port catheter in his chest and his metal pole, Dashiell thought about the first time he'd entered that room full of other gay Republicans, all of them enraged by the sniveling of the left, the ever-expanding government that could simply go wherever it wanted, encroach upon you like some sort of lawn infestation. He was a gay man and he wanted the government out of his life; he wanted to be left alone to make his money and spend it, to make his decisions and fuck someone of his choosing in a state of exquisite joy.

But what Tom had been telling him—and what he'd been seeing on the news every night before he went into the hospital—would have created a chill in even a lifelong member of the GOP. The Iraqi war was a drawn-out mess; there seemed to be no plan; the White House was helpless but angry, much the way that Dashiell had been throughout his childhood. Belligerent, simmering, wishing for things that might never happen. The GIs were dying in their helicopters and their convoys, or while standing sentry at a bank or a school or a grocery store, or while lighting a cigarette outside the gates of a compound. They were dying, these men, these boys, including Mary Ann McCullough's unfortunate son, thus turning his mother into an accidental activist chasing candidate Robert Wyman around the tiny state of Rhode Island.

So the men of Washington had pulled down the dusty maps with their faded blues and their yellow land masses. The maps were so fucking old, they probably had words on them like "Persia" and "Constantinople." Quickly, quickly, the men had to learn, and then the world had to be told what the men had learned. Dashiell couldn't trust these men, he knew, at least not with this particular task. He could trust them with his bankbook, his wallet, with a waterfall of cash, but he would never let them send him out into a world they were too arrogant to understand. The whole country was suddenly loathed in ways that were incomprehensible to Dashiell. *We have lost our special place,* he thought. We've lost the perfection that allowed us to be boyish in one way and manlike in another; we've lost the shining maleness that shimmered everywhere, and was sometimes resented but tolerated, and more often than not was *loved.* We have lost it, and it can never be returned to us. We no longer have our position, our corner booth, our distinction.

Dashiell knew famous stories of Republicans who'd converted to the other side when they became critically ill. These changes were legendary; bombastic types who for years had been working to defeat the Left now wept with sorrow at the zero hour and asked for forgiveness. He would not become one of them, no he wouldn't. He wouldn't change sides merely because he had seen some of the ugliness of his own side. He'd seen it and he could never unsee it, just like his parents' book. It disturbed him, but he had to live with what he was and what he'd made himself into all these years. He couldn't conveniently change, when push came to shove. He was a Republican, he was one of *them,* but he could loudly complain about *them* too. He could complain when they were boorish and ignorant, and he could keep on complaining for the rest of his life and never shut up.

Dashiell was tired now, but his feet kept moving, shuffling along the road. *For there's a farmhouse up ahead, and a light is burning in the window, and they're waiting for you,* Trish Leggett had said to him in the hospital room. She was gone now, had slipped into the darkness and couldn't be found, but up ahead he saw something, and he realized it was a light.

Of course, he thought, and he lifted the metal pole up from the ground and carried it over his shoulder, the way he'd done with that little hobo stick in his dream when he was a boy. And soon enough he had arrived at the farmhouse. It had a thatched roof and leaded glass windows. *I see, this is all just another hallucination,* Dashiell thought. *I've had them before, but this one is different.* It was the kind of extended-narrative hallucination that people get when their immune system is turned off and the fevers spike and the drugs are poured in like water on a fire.

He now knew that this was the case, and that in actuality he was still in his hospital bed, lying there with his legs moving slightly under the extra blankets that the nurses had thrown over him when he'd started to shake. But knowing it didn't change anything, for here was the farmhouse, appearing before him with clarity.

He tried the door and found that it was unlocked. Inside was a simple and beautiful room with a wooden table and chairs, and a hearth that was lit. Waiting for him in the middle of the room was someone who was neither the farmer nor the farmer's wife; neither death nor life, though perhaps both, but the thought was too complicated to understand in his current state. During the bout of hallucinations, his fever, which was being monitored continually by the nurses and by Drs. Chang and Balakian, had now reached 105.2. A special ice blanket was being filled for him right now, and it would bring the fever down to a safer level fairly quickly. Dashiell Mellow would recover from the transplant, and he would go into the remission that everybody had hoped for. But he didn't know any of this yet. He was still in the farmhouse, and the light was on, and someone was waiting for him. He stepped inside and let his mother take him in her arms.

Chapter Eleven

UPON HER return from Providence, Roz Mellow found that her husband had cleaned all the closets in her absence, as much to please and surprise her as to do something with his own anxiety. Deep into the closets he'd gone, scooping out the detritus of this marriage and the one before it. By the time Roz looked, flashlights had been loaded with fresh D batteries and upended on shelves in the utility closet, and old, ignored shoes and boots had been lined up in rows on the floor of the front hall closet, as if waiting for feet that hadn't come to claim them in many years and maybe never would. The sense of order, even if it wouldn't prove to be particularly useful, was still soothing to Roz, as Jack must have hoped it would be.

She had gone to Providence to take care of Dashiell by herself; there was no point in Jack coming with her, she'd said. He wouldn't be any help to Dashiell, and he wouldn't really be any help to her either. Besides, after a day spent watching her son be transformed, purposefully turned even sicker than he already was, she had secretly wanted to be alone at night in her room at the Biltmore, watching endless loops of CNN's *Headline News* and eating a standard room-service Asian chicken salad with its empty crunch of noodle and canned water chestnut. If she lost Dash, then *she* would die too, and she knew this but didn't want to discuss it with Jack, for saying it was so melodramatic, so attention-getting. Instead, she came back to her hotel room each night, slid her card into its horizontal slot in the door, waited for the green light, and was gratefully alone.

Now it was over, Dashiell would be all right, and Roz was back in the house in Saratoga with its collection of beautiful, deep closets. Jack stood beside her, hands in his pockets, watching as she inspected each one.

"I can't believe you took it upon yourself to do this," she said. "It's just about the worst chore there is. So how can I thank you?" she asked him.

"Ah, why even try?" he said.

She knew that some of her friends at the college saw Jack as a slightly amusing figure, a house-husband whose steady, low-key presence served to counterbalance Roz's own dynamism and emotionality. Roz was home with him now in this house of clean closets and temporary peace. It wouldn't have to be a place of grieving and suffering, for Dashiell's Hodgkin's disease had been forced into remission by his own cells. He'd saved himself.

On her three-and-a-half-hour drive home today on I-90 and I-95, those flat, dead strips with their rumbling eighteen-wheelers, Roz was manic and excited with relief. She'd walked in, and there had been Jack, and all those closets, with their promise of a new start, a new chance for something good to happen. He'd even put fresh shelving paper down. Jesus, fresh shelving paper. What kind of man did such a thing? Her friend Constance Coffey was right; she was very, very lucky.

The first time Roz Mellow had ever heard the word "uxorious," she'd had to look it up in the dictionary. This was way back in 1961, when she was married to Paul, and someone they knew had accused him of being "uxorious," which had only made Paul laugh. "I couldn't agree more," Paul had said. Later that night, Roz had discreetly looked up the word in the dictionary.

"Excessively fond of one's wife," read the definition, and at first Roz was puzzled by this, for how could a husband be *too* loving? She was twenty-five then, and mostly she still liked the special place she occupied in Paul's life. When he made love to her she sometimes felt that he wanted to lap her up, to get every last bit he could out of her. This could be exhausting, but often it made her feel valuable, even relieved.

By the time Roz and Paul posed for the drawings that would accompany the text of *Pleasuring,* they had been together for almost fifteen years, and she had long grown accustomed to his unwavering attention. Though she found herself irritated by it at times, she had simply absorbed the fact of it and rarely thought about it. But the first day they were to pose for the drawings for the book, she became aware that Paul's absorption with her would be highlighted in front of the artist. Suddenly she became embarrassed; not just for herself, but also for Paul. During the nine months that she and Paul were his subjects, though, John Sunstein simply sat behind his easel, working and not commenting on the dynamics he witnessed between husband and wife. Roz found herself able to relax. She wanted Sunstein to admire her too, in a way, though he only offered the mildest, most generic of compliments, so different from Paul and how he continually hailed her. Roz loved her husband and was still sexually aroused by him, but she had once read a line in a book that she'd never forgotten: *"Women have sex so they can talk, and men talk so they can have sex."* Yes, she wanted to talk more than he did, and yes, he wanted to touch her body more than he wanted to talk. Paul was slightly obsessive and anxious, she realized, and he'd always approached sex with her with the kind of interest that men sometimes had in wines or stereo equipment or cars. How did they taste, sound, run? Which was the best one, and what was the best way to try it out?

One day she entered the white studio a few minutes before Paul did, for he was still trying to find a parking spot on the street. As Roz began to remove her clothes for the session, an exterminator suddenly walked out of the bathroom carrying his canister of poison, and John Sunstein leaped up and placed himself between the man and Roz. "I forgot he was here," John said. "I'm so sorry. We had a little cockroach situation."

Roz quickly slipped into her robe, but the exterminator seemed unfazed by her nudity. When he turned to leave, she and John saw that the words "We Zap 'Em" were stitched across the back of his jumpsuit, and for some obscure reason this cracked them up. They sat together and laughed, and when Paul showed up and wanted to know what was funny, neither of them could really explain it. You had to have been there, they said. Throughout the rest of the day, Roz thought about how chivalrous John Sunstein had seemed, as though he understood that the sight of her naked body was not something to take lightly, but not something to exclaim over mightily, either.

At the end of the nine months, after all the artwork was complete, Roz and Paul brought John a bottle of good champagne as a present and thanked him emotionally for his beautiful work. "I used to be so mortified when I came in here," Roz said to him as the three of them stood together drinking the champagne from the coffee mugs that Sunstein quickly had to wash in his kitchenette. "I thought I had no right to show myself like that," she went on. "But it's as though you gave me the right. You gave it to both me and Paul. So thank you." They lifted their mugs and Sunstein lightly, awkwardly hugged them, and that was the end. Their work was done.

As it happened, Roz and Paul met John Sunstein again several times over the next couple of years, first with the editor and the art director to discuss the book's layout and to make decisions about the inclusion or exclusion of particular drawings, and then, when the book appeared and quickly became such a freak success, Sunstein was occasionally interviewed along with them. Sometimes, if there was an article about the Mellows in a magazine, a sidebar would appear about the artist. Roz was always glad to get another glance at his shy face and pained smile, the slightly jagged part in his long hair. Day after day he had made himself invisible so that they could be more visible. One article said that he had gone back to drawing album covers now; the Kinks were interested, and his agent was in negotiations with Jefferson Starship.

"So, any more nudity in your future?" an interviewer asked.

"I hope so," John Sunstein had answered, laughing.

After that, there was no more contact, no more need for them to see him, and the continuing success of the book took Roz and Paul everywhere, kept them twinned and intertwined, with little time to imagine a world outside the sexual landscape they had created. Their children, busy with homework and one another in the house in Wontauket, grew and grew.

In early summer 1977, when a magazine asked for a few new drawings of the couple for a feature article, Roz and Paul returned to the studio. This time, Sunstein had a new studio apartment, located all the way downtown. In the distance stood the massive, four-year-old towers of the World Trade Center. Roz and Paul had been photographed on the observation deck a few months earlier, with the wind in their hair and Paul's arms wrapped around her. "Who's on top?" read the caption.

When they arrived to pose for him this time, Sunstein seemed different, more subdued than ever. He looked older too, Roz thought, for he'd cut his hair so that it only came down to his chin. His face was still shy and closed up. He had gotten very rich over the past two years from the book, though not nearly as rich as they had. Roz wondered what he spent his money on; surely not clothes. She wondered if he lived alone, and then she realized that in all the time of posing for him, she'd learned very little about him. She and Paul had never asked, and John had never offered. That was one of the side effects of continual and labor-intensive sex tableaus; they didn't allow for anything else. There was no world beyond the boundaries of the bed.

Today, Sunstein's bed awaited them. It was different from the one they previously used. "The sheets are clean; I just changed them this morning," he said. "But anyway, I'll draw the old bed. This is just a stand-in."

"Can I have a stand-in for myself?" Roz asked.

"Thanks a lot," Paul said, and he absently began to unbutton his clingy blue shirt. Chest hair sprang out as the buttons were opened. He was wearing striped briefs today, and she felt, looking at him critically, that success had rendered him well fed, that he had the appearance of someone who had been corrupted by too many interviews and audiences.

"Please," she said to Sunstein, "I'm serious. Couldn't you just use the other sketches of us as a starting point? Couldn't you imagine what we'd look like?"

"Yes," he said. "I could imagine it. But I don't think I could draw it. They're different things."

"Oh," she said, not really understanding the distinction.

"Roz, what's the problem?" Paul asked. "It's just John. Is it because you're so famous now, is that it? You feel different?"

"I don't know," she said.

Paul put his hands gently on her shoulders, rubbing lightly. Roz slowly undressed, full of dread, the way she'd felt the first time they'd posed for the artist, except back then she'd also felt a kind of excitement, while now she only felt ashamed. She lay upon the bed with Paul, and in this new shade of white light, subtly different from the one in the other studio, what they were doing seemed different. Or maybe she was different. Paul's hand cupped her breast, and she looked dispassionately at the sight: Still life with hand on breast.

What was it I wanted, again? she wondered. A long time ago she'd wanted Paul, and that was it; and then she'd gotten him and kept him. It had been exciting to know that she wouldn't have to live the stiff, walking-stick life her parents had led. Her marriage to Paul was a response to theirs, just the way all marriages are a response to those earlier ones, with corrections made in the flawed texts, only to be corrected again, and yet again, over time.

So Roz closed her eyes when posing in bed with her husband now, the way a baby imagines that, upon closing her eyes, no one else can see her. Paul's hand found Roz's breast and curved around it, accommodating to the shape, which had changed in the slightest way over these two years, the edges loosening, the tissue shifting, the formed sand pies giving way to something a little more gelatinous, though this was not yet apparent to the human eye, only the human hand. The husband's hand.

"All right," Roz said. "It's fine. We'll just do it, then. I don't want to make a big deal out of it."

"You know how to make a man feel good inside." Paul laughed.

But later, when they were done posing and Paul had stepped into the kitchenette to make a phone call about the lecture they were going to give tomorrow in Boston, Roz and John Sunstein were briefly alone. They were standing together, and she was dressed again. Roz had tucked her silk blouse into her skirt, zipped up her boots, and was now looking for a mirror so she could brush her hair.

"In there," said John, pointing to the bathroom.

She took out a hairbrush from her purse as she walked, and it wasn't until she was inside the small white bathroom that she saw he had followed her. She turned to him in puzzlement, her hairbrush raised reflexively, and Sunstein came very close in one swift movement and quietly said, "I love you, you know."

"Pardon?" she said, rendered so stupid so quickly.

"I love you," he said flatly, as if his punishment for saying it once was to have to say it immediately again.

She just gaped at him, completely defenseless against these

words that seemed almost another language, as though he'd said to her, *"Yb lff gruxtyl,"* and she needed a moment to translate.

"No," she said involuntarily, "you don't. You don't even know me."

But she saw that his face was so completely focused now, so full of feeling that she had to look away from him, and she heard him insist, "Yes I do." And of course, yes he did. All that time they'd posed for the book, he was right there, seeing how she operated, what excited her, what made her shy or amazed. He was there all that time, watching her, knowing her. "It's true," he went on. "And I'm in love with you. I had to say it."

"When?" she asked in a whisper. "When?" As though she were inquiring about two other people, as though this were separate from them and she was just curious.

"I don't know," he said. "Always. I'd come to work, and I'd sit there drawing you, looking at you, and I'd be really happy. I just had to tell you. I know you probably can't feel it too, but I had to say it once, so you'll always know. I won't bother you with it again."

She was like an appliance stirring to attention; she felt something move and heard its drone. *Oh,* this *feeling again,* she thought as it attached itself predictably to her abdomen. But it wasn't only arousal, or even exactly arousal. There was some other element, too, but it couldn't be corresponding to love, could it? How could it be, when he was just "John Sunstein," or just "the artist," or even just "the man behind the easel"? *Pay no attention to the man behind the easel.* And she hadn't paid attention, mostly, throughout the years since she'd first met him up until now, at this particular moment, though of course she'd admired him physically because he was young and unspoiled.

Here, then, was John Sunstein, out from the shadows, and his hand was on her face. She took his hand in her own and moved it to her mouth. Slowly, thoughtlessly, she kissed his fingertips and let her mouth go around them one at a time. *What are you doing?*

she asked herself, and she could only answer: *I have no idea, so don't ask again.*

He drew her close to him in one swoop, and the hairbrush flipped out of her hand, landing on the tiles with a clattering sound. It was as if, in the small silvery bathroom with the mirror right there to record their actions, she could see how much he was not her husband. His face was still so young; he was thirty now, to her forty-one. Here was a face that couldn't be hidden behind an easel and a sketchpad any longer. He was right in her line of vision, the way she'd been all those years in his.

John moved Roz deeper into the small room, and she leaned against the pocked glass of the shower stall, which shook on its metal track. She put his hand against her heart, and suddenly she was the one demanding and wanting, when moments earlier she had wanted nothing. We're so simple, we human animals, she thought; no, we're not animals, we're evolved race cars, and we go from zero to a hundred in no time at all, not caring about danger. We spring into action because an idea is planted in our heads by someone else, and then all of a sudden it seems like it had been our own idea all along, and so we take full credit for it.

In the recesses of the studio, Paul's voice lifted and they could hear him talking on the phone. Since he clearly wasn't yet using the wrapping-up cadences at the end of a phone call, John Sunstein took the opportunity to kiss Roz Mellow. The kiss was hard and deep but somehow also chaste, as if he wanted her to know that he wasn't only about sex, and that he would never see her as mainly a sex partner; yes, she would be that too, and both of them could imagine what it would be like to move this state of high excitement onto a bed; but no, he would not be like Paul, always saying *Look at you.* Or *Roz, try it this way.* John had seen everything; he knew what Roz looked like in orgasm, and at rest, and in tears. He knew it and he'd seen it and she would never have to prove anything to him. This, it seemed, was what he wanted her to know right now.

His body was narrower and much more hairless than Paul's, different in all ways. John hadn't sloughed off youth yet, even though he'd cut his hair. His jeans were low-slung; he was fluid and rangy. Roz, too, knew that she was different from the women John had been with. She was older, she had done things, she was a mother, she was responsible and reliable, and what a relief that might be to him. He was happiest in her company, sitting quietly and drawing this woman who lay on a bed in various poses that displayed her beauty, yes, but also her energy and her warmth, and, once in a while, her unhappiness. This young, mostly silent man was in love with her.

Paul was still talking on the telephone now. "Yeah, we're just about done here," she could hear him say. "We'll be out of here soon. . . ." And then his laughter, easy, so purely unaware.

"John," said Roz into his neck. He smelled like fruit, and she thought that he probably washed his hair with one of those shampoos her daughters used, meant to evoke a distant orchard visited in childhood, or in a dream. "I don't know what I'm doing," she said, "and I don't know what to do now."

"I know," he said. "We'll figure it out."

They stood in silence for a few seconds. "So have you figured it out?" she asked.

"Not yet," he said. Then he pulled back and looked at her. "Oh, I should tell you something," he said. "Nobody really calls me John. I mean, in business they all do. But usually I'm Jack."

So Jack's big boots sat on the newly clean closet floor twenty-six years later. His feet no longer fit into them; like most people, everything had gotten slightly larger with age. He was still slender and looked younger than he was and he was still intact, had remained himself, but he'd lost almost all of his beautiful boyish hair and that had changed his appearance completely. The boots in the closet were trappings of a younger persona, but Jack couldn't throw them out, and there they sat among Roz's wavy old wooden Dr. Scholl's sandals and some discolored high-top sneakers that had belonged to one or another of the children over the years.

In the first two weeks after Jack had kissed her in the summer of 1977, Roz had gone back to the city to see him several times, at first in a trance of trepidation and thrill. She and Jack went to bed and made love easily, affectionately. She liked his taste, the sweetness of his clean skin, the way he kissed. He put his hands on her, his head between her breasts, his finger on her clitoris, as if stirring a little pot. She was delirious, and then somehow calm. He knew when not to touch her, too, when to almost ignore her. She went with him to Pearl Paints, where he purchased new brushes, cans of fixative, and canvas by the yard. The store smelled so strongly of him that going there was erotic. They talked at a rapid pace, trading stories of her past and her marriage and his own past and his various relationships with women. Jack was Jewish, the son of a rabbi from Plainfield, New Jersey, and at her coaxing he brought her a snapshot of himself at his bar mitzvah. There he was with his hair as long as a girl's, his teeth encased in braces; behind him were a mother and father with their hands on his shoulders, urging their son into the future and manhood and eventually into an affair with a married woman much older than himself.

Every day, those first weeks, when Roz came to see Jack, she was not sure how long this could last. There were no plans, and she warned him of this. "I have been married for almost twenty years. I'm married. I have four children." As though being planted deeply into a life meant you could never uproot it. He didn't try to change her mind, but simply accepted what she said, while adding that he wanted to be with her, wanted to marry her, and all she had to do was say the word. His ardor was reliable, and unlike Paul, he didn't pour himself all over her. She was so grateful for Jack's *quiet*.

Being at home with Paul at night made her jump out of her

skin, but she endured it. One night in the den, Paul showed Roz a magazine ad for a record album. The cover art was a highly stylized drawing of the band. "Doesn't that look familiar?" he asked her.

"It must be Jack's," she said.

"Who?"

"John. John. Sunstein, I mean."

"Since when is he Jack?" asked Paul.

Despite herself, Roz stammered, her face aflame in this moment of having been caught. "He said his friends call him that," she said, and she thought: *Can I give myself away any more than this? Can I possibly be any more obvious?* Despite the intensity of Roz's response, Paul said nothing to her. But one afternoon the following week, when she told him she was going to the city to have drinks with her old friend and roommate Vivian, who was now a style writer for *Vogue,* Paul followed her. She took the new car into the city, a red high-end Volvo they'd recently purchased, and he drove the old one. Vivian's office was in the Condé Nast Building on Madison and 44th Street, but Roz headed downtown, and found parking on Greenwich Street. Later she learned that Paul double-parked out of her line of vision, seeing that he was *right* about her, and watched as she stood at the entrance of the artist's studio, where she pressed one of the row of crude metal buzzers, then waited. In a second she went inside the building, and the door clicked shut behind her. Paul stayed out on the street, sweltering. He punched the palm of his hand hard, smashing against it, and then he shook his hand in the air while it throbbed. For twenty minutes he stood on the street, and finally he went to the door and pressed the buzzer that his wife had so recently pressed.

"Yeah," Jack's voice said, all fuzzed over.

"It's Paul."

"Who?"

"Mellow? Paul Mellow?"

A long, meaningful, *oh Christ* pause. Then the buzzer rang and the door lock clicked its permission, and Paul trudged up the wide, sagging wooden steps, his poor cuckold's heart rising. By the time he reached the door of the studio, Jack Sunstein was standing there shirtless, and Roz, in a robe, was right behind him. She'd had no time to change into clothes. She was frantic, desperate, her skin pink and splotched; she could feel it even without looking in a mirror. She hadn't wanted to say anything to Paul yet, but here he was. If he hadn't come here, would she have ever told him? Would the affair have simply died off? She never found out, for here was Paul, blustering and falling apart in front of them.

"What are you doing?" he said to Roz.

"I'm sorry. I'm so sorry."

"All right," he said. "So I've seen it. Great. That's fine. Can you please come home now?"

She nodded to him, wordless, threw a look at Jack, and went to get her clothes. She and Paul drove their separate cars home, and it was a wonder neither of them crashed. Roz felt as though she were hyperventilating during much of the ride, and had to talk to herself to stay calm. Once inside the house, they fended off the children and disappeared upstairs into the bedroom. His questions to her were relentless, battering, justified. *"How long?"* he thundered. "The whole time? The whole time we were posing for him? You were screwing him *then*?"

"No, no, of course not," she said. "It's new. It's very, very new." *It's so new,* she could have said, *that I don't know what I'm doing, and I am simply improvising even as we speak.*

How often, he persisted, and when, how, why? *Why?* She was unable to answer, so he tried to. "You need to do this, you need to get it out of your system, and you want me not to make a big deal out of it, is it something like that? A midlife crisis?"

Paul was desperate and grasping. They sat on the brass bed; from somewhere up above them came a thump of bass and a shriek of music, a slamming door. The children were roaming, restless, ignorant of the drama taking place below them on the parents' floor, or maybe not so ignorant. Roz kept sighing throughout the conversation and looking down at her hands. "I'm in love," she finally told her husband, testing out the new, shocking words and feeling a small, proud, shameful thrill upon hearing them and realizing they were true.

Paul was so stricken by this that he began to clutch at his heart, his hand buried under his shirt, deep in the curls of his chest hair, Napoleonic, struggling for dignity and composure. "Oh no," he said in a soft voice. "Oh no."

"I know," she said. "I know. I'm sorry."

"Can't you just keep *fucking* him until you get tired of it?" he wailed. "It wouldn't be the end of the world. I'd live with it; we'd go through it, and that would be that. Everybody would come out okay in the end."

She was shocked to see him so desperate. "I didn't mean to do this," she said, and at this point, predictably, she began to cry. "I didn't mean it," she said, her face collapsing. "I didn't mean it, Paul. I didn't ask for it. It just happened, the way these things happen. There was no . . . premeditation on my part. There was no anything, if you want to know the truth."

"So then stop it," he said. "Just have your little thing, your affair with him, your fling, whatever it is, and then just stop it. Just come back home to me."

But she shook her head. "I can't. It's already started. It won't stop. I love him now."

"And what, that means you don't love *me*?"

She closed her eyes. "Of course I love you," she said carefully. "That doesn't just end. But it's different."

"How long has it been different?"

She thought of Paul on top of her, then below her, guiding her hands, arranging their two bodies, regarding her with a gaze that was relentless, and that he'd always thought she liked because she'd never told him she hadn't liked it. She thought of all the configurations their joined bodies had made, like two people using semaphore signals. They had let their bodies attach and detach, skin clinging to skin with suction-sounds, ingenious moisture and friction and texture, and for her to pull away now, after he'd done so much with her, after she'd let him touch and explore, and had gamely done it to him as well, after he'd looked and looked at her for so long a time, was an aberration, was a crime.

"I'm going out," Paul said. His face was hard now. His face and beard and mustache were wet with tears, but he was no longer crying. "And I'm taking the kids with me." He found his keys and started out of the room.

"What are you going to do?" she said, hurrying after him. "Are you saying something to them? Paul, don't say anything to them. I'm not ready for this!"

"Yes, well, I wasn't ready, either!" he called back to her, but he didn't stop. She was still shouting entreaties as he stood at the foot of the stairs that led up to the children's floor. He himself was now shouting to *them*: "Kids! Come down here! We're getting Carvel!" One by one they straggled down.

"Paul, don't go out," Roz begged. He looked at her now with an expression that she'd never seen, for it strove to be the opposite of the way he'd always looked at her. Hatred mixed with loss of interest. He was saying something to the children as he herded them down the stairs and out the door. Only Michael paused in the front hallway and looked up at his mother, but Paul ushered him outside into the car.

They were gone for more than an hour, and at first Roz sat on those front hall stairs with her head in her hands, and she assumed that she'd still be sitting there when they returned. But then she remembered that she could call Jack now. Her heart unexpectedly lifted. Roz Mellow left her perch on the stairs and went to call her lover.

The Mellow marriage lasted for one more week, choking and dying. Roz spoke to Jack each night on the telephone, and once Holly heard her and then Paul walked into the room too—and Roz found herself at the terrible center of her family's unhappiness. Something would have to be done, and done quickly. Roz and Paul sat all four children down the following Wednesday night. Michael attempted indifference; Holly was clearly stoned, her eyes boiled and red. She had been spending a lot of time at the railroad station, and sometimes at night in recent months Roz and Paul would drive by just to have a look, for this was the closest they could come to checking up on this wayward child, the way they used to do when she was young and lying in bed at night. Back then, they would come home from one of their days in the city and walk upstairs, going from room to room, checking on the children, but really, more importantly, supping freely of the pleasure of ownership, treasureship.

The two youngest ones were restless as they sat on the brown couch. Dashiell bounced up and down, as though the velvet were hot underneath his body. "Look, you know things haven't been very happy between Dad and me," Roz began. Paul didn't say a word. He didn't have anything to add; this was Roz's show, and he let her talk. He was numb and defeated, his face slack. The older children just sat sullenly, and Dashiell seemed to be humming to himself. Was he even *listening*? Only Claudia seemed affected by what Roz said.

"What?" Claudia said in response. "You're getting a divorce? Oh no, you can't. You can't. Ariel Spitzer's parents are divorced, and she says it's terrible!" Claudia wasn't jaded, Roz realized. Unlike the others, Claudia was still capable of shock and outright sorrow.

The Mellows separated two days later, a fact that was published in the newspaper and snidely referred to in print for months, and it was furiously discussed among all the people who knew them. Paul moved out of the house, renting a tiny place on the water in nearby Marburne, close enough to allow him to see the children every weekend. Slowly, over the following year, Roz allowed Jack Sunstein to come and visit her in Wontauket once a week. She didn't want him to live with her, to pretend to be a father. He wasn't their father; they already had a good one. She would keep Jack separate, just for herself. She would not be sexual with him in front of the children. She would just be a mother to them.

But the children knew about their mother's lover, and it drove them deeper into their own lives. They *knew*, and she knew of their knowledge, and no one ever said a thing, except for Paul, who in his despair and rage at suddenly losing his wife sometimes said inappropriate things to the younger children about their mother. Roz later heard that over a sloppy-joe dinner at Paul's rented house (the sloppy joe being his signature dish, his only dish) he had called her "a common whore," and then immediately burst into tears and said to Dashiell and Claudia, "I take that back. It isn't true. I don't know why I said it. Your mother is a wonderful woman." Over time he grew used to the separation, even though it had effectively ended their career as a couple. It ended the run they'd been on, the nearly two years of being known as "those Mellows." It was over, it was *over*, and Roz had caused it. Paul still couldn't understand why, and as the years went by, though he remarried twice, he could never figure out what that quiet, inarticulate artist possessed that he lacked, and he never could accept it. Sometimes Paul Mellow just shook his head, thinking about it.

In 1986, when Claudia graduated from high school and enrolled at Hampshire College, an experimental school in Massachusetts with its share of students like Claudia, who seemed eccentric or internal or even just a little lost, Roz put the house up for sale, and she closed the deal with the Chinese couple named Feng soon after. It was a sad time of continual activity, as all of the children except Holly came home to help their mother dismantle the past, each of them taking some of it into their own dormitory room or studio apartment. They all pored through the books from the den because Paul wanted none of them. To Roz's mild surprise, the children seemed to feel sentimental about items that she'd never thought they would. Michael, for instance, wanted *Diet for a Small Planet*, even though he was a real carnivore, and Dashiell asked for that oversize book about golden retrievers.

Roz put most of her belongings into storage when she finally went to live with Jack in the city. Two years later, when she was offered the tenure-track job at Skidmore, she took those things out of storage and was reunited with the life that had been packed away in boxes for so long. Now that earlier life partly filled the house in Saratoga Springs, but it had been meshed with her life with Jack. The closets here were crowded with life upon life: his old boots, her shoes, a daughter's rain poncho, a son's summer-camp flashlight, another son's ukulele, a former husband's umbrella, something whose provenance no one remembered anymore, and then something else, and something else too, and so many things that might have belonged as plausibly to one life as the other. Because the truth was that there were just so many ways you could spend your life; though the characters changed, and the rooms and the objects, if you had been married once you knew what it would be like to be married again. It involved being *next to*, being *near*, just the way that being in any family meant being *among*. You waded through slowly, and along the way things drifted past, and some of them you recognized, and a memory was sprung.

Roz knelt before the downstairs hall closet now. Here was a red plastic lunchbox from the Cenozoic era. Immediately she remembered that it had once belonged to Dashiell. *"The Six Million Dollar Man,"* it said on the front, and there was a crude picture of the hard face of its star, Lee Majors, scowling. How proud Dashiell had once been of this lunchbox, she thought, and she saw him carrying it to and from Bolander, his fingers curled around the handle. It was almost impossible to connect that boy with the man in the hospital bed—almost, but not quite, for the trajectory that any child made was free of angles and turns. It was one long curved line that led from there to here. You knew them then as best you could, and you still knew them now. They didn't even have to tell you much about their lives, they could keep it a secret because it wasn't your business anymore, but still, somehow, you knew.

She had left Dashiell with Tom in his apartment in Providence, left him there to carry on, to have visiting nurses stop by period-ically, to let the transplant continue to do its work inside him, his immune system to continue growing and returning, like a baby dinosaur stumbling out of its shell. He would be okay, his doctors had told her, and therefore, so would she. All right, there would be no reissue of the book. Michael had made no headway with Paul; none of them had. The book was dead; she'd have to accept it once and for all.

Fuck the book, Holly used to say. Yes, that was about right: *Fuck the book*.

Roz closed her eyes for a moment, and then she let them fly open, wanting to be surprised all over again at the way Jack had sifted through their things and ordered them while she was gone. She also wanted to look more closely at all the things they had gathered over time, or that had incidentally gathered around them. It seemed that Roz Mellow was looking at time itself now, which had somehow expanded so greatly that it had managed to fill every closet and room and hallway of this house.

Chapter Twelve

FATHER AND SON were going out on the town together. They were going because Dashiell had pulled through his transplant and would be all right, and because it was Michael's last night in Florida, and because they needed to drink jumbo Blue Floridians and eat fried things from plastic baskets, and grow tearful and sappy with relief, and talk, and talk, punctuating their conversation with occasional expressions of their manhood in ways that fathers and sons occasionally do, like a mutual inspection of automobiles.

Michael would leave in the morning, after what had turned out to be a fifty-four-day stay in Naples. He'd taken every vacation day and every personal day he'd ever had coming to him; he'd also called DDN and asked for a leave, and his superiors had granted it because they couldn't afford to lose such a gifted person in the long run, and they wanted him to do what made him happy. Still, product manager Rufus Webb had emailed Michael with frantic regularity over all these fifty-four days, and for a long time Michael had written back to him immediately. "THE TWINS

HAVE LANDED," Rufus had written on the day that the owners had arrived; he always typed in upper case, as though to convey the sense of emergency he felt. "I AM DEAD." To which Michael had responded, lower case, gently, "You are not dead. Relax."

Relax. This was a new idea. After the initial, ferocious withdrawal from the Endeva—the charging anxiety, the dizziness whenever Michael stood, the sweating that woke him at night in the guest room, and the strange *zhzhzhzh* sound he heard whenever he turned his head either to the right or the left—he started to detoxify, to come down. One morning, about two weeks into his stay, he realized that the drug was gone from his body. He would be going it alone now. No antidepressant, no help with his misery. No net. Just himself, alone, here in Florida. Being alone, unglazed, unprotected, was like lying naked in wet leaves. Not unpleasant, just very, very strange. *Feel the leaves,* he ordered himself. *Roll around in them.*

He telephoned Thea one night close to midnight because she liked to stay up late and he wanted to tell her about the wet leaves analogy, and also that he loved her. The telephone rang and rang, until finally the machine picked up. There was his own awful voice, sounding nasal and robotic, and Michael just hung up quickly without leaving a message. He thought about calling back the next night, just to see if she was there, but he decided that he really didn't want to. He remembered his father, bellowing like a moose in the house in Wontauket after Roz said she was leaving him. There was nothing worse than a man in pain. It was worse than a woman in pain, if only because it was so much louder. *Relax,* he told Rufus Webb, and perhaps for the first time in his forty-one years, it was a concept that Michael could comprehend. He wasn't cured of depression, not at all; his brain chemistry left him vulnerable to it, but for now he liked the idea of being on nothing.

So the twins had landed, and so what? After a while, Michael stopped replying to all the hysterical urgent chirps and squeaks of his PDA. There was one day when he actually ignored all his messages from Rufus, and then another day, and another. He wondered how he could bear to go back to work there, for though he liked the company and the fact that his work, astoundingly, seemed to do some good somewhere, whether it was Kenya or Chechnya or Appalachia, the idea of being in those muted offices among that same group of intelligent but anxious people threatened to bring back his despair with the force of the waterfall that poured its noisy, pointless heart out in the Strode Building lobby.

The trip to Florida was a failure, at least technically, though it didn't feel that way. He'd tried many times, but he hadn't been able to get his father to agree to let the publisher reissue *Pleasuring*. But he and Paul had been through so much here, what with Dashiell getting sick and having the transplant, and everyone worried to death about him. So now, at the end of the stay, Michael and his father would unwind and have something to celebrate.

Tomorrow morning, he'd be back on a plane bound for New York and Dimension D-Net and Thea Herlihy, whatever that might mean. His father would return to the condominium, where right now his wife Elise/Elisa was sitting in bed watching the nightly news and applying cracked-heel cream to her feet, the scent of peppermint infusing the bedroom like potpourri. Elise/Elisa would put fresh Wamsutta sheets on the bed in the guest room where Michael had slept for fifty-four nights, and there would not be another actual guest there for months, or even years. His father and stepmother would take another class in the Gathering Room; maybe they'd learn Italian, like many people did, stirred by the lilting syllables, the olive oil poured from a ceramic decanter, and the Annunciation paintings with their delicate crackage. A sense of calm, almost a loneliness, would steal over Paul, and there wasn't a thing that Michael could do about it, because he knew it would steal over him as well tomorrow morning as he headed home.

Michael felt a sense of dread at the thought of returning to his apartment, putting the key in the lock, entering the clean, high-polished place. "I don't know what I'm going home to," he told his father in the dark bar after one Blue Floridian, which was served in a glass the size of a dog's water bowl. Suddenly, the night before he was going home, he wanted to talk about this.

His father looked at him for a long time and then said, "Well, what are you afraid of?"

"That there's nothing there anymore. Work. My love life."

"Was it there before you left?"

"I'm not sure. And if it wasn't, then why wasn't it? DDN does authentically useful things, but I can't stay there. It lulls me."

"Florida," Paul sighed quietly, nodding.

"What's that?"

"Nothing," said his father. "Go on."

"Okay. I mean, as far as Thea goes, here's the story. I'll tell you the truth, and you must swear that you'll never, ever tell anyone, Dad, not even Elis—even your wife." He took a mouthful of his drink. "I couldn't *come*. I couldn't do it." He shook his head. "It was the fucking antidepressant I was on," he said, "and I know I never told you about that either. When I got here I was starting to get off it. That's why I seemed so wierd, remember? I wasn't doing well. And it was as if a message was being sent to me, telling me *not* to come. Because it wouldn't lead to anything, finally. It wouldn't become happiness."

Paul Mellow shook his head. "I'm sorry," he said. "It sounds like no fun at all."

"That's right," said Michael. "No fun."

"But the thing is," Paul went on, "*not* having problems is no guarantee of anything. Even though I never had any overwhelming sexual problem that I can think of, it didn't really matter in the end. Because in the end, your mother left me for Jack Sunstein."

Time for another drink, and fast. Paul formed his lips into a kiss-shape as he drank off the sea foam on the surface of the next Blue Floridian. "So that's really why you can't have the book reprinted?" asked Michael. "It all comes down to that?"

"Pretty much. What can I tell you? I'm not a very complex person. You kids are the complex ones."

Michael took another slurping drink from the dog bowl and thought of his father and mother when they were married. He remembered the way they had sat on the couch in the den together, sprawled out like children. Michael often thought of those beginning days, when his father had a proprietary quality regarding his mother, and it seemed so admirable, so affectionate, something to aspire to yourself. But what you really ought to aspire to, he thought now, was reciprocity. That was what he'd thought he'd had with Thea, though mutual absence of feeling apparently didn't count.

He thought of his siblings: Maybe Dashiell had found his version of balance over the years; certainly he'd seemed to be looking for it enough. And Claudia—she had been calling throughout Dashiell's hospital stay, and over the course of the very last call she'd happened to mention shyly that she'd "sort of gotten together" with that person she'd been emailing for a while. "You know, the one from the house," she added. "The one whose parents live there now."

"I know who you mean. Good for you," Michael had said magnanimously. It had always been so hard for his little sister to meet people, to get along on her own, and he was impressed that she'd actually followed her email flirtation into the actual world.

Were they complex, any of them? "Only Holly's complex," Michael said to his father.

"You mean because she took off?" Paul asked.

"No. I always thought so."

His father nodded in the melancholy manner of a man calculating his own personal failings. The image of Holly danced briefly between them, tiny as Tinkerbell, then leapt away.

Maybe, Michael thought, Holly was the only one he would have to worry about. It didn't seem likely that you could find contentment in your life when you were married to a man like that doctor-husband of hers. The one time Michael had met him, Marcus Leeming had seemed weird and elliptical. Michael couldn't imagine that much love existed between those two, and it was excruciating to try to imagine them sharing a dinner table, or, even worse, a bed.

One night, when Michael was twenty-two years old and had just moved to New York City after college, his telephone had rung in the dark railroad apartment he shared with two friends on Riverside Drive, and there came Holly's voice. "Hey," she'd said, and he'd been shocked, and even though he'd been reading deeply on the futon in his tiny, hammered-up-Sheetrock-wall bedroom, he'd thrown aside his book and snapped to attention.

Half an hour later, Holly was shaking when she came upstairs, and Michael's roommates regarded her with suspicion and interest. She was crying, talking about her failed love life, her general despair. Clearly she was high—the stink of pot was all over her, "a ropy smell," they'd been taught during drug films in junior high, as though everyone knew what burning rope would smell like. "Shhh," he'd said to his sister, for lack of much else to tell her, and he lent her a Princeton Ultimate Frisbee T-shirt to wear as a nightgown and gave her the mattress to sleep on. They faced each other in the darkness of his room, on different levels. There were no curtains on his window yet, but he'd tacked up a dark blue sheet that had once graced his bed in Wontauket, and the bedroom felt as though it were an aquarium.

"I hate myself," Holly said.

"Shh," Michael said. "You're okay, Holly. You don't think you are, but you really are."

"I haven't done anything with my life, Michael."

"I wasn't aware that it was over already."

"You know what I mean."

And all he could say again was "Shhh." She lay inches from him in his own Tide-with-booster-bleach-smelling shirt. Her hair was long, a little stringy, but still so golden, and her eyelashes had never lost their near-albino whiteness. Holly Mellow was then such a beautiful woman, age twenty-four, on her way to being ruined, and he couldn't stop her because he couldn't claim her. He had no rights to her, she would never be his.

Michael, in his drawstring pants, shirtless, rolled over and faced the wall. "Good night," he said. "I'll make you breakfast in the morning."

But she was gone before breakfast, and the next time he heard from her, an entire year had passed, and she had moved to Nevada.

He sipped the big Blue Floridian, now, that pond of alcohol that never seemed to drain. "So, what are you going to do, Michael?" his father suddenly asked, himself soft-headed and unfocused enough to jump into a conversation like this.

Michael shrugged. "What can I do?" he said. "I can go home and figure it all out. I'll have some conversations at work. I'll have a conversation with Thea. She's all wrapped up in her Dora play. We've talked, and she's written me, but I have no idea what she wants from me anymore."

"You know, I feel that way with Elise," said his father.

Once again, Michael missed the end of the last syllable in the sentence, wasn't sure whether his father had said *Elise* or *Elisa*; would he ever know his stepmother's name? It was far too late in the game to ask. "She sleeps a lot," Michael said carefully. "Is that the problem?"

Paul shook his head; it wasn't a yes or a no, and he closed his eyes, fighting tears. *Oh no, my father is going to cry*, Michael thought, and a kind of panic overcame him, for here would be an awkward moment in which he would have to reach out and pat the upper arm of his father, maybe pat his back too; he would do it with the gracelessness of a young father burping a new baby, wondering, Is this too hard? Too soft? Am I ineffectual? Will it be over soon?

But Paul Mellow didn't cry; like most men, he held himself

together, then he reached into the basket of fried mushroom caps, each one transformed into an object twice its original size once the breading had been applied, and he ate for sustenance. Michael would have liked to hear more, but at that moment three women approached the bar table with sharklike single-mindedness. *Eet eez deeficult to know when zee white shark she weel attack.* Michael had been the recipient of such women before, but never in the presence of his father, and not since he had been living with Thea, for he almost never went out to bars anymore.

The three women were all pretty in some historical way, channeling a past that had disappeared but was not forgotten; the 1980s, he thought, with those feathered and spiky hairdos, a bit of henna, and some mousse from a can whipping the whole thing up into a thorny crown, and then some dangly earrings that someone's friend might have made as a Christmas present. Of the three women, one of them hung back. She was the shyest, the most tentative, and the least pretty, and it was she who in this Darwinian moment did not last, but self-selected and was then sucked back into the room at large, sensing the inevitability of it all. She wound up at the CD jukebox, where she stood with a five-dollar bill, flipping at great length through the stiff metal pages of jukebox choices. This, Michael realized, was the bar equivalent of someone standing by a bookshelf at a noisy party, picking up a book, and starting to read it, actually pretending great interest in order to hide social awkwardness. He felt sorry for this woman, and he thought about going over there and talking to her, but he found that he was really drunk and couldn't quite get up, and so his burst of sympathy dissipated.

"We have a bet going," the blonder-headed of the remaining two said to Michael.

"Oh yeah?" he said, lifting his head slowly. "And what's that?"

"I bet," said the other one, whose hair was darker and whose entire look was sleeker and less trustworthy, "that you two are father and son. But my friend Sabina here says that's crazy, that you two are just friends, and that you really aren't all that far apart in age."

"Father and son?" said Paul, joining in. "That's ridiculous."

Michael regarded his father with surprise and new admiration. A look passed between them, like two glasses lifted and clanged together in a toast.

"I knew it," said Sabina. "Lindsey, you owe me a drink. That looks good. Is it a Collateral Damage? Because those are awesome."

"No. Blue Floridian," said Michael. The drink was actually sort of wretched, sweet and thin like Gatorade, but the sweetness seemed to try to hide rather than complement the alcohol. It didn't work, but still he drank it, as did all the people around him, and the cheerful young bartender kept taking a cocktail shaker and a strainer and pouring drink after drink into an endless supply of enormous glasses.

"So, do you both live around here?" Paul asked.

"No, we go to college up north. We're on winter break," said Lindsey. "But Sabina's mother has a condo here, right across the highway, and she lets us use it every year. We came down last winter, too, and it was really fun. The weather's so great, and sometimes I have to wonder why we live where we do, when life is so much easier down here."

Paul stood up then, and Michael saw that his father was drunk, even drunker than he was. Paul's head circled lightly, like that of a boxer in a cartoon. "We've got to go," he said. "It's late, I think."

"Actually, no, it's pretty early," said Lindsey. "And to be honest, you don't look like you should drive. Either of you. You both look pretty plastered. Do you guys want to come across the highway to the condo and hang out?"

Michael followed his father and the two women out the door of the ferny and mahoganous bar and into the dark balm of the night. They dodged traffic, they held hands with the women and skipped sloppily across the highway, obviously looking absurd, but feeling free, for the first time ever, of their father-and-son-ship.

This was a greater release for Paul than it was for him, Michael knew, but it was interesting to see the way his father, though quite drunk, seemed to improve under the gaze of these young and interested women. It would go nowhere, of course; both men were attached to other women, and these particular women were so absurdly and bruisingly *young*, but there was no harm in the suggestiveness of it all. No harm in sitting in their condo—which, as it turned out, was yellow and green and resembled nothing so much as a patio-furniture store. The condominium was a dead ringer for Paul's home in Laughing Woods, except this community was called Conch Haven, a name that made no sense, Michael thought, as though conches needed a haven, or that this was a "haven" for conch lovers. Neither image could be easily summoned, and he chalked it up to the general off-kilter quality of many things he'd found here in Florida.

Sabina put some music on, which Michael recognized as old Steely Dan, and he understood that this was in deference to the two men and their age. Michael was interested but anxious as he watched his father lean back against the couch and appear to be in danger of falling asleep, but when one of the women pulled a tightly rolled joint from a small makeup bag and lit it, Paul Mellow came fully awake, sitting up and leaning toward the direction of the smoke.

Michael himself almost never went anywhere near dope, though some of Thea's actor friends smoked sometimes when they came to the apartment to work on a scene. Michael would usually go into the bedroom and shut the door, listening to the muted sounds of people putting on accents and trying on emotions freely and then casting them off again moments later in peals of laughter.

Back when the Mellows lived together in the house, Michael knew that his parents sometimes got high, and he'd never liked it. They had written about it in their book, a fact that had only increased the scandal level among the disapproving. The drawings that accompanied the section on recreational drug use featured Paul and Roz with, if you looked closely, the vaguest bloodshot eyes, as though Sunstein had applied a faint pink wash to them. Paul's eyes were quickly turning that way now in real life, Michael saw. His father was drunk and would now be stoned, and Michael, whose drunkenness would abate, would have to drive them home tonight.

Someone brought out a store-bought chocolate icebox cake, and they all ate, not out of hunger but simply from the stoned desire to graze. *We ought to leave soon,* Michael thought when the entire thing had been demolished. There wasn't any danger of Elise/Elisa waking up, but Michael had to go to the airport first thing in the morning, and he was agitated. He knew that this could lead to no good.

"Paul," he said, using his father's name deliberately and archly, here in this place where a father and son were merely buddies and where an actual drink bet rested on the nature of their relationship. "We should go."

But his father wouldn't hear of it. He was listening to Steely Dan with the intensity he usually gave to jazz. At some point, Sabina, whose condo this was, sat down beside Paul and whispered something to him. He laughed and Michael looked away, and he was looking away still when the young woman led his father out the sliding glass doors of the house and into the gated garden. Michael was left sitting with Lindsey, and he shifted on the couch, sitting up straighter. His father had put him in a terrible position. His father, his married father, was off with this girl, this person who could easily have been one of his own children or even grand-children. *You cliché,* was what Michael thought, and his jaw felt stiff, so he massaged it with one hand, working his fingertips into the side of his face so deeply that it hurt.

"So," Lindsey said, "I guess they've gone outside."

"I guess so," Michael said.

"You don't look very happy to be here," she said, and then in that instant her eyes seemed pleading and urgent. "Is it that you were hoping for Sabina?" she asked with what struck him as touching bravery.

"What? No, of course not. I wasn't hoping for anything. I'm going back to New York tomorrow morning."

"That's all right," she said softly. "It's what I figured. God knows I'm not looking for a relationship. I *have* a relationship already," she said, and she rolled her eyes. Michael imagined a sweet but dim stoner boyfriend up in college, keeping her warm for the winter.

"You want to see the bedroom?" she asked, and Michael nodded as dumbly as that boyfriend would have, and then, without even thinking about whether or not he ought to do this, he followed Lindsey into a room that held two pushed-together beds with floral coverlets. She closed the flimsy door behind him and then turned around, her hands against the door, and smiled broadly.

"You're a cute one," she said. "Come here."

He obediently moved toward her, and as soon as they kissed he had an erection that pushed against his pants. No one had ever said he was cute before. Handsome, yes. Serious. Soulful. Brainy, brilliant, Phi Beta Kappa, "summa," moody, tense, gloomy, achieving, good-looking. But never, ever cute.

They climbed onto the twin beds and Lindsey lay on top of him, a lightweight presence like a summer blanket. She nuzzled his neck and kept saying "Mmmm," running her hands with their curved, manicured nails up and down the length of his chest. He realized that he didn't really like the way she smelled, that her perfume was something generic, the kind of scent that hit you when you opened a magazine. But even though he didn't like Lindsey's smell, he was still excited. It was female; he thought of her breasts and the wet depth between her legs. He realized that if he wasn't careful, he was going to come right now. He'd shoot out right into his boxers, something he hadn't done since he was a pubescent boy.

He could come now; he knew he could. He was convinced of it. There would be no hesitation with this orgasm, but it would simply fly out of him without even thinking. No worries, no nothing.

"Mmm," she kept saying, and he remembered his own "Nnng" sound during lovemaking with Thea, and he was aware that he was making absolutely no noise at all right now. He could have an orgasm if he wanted to, yes he could, but he had very little interest in having one. Michael shifted on the bed, wondering what to do, when suddenly the solution was thrust upon him accidentally, for as he moved slightly, the two pushed-together beds separated like seas parting, and as the gap widened, Michael and the college student on top of him fell to the carpet below with a soft and painless thud.

"Oh my God," Lindsey said, laughing. "I can't believe this."

They lay in the dark alley between the beds, and it took some maneuvering to get up again, to stand and get their balance and then to push the beds back together again. Lindsey kept laughing and laughing, and Michael did too. But when she tried to pull him down again and start things all over, he shook his head lightly no.

"You know, I think I'm too high for this," he explained, for he felt it was essential that he not hurt her feelings. All he could think about, though, was the orgasm that could have been—the one that was there, waiting for its moment—and the ones that would happen in the future, with Thea maybe, or perhaps with someone else, with another woman, with many of them. He saw himself at his laptop, watching Internet porn and getting off on it and not feeling that he'd committed some act of soul murder. He saw himself corresponding electronically on a personals page with a woman he hadn't met, and even though he ought not to like this image—even though it was against everything that his parents' book had once been about, against love and comfort and intimacy, and all that was long lost—he wanted it for himself, for the possibilities were endless.

"No problem," Lindsey said, containing whatever degree of hurt she actually felt, and she and Michael self-consciously made their way out of the bedroom and back into the living room just in time for the front door of the condo to open and the third friend to enter, the one who'd been left behind to look through the CD jukebox.

This friend took a few steps into the living room, staggered slightly, leaned against a wall for support, and then said, "I can't believe you guys just *ditched* me like that."

"I feel bad about it," said Lindsey.

"Well, you should," said her friend, and then without warning she vomited in a neat blue arc onto the carpet. "Oh Jesus, I'm so sorry," she said immediately, and she began to weep. "I never do anything right."

"It's okay, it's okay," Lindsey said, and the two women came together for an embrace. Michael was desperate to leave, and he was grateful when soon enough the sliding glass doors to the garden slid open and Paul walked back inside, Sabina following a few feet behind him. Something had happened, he could see from his father's slightly shaken expression, and Michael knew that in all likelihood, his father would tell him. But now it was time to go.

They thanked the women for their hospitality, their pot, the cake, the kindness they'd shown them. They wished them a pleasant remainder of winter break and best of luck in all their studies. This had been such a mistake, such a misfire, a weird evening spent in the company of two people they would never see again, which in itself was enough to give Michael a case of existential melancholia if he let it, but he wasn't about to let it.

"Dad," he said as he trundled his father into the front seat of the car beside him, "what happened to you?"

The ride home was long, and with the window down and his head leaning out, Paul Mellow felt like a dog being taken somewhere by his master, unaware of their destination, and unconcerned. There had been a great sense of relief merely in handing over the keys to his son and stretching out in the passenger seat, a place he had almost never sat before. This was Elise's seat. It had been pushed so far forward that it had to be moved back for him. Now it was his seat, and he was letting his son drive him along the highway, and what had happened this evening was something that he would have to talk about, but did not want to, at least not with Michael.

"I need to sleep it off," he told his son, and then he closed his eyes with his head tilted out the open window and the wind roving through his hair, the conversation with that girl Sabina still inside him like a song.

He and Sabina had talked about his life down here in Florida, and about the adult ed courses he was taking at the condo, which then led her to tell him about being a Sociology major in college up north, and how she wasn't sure what she could possibly do with that degree, but she enjoyed the classes so much that she didn't want to worry about the rest of her life just yet.

"That's a good philosophy," he said, with a certain natural avuncularity that he was unable to suppress. And then, innocently and politely, he asked her where she went to college.

"Skidmore," she said, her voice cheerful and maybe proud, and he felt himself seize up inside.

Did every road in the world lead to Roz? Was that really possible? Why did this happen, why must he be chased by her for the remainder of his life on earth? But no, of course, even as he asked this perfectly sweet girl Sabina if she had studied with Professor Mellow in the Psych department, he knew what the answer would be, and he knew that he had brought this on himself. Roz was not chasing him at all; he was doing the chasing, and that had always been the case.

But he wasn't prepared for the delight in Sabina's reply to his question, when she turned to him with bright eyes and said, "Oh, I can't believe it. She's my adviser." And she explained that even though Professor Mellow wasn't *in* the Sociology department "per se," Sabina had taken three of her psychology classes and had made a special request to be her advisee. "She's such a wonderful teacher," Sabina went on. "Really cares about the students. And I see her all the time in town with her husband, that younger guy who's kind of bald. Do you know him? They're always holding hands. They look so happy together. I've never seen my parents like that. How do you know Professor Mellow again?"

This information was revealed in a long unbroken sheet, and Paul reared back and immediately composed himself, saying inside: *I will betray no emotion.* But all he could think about was that Roz and Jack looked happy together in town, and he felt a completely senseless swell of rage. He turned away from the young woman slightly and put his hands around the sides of a clay pot that was filled with some variety of bright tropical flowering plant.

"She's an old friend," was all he offered.

Oh, she was his old friend, she was. Roz Mellow, his beloved, the woman with whom he had done everything. He thought about the day they had come up with "Electric Forgiveness." And later on, re-creating it in the studio, lying on that enormous, blindingly white bed whose sheets were changed daily and that gave a continual impression of sun-burst, gleeful sex, Paul and Roz had carefully arranged themselves the way they had done at home in their own brass bed.

"It's like Twister," she said to him as they tried to get into position.

"What?"

"The game Twister. That our kids play."

"Yes, you're right," he'd said. Left hand red. Right foot green. They interlocked carefully and studiously. He had an erection then; he'd never failed to have one throughout the entire creation of the book. There it was, full, curving, and he slowly and nervously entered his wife according to the plan that they had written themselves.

"Wait, slow down," she'd said, laughing a little. "I might fall over."

"I won't let you," he'd said. "I'd never let you."

In his corner, behind the oversize easel, the artist sat with pen and ink at the ready. Paul moved against Roz, amazed and relieved that they hadn't toppled over after all. At the time, poor old Electric Forgiveness had seemed inspired, with its implied, hot shades of psychedelia, its hint at something from an altered consciousness, one that could be brought on not through a tab of blotter acid on the tongue but through the stroking of skin, the arrangement of forms, the wreathing and suspension of your aging selves, the triumph over death that this certainly was, for without the willingness to *engage* in difficult, precarious ways, without the bargain struck between you and another person, there was really nothing much left in life to be all that excited about. After all, you'd read the great books already in college, at a time when the mind was open, baby-bird-beak-wide, and you'd listened again and again to the depths of Mahler, and now the rest of life awaited. You still had a body, and it could still do things, perhaps not with the same relentless, no-return vigor it once possessed, but here it was for the long run and still it had to run and run, and if you left it to idle, it would be your loss, and it could never be recovered, never.

To think he might be in bed with Roz again was an idea that Paul hadn't had in ages, but it wouldn't happen; she had unwrapped her legs from around him, unwrapped her arms, moved out of the way. He couldn't remember the very last time they had made love, but he was sure that he hadn't known it would be the last time. If only he could go back to that salty neck-skin, the heft of breasts— *and yes, Roz, they* were *sagging*, Paul thought; *I lied a little when I said they weren't*—and the scribble of reddish pubic hair that he had parted with his fingers so many times, which he had loved because it was hers, it belonged to her, was part of the ridiculous and fragile ornament of human beauty.

"Are you okay?" Sabina the college student asked him.

"What? Oh yes, yes, I'm fine."

He returned from that faraway bed to this strange and unfamiliar garden with this woman he did not know, and when he looked at her now, taking in a few bare details—the slight constellation of acne on her forehead, her spiky moussified hair, the tiny tattoo of a bluebird on her wrist—he instinctively backed away and said, "You know, I have to go." She was so young, and he had no business here, and he could taste the individual components of cake in his mouth—the granulated sugar, the butter, the egg, the white flour, even the cream of tartar—each one articulated by the marijuana he'd smoked.

Then he was in the car again with Michael, his head leaning out into the wind, and his thoughts were of lost Roz, lost only to him and to no one else. She was his grown children's mother forever, and she was Jack's wife, but she was nothing to Paul. There was no overlap anymore. As the car went fast over dark roads, Paul remembered the night he'd first found out that his wife was in love with the artist whom they knew then as John. Paul had been wild, practically foaming at the mouth, and he'd gathered the kids up and said he wanted to take them out for Carvel. No one was hungry, no one wanted to go, but still he herded them into the car and drove sixty, seventy, eighty miles an hour along the turnpike.

"Oh we're the Mellows," he roared. "Your mother's got a fellow . . ." No one said anything, but he was aware of Michael sitting in the passenger seat and studying him. "We're not the Rinzlers," Paul went on, "'cause we'd be . . . Pinzlers!" Then he couldn't sing anymore, because he was crying. Briefly, he'd imagined cracking that green Volvo station wagon up, driving it into a wall—no, better yet, into the slanted glass façade of Carvel itself, killing himself and all four children, as if to say to his wife: *Look at us. Just look at us.*

But of course he could never harm his children, his babies. He was immediately ashamed that the thought had even been allowed to flit through the curves and ridges of his brain. Michael, self-important at age fifteen, had sat beside him in the front seat, and Paul was an endless loop of despair. "We're just going for a drive, kids," he'd said. "We're just going to drive and drive until I run out of gas."

"You're not serious, Dad," Michael said.

"No, I'm not serious. I'm just joking. I'm a real joker. Tell your mother what a joker I am. How hilarious. Maybe then she'll come to her senses."

"Are we getting the ice cream or not?" Claudia called out from somewhere in back.

"Of course, honey, of course." He pulled the car into the Carvel parking lot, handing the children a bloom of bills and sending them out. Holly shot him a furious look, but off she went. Only Michael stayed behind. "Aren't you getting something?" he asked his son.

Michael ignored the question and just said, "What are you doing, Dad?"

"Nothing," he said. "Nothing, I guess. Nothing that's going to work." He sighed and nodded in the direction of Carvel, where three of his children stood clustered under the light, giving their orders to a woman whose head poked through the sliding window. "Go get yourself something. Get me something too."

The drive back to the house was quiet, thoughtful, much slower, as all of them ate their cones. Paul fell asleep that night on the couch with the headphones on, Gustav Mahler soothing him to sleep.

He'd been brooding over Roz for more than twenty-five years now, brooding and muttering: The way she'd once loved him. The way she no longer did. The fact that she'd fallen out of love with him. The fact that she'd fallen in love with someone else. The fact that she used to crack her knuckles in bed. The fact that she had put on weight over time. The fact that she existed. The fact that she existed without him. Paul imagined her traversing a leafy upstate New York campus with that husband of hers, the two of them with their arms linked, talking about dinner, or, worse yet, about *sex*, maybe even reminiscing about the first time they had gone to bed together. Paul closed his eyes and tried to put on an overlay, a superior image of Roz and himself above the one of Roz and Jack, but the image wouldn't take; it flew off, would not be smoothed down where it didn't belong.

How, he wondered suddenly, had Elise put up with him these last seven years? How had she tolerated being married to a man who was so internally involved with his ex-wife that he spent a great deal of his day thinking of ways to profess his indifference to her? Keeping *Pleasuring* out of print forever was the least he could do, for she needed the money and she needed the attention again. Roz had always loved attention, even back at the very beginning, when she was his misbegotten psychoanalytic patient. She would lie on the couch in his office and arrange her skirt around her in a girlish manner that she had to have known would be arousing to him. And she would talk about her childhood and tell her dreamy sexual stories, and it was as though there were a spotlight on her and she craved it, and she never wanted to give it up. Maybe she was disappointed to leave analysis and be his lover. Maybe he should have held back. *Of course* he should have held back, but he'd had no control over that back then; he was weak. Sex made your cranium soft and porous, open to the anticipation of experience. In the beginning with Elise, he'd felt it was possible to be attentive to her and to stop thinking about Roz. Sex was good, and when Elise turned to him in bed sometimes, her breasts were warm through the thin skin of her nightgown. Afterward, she would often cling to him and say, "Paul, that was just great."

Her voice indicated that she meant it. So did her eyes. She was a compassionate person, but needful, too. Both sides had been in balance, at least until he came into her life. He had never hidden his ongoing preoccupation with Roz, and as time passed, Elise simply gave in to it, and the degree of her need for him was tempered by a newer desire for sleep. He saw that he had done this to her; that she wasn't a narcoleptic, that she wasn't in the thrall of her red-rice pillow, that she wasn't a zombie. God, he was such a narcissist, such a baby, and still she had stayed married to him. It was almost miraculous.

Three days a week, Elise drove to the nearby town of Corliss and worked as a clinical social worker, attending to families that had been torn up and demoralized by drugs and poverty and mental illness. She sat in their apartments with her casebook open and she spoke to them in English or in Spanish. She worked for these people as hard as anyone could, and sometimes she changed their lives.

Occasionally in the evening Elise would tell Paul about a case she had worked on that day. They were illegal immigrants from Cuba, perhaps; the father had lost his job at the Hormel processing plant, the younger child had cystic fibrosis, and the older child, a teenager, was breaking into homes and stealing stereo equipment. How could this immigrant family survive in this country where none but the best, the top, the richest, the most blessed, could even manage to scrape by? Elise had been known to secretly slip money to her families; a little cash here and there for diapers or milk or even just for movie tickets.

Paul was well aware of her goodness; it had attracted him to her when they'd first met seven and a half years earlier at a cocktail party in New York. "Do you know Elise Brandau?" their mutual friend had asked, a woman from the old days who had taught sex education to kids in a variety of terrible public schools, and who had been the subject of a PBS documentary.

"No, I don't," Paul had said, and Elise Brandau had smiled at him with genuine affection. She was extremely pretty in the slightly self-deflecting way that women in the helping professions sometimes were. She wore a calf-length cowgirl skirt, a soft scarf, and a slight, almost accidental touch of makeup. Her rhinoplasty registered with him, and he imagined the previous, less perfect version of her; he saw a bookish though not brilliant younger person with a slightly large nose that she sometimes pressed one finger against when she was thinking, as though trying to push the bump on the bridge back down. The newer, older self, without the bump, was probably less interesting-looking, but also probably felt more relaxed and perceived herself as more attractive to men. And men *were* often attracted to sameness, he well knew. Paul wanted, in that one moment, to let her see that he wasn't one of those men; he would have loved her even without the nose job. But all he could do was shake her hand and make eye contact and imagine what she looked like under all those flowing clothes.

He found out merely three nights later, when he took Elise Brandau out for a steak dinner and then to bed. After the meat and the wine and the perfectly exciting bout of sex, she told him about being widowed young, and he told her about his two marriages, working backward in time so that he could say just a little about wife number two, Elisa. Then he slowed down slightly to lavish a lot of anecdotal space on Roz, as he always did.

"We were very much in love," he said. Maybe not a great opening gambit when at that very moment you're in bed with someone else, although at least, he thought, it would show that you are a man who is capable of being in love.

"So why did your first marriage end?" Elise Brandau asked, her voice soft but curious, the way it must sound when she asked a client: *Why do you want to regain custody of your children?* Or *Cuántas veces a la semana fuma "crack cocaine"?*

"Why?" he said, and he felt a sudden, terrible, physical memory of the end of his marriage to Roz, and he covered it with a strange little sniveling laugh, one that he'd perfected over the years when asked this very question. "Only one reason," he said. "Because she fell in love with someone else."

"Oh. Oh. I'm sorry," Elise said, and then she did something that surprised him: She rolled over on top of him and stirred him into arousal again. He thought for a while that this would help him get over Roz in a way that wife number two Elisa hadn't been able to do. Elisa had actually made him more absorbed in the drama of Roz because she herself was so inadequate that her flaws set Roz's attributes into relief.

But Elise Brandau's sympathy was genuine. When they were done making love again—and he had to assume that she was impressed at his ability to perform so quickly after the first time, and at his age, too—she asked him more about himself. He couldn't believe his good luck, that this woman was willing to listen, was perfectly *happy* to listen to the story that he so desperately wanted to tell. And though her good listenership could have been used in dozens of other ways over time, could have been used to speak about his marriage to *her*, his hopes and his disappointments, it hadn't been. Nor had he tried to find the flip side of it, either, the side of her that wanted to talk and talk and tell him about herself. Okay, his first wife Roz had been singular. You could not compare her with anyone else. But so what? So what, so what, *so what*?

There at home in unit 3A in Laughing Woods lay his wife Elise, his third wife, yes, but his wife nonetheless. Seven years ago on a Friday she had gotten all dressed up in a violet crushed-velvet dress and matching handbag and married him in a civil ceremony in front of a few friends, and then they'd gone out to lunch, and then it seemed he'd promptly forgotten he'd married her, that they were a couple. He couldn't tolerate being alone. Loneliness swept across him and rattled the windows. He would have been in a state of perpetual terror without Elise, and instead he had remained in a state of perpetual distraction.

Riding along the highway with his son driving, feeling inert and out of commission, Paul was prostrate with regret. He was a *hub* of regret, a switchboard lighting up in hundreds of bright and urgent little lights, each one a moment that he could have kicked himself over, he had been so stupid.

Roz was gone and that was that. He regretted what he had done and what she had done, but it was dead and over. Elisa was gone, too, was barely regretted by virtue of having been barely remembered. But *Elise* was still there, fast asleep in the home they shared, and that he had chosen to share with her. So maybe it hadn't been for the right reasons; that day in New York City when they'd been introduced, he hadn't thought ahead, or even thought back to his history of mistakes and regret, or informed her of this unfortunate history. *I loved the first one too much*, he could have told her. *And*

I'm afraid my love is all used up now. She'd trusted his interest and his smile and his kindness and his beard—that beard, which women seemed to go for because it seemed to signify a kind of sensitivity, a closeness to the earth or something. You got away with murder if you had a beard. He'd always been kind to women. He'd never raised his voice to them—except to Roz at the end, but that had been different. When your wife says she's leaving you, that she's in love with someone else, then you're entitled to raise your voice, to let it paper entire rooms.

"Are we almost there?" Paul asked his son now, bringing his head back inside the car. He had lost track of where they were.

Michael turned slightly toward him. "You've got clown hair, Dad," he said.

"The wind," said Paul.

"Yeah. Why don't you keep your head inside. We've got about ten minutes more. You okay over there?"

"I'll be fine," Paul said, and he flipped down the mirror that his wife often used to look at herself when they went out somewhere. He'd never sat in the passenger seat before, and he had certainly never used this mirror. It had a small light on it, and in the darkness of the car at night he could only see the barest outline of himself, but it was enough. Paul Mellow watched himself smoothing down the loose tangle of gray hair that ringed his head and that, he was sure, only advertised his aging maleness, the inevitable intertwining of his vanity and his mortality.

In the morning Michael would leave. Good luck to both of them, as they sallied forth toward their women, like knights riding great distances to return to their Ladies. Good luck to them, for you never knew how you would be received until you actually arrived. Oh, he would miss his son so much; he would brood about it after driving him to the airport. He would miss him and call him more often from now on, just as he would call the other ones, too, making a point to force himself outside that fortress of his own battered and solipsistic self. He would *haunt* them: the steady, newly recovering Dashiell and his dreadful politics; Claudia, who was still a baby as far as he could see; even Holly, who did not need him at all, or at least who said she did not, but it was too bad, she'd get him anyway. He would claim just to want to hear her voice on the telephone. Don't worry, he would reassure her, nothing would be required of her, no trips back east to be with him or with any of them.

How did children raised in the same family end up so different from one another? How did they end up *away* from one another? But he wouldn't weep on the telephone to his children, for they would only find him pathetic, a sex-educated Willy Loman figure, and he never, ever wanted to be seen like that.

They thought he was bitter, and this he regretted too. He would not be bitter; that was over. "All right," he said suddenly. "If it really means so much to you."

"What?" said Michael. "If what does?"

"The book," said his father, suddenly animated, sloughing off his windblown, drunken self, the sad old Arthur Miller character that he was afraid he'd already become. "I'll do the book," Paul went on. "The reissue. Whatever. If it will make you happy."

"You serious here?" Michael asked, and Paul said he was.

"I see," Michael said. "So the secret was for me to stop discussing it entirely with you. To let it be forgotten. Is that it?"

"No," said Paul. "That's not it."

"Well, whatever the reason, it's great," said Michael. "It really is. Thanks. Thanks a lot, Dad."

"Don't worry about it," Paul said, and he waved a hand vaguely in his son's direction. Michael pulled the car into the garage, and the attendant seemed to raise his eyebrows slightly when he saw that Paul had not been driving his own car, but he said nothing. It was almost midnight; the garage here did not see much late-night action.

Inside the condo, the lights were all off except for the pale bulb they kept on at night for the little plants in the kitchen window, as though to soothe them like sleeping babies. Michael said good night to his father and retreated down the hall into the guest room, and soon Paul could hear the thump of shoe-removal, followed by the rush of water in the bathroom pipes. Deeper into the condo Paul walked, across the thick, sound-absorptive carpet that seemed specifically designed for sheepish late-night returns. When he opened the door of his bedroom, there was no light whatsoever. Elise slept in a bedroom that was little more than a black, airless cave.

He made his way across the room in the shaft of light that he'd brought in with him from the hallway. On the left side of the bed his wife lay on her back, her hair loose around her head, one breast slightly rising up out of her nightgown, and a round, white knob of a shoulder showing above the edge of the quilt. The pillow cradled Elise's head; even in the dim room he could see the slightly raised, individuated bumps of grain beneath the surface.

His wife slept on, unaware of his presence in the room, and Paul Mellow stood over her for a moment, hesitating, before he sat down on the edge of the bed, touched her arm, and said, "Please wake up."

Chapter Thirteen

PICTURE THEM, then, these two estranged lovers of a certain age, connected through four children who were themselves getting on in years. Picture the man and woman in their best clothes and a light layer of pancake makeup, sitting at a round table separated by a neutral, ageless television host who had sat with them thirty years earlier at this very same table, or one just like it. Back then, during the first interview on *Ken London's Night Owl*, it had seemed as though the host was doing his best to keep the husband from taking the wife and bolting from the table to go off and make love in a nest of television cables and klieg lights. The camera had come in tight upon them then, picking up facial cues, marital exchanges, and holding for an extended moment on Paul Mellow's face as he gazed in devotion upon his wife, then shifting away from Paul and over toward Roz, holding on her blue eyes, her mouth, then moving slightly downward to honor the cleft between her breasts.

But now the camera was far more chaste and withholding, giving this aging but still attractive couple their dignity, and somehow attempting to ignore the suggestion of animus that existed between them, even here in the dead air of the television studio. It was late on a cold Monday afternoon, not a time for night owls at all, but the show would not appear until later in the week, at 11:30 P.M. Just outside the television studio on the corner of West 58th Street and Tenth Avenue, the street was lit with cars and taxi-hopefuls with arms swaying upward like people drowning, but here inside the studio, all was calm. An estranged husband and wife found a way to sit at the same table, and the host found a way to ask them questions, and the cameras were readied and pointed.

The tech crew looked too young for their jobs, even collegiate, and if any of them had ever heard of the original version of *Pleasuring: One Couple's Journey to Fulfillment*, they certainly didn't show it. None of the young men in work shirts and headphones looked at all interested in the discussion about sex that was taking place in front of them. There, propped up on the table, was the thirtieth-anniversary edition of the book, with its newly pink cover and its stylized bed, the sheets a subtle shade of rose now, the whole thing weighing a full quarter-pound more than the 1975 version.

It was amazing to many of the people who knew them that the Mellows had managed to make their way here, to this moment, Roz perhaps a touch smug about her triumph but careful not to display it, and Paul overtly ambivalent and abashed but still here, and the fact that they were here was what mattered. Over the past two years, overseen by Jennifer Wing, the book had been revised and produced, and an entirely new set of illustrations had been created by a young artist named Harris Glynn from Phoenix, Arizona, who could draw perfect reproductions of the human form, but whose abiding passion was for Japanese *animé*, which perhaps explained the slightly wide-eyed, startled look his depicted lovers had no matter what act they were performing.

So here they were, Paul and Roz, answering the fairly intelligent questions of Ken London, whose 1970s Prince Valiant haircut and velour blazers had been exchanged for a more softened gray head and conservative black suit that gave him a kind of sudden, late-life gravitas that no one could have expected. The questions he asked were about the old version of the book, the new version of the book, about how sex had changed over the decades, what with the country's fixation on Internet porn and Internet dating, and violent, graphic movies and video games. He asked how they thought love had changed over these years since Paul and Roz had lain in a bed together and showed other people how it could be done.

Seeing them together after all this time, it was possible that someone watching the show who had watched them on it thirty years earlier might still wish for a sudden on-air sea change. Might wish for an ex-husband to turn to his ex-wife and tell her he loved her, and for her to say she still loved him, and for the two of them to push a bewildered Ken London away, to shoot him back in his swivel chair with one swift shove, and for them to move together, chairs colliding as they found each other's mouth, unclipping the raisin-size microphones on their collars so that the audience could not hear the things they had wanted to say to each other all these years, and hadn't been able to say until now.

Everyone wanted closure; that was the reached-for word. Closure was asked for during the penalty phase in the trials of child-murderers, closure was required when the new memorial staggered up at Ground Zero. There was closure in every divorce, but a new fissure opened up each time too, a pit that could never be filled in, for just look at those bitter or mournful faces, years later. Just look at those grown-up children, lumbering around the earth with their freight of sadness and detachment. What babies they were, those children, all children, for no one forgets the early pleasure of seeing two parents together; no one forgets the incomprehensible safety and symmetry of that image. For children, parents aren't a two-backed beast but instead an enormous two-winged bird, each parent represented by a wing, with all the children riding on top, holding on by grabbing tufts of feathers, letting themselves be carried aloft.

Inevitably Ken London did ask Roz and Paul about the breakup of their marriage, lowering his voice to a slightly mournful timbre, as though the divorce still stung, which it did in a way, and both of them spoke, using the answers that they'd agreed upon during several telephone calls in recent weeks. It was important, they had decided, that their responses be coordinated, that one of them did not seem more wounded or angry or lost than the other. If they were going to go through with the interviews, the articles, the lecture tour redux, then they needed to seem, if not exactly together, then at least equal. So now, when Ken London asked Paul Mellow how he had felt when his wife fell in love with the illustrator of the original book, he knew what to say.

"It was very painful," Paul said.

"A painful time," Roz echoed before his sentence had been finished.

They turned slightly toward each other, and in a moment that had not been prepared in advance, he nodded. She wasn't sure what the nod was supposed to mean, though, and she was flustered. But she had no time to figure it out, for London was now on to something else. He was asking about "the landscape of AIDS," and how it had changed the nature of sex in America.

"I think I can speak to that," Paul said, and Roz sank back slightly in her leather swivel chair, letting him take the lead.

Afterward, the publisher gave them a dinner at an expensive midtown steakhouse called Plank's, and the Mellows and their entire party arranged themselves at two long tables that were soon lit with little candles and covered in bread baskets and enormous menus and plates of beef. It was *sumptuous*, that was the word, Roz thought, when she looked down the long airstrip of a table and saw her family there, or at least most of them. Claudia sat with her fiancé David Gupta, a man she would marry in May. When you have a shy child, Roz thought, you are forever worrying: Will anyone ever see her for her special qualities? Will the world ever get to know her? Will she be trampled on by the louder ones, the ones who ask for what they want, and inevitably get it?

But last year Claudia had stood up in the front of a screening room at a small film festival in Philadelphia, in which *K Through 6* had been entered into competition, and she'd spoken to the seventy-five people in the audience about what it had been like to shoot her first film. No one had mocked her, and everyone had applauded when the screening was through. To Claudia's own astonishment, the film hadn't been half bad. David had watched all the footage with her as she was working on it, encouraging her to keep it serious and funny, and never condescending. She felt that she'd salvaged it in the editing room; maybe that was where her real strengths lay. She was taking a class in film editing and hoped to be able to get a job on someone else's film when it was over; her instructor had given her the name of an independent filmmaker who might be willing to hire her. Beside her now, David Gupta, the intellectual property lawyer, was whispering something into Claudia's ear, and she was laughing.

Three of the four Mellow children had made it their business to convene in New York City for the week of activities surrounding the reissue of the book. There had been a vague possibility that Holly might even fly in from L.A., but after a long, mumbled phone conversation with Claudia two days before, during which Holly had said yes, all right, she would agree to come to New York for this fucking celebration, she would come to see her parents in their last blaze of glory, she freaked out and in the end did not come. "I'm sorry, I'm sorry," Holly had said to her sister that very morning on the telephone from California. "I can't get on that plane. I can't do it."

"Why?" said Claudia. "You're afraid it'll be blown up or something?"

"Of course not," said Holly. "I just can't deal with it, okay? With the family."

"Fine," said Claudia. "So don't come." And then there was

silence, and a slightly wet sound that might have been a nose being blown, and Claudia added in a quieter voice, "Just tell me why. Why can't you deal with it and we can? What makes you so different from us?"

"I don't know," said her sister. "I really don't know. It just worked out that way, I guess. I have a very toxic reaction to this family. I get too upset; I think about things. I can't deal with it. Anyway, tell them hi."

So Claudia had actually walked up to her mother and father separately before the taping, and said, "Hi," paused, and added pointedly, "That's from Holly."

Holly, who could not deal with it, was an apparition here. Michael had always been considered the one who understood her, but this was a by-default role, and his understanding was incomplete. It seemed that most families had one person who "could not deal," to some degree. Holly, he knew, had found an early pleasure in Adam Selig's hands and mouth, and then in damp, poorly rolled joints, and from there it had been a long collapse. As a teenaged girl Holly had told him long stories about life and her future and what she and Adam did together. Her brother had listened, impressed and jealous and riveted by who she was. His love for Holly had burned on and on, and then it just didn't burn anymore, giving out with no warning.

It was difficult to hold two simultaneous images of Holly: one young and smirking and excited, the other older, harder, lost, furious. She continued on as the missing person in the family, though it packed less punch now. What power her absence had anymore was forlorn and almost touching. Imagine: still, after all this time, being so angry at your parents for their foibles and their selfishness and for letting you think that love could gratify a person forever. Imagine: caring so much that you had to stay away from the family forever. Holly's isolation was almost religious.

Michael was eating a sixteen-ounce Wagyu steak tonight, one of the highest-priced cuts on the menu. He had been living in Wise

County, Appalachia, for the better part of a year, working in the field for DDN. It had been his choice to be transferred, and he'd gone right to the twins with his plea, aggravating his closer superiors. But the twins had been receptive and had arranged for Michael to supervise the operations out of an office in an old, modest building in the town of Norton, Virginia. He had an assistant and a secretary, but some of his day was spent out of the office and in local schools, shelters, and churches. He found himself wading into real poverty, with its empty, abandoned factories and entire dead-eyed families sitting on broken couches that had been dumped onto weedy front lawns. Michael drove around, taking notes, being overwhelmed, but somehow he found it far better than being back at DDN, though of course there were times when his loneliness was spectacular. He had an apartment that took up the top floor of an old frame house in Norton; he had a car; he had few friends. He'd gotten to know a couple of faculty members from the nearby university, and they'd invited him into their homes for dinner, eager for new companionship, new blood, but mostly he came home and ate by himself. Because he was working on a hunger initiative, he could not bring himself to cook meals that seemed too elaborate or vulgar. He'd go to the local Kroger and buy hamburger meat and a sad head of lettuce. Occasionally he'd buy a sack of brown rice and some cheese and lentils, and when he got home he'd pull out *Diet for a Small Planet*, that relic from his family's shelf, that book that had been pressed up against his parents' book year after year, and from its crisp, discolored pages he would create a vegetarian meal for himself, potentially unsatisfying but somehow creative. He'd eat his steaming mass of dinner in front of the computer screen, instant-messaging Claudia or Dashiell, feeling almost as though he were sitting across from them at a dinner table. At night he'd lie in bed and listen to old Pink Floyd CDs and think with astonishment: *What have I done? I am living in Appalachia.*

But really, he hadn't done anything all that shocking, for he'd held on to his apartment in New York, and he returned there about once a month for meetings. Sometimes, during one of his trips to New York, he would get involved with a woman, though nothing serious. He didn't know how long he would continue to live and work out in the field, but there was some talk that he might get to go to Kenya for a while in the spring.

Two years earlier, after Michael had returned home from his trip to Florida, he had found, to his modest surprise, that his girl-friend Thea Herlihy no longer loved him, and that instead she loved the former television actress Anne Freling. They fought in the obligatory way, and he was wounded but not mortally. Thea moved out not long after his return and moved in with Anne Freling at once. The Dora play, *Hysterical Girl*, opened to respectful reviews, but Michael did not go see it. The play closed after a brief but noble run. The two women still lived together, and occasion-ally Thea emailed him a few innocuous lines. She'd asked him to stop by their Gramercy Park apartment when he was in town, though he had no desire to do so. Claudia told him she'd seen a picture of Anne and Thea in a gossip column in the *New York Post*. The two women had been shopping at an outdoor greenmarket, and the caption referred to "former *Classic 6*-er" Anne Freling and her "lady friend." He liked that description of Thea, for it seemed to capture some of her aloofness: She was a lady, and a friend, and she'd never been all that loving to him. She was cur-rently playing Peter Pan in front of child audiences. That was a good role for her, Michael thought, the eternal androgyne; it was as though she thought that leaving him could allow her to fly any-where she wanted. How could she possibly love the self-absorbed Anne Freling? *That* was where she wanted to fly?

But anybody's choice of lover was always mystifying: why one appealed and another did not—why a flavor tasted good when another one was repellent. Why, right now in this restaurant with his family, Michael Mellow wanted nothing more than to push his knife into the flesh of a sixteen-ounce Wagyu steak from Japan and feel how easily and deeply it went in, and how sad he felt each time he had to actually chew and swallow the soft meat, losing one more moment of the joy that was found in eating it. There was no Wagyu in Appalachia.

After dinner he'd leave the restaurant and head east, going to a bar on Second Avenue called, paradoxically, Smoky's; by law no smoke had blown through these New York establishments in years. It was a young-professionals kind of place, with men in shirtsleeves and women in the snappy, tight outfits of young lawyers and marketing executives. A year earlier, during one of his trips to New York, Michael had met a woman named Lucy Sherkow at this bar. She was an assistant DA, ten years younger than he was, and they'd had some drinks and talked and then gone home to her loft in Noho. The sex was easy, playful, and with the Endeva long purged from his system he'd ejaculated without worrying about it. He'd almost wished he could call up Thea at Anne's place, and say to her, "Hey, guess what I just did," as if, even now, she would be interested.

Recently, on another visit to the city, Michael had been to see the pharmacologist Snell again. His depression was waving feelers at the edge of his vision, and he was slightly alarmed by it, fearing that it would encroach upon his life and make it unbearable. "But I'm hesitant to go back on anything again," he told Snell.

"I understand," the pharmacologist said. "Many of these drugs have sexual side effects."

"It almost seems to me," Michael had said, "that in order to neuter the depression, you have to neuter yourself."

"That can unfortunately be the case. We've had luck with a few of the more recent SSRIs, though like most of them they take a while to build up in your bloodstream. But there's a new drug," Snell offered. "It addresses these concerns. Doesn't seem to interfere with sex, and it's unusually quick to take effect."

The drug was called Relīzon, another strange, futuristic name, and this time, after Michael began to take it, there were no egregious side effects. He had an orgasm on the occasions when he went to New York and slept with Lucy Sherkow, or other women. He could come easily, thoughtlessly, even though he was on an antidepressant, and even though he wasn't in love. As though love had anything to do with it. When Michael was young and had looked across a room at his sister Holly, he'd seen the way her own eyes were often looking elsewhere, on to the next thing, and the next. Love was a food chain, a desperate gobble, a grab.

"How's that Wagyu?" Jack Sunstein asked him, and Michael let Jack taste it, passing him the plate in the din of the crowded table.

Jack was a floater here tonight. His feeling of disappointment or even anger at not being asked to illustrate the new edition of the book was something he tried not to talk about, and which he'd been able to accept over the months. Just as, tonight, he was able to accept that for this brief period of time his wife belonged to her first husband again. They sat side by side, those sex Mellows, and both Jack and Paul's wife Elise knew enough to give those two plenty of room, to let the reissue of the book and its attendant reunion happen in all its nostalgia and discomfort. In the years since the family had lived in Wontauket, their ranks had shrunk and then swelled. Almost everyone here was paired off, as if there would be dancing. Except for Michael, no one had wanted to come alone tonight. When you were with your family—your "family of origin," people called it—you needed someone from your new life, your replacement life, to provide sustenance and comfort. You could not make it alone. Jack was alone, but not really. Across the table, he saw his wife smile and touch her children's hands and arms, and laugh at something that Jennifer Wing had said.

Later, Jack knew that he and Roz would sit on the king-size bed in their Helmsley-monolith hotel room, and they would undress and talk about everything that had happened tonight, everything that had been said at the restaurant.

"So how was I on the show?" Roz would want to know, and Jack would tell her that she had been beautiful and intelligent, and that it had gone wonderfully. What he would not tell her was the fact that he had stopped listening in the middle of the taping. He hadn't been planning on it, but before he knew it he was thinking of something else and had lost the thread of the conversation. It was probably hostile that he hadn't listened all the way through. But there was just so much he could take. For always that earlier marriage was calling from the back of the room, and always its companion text was on the coffee table, a handbook for all the ways a man and a woman could express their love.

Jack Sunstein knew he could never keep up with how Paul and Roz had loved each other and had had sex all over creation; he himself had never been one of those restless, perpetually horny satyrs who women seemed to go for, but who ultimately made the women unhappy and kept them desperate to be alone for a while. He'd been into women, always, but in a more modulated way. And now he and Roz were older, slower, and their sexual life had simmered down over the years. How sad that this had happened, but he knew it happened to all couples; one by one they succumbed, unless they worked at it. And if they *worked* at it, that meant that they had already succumbed. When Paul and Roz began talking to the TV show host about the sexual climate of the 1970s and how they had come together in it and lain down on a white bed, Roz's kind and somewhat passive second husband had felt a primitive anger developing in him, and he knew that he could either force himself to keep it down by maybe drinking a lot at the steakhouse after the taping, or else he could simply stop listening.

So as his wife continued to talk, and he heard the lovely, soft scrape of her voice accompanied by the deep complement of Paul's voice, Jack started thinking about something else: a project he was going to begin on Monday, a CD cover for a New Wave band from the early '80s that was trying to make a respectable comeback.

They were all there at dinner, Claudia and David and Michael and Dashiell and Tom and Jack and Elise, she who sat on Jack's other side, buttering her bread with such an intense degree of attention to something inanimate that it seemed almost autistic. "How are you doing there?" Jack asked, turning to her out of kindness.

Elise looked uncertain and anxious here in the big meat cavern in which they all sat. In Florida she was a social worker, he remembered, but he knew nothing more about her and therefore had no idea of what to say to her.

"I'm okay, thanks," she said. And then she added, "I think you and I should order a couple of really stiff drinks."

Jack laughed in surprise. "Yes," he said. "Yes, we really should." He raised a hand for the waiter and got them two Ketel One martinis. Elise seemed pleased that he understood what she had meant, and that her remark had not been met by puzzlement and silence.

"Thank you," Elise Brandau-Mellow said when the drinks came. They lifted their glasses and touched them together.

"To marriage," Jack said.

"To marriage," said Elise, though each of them really meant *To the end of marriage.* For those other marriages had had to disintegrate in order for theirs to exist. These two spouses who wanted to be the last ones—the only ones from now on—drank from their martini glasses, and then, after a moment passed and it wouldn't seem too rude to the other person, they discreetly looked across the table to see what their husband and wife were doing, and what they were saying to each other.

What Paul and Roz were saying was this:

"Is everyone having a good time, do you think?" Paul asked.

"I think so," said Roz. "Look at Claudia. She's so in love. I could cry."

"You can't cry at this dinner," Paul said. "Jennifer went to all this trouble. And anyway, people would just assume that we were being overly nostalgic."

"Well, this whole thing does require a certain degree of nostalgia," Roz said.

"A certain degree, okay," Paul agreed. He kept looking up and down the table. "Dashiell looks pretty good. He and Tom keep in shape. I gather they have access to the gym at Brown or something."

"Is he eating anything over there?" asked Roz. "I haven't seen him pick up his fork."

"Who, Dash? Of course he is." But Paul couldn't really see whether or not Dashiell had eaten anything. His son was sitting at the far end of the table, and there was food on his plate, but it might have been left there untouched. After the transplant two years earlier, the disease had soon transformed into non-Hodgkin's lymphoma, and had been treated successfully with a second transplant. Dashiell had recovered fully, and though he was well, his appearance was perhaps permanently sculptural and elegant, *homosexual,* Paul thought, though he wouldn't have said that out loud. He knew that for all his own sexual openness, his own understanding of two men in bed together would always be willfully incomplete. He was still a little squeamish about the matter. Dashiell and Tom did not want to lie down with women; they didn't want the taste and smell and texture and meaning of women against their bodies. But far more alien to Paul was the idea that Dashiell and Tom somehow agreed with the stringent, coldhearted beliefs of the Republican party. They stood behind those wild tax cuts, the bullying defense policies, and all else, but surely, as they stood there, they had to wince a little, didn't they? Robert Wyman, U.S. senator from Rhode Island, was planning a presidential run in 2008, Dashiell had said a few months ago, and he and Tom were certain to be high up in the campaign.

Paul looked across the table at his younger son in candlelight and took in the bones of his head, the crispness of his collar, the way his arm brushed against the arm of his lover, but strayed no farther. They were careful, those two, slightly stiff and courtly. Tom and Dashiell were talking to Claudia and David Gupta and Jennifer Wing; everyone seemed to be having a very good time.

Paul felt suddenly tired, and he wanted to go back to the hotel room right now. Elise would be happy to leave when he left; she wasn't the kind of person to stay on alone at a party. Even down in Naples, when they attended a reception following a poetry reading in the Gathering Room, she would stay very close to him as he circled the room, meeting the people he met, saying good-bye when he did. You would think, from observing them in those moments, that their marriage was as close as any couple's could be, and that they stayed together because they made each other happier than anyone else could. *Oh, I wish that could be true,* Paul thought, and he hoped there was still a chance that it might *become* true. Over the past two years his wife slept significantly less, and they took more walks together and played Scrabble competitively, tried some new things in bed (old things to Paul, but new to them as a couple), and who knew what might happen? There was time.

After coffee and cheesecake were served at the table, and enough fat had been packed into the arteries of the Mellow family to stop all of them at once in their tracks forever, they retrieved their coats and stood in the vestibule, saying their good nights. Always there was an awkward moment at the end of an evening; how much better it would be, Dashiell thought, if you just plunged your arms into your sleeves and grabbed your lover's hand and rushed headfirst into the night without having to linger, or say pleasantries, or make things worse. This wasn't really good-bye, for everyone would be together in the city for the rest of the weekend. Roz and Paul were giving a talk at the 92nd Street Y tomorrow afternoon, doing a signing at a midtown bookstore, and sitting for several print interviews over the next couple of days. The family would meet and re-meet. It wasn't good-bye at all.

"Good night, Mom," Dashiell said, and his mother took the opportunity to step forward and kiss his cheek hard. She still wore the makeup from the television taping and so did Paul, rendering them both slightly theatrical, like two old troupers coming together for a benefit performance of some chestnut of a play.

"Good night, my dear," she said, and then she turned to Tom and kissed him too, with equal effusiveness. "See you both tomorrow. Is the hotel all right? You asked for a smoke-free floor?"

"It's fine, totally fine," said Tom, whose life was often spent in hotels, as he shadowed the senator around the Northeast. Often Tom brought Dashiell gifts from hotel rooms: jars of macadamia nuts sealed like crypts, little bottles of Johnnie Walker, pens that read "The Centurion" or "The Inn on Castle Park." When Dashiell wrote political speeches, he still wrote them out by hand, so the pens were useful. But he hadn't written much lately.

Claudia and David Gupta and Michael all had their coats on now, and David was even putting on earmuffs—God, who at that age wore earmuffs?—so Dashiell had to speak to them all quickly and casually, but somehow effectively. "Listen," he said to his brother and his sister and her fiancé, moving them slightly away from the sets of parents. "You want to get a drink before we all split up?"

Claudia and David looked at each other and shrugged, and Michael checked his watch and then said something that sounded like, "Well, okay, I guess," and then the Mellow children said the rest of their good-byes to the parents, and left in a cluster.

"Look," said Paul to Elise and Roz, who by sheer chance were standing beside each other, the two women winding long, beautiful scarves around their necks and peering into the mirror in the dark red vestibule for one final glance at themselves, making that sucked-in face that women always made. "The children are all going somewhere together now. I love that, don't you?"

"Yes," said Roz. "It's like they've got their own society."

"'The Soul selects Her own Society,'" Elise recited quietly.

"What?" said her husband.

"It's a line from a poem."

"Emily Dickinson," Roz put in. "I always liked it too." And the two women smiled at each other now in the mirror.

But out on the street, the children and their partners walked in a loose pack, Michael and David slightly annoyed that Dashiell had suggested this, both of the men feeling full of food and wishing they could simply say good-bye now, like they were supposed to. But no, for some reason they couldn't. *All right,* Michael thought, *one quick drink.* With Dashiell in the lead, they followed him into a dim and narrow sports bar on the corner, where television sets were tuned to the game du jour, and heterosexual men sat with chicken wings in hand and heads upturned. What an unlikely place for Dashiell to want to be, Michael thought, but he said nothing. Briefly, he thought about Lucy Sherkow, the woman he'd called on his cell phone from the restaurant, and who would be waiting for him now in another bar, one much more appealing than this one, but she would have to keep waiting a little longer. He fervently hoped she wouldn't leave before he got there.

The five of them sat at a booth in the front, away from the television sets, and no one wanted to drink any more alcohol, so they all just ordered waters or Diet Cokes, and the talk was subdued for a moment, until Dashiell began to speak.

"I had to ask you to come here," he said, "because I didn't want to say any of this in front of Mom or Dad. I didn't want them to know. Not now. Not ever, if I can help it, but I don't think I can."

Tom took his hand at that moment, and Michael first thought, *Are Dashiell and Tom having a wedding?* But within an instant he realized this was not the case at all, and his stomach swung violently.

"The cancer came back," Dashiell said. "It's everywhere. The second transplant stopped being successful. The remission's over."

They were all silent for the brief knockout, seeing stars. Then Michael said, "What? But you said this time it worked for good, and that was supposed to be that. End of story."

"It can sometimes happen this way," Tom said. "It's very unpredictable."

"So they can do a third transplant, right?" asked Claudia in a voice that threatened to break at any second.

Dashiell shook his head. "No," he said, and he worked to sound level and steady. "Apparently I won't respond to it. The disease is too aggressive now. I could get more chemotherapy if I want, Dr. Balakian said, but only to get some more time. Not much more, anyway. Five or six months, he estimates, and we discussed it, and I decided it wasn't really worth it. Quality of life, and all that." He paused for a moment, then added, oddly, "If anyone asks you if it was AIDS, I want you to know that you can tell them anything you like. I've decided that I really don't care."

"Five or six months," said Claudia. "Oh no, oh no," and she began crying so hard that David Gupta looked around the table helplessly, as if trying to find guidance about how to handle a woman in this state. No one could help him, so he just threw an arm around her shoulders and kept her close.

Are you sure? they all kept asking. *Are you sure?* Dashiell and Tom individually and patiently said yes, they were certain, this was the way it was, there was nothing to do about it.

"Dash, do you feel very bad, physically?" Michael asked, and Dashiell told them no, he was mostly pretty tired, but it wasn't terrible, he could still get up in the morning, and he'd been able to come to New York, after all. It was the strangest thing: He hadn't even known he had relapsed at first, he explained. He'd gone to the dermatologist because of a rash on his chest, just a pink pinprick spattering, and he'd assumed he would be given a tube of cortisone cream and sent on his way, like everyone else in the world. But the dermatologist, who knew Dashiell's medical history, had been troubled by the aggressiveness of the rash and wanted to run some tests. Two days later, the blood told the story of the disease, which was swarming, overrunning the body, and would soon be winding it down.

Michael began crying almost immediately after Claudia, and then Dash followed, and Tom too. David's mouth was pulled into a tight line, and though he was stunned and aching he didn't feel he had to cry. It wouldn't do any good, he knew. He held on to

Claudia and rubbed her back, kissed her hair. Michael, in tears, removed his eyeglasses and put them on the table beside the Cokes and waters and Gupta's earmuffs. The waiter, who was about to ask if they wanted anything else, suddenly hung back, startled by the scene.

"Oh shit. Oh fuck. I hate this, I just hate it," Claudia said repeatedly. "I hate it so much." And then, finally, she asked her brother, "Dash, what can we do for you?" Her voice was so thick it was almost impossible to hear, but Dashiell leaned across the table and took her hand. *Nothing* was the real answer, but he just shook his head and shrugged and didn't know what to say. "I love you, Dash; I love you so much," Claudia went on. "We all just love you, we do." And she blew her nose into a green cocktail napkin and said, suddenly, "Remember the day we first read the book? And then I rode you around the kitchen like you were a horse?"

"Yes," Dashiell said, nodding. "We went around and around on the floor." He turned to Michael then, and asked him, "Why did you make us look at the book, anyway? We were so young. It could have warped us."

"It did warp us," said Claudia.

"Because I'd already looked at it," Michael said. "And I didn't want to be alone with it."

"Someone has to tell Holly," Dashiell said. "Claudia, you should tell her. She and I basically have no relationship."

Claudia nodded glumly and blew her nose. Sure, why not, she could tell Holly; this whole situation was so terrible that nothing could make it either better or worse. She could tell Holly and it wouldn't matter. Who knew what her sister would say, or think, or do, whether she had any genuine feelings inside her anymore, or whether they'd all been burned out over the years by the corrosiveness of nonstop drug consumption, and then replaced by feelings for a husband and a baby who was now not such a baby anymore, but who none of them had met more than twice.

"What about your parents?" David Gupta suddenly asked, he

who hadn't said a word until this moment. "You're really not going to tell them?" There was silence for a moment; each of them pictured their poor parents, and they froze in a tableau of guilt.

The parents were right now walking along West 57th Street, had in fact moments earlier gone right past the bar where the children sat, not realizing they were all inside. Paul and Elise and Roz and Jack were in a foursome, like two long-married couples out on the town for the evening, taking a stroll after dinner, checking the sky and seeing its strange lightness. It was supposed to snow tonight, Jack had heard on the radio. The sky had that nearly-snow look about it, a pale purplish color, and the wind seemed to be pausing, as if waiting for something to happen.

Roz fretted about how she'd looked on television and whether she could bear to watch herself later that week on *Night Owl*. Yes was the answer, of course she could, but she needed to pose the question, even to herself.

Paul thought about the moment when he'd nodded at Roz during the show, and how surprised she'd been at the brief acknowledgment that, yes, it had been painful to lose her, but he had managed. It had been a long time since he'd had a chance to surprise her, even so slightly.

Elise thought about sleep, and then stopped herself, thinking: *No, think of something else.*

Jack thought about how he used to draw Roz for hours at the studio, back in the beginning, and would then put Paul into the drawing only at the very end, with haste. He thought about the piece of Wagyu steak he'd tried tonight, and how delicious it had been, and he wondered whether such steak was available up in Saratoga Springs.

As the two couples said good night on the corner of 57th Street and Fifth Avenue, going off in different directions toward their separate hotels for the night, the snow, the first of the season, came down lightly at first, then harder. It was covering their hair and shoulders within seconds, though the temperature did not feel very cold. Paul gathered Elise against him; Roz took Jack's arm and then turned him toward her and kissed him, already tasting snow.

They thought briefly of their children, as all parents do, picturing a scene of laughter and drinking and jokes with cultural references that neither Roz nor Paul would understand, for references had changed, and jokes had changed, and after a certain age it was just impossible to keep up, and then after a while you didn't want to try, but left the new references to the newer people and simply kept thinking about the old references, the names from past decades that still rang inside you.

It was as though, on this first night of snow in New York City, the Mellow family came to life one more time, like an antique wind-up clown toy that's been sitting untouched and still for decades, only, for no reason at all, to suddenly have a shift in some internal workings and to spontaneously make noise, the clown's cymbals clapping together in a fever of brief and inexplicable activity.

"Let's go to bed," Paul said to Elise, with feeling.

"You know, I can't wait to get into bed," Roz said to Jack, and she yawned for an extended moment, and the two couples kept walking, one heading east, the other heading west, as the snow came down harder.

In the sports bar, men roared at a football play, and the crying group sitting at the front booth leaned in closer, as if trying to become one organism. *What about your parents?* David Gupta had asked.

"I'm going to have to tell them sometime," Dashiell said. "But not now. Not this weekend. Not this week. Not while all of this is happening to them."

For his parents were as mortal as he was, he wanted to say, and this was their moment, and in a sense they were back in a bed, and there was no end to the things their two bodies could do together. Leave them there, Dashiell thought. Leave them in the bed. Close the door and let them enjoy what remains for them, because the body is temporary, and of course his parents had always known that, urgently touching each other as though they had very little time, knowing that one day they wouldn't touch each other ever again.

Which was something every couple knew about, and the future heartbreak was briefly revealed, then by necessity it was banished from the conscious mind. But they all saw it, if only for a second:

Claudia and David Gupta did; and so did David's parents Vikram and Preethi; Roz and Jack; Paul and Elise; Holly and her husband Marcus; Ken London and his wife Helene; the Rinzlers from down the street in Wontauket; the kindergarten teacher Doreen Pernak and Russell Corcoran, the AV specialist at the school; Jennifer Wing and her boyfriend Corey Xu; the waiter at the sports bar and his partner Lowell; Warren Keyes and his wife Margaret; Senator Wyman and his wife-in-name-only Susan; the Dibbler twins and their various good-time women; L. Thomas Slocum and his fourth wife Maureen; Ricky Lukins and a closeted young male movie star; Thea Herlihy and Anne Freling; Dr. Ham Kleeman and his boyfriend Douglas; "Hojo" Westborn and his drug-addicted wife Nona; Trish Leggett and her lobbyist husband Todd; the man and woman at the next table in the restaurant tonight who were holding hands in the candlelight; the teenaged lovers who walked the Skidmore campus at dawn; the grand-parents of one of those teenagers, lying together in a house in Maine; the men and women, and women and women, and men and men who were about to meet one another for the first time through a chat room, an online ad, at a dinner party, an antiwar march, the Motor Vehicles Bureau, a bus stop, by accident, by chance, and deliberately and stunningly let themselves fall.

Roz and Paul Mellow were briefly together again tonight after a long absence from each other, though they alone were well past the slightest possibility of shared heartbreak. They were immune to it now, and felt fortified by the idea of their invulnerability to this particular human disorder. There they were, speaking eloquently to

various interviewers about love, and sex, and the capacity for intimacy, and the subtle and less subtle shifts that took place over time
and across broad cultural landscapes. There they were signing
copies of the brand-new, good-looking, and up-to-date edition of
their book, sharing a table at dinner, even sharing an imaginary
bed, one with a brass headboard that reared back against a wall
again and again, as if tapping out a code that no one else could ever
decipher.

Much later that night, Claudia Mellow and David Gupta tried to
find a comfortable position in which to sleep, but the bed in her
apartment on East 7th Street wasn't really meant for two people.
The routine was that David took the train up from Philadelphia to
visit her on alternate weekends, and just last week they had put a
down payment on a place in Prospect Heights, Brooklyn, while he
applied for jobs at various medium-size law firms here in New
York. The apartment would be ready in time for the wedding,
which was to be held in the Puck Building on May twelfth. They
planned to travel to India and Pakistan for a two-week whirlwind
honeymoon and meet David's relatives, all those many Guptas
who he himself barely knew.

Now they turned and turned throughout the night, and at
times Claudia fell into sleep only to be awakened by her own crying, which came involuntarily. "Talk to me," David whispered to
her, and she said no, she couldn't bear to talk any more tonight. At
three in the morning, though, desperate for some kind of comfort,
she threw a leg over his, waking him, and he put his hands on her
waist and braced her against him.

"Let's try something," he whispered.

Outside, on Avenue A, there was some kind of commotion
involving a car alarm and two drunken, shouting men, but it
wasn't too bad; snow softened everything. "Try what?" she asked.

"'Electric Forgiveness,'" he said. "You know."

"Oh no," she said. "Please, not that. There's nothing to forgive, anyway."

"There's always something to forgive."

"In a general sense, yeah."

"Well, fine," said David. "That's good enough."

He took her copy of the old edition of the book out from a box under the bed, where he knew she kept it so no one would see. The thirtieth-anniversary edition no longer had the position in it, for it had never really caught on after all, despite the Mellows' insistence, in print, that it was "a wonderful way to achieve climax quickly and lovingly after a scene of anger or stress." David propped the old book up on the windowsill by the bed, and in the stuttering light from the 24-hour check-cashing store across the street, he found the page where it was explained and illustrated. Claudia had read the description before, but had never memorized it.

"'Sit in the very middle of your bed, facing each other,'" David read aloud. "All right, that's not hard. Hello, you."

"Hello," she said.

"'The woman should wrap her legs around her lover in a grasp that is as tight as a hug, and no tighter.'" Claudia did as he said, her legs containing him, and then she waited for further instruction. "'Then she should take her left hand,'" David said, "'and place it on his sternum, exerting a gentle pressure, while at the same time . . .'" Here he paused to turn the page, and then continued. "'. . . she places her right hand on his lower back, at the sacroiliac joint.'" He looked at Claudia and asked, "Do you know what that means?"

"Base of the spine," she said.

They got into position, slowly and carefully, as though building a house of cards that might topple at any given moment.

"'The man does the exact same thing to his lover,'" David read. "Oh, *now* you tell me." He shifted on the bed, squashing Claudia's foot briefly, and extricating a hand that had gotten caught in the sheets. "'He should bring his penis forward into his lover so that the exact degree of slant exerts as much pressure as possible on her clitoris.' There," he said, entering her quickly and slightly awkwardly. She felt him poking against her. There was nothing natural here, nothing familiar, just an odd translation of an age-old tale. "'Rock together very slowly at first,'" David said. "Okay, I'm perfectly happy to do that. 'Build up speed and vigor as you remember how much you love each other, and how you forgive each other for the ways that you have accidentally or perhaps even purposefully been unkind to each other. Life is too short to hold on to rage and disappointment. Continue rocking, mouths joined, until both of you reach climax. And when you are done, gently part, falling backward onto the bed.'"

They continued to arrange themselves as best they could, given the narrow space and the time of night and how much she'd been crying. Claudia's body fit snugly against David's; he was so warm, and she was so warm, and it was astonishing to her that they could approximate the mechanics and make themselves actually fit. They did fit, though as they rocked slowly she worried that David would fall right out of her, or that she would fall off the bed, or that the pressure she was applying on his sternum was uncomfortable for him. Their kiss was long and arduous; they were both nervous, but they had done it, they had really done it, and for a few minutes she forgot that simply being able to do it doesn't mean that it's at all worthwhile. For the pleasure she felt was minimal; there was friction, an uneasy fluctuation of pressure, and the sense of continually being prodded, told to move along. If she even breathed too hard, she feared he would be forced out of her, so she hardly breathed as they rocked.

After a while, they both stopped their rocking and kissing, taking a breather. "So, do you like this?" David asked, deadpan. "I mean, does it *work* for you? Is it everything you hoped for?"

"Actually, it's kind of boring," she said.

"I know."

They stayed in that clumsy stance for just a few seconds more, and finally neither of them could take it. So this was "Electric For-giveness," this was the thing the parents had invented, the thing that long ago they had tried and decided other people would like. Claudia hadn't known how slight and uncomfortable and how ridiculous it would be, but now she did.

And suddenly they were laughing, despite their earnest attempts to try this, to get something out of it, and despite the unbearable news they'd heard tonight. "This position is terrible," David said. "I think I'm going to be castrated. We'll have to adopt. I'm sorry I sug-gested it."

"We can at least do the falling away onto the bed part," she suggested.

"Yeah, let's do that." So they let themselves fall backward, away from each other, drawing their legs up, everything exposed, hold-ing their knees like two tumblers hurtling through the air.

"What were they thinking?" Claudia asked him a little later. "Did they really imagine that anyone else would enjoy this? Did *they* enjoy this?" But it didn't matter what the parents had been thinking, she knew; it was a riddle, a puzzle, a thing conjured up in darkness, and she could never solve it, and she knew that she didn't even want to because, after all, it was about them, not her.

She and David both lay on their backs now, stretching their legs out fully, their laughter dying down. The drunk men on the street had wandered away, together or apart, and the car alarm had finally been silenced. At dawn the light would climb the side of the brick walk-up building where Claudia Mellow and David Gupta slept, and it would enter through the window glass, and she would be awakened, and there would be things she would have to remem-ber, but not yet, not yet. The narrow bed held them fast until morning.

About the Author

MEG WOLITZER is the author of six previous novels, including *The Wife; Surrender, Dorothy;* and *This Is Your Life.* Her short fiction has appeared in *Best American Short Stories* and *The Pushcart Prize.* She lives in New York City.